FINDING CARLY

SEAL Team Hawaii, Book 5

SUSAN STOKER

CHAPTER ONE

Carly Stewart sat with her back against the wall in the corner of her bedroom. She'd heard a noise in the hallway earlier and it sent her into another panic attack. She'd hidden under her bed like a five-year-old for a while, then finally scooted out and was currently clutching her knees to her chest, trying to breathe.

A funny thing was happening though. Something new. Something that hadn't happened since the evening Kenna had been kidnapped by Carly's ex-boyfriend and almost blown to pieces by the bomb Shawn had strapped to his chest.

In addition to the paralyzing fear she'd experienced almost every day since, Carly felt anger boiling deep within her.

Neither emotion was common for her. She wasn't the kind of woman who stressed over every little thing. She was generally a happy person...or at least she used to be.

Dating Shawn had been good at first. He was older than she was, by two decades, but that hadn't bothered them. But it

1

wasn't long before he'd changed from the kind, romantic man she'd thought she knew into a controlling abuser.

It had taken Carly far too long to finally come to her senses. She was just thankful she'd never moved in with him like he'd begged her to.

But he'd refused to accept their breakup, which was crazy. He began stalking her, making her life a living hell. She'd taken out a protective order against him, and even though she knew he wouldn't like that, she'd never expected he'd want to kill her.

She'd gone home early from work the evening he'd shown up at the restaurant, bomb strapped to his chest, prepared to kidnap and do who-the-hell-knew-what to her. He'd ultimately kidnapped her friend, Kenna, then blew himself up.

That should've been the end of it. But instead, it was just the beginning of her nightmare.

It was one thing knowing who to look out for, to know who hated you. But it was another to realize someone had been working *with* Shawn that night. Someone willing to aid in her torture...and not know who that person was for sure.

Carly and the cops were fairly certain it was Shawn's son, Luke. He'd hated her from the second they'd met, and hadn't been afraid to show it. During the kidnapping, Shawn had inferred someone was out in the ocean in a boat, ready to pick him up from the beach outside of Duke's restaurant. But the police couldn't find proof of Luke's involvement...or that anyone else had been working with Shawn.

Ever since that night, Carly had been paranoid. Scared out of her mind. Terrified that whoever was working with Shawn would finish what he'd started. She'd quit her job, stopped seeing her friends, and become a shell of the woman she used to be.

She would've become a *complete* recluse if it hadn't been for Jag.

Jagger Bennett was a Navy SEAL. She knew him through Kenna, her friend and fellow waitress at Duke's, who was dating Jag's teammate.

Jag literally wouldn't leave her alone. He texted and called and even came by to check on her. He was annoying, persistent, bossy...and Carly didn't know how she would've made it through the last couple of months without him.

She wanted to hate him. Wanted to resent his interference in her life. Wished he'd just let her hide in peace. But she couldn't. He'd kept her sane, kept her from completely freaking out.

And there was the fact that Carly had developed the biggest crush on the man, even before Shawn's kidnapping attempt.

But she'd learned her lesson about dating older men. Granted, Jag was only ten years older, and was nothing like Shawn, but still.

As Carly sat on her floor, her ass numb, thinking about the last couple of months, the anger in her belly continued to grow. Shawn was an asshole. He'd never taken responsibility for his own actions, instead blaming everyone around him. And when they'd started dating, Carly had soon found herself the recipient of most of his anger. She couldn't do anything right. Was immature and stupid and irresponsible.

She was ashamed to admit that she'd started to believe him.

No one knew exactly what she'd been through with Shawn. She kept it to herself. Smiling and joking at work, yet feeling beaten and broken inside. Then he'd almost killed her friend. It had all been too much.

Carly desperately wanted her life back. She was broke, lonely,

and terrified to step outside her apartment, in case Luke was waiting to get revenge for his dad's death.

A week and a half ago, she'd actually let Jag talk her into going to Kenna's wedding. It was the first time she'd willingly gone out in public in months...and one of the most painful days of her life. Kenna was beautiful. She'd looked so damn happy. Carly was happy *for* her, but sad for herself. She no longer knew what was going on in her friend's life. Or the lives of *any* of the new friends she'd met through Jag's team. And she didn't know Monica at all, who'd recently joined the small circle of women Carly had just started to get to know.

Attending the wedding had hammered home that life was passing her by. She missed her friends. She wanted what they had. And she wouldn't get any of it by sitting on her ass shaking like a leaf in her apartment.

Feeling as if she were a hundred years old, Carly leaned over and picked up her phone, which was sitting on a small table next to her bed. She gripped it tightly and unlocked the screen, staring down at her contact list.

Elodie. Lexie. Kenna. Jag. The rest of Jag's SEAL team was programmed in as well, but Carly had never called or messaged them. She clicked on Jag's name and scrolled up. There were hundreds of texts from the last few months. Most from him, asking how she was, if she'd eaten, if she needed anything, or if she wanted him to come over. Even though she rarely allowed herself the luxury of inviting him over, when he did come, she felt a short-lived relief.

She'd last seen him at the wedding. He'd gotten upset with her for wanting to leave early. She'd been frustrated with *him* for not understanding how hard it was for her to come to the ceremony in the first place. She'd had only one text from him since.

The following day, short and to the point. Carly stared at the words he'd written.

Jag: Headed out on a mission. When I get back, we're gonna talk.

For the first time in a while, Carly worried about someone other than herself. Was he okay? She had no idea where he was, which she knew wasn't something she'd *ever* know, since he was a SEAL, but what if he'd been hurt? Or worse, killed?

That thought sent a pang of dread straight to her heart. And it wasn't like the dull, constant fear she'd experienced over the last few months. It was all-encompassing.

Without thought, Carly's thumbs flew over her keyboard as she typed out a message. It was long, much longer than the few words she usually used to communicate with him. She wanted— no, *needed* him to know she was thankful for his presence in her life. That without him, she didn't know if she would've been able to handle what had happened to her. Not that she was handling it very well, but without Jag, she had a feeling she'd be in even worse shape than she was right now.

Carly: I'm sorry I've been a bitch to you. There are some days when your texts are the only thing that keep me from doing something drastic to stop the never-ending fear I've been living with. Thank you for forcing me to go to Kenna's wedding. I would've hated myself if I'd missed it. I'm assuming you're still gone, at least I hope that's why I haven't heard from you in a

week and a half. I'm so tired, Jag. Tired of being a coward. Tired of being scared all the time. And I'm angry. Pissed. You're right. Hiding isn't going to make Luke go away. I want to live again. I want to be *me* again. When you get back, will you go to the police station with me? I want to talk to the detective. Want to find out what he's discovered about Luke. How close they are to arresting him. I know it's cowardly of me to use you as a crutch, but I swear it'll only be until I'm on my feet again. I realize I've been selfish, and I'm going to try to change, to not think only about myself. I'll get better, I swear. Please don't give up on me.

Carly hit send before she could chicken out. Then she typed some more.

Carly: I hope you're okay. I don't know where you are, if you're back in Hawaii or what, but now that I've realized how long it's been since I've heard from you, I can't help but think the worst. I hope your friends are okay too. I can't even imagine something happening to Kenna's new husband or the other guys. I miss you, Jag. I never realized how much your notes meant to me until they weren't coming anymore.

She sent that text then clicked off her phone. She kept it in her hand and rested her chin on her updrawn knees. She had no idea what her future held, but she was going to do her best to stop hiding away like a coward.

* * *

Jag was exhausted. The mission to Tajikistan had been frustrating and lasted longer than any of the team had wanted. In the end, it was successful, but they'd had to deal with delays and red tape that dragged out the situation.

Now they were finally home. Aleck was more than ready to see his new bride, and Midas, Mustang, and Pid were just as anxious to get home to their women.

Even Slate seemed impatient. Of course, that was practically his permanent state, but Jag knew this time it was because he wanted to touch base with Ashlyn. The two hadn't admitted their bickering and teasing was a form of foreplay, but it was obvious to the rest of the team it was only a matter of time before one of them broke and admitted they were interested in the other.

But Jag's exhaustion took second place to worry for Carly. When he'd left a week and a half ago, he'd decided that he was done going easy with her. Yes, she'd been through something traumatic, and yes, whoever was working with her ex was still out there, possibly watching and waiting to get his hands on her, but she couldn't live her life in hiding.

The second the plane landed, Jag pulled out his phone. The other guys did the same, eager to let their women know they were back. Jag tapped his foot as he waited for his cell to power up. He knew the battery was low, but hopefully it had enough juice for him to at least send a quick text.

But the second the phone turned on, sending a text flew from Jag's mind. He read the messages Carly had sent not even three hours ago...and his exhaustion fled. Adrenaline shot through his veins.

"Everything okay?" Mustang asked.

Jag nodded. "Yeah." He looked into his team leader's eyes. "Carly asked if I would go to the police station with her."

"That's awesome news," Mustang said. In their downtime over the last week, Jag had opened up to his teammates. About his worry for Carly. About what she'd been going through and how he might help her. Everyone agreed the first step was to find Luke, to figure out if he really was a threat, so she could put what happened with her ex behind her.

"This is the first time I've heard her sound so..." His voice trailed off. He wasn't sure what word he was looking for. Her emotions in the texts seemed to be all over the place, but that was better than the abject fear he'd seen in her eyes since Kenna had been kidnapped by her ex.

Mustang nodded as if he knew exactly what Jag was trying to say...and he probably did. "It's gonna be a roller coaster as she deals with this. You ready for that?" he asked.

"Fuck yes," Jag said without hesitation. He'd been attracted to Carly from the moment they met. She'd been their waitress when Aleck had gone to Duke's to meet Kenna for the first time, and the rest of the team had tagged along. Her petite frame, her blonde hair and blue eyes, her friendliness, her genuine affection for Kenna and her friends at Duke's...it all appealed to him. He'd hated to see the spark within her dim the last few months.

He was determined to bring it back, no matter what it took.

"You finally going to stake your claim?" Aleck asked, obviously having overheard some of his conversation with Mustang.

"Yes," Jag said. He knew it was chauvinistic to stake a claim on another person, but he didn't care. He wanted Carly for his own. The fact that nothing about a relationship with her would be easy wasn't a turnoff.

"Good," Aleck said. "Kenna misses her friend. Wants to see

her again. I'd be forever in your debt if you could help facilitate that."

Determination rose within Jag. He wanted to help Carly so she'd hopefully feel comfortable enough to start a relationship, but also because she needed her friends. She thrived on being around others. He could tell just by how depressed she'd gotten after she'd quit working at Duke's.

"I'm heading over there now and will take her to the police station tomorrow," Jag said.

"Um, you know it's three in the morning, right?" Midas asked, as they began to walk off the plane.

"Shit," Jag mumbled.

His friends laughed.

He'd been so pumped that Carly had asked for his help and was finally willing to hopefully move on with her life, he hadn't even considered the time. To be fair, his internal clock was all messed up after spending several days on the other side of the world and after traveling, but still.

"I'll talk to the commander, get you a few days off," Mustang told him.

"I want to know what the detectives have found," Aleck added. "I've got as big a stake in this as you."

Jag wasn't sure about that, but he understood where Aleck was coming from. It had been *his* wife who'd almost been blown to pieces on the beach when Shawn had kidnapped her. If it hadn't been for her quick thinking, the outcome could've been devastating.

He nodded at his friend.

"Call Baker," Slate said, piping up for the first time. "You know he's been looking into the situation, and he's frustrated he hasn't found Luke yet. He'll want to know anything new the

detectives tell you too."

Slate was right. He knew Baker was already looking into the situation with Luke. The retired SEAL was a damn good person to have at his back.

"I will," he said.

After collecting his duffle bag, he said goodbye to his teammates and headed for his black Volkswagen Jetta in the parking lot. It was a reliable car, but not one that would stick out on the streets or at his apartment complex. Jag liked to fly under the radar, didn't like to be noticed if he could help it. It was a handy skill to have as a SEAL...though he'd actually learned to dislike attention from a young age.

Jag sat in his car for a moment, trying to decide what to do. He knew it was way too late to be going over to Carly's apartment right now, but he wanted to. Needed to see her.

He reached for his phone and typed out a text before he thought better of it.

Jag: I just got back. You up?

Of course Carly wasn't up. It was three-thirty in the fucking morning. She was asleep, as were most of the other residents of the island. It was stupid to think—

Jag blinked in surprise when three dots flashed at the bottom of the text message box. She was up and typing a reply. His heart started beating a bit faster. He was exhausted, as he always was after a mission, but at the moment, he felt as if he could easily stay up another three days without any problem whatsoever.

· · ·

Carly: I'm up. I'm glad you're back safe.

Jag wanted to ask *why* she was awake, but he had a feeling he knew the answer. He was aware that Carly didn't sleep well. She'd told him once that ever since Kenna had been taken hostage by Shawn Keyes, she could only sleep a few hours a night, too worried that Luke would break into her apartment and finish what his dad started.

Jag: Can I come over?
  Carly: Yes.

One word. Jag felt as if it was a sign of his life changing, hopefully for the better.

He'd been to Carly's apartment many times over the last few months, but this felt different somehow. Maybe it was because he'd already decided to do whatever it took to make Carly feel safe again, to help her get her life back. Maybe it was because he'd just gotten off a gnarly mission. Maybe because he was going on seventy-two hours without sleep. Whatever the reason, he felt just as amped up as he would in the middle of a firefight. He couldn't start his car fast enough.

He'd never felt this way about a woman before. After—

No. He wasn't going there.

Women weren't really a part of his life. Never had been, by his own choice. He'd never gone through the phase that a lot of young SEALs had, where they were happy to fuck anyone who

showed the least bit interest. He'd never even had a girlfriend. Never wanted one.

Jag hated thinking about his past, but for once in his life, he mourned not having more experience when it came to women. He wanted to say and do all the right things with Carly, but didn't know what those things were. He was going to have to wing it—and pray he didn't make her life more miserable than it already was.

Taking a deep breath, Jag did his best to calm himself down. He'd just follow Carly's lead. She'd taken the first step by asking for him to go to the police station with her, he'd see where things went after that.

Twenty minutes later, Jag pulled into the parking lot of Carly's apartment complex. It wasn't in a bad part of Honolulu, but it wasn't exactly luxury either. The building was three stories high, and Carly was on the top floor, for which he was glad. There was no security and the resident doors were all outward-facing, which meant anyone could walk up to her door without any problem whatsoever.

It wasn't ideal in Carly's situation. Luke could sit right here in the parking lot and watch for her to leave and grab her. It was no wonder she didn't leave the safety of her apartment. And moving wasn't exactly a viable solution, as she currently wasn't working and Jag knew her funds were low.

Everything about Carly's situation grated on his nerves, and he was extremely thankful she was ready to make a change. He'd made the decision before his latest deployment to shake things up. To try to encourage Carly to start living again. The relief he felt at getting her text was immense.

Turning off the engine and reaching for his phone, Jag sent a quick text as he always did when he arrived to see her.

. . .

Jag: I'm here. I'll be at your door in less than a minute.

He didn't wait for her to respond. He headed up the stairs in the center of the complex. He took them two at a time before striding down the concrete walkway to her door. Taking a deep breath, he raised his hand to knock. But it opened before he could make contact with the wood.

His first glimpse of Carly made Jag's heart hurt. She looked like hell. Her hair was limp and greasy around her face, as if it had been several days since she'd showered. She had dark circles under her eyes and wore an oversized T-shirt and a pair of extra-large sweatpants that swam on her petite frame.

But it was the combination of relief and desperation in her eyes that affected him the most.

Jag took a step forward, and she backed up. He shut and locked the door behind him, all three deadbolts that he'd put on for her not too long ago to help her feel safer, then he gathered Carly into his arms without saying a word.

CHAPTER TWO

Carly had never been so glad to see anyone in her entire life. Making the decision to try to move on with her life wasn't easy. She was petrified. But the second Jag pulled her into his embrace, she felt as if she could breathe for the first time since... well, since the last time she'd seen him at Kenna's wedding.

Her hands clutched the material of Jag's shirt at his back and she rested her cheek on his chest. His hair had gotten longer since she'd seen him last, almost hanging into his eyes. He had a scruffy almost-beard on his face, and his eyes were bloodshot... but Carly had never seen anyone as handsome in her entire life.

Jag wasn't a talkative man. She'd noticed that about him the first time she'd met him at Duke's. He was content to let conversation flow around him. But she didn't need words. She just needed his strength. His competence. He made her feel protected simply by being near. It was a mistake to fall for this man, Carly knew it, but she had a feeling it was too late.

Kenna had told her once that Jag was extremely mysterious.

That Aleck had mentioned no one knew much about his child-hood or his life before joining the SEALs. But she didn't care if he was raised by a pack of wolves in Siberia...the man he'd grown into was honorable and trustworthy. Maybe even a bit scary, but frightening only in the sense that Carly knew he wouldn't hesi-tate to do harm to anyone who dared hurt someone he cared about. And that was what Carly needed right now. To feel safe. Jag did that for her.

She felt him shuffling them backward, but she didn't let go, didn't lift her head from his chest, wasn't sure she could. All of a sudden, her sleepless nights seemed to catch up with her. She had no idea what time it was, but she knew it was late...or early. Time had ceased to have meaning for her. She muddled through her days and nights trying not to think about what Luke would do when he finally got his hands on her.

When she did fall asleep, her dreams were full of terror. Of Shawn yelling at her, telling her she was pathetic and useless. Of blood, as father and son tortured her with knives and laughed as she begged for her life. Needless to say, she hadn't had a good night's sleep in a very long time.

Jag moved them into her room and took hold of her shoul-ders, forcing her away from his body. Carly shivered at the loss of contact.

"You need to use the bathroom?" he asked.

Carly wanted to smile at how blunt he was. But she didn't have it in her. She shook her head.

"I do. It's been a long day and night for me. Climb in. I'll be back in a moment."

Carly swallowed a protest and nodded, reminding herself that she'd made a decision to stop being so damn cowardly.

But Jag seemed to read her mind. He leaned down and rested

his forehead on hers. He kept his hands on her shoulders, and Carly couldn't help but grab hold of his shirt at his sides. They stood like that for at least a minute or two before she took a deep breath.

"I'm okay," she whispered.

Jag lifted his head and studied her. In return, Carly took her own long, hard look at him, as well. She knew she looked rough, but he looked absolutely shattered. She could see the strain around his eyes. His clothes were wrinkled, and he actually swayed in front of her slightly.

"How long has it been since you've slept?" she blurted.

His lips quirked. "What day is today?" he asked.

Which answered her question. For the first time in a long time, something shifted deep inside her. She wanted to take care of him, which was kind of ridiculous because Jag was obviously a man who could take care of himself, and everyone around him. But it didn't stop her from wanting to do it.

Forcing herself to let go of his shirt, she took a step backward. "Go," she ordered, gesturing toward her small bathroom with her head. "If you want to shower, feel free."

Jag shook his head. "Would take too long," he muttered. "I'll be out in a minute or so."

He waited until she took a step toward her bed before heading for the bathroom.

Carly's heart beat hard and fast in her chest as she pulled back the sheet and climbed onto her bed. She lay back and stared at the mostly shut door across the room. She heard the toilet flush and the water in the sink come on. The unmistakable sound of Jag brushing his teeth met her ears. He'd obviously found the unopened toothbrush she'd gotten the last time she'd been to the dentist and hadn't used yet...at least she hoped he

had. She liked Jag, but the thought of him using her toothbrush was kind of gross.

But she had no time to think about it anymore when the door opened and the light from the bathroom shut off. Jag reappeared, striding over to the wall next to the entrance and turning off the overhead light.

Carly blinked in the sudden darkness. She'd been sleeping with the light on, because the dark seemed to overwhelm her. Just when she was about to tell Jag to turn the light back on, he left the room, then she saw a soft glow coming from the hallway. Jag had turned on a light in her living room. When he returned, he kept her bedroom door open, letting just enough light in to make her feel more comfortable.

To her surprise, he then reached for his shirt. He peeled it off over his head and leaned down to untie his boots.

"Um, Jag?"

"Yeah?"

"What are you doing?"

He stopped mid-stoop and looked up at her. He slowly straightened. "Getting ready for bed."

"Here?" she couldn't help but ask.

"Yes."

Short and to the point. No beating around the bush.

"Oh. Okay." What else could she say? Jag needed rest, and if he wanted to sleep in her bed, she wasn't going to say no.

He finished taking off his boots and socks and strode toward her bed still wearing his cargo pants. He reached out to lift the sheet and she blurted, "You aren't going to take your pants off?"

His lips twitched, but he shook his head. "No. I feel more comfortable with them on."

Carly blinked in surprise. He didn't say *she* would feel more

comfortable if he left them on, but that *he* would. She didn't get a chance to say anything else before he was suddenly lying next to her. Then, without asking, he reached for her and hauled her against his side.

She found her cheek resting on his chest, and the skin-on-skin contact felt so good. Snuggling into him, Carly tentatively rested her arm across his belly. She felt Jag's stomach tighten for a moment, before he lay a hand on her forearm and let out a long breath.

"You have no idea how good this feels," Jag said softly.

"Long mission?" she asked.

"Yeah."

Again. One word said it all.

"I'm proud of you," he said after a moment.

Carly huffed out a small laugh.

"I am," he insisted. "Your text was the best thing I've ever read. I'm too tired to talk right now, but we're gonna find him, Carly. You're gonna get your life back. I swear on it."

Carly closed her eyes and did her best not to burst into tears. She'd felt broken for so long. So unlike the Carly she used to be. And she hated it. She did want her life back. It scared her to death, but she couldn't live like she had been for much longer. Hiding out, panicking over every little sound. Scared of her own shadow.

If anyone could help her, it was Jag. She knew that down to the tips of her toes.

"Okay."

"Sleep, Carly," Jag ordered. And there was no doubt it *was* an order.

Carly smiled. When was the last time she'd smiled about anything? She couldn't remember. "Yes, sir," she quipped.

"I'm here. You're safe. Nothing and no one's getting through me to get to you," he added.

His words settled in her soul. Carly was fairly certain she wouldn't be able to fall asleep, even though being in his arms was one of the most comfortable places she'd ever been in her life, but she nodded anyway.

Jag's thumb brushed back and forth over her forearm rhythmically. To her surprise, her muscles relaxed and her eyes closed.

"That's it, angel. I've got you."

"Jag?" Carly mumbled.

"Right here."

"Thanks for coming."

"Nothing would've kept me away," he said.

Carly could've sworn she felt him kiss her forehead, but decided she was hallucinating. Jag had never crossed a line between them. Had always treated her like a friend, a buddy.

Then again, he'd never climbed into bed and held her either.

Before she could think about it anymore, however, Carly fell into a deep, healing sleep.

Carly stirred, and when she opened her eyes saw that it was no longer dark outside. The sun was shining so brightly, her cheap curtains weren't able to keep the light out. She couldn't remember the last time she'd slept so late.

"Good morning," a deep voice said from next to her. *Right* next to her. "Or should I say good afternoon?" Jag asked with a chuckle.

Carly would've been alarmed, but she'd known whose arms

she was lying in. Coming up on an elbow, she looked at the man next to her.

His hair was mussed, but his eyes were no longer bloodshot and he looked a hundred times better than he had last night. Grimacing, Carly had a feeling she probably looked a hundred times worse. She couldn't remember when she'd last showered and her mouth felt like she'd been sucking on cotton balls all night.

"What time is it?"

"A little after one," Jag said.

"In the afternoon?" Carly squeaked in surprise.

"Yup."

She couldn't believe she'd slept that long. Or at all. "I slept," she said in surprise.

"Yeah, like a rock," Jag agreed.

"No, you don't understand. I haven't slept since...I don't know when," she said. If she hadn't been so surprised at the late hour, she probably wouldn't have admitted it. "I didn't dream at all."

"Good," Jag said sincerely. "We need to talk, but first you can shower, put on some clean clothes, and I'll make us something to eat."

"Um...I don't know what I've got in my kitchen," Carly admitted.

Jag's brows came down. "When's the last time you went shopping?" he asked.

Carly wrinkled her nose and shrugged.

"Carly..." he said in exasperation.

"I haven't been hungry," she told him. "And the last thing I felt safe doing was going to the store. I've been using a delivery service. But, um, since I haven't been working, I've had to really

watch my budget. I haven't had an appetite though, so it wasn't a big deal."

Jag's frown deepened. "Change of plans. Gather some shit together, don't shower, I'll take you to my place. You can shower there. I'll make us breakfast, then we'll talk."

Carly blinked in surprise. "Your place?"

"Yeah. I've got plenty to eat and my shower's bigger."

"I can't go to your place," she told him.

"Why not?"

Carly opened her mouth to answer, but she couldn't think of one compelling reason why she needed to stay in her apartment.

"Exactly," Jag said a little smugly. "You've been holed up here for too long. This place represents fear to you now. A change of venue will do you good. Trust me."

Carly stared at the man next to her. The man she'd slept next to. She hadn't dreamed last night, and she knew it was because she felt safe with him there. He didn't have to come over. He'd been exhausted...and yet he'd still come.

And he wasn't wrong. Her apartment had started out as her refuge. She'd holed up in here and, slowly but surely, the outside world became more and more menacing the longer she hid out. Until her apartment felt more like a prison.

Carly felt another twinge of anger deep inside. Anger at herself. Anger at Luke. Anger that she'd allowed herself to become so pathetic.

"Okay," she blurted.

The smile that spread across Jag's lips was all the reward she needed for agreeing to step *way* outside her comfort zone.

Jag lifted a hand and cupped her cheek. Carly held her breath as the warmth from his skin seeped into her own. She tilted her head into his hand.

"It's going to be all right, angel," he soothed.

Carly believed him. She nodded.

He leaned in and kissed her forehead tenderly before turning and climbing out of her bed. Carly watched as he grabbed the same shirt he'd had on last night and pulled it over his head. The muscles in his stomach flexed and her fingers curled into fists. The visceral reaction to seeing him was surprising. As was the way her thighs clenched together under the sheet.

Jagger Bennett was one hell of a sexy man, and last night she'd been plastered against his side. If she was a swooning kind of woman, she definitely would've swooned right then and there.

"Get up, lazy bones," he teased as he leaned over to put on his shoes and socks. "I'm starving. And you, my friend, need a shower in the worst way."

Carly couldn't help but laugh. This Jag was a surprise. She'd never heard him kid around before. Not with his friends and definitely not with her. She scooted over and stood up.

"Here, use this," Jag said, stepping into the closet and pulling out the large suitcase Carly had brought with her when she'd moved to Hawaii. It had sat unused since then in the back of her closet. He'd obviously seen it at one point or another, because he hadn't hesitated to grab it.

"That's way too big, Jag. I've got a smaller bag I can use to throw together a change of clothes and some toiletries."

He met her gaze and shook his head. "No. Pack as much as will fit in here. You're gonna be at my place until we figure out your situation."

Carly stared at him in surprise. "Jag, we have no idea how long that will take. It's been months as it is."

He didn't comment, merely lifted an eyebrow at her, then walked over to the bed with her suitcase in hand. He laid it

down and unzipped it. "Fill it," he ordered, then, ignoring her gaping, turned and walked out of the room.

Butterflies swam in Carly's stomach as she stared at the extra-large suitcase. She was so conflicted. She wanted to protest. But at the same time, a part of her was jumping up and down like an excited kid on Christmas Day. Her apartment had so many bad memories.

Every moment she'd hid in her room with a knife in her hand, because she thought she'd heard someone trying to break in. Every sleepless night. Every day she'd spent filled with despair over how horrible her life had become.

But move in with Jag? Could she do that?

Her phone vibrating on the table next to the bed made Carly jump. She walked over and picked it up, and saw a text from Kenna.

Kenna: The guys are back! And Marshall said Jag went over to your place. You can trust Jag, he's a good guy. You know that. I know we don't talk as much as we used to, but I miss you, Carly. Work isn't the same without you. If you need anything, I'm just a phone call away. But then again, you've got Jag. Do what he says. Even if it seems crazy and you have no idea what the hell he's thinking. Our SEALs know what they're doing. Promise.

It was the nudge Carly needed. Hadn't she just decided to do whatever she needed to do in order to move on with her life? And staying with Jag for a while would definitely rip her out of her comfort zone and get her back on a path to normal.

She put the phone down and headed for her closet. Jag

was hungry and she needed a shower. She wanted to pack quickly so they could get out of here. The upcoming talk he insisted on having would be uncomfortable, not to mention the visit with the detective assigned to her case, but she'd wanted Jag's help, and it looked like she was getting it.

Carly knew she had to be open and honest with him. Doing so might end any chance she had of becoming more than friends with the man...but so be it.

Carly was done being a coward. Even if it was easier said than done, she was moving on. Shawn Keyes had taken enough from her. It was time to put everything that had happened behind her and take back her life.

She wasn't an idiot, she knew she could still be in danger. Luke was still out there somewhere, probably waiting for the perfect time to take his revenge for his father's death, but determination rose within her. Somehow, with Jag by her side, she felt as if she could take on the world.

But with baby steps. First step, put the toxic environment of her apartment behind her for a while. Second step, shower and eat something besides ramen noodles. Third step...well, time would tell what that would be. But it wouldn't be cowering in her apartment anymore.

With renewed determination, Carly continued to fill the suitcase.

* * *

Shawn's accomplice stared out a window in his condo and scowled at the beautiful day. It wasn't the sun he was pissed at, it was *her*. Carly Stewart.

Shawn had died because of that bitch. And she needed to pay for his death.

He'd been watching her, waiting for an opportunity for months. But she never left her fucking apartment.

At first, he assumed avenging Shawn would be easy. He'd planned to offer Carly a ride home from his friend's memorial service and quickly finish what he'd started. But she hadn't even shown up! The utter disrespect infuriated him.

Shawn had taken her in, a naïve twenty-something, and tried to mold her into a mature woman. Someone who would be there for her man, stand by his side, see to his every need. And in return, she'd metaphorically spit in his face. Rejected him in the most humiliating way possible. She'd taken out a *protective order* against him. It was complete bullshit.

Shawn had been a good man. The very best. That slut didn't know how good she'd had it. If he could be half the man Shawn had been, he'd consider himself lucky. But the dumb bitch hadn't appreciated him. Hadn't respected him and all the things he'd done for her.

And no matter how many times Shawn had tried to talk to her after she *dared* to walk away, no matter how often he'd explained that if she'd just listen to him, she'd go much further in life, be more than a lowly waitress, she'd ignored him.

It was no wonder Shawn had to discipline her. She was a wild animal who needed to know her goddamn boundaries.

Women shouldn't be allowed to go *anywhere* without letting someone know where they were, who they were with. It was a dangerous world out there. If men like him and Shawn were going to protect their women, they had to know their every movement, at all times.

It made perfect sense.

He'd learned so much from Shawn. Including how to be a *real* man in a relationship, how women just needed to be shown the correct path in order to be a good girlfriend or wife. Women were fundamentally weak. They needed men to lead them. To keep them safe.

And the bitch was not only too stupid to see what a good thing she'd had with Shawn, she was disrespectful to the nth degree.

The fact that she'd refused to move in with him was the final straw. How could Shawn continue to mold her properly if she wasn't sleeping by his side every night? A man had needs, and Shawn told him all about how Carly had refused to sleep in his bed at the end. Had refused to kiss him. It was unacceptable. She was a disgrace. And she had fucked up everything—for both him *and* Shawn.

When his friend came to him, upset and angry after being served with the protective order, they'd discussed what his next steps should be. It felt so good that his friend had opened up to him about his problems, trusted him to help. He'd been truly honored. They'd decided Carly needed to be taught a lesson, of course. *No one* said no to Shawn Keyes. He was the best the bitch would ever get, and she needed to understand the mistake she'd made by throwing him away.

The plan was perfect...except the evening they were set to carry it out, everything had gone wrong. The bitch had left work early because she was sick and the biggest storm the area had seen in years rolled in.

In the end, Shawn had died.

It wasn't fair! Carly hadn't been taught her lesson—and it was now up to *him* to finish the job. He would honor his friend by making Carly pay.

The original strategy had to change, unfortunately. There was no time for days of torture. Snatching her from work was no longer an option. And he wasn't interested in fucking the bitch, as Shawn himself had planned to do; no way in hell would he get his cock anywhere near her poison pussy.

No, she just needed to die. Disappear without a trace.

There were plenty of places he could dispose of her body where it would never be found. The most effective option was the sea. The millions of gallons of water would swallow her up and never spit her out.

Anger churning at the delay, he vowed to avenge his friend. Carly Stewart would rue the day she'd rejected such a fine man. Then, and only then, could he go on with his life with a clear conscience.

Regrettably, he knew he had to wait even longer. Wait until the right time. When her guard was no longer up. The bitch hadn't left her apartment in ages—and he would know. He was at least thrilled that she seemed to be so terrified; she should be. Danger was coming for her.

But vengeance would be so much sweeter if it struck when she least expected it.

She couldn't hide out forever. And when she finally crawled out from under the rock where she was cowering, he'd be there. Waiting and ready to strike.

The man turned from the window abruptly. He knew exactly how he would end Carly's life. He couldn't wait.

CHAPTER THREE

Now that Jag had gotten Carly to his apartment, he wanted to nail the door shut and never let her leave. He'd dreamed about her being here more nights than he could count. If it was up to him, she'd never go back to her own place.

He'd been interested in Carly for months, and watching her suffer had been extremely painful and frustrating because he hadn't been able to do much to help her. But now that she'd reached out to him, he wasn't going to let her down. The thought that he wanted her to stay with him permanently was crazy, but Jag had seen this exact thing with his friends. Once they'd gotten their women into their lairs, so to speak, they'd never left.

And that's what he wanted. Carly was his. He felt as if he'd known her forever and he couldn't seem to shake her. Didn't *want* to shake her.

The thing was, Jag knew she could do so much better than him. He was broken inside. He wasn't sure he'd ever be able to

have a normal relationship, not after his childhood. But for Carly, he wanted to try. Wanted to rise above the shit swirling in his head and be the kind of man she could rely on.

He just wasn't sure he could.

Pushing away thoughts of his past, Jag did his best to concentrate on the here and now and the meal he was making. The waffles were almost done, then he'd scramble a few eggs. Carly needed to eat. She'd lost some of the lush curves he admired, and the thought of her skimping on food because she didn't have enough money made him almost physically ill.

He'd given her *too* much space. He wanted to help her, but he should've done more, considering how bad her situation had gotten. That was over now. She was here and they were moving forward.

He'd slept like a rock last night. Yes, he'd been exhausted from the mission and traveling, but it was more about having her in his arms, knowing where she was and that she was all right, allowing him to finally let go and fall into a deep sleep.

He'd felt a hundred times better this morning, enough to suggest she pack and come to his place. Jag was actually surprised she'd agreed so easily, but he'd seen the determination to move on in her eyes. Less than two weeks ago, at Kenna and Aleck's wedding, he'd seen a spark of anger, and he'd actually hoped to work with that. But as it turned out, Carly didn't need him lighting a fire under her ass. She'd decided for herself.

She was strong as hell. He just needed to help her see that.

"Your shower is amazing."

He turned to see Carly walking toward him. Her blonde hair was still damp around her shoulders. She had on a pair of shorts and a long-sleeve T-shirt. Her feet were bare and the sight of her toes made him smile.

"What?" she asked.

He shrugged. "I don't think I've ever seen anyone with ten different colors on their toenails before."

Carly gave him a sheepish grin. "I had to do something all day while I was cowering in my apartment."

Jag put down the spoon he was using to scramble the eggs before pouring them into the pan, then walking over to her. He put his hands on her shoulders and waited until she met his gaze. "Don't," he said in a low, earnest tone. "You did what you had to do in order to survive."

"Jag, I hid out in my apartment like a kid hiding from the boogeyman. It was...pitiful."

He shook his head firmly. "No, it wasn't. You just needed some time to process. And I happen to think it was smart. I hate that you were scared, *are* scared, but I'm going to do everything in my power to make sure that asshole doesn't get anywhere near you."

"If he really wants me, there's not much anyone can do. He'll find a way. You and I both know that."

"Then I'll do what I can to teach you how to defend yourself," he said easily. He hated it, but she was right. If he'd learned nothing from his teammates' women's situations, he'd learned that he couldn't be by Carly's side 24/7 and there was a better-than-average chance Luke *would* be able to get to her eventually. "You've been a prisoner in your apartment long enough. You need to start living again. Fuck him," he said harshly. "You can show him that you're stronger than he or his father thought you were. Nothing will get you down. And if he does decide to be an idiot and pick up where his dad left off, he'll be sorry, because you'll kick his ass and make him wish he forgot your name."

Jag hadn't meant to be so blunt, but he couldn't help it. The

thought of Luke, or anyone else, getting their hands on Carly made his blood curdle. He knew with a bit of training, Carly could outsmart him and prove he'd picked the wrong woman to set his sights on.

She gave him a small lopsided smile. "In case it's escaped your notice, I'm not exactly SEAL material," she said with a shrug.

"You don't have to be," Jag told her. "You can use his size against him. He won't expect you to fight back and...don't take this the wrong way, but because of the amount of time you've spent hiding, he'll think you're too terrified to do anything to help yourself."

Jag could tell Carly wasn't fully convinced, but he did like how she seemed to stand up a little straighter.

"It smells good in here," she said after a moment.

She was obviously done with this particular conversation, so he let her change the subject. "What do you like in your eggs?"

"Um...what do you have?"

"Everything." Jag let his hands drop from her shoulders and he took a step back. What he really wanted to do was pull her into his embrace and tell her that everything was going to be all right, but he didn't want to make her even more uncomfortable.

Carly chuckled. "Everything?"

"Yup. Bacon, green or red peppers, cheese, salt and pepper, salsa, chorizo sausage, mushrooms, onions, tomatoes, spinach, ham, sour cream, hot sauce. I think the sour cream and cheese are still good, and frozen veggies will have to do until I can get to the store."

"Holy crap, people put all that on their eggs?"

"Well, probably not all of it at the same time." Jag grinned. "And usually those things go into an omelet. But I can never get

omelets to work right, so I usually just mix everything together with my scrambled eggs. I figure it's the same thing, even if it doesn't look as pretty. So...what's your preference?"

"Can I have green pepper, cheese, tomatoes, mushrooms, and sour cream?"

"You can have whatever you want, angel," he told her.

"Can I help?" she asked next.

"Sure. You can shred some cheese."

They worked together making their breakfast, and Jag felt a pang of longing so intense it almost made his knees buckle. He wanted this. Wanted her right next to him, smiling and relaxed as they made breakfast together in the future.

The meal was done in no time and they settled at the small table next to the kitchen. Jag didn't usually sit and eat there, he ate most meals standing up in the kitchen or in the living room as he watched TV.

There was something so...homey...about sitting at a table with Carly.

She stared down at the plate in front of her in disbelief. "You don't seriously think I can eat all this, do you?" she asked.

Jag winced at the amount of food he'd made for her and shrugged a little self-consciously. "I hate the thought of you being hungry," he admitted. "Just eat what you can. I'll finish what you can't or put the leftovers in the fridge."

They ate in silence for a moment before Jag broached the subject he'd been thinking about since he'd received her text after returning from his mission. "I'm happy to go to the police station with you. Thrilled actually. I want to find out what they've been doing to find Luke and to end this limbo you're in. But why now? What changed?"

Carly chewed and swallowed the bite of eggs she'd just taken,

then put down her fork and leaned her forearms on the table. "I got tired of being pathetic," she whispered.

"You are *not* pathetic," Jag told her.

"I am. Was," she said firmly. "I realized that hiding out in my apartment being scared wasn't solving anything. I've been miserable and I miss my job, my friends. I miss *people*, Jag. Going to Kenna's wedding was so scary. I kept thinking Luke was going to jump out from behind a tree or something with a bomb strapped to him and try to kidnap me. Or blow up everyone I love. By the time I could concentrate on the ceremony, it was over. I'd completely missed it because I was stuck in my head.

"I saw Monica with the others—with Kenna, Lexie, and Elodie—and realized I don't even know her. Ashlyn and Lexie talked about Food For All and the great things they were doing, and want to do, and it upset me that I had no idea what they were talking about. And the fact that Theo kept his distance from me...kind of hurt. I haven't been around for so long, he's practically forgotten me. All of that stuff sort of piled on, and I started to get mad."

Carly took a breath, and Jag couldn't help but reach out and take one of her hands in his. He needed to touch her, to let her know that he was there for her.

She squeezed his hand and didn't let go when she continued. "But even then, I was still terrified. The only place I felt safe was locked inside my apartment, and I knew that wasn't healthy. Is it crazy that I wish Luke would just make his move already? Do whatever he's going to do so I can move on with my life?"

"It's not crazy," Jag reassured her. "And believe it or not, what you're feeling is normal."

She rolled her eyes.

"It is," he insisted. "You've been through a trauma and you have to heal from that before you can move on."

"First of all, *I* didn't go through a trauma," Carly said a little belligerently. She removed her hand from his and crossed her arms with a huff. "Kenna did. She suffered in my place and that eats at me. And secondly, I don't even know why I'm trying to explain. You could never understand."

It was the second time she'd said something like that. The first was at Kenna and Aleck's wedding. She'd said that he wouldn't understand what it felt like to be vulnerable.

Jag hadn't told anyone what happened to him when he was a kid. Not one person. He suddenly had the urge to confide in Carly. Tell her just how wrong she was.

But instead, he swallowed the words and kept his gaze locked on hers. "You'd be surprised at what I understand," he told her. "But the bottom line is that you *were* traumatized by your ex. And I'm not talking only about that night he took Kenna hostage either."

Carly stared at him warily. "I don't know what you're talking about."

"Yes, you do. I don't know the details, but a man like Shawn doesn't go from being a model boyfriend to strapping a bomb to his chest to kidnap and torture you in the blink of an eye. And you're too smart to get involved with someone who treats you like shit. I'm guessing he *started out* as a good boyfriend. Treated you like a princess. Made you feel great. Then he probably slowly started to change. Make comments here and there that were belittling. Nothing that a quick apology wouldn't fix.

"From there, he probably said shit about you to his friends and son behind your back...making you feel uncomfortable when you were around them and they starting looking at you weird.

Then those comments might've continued when you were right in front of them. He'd say something awful, apologize profusely later. The cycle would continue, may even escalate to him getting physical. I'm guessing that's when you'd finally had enough. But by then it was too late. Shawn had already decided he owned you. That you were his. And thus the need for the protective order and his descent into bat-shit crazy."

Carly's mouth was open and her arms had uncrossed and fallen into her lap. She stared at him in disbelief.

"I'm right, aren't I?" Jag asked.

"I...Yeah, pretty much," she whispered.

Jag reached out and picked up one of her hands again. He held it tightly, resting their hands on the table. "*He's* the asshole here, angel, not you. He had something precious and he treated it like shit. He deserved what happened to him, and I'm not in the least sorry that night ended with him being blown to pieces. I hate thinking about what you went through with him, and the fact you had the strength to leave, to tell him to go fuck himself, makes me proud as hell."

He watched her swallow hard. "He changed so much," she said quietly. "I never would've dated him if he'd shown me his true colors from the start."

"I know," Jag soothed.

"I feel so stupid."

"You shouldn't. Not at all. Again, he's the asshole, Carly. The guy who put you in this position. Remember that, okay?"

She tilted her head and said the last thing he expected to hear. "Wait, is that a quote from the movie *Speed*?"

It was Jag's turn to look confused. "Um...I don't think so?"

"I think it is. It's right after the old woman got blown up on the steps and smushed by the bus. Annie, the heroine—you

know, Sandra Bullock? Anyway, she's upset and driving the bus and Jack, the hunky Keanu Reeves, kneels by her side and says almost exactly what you just said to me."

Jag grinned. "Yeah?"

"Uh-huh."

"And did his words help?"

A small smile lit up her face. "Yes. She said something like, 'Yeah, he's the big asshole,' or something like that."

"I haven't seen the movie," Jag admitted.

Carly's eyes nearly bugged out of her face. "You haven't?"

"No."

"Well, *that* needs to be rectified immediately. You remind me a lot of Jack. Your name even kinda sounds the same. Jag, Jack. He's brave, selfless, and sometimes funny."

"I'm not funny," Jag said with a straight face.

Carly giggled.

The sound shot straight to his heart. He much preferred Carly laughing than looking as stressed out and scared to death as she'd been last night when she'd opened her door.

Jag squeezed her hand. "You aren't alone, Carly. You've got me. And my team. And Baker. We're gonna figure this out. Together. Okay?"

She nodded.

"But first...you need to finish your breakfast."

She snorted. "You have an obsession with me eating," she muttered as she picked up her fork.

Reluctantly, Jag let go of her hand and sat back. "The thought of you being hungry doesn't sit well with me. So yeah, I'm probably gonna be overly obsessed with making sure you're getting enough to eat for a while, so you should get used to that," he told her.

Carly paused with a forkful of eggs halfway to her mouth and asked, "Why do you care so much?"

"You've gotten under my skin, angel. And I kind of like you there," Jag said baldly before putting a large bite of eggs into his own mouth.

She stared at him for a beat, before lifting her fork. She chewed and swallowed then admitted softly, "I think I like being there too."

They finished their eggs and waffles without any more heart-felt admissions, and Jag had never felt more settled. If this was what Mustang, Midas, Aleck, and Pid felt when they were with their women, no wonder they were so deliriously chipper all the time.

Jag hated that he'd waited so long to try to help Carly. He'd only guessed that Shawn had emotionally and physically abused her, and when she'd admitted he was right, it had taken every-thing within him not to leap up from the table and head out to find Luke himself. The man probably knew what his father was doing to Carly and did nothing to stop it. That alone made him a shitbag of the highest order in Jag's eyes.

Abusing women was a close second in the worst crimes someone could do to another. The first was the abuse of chil-dren. In Jag's opinion, nothing would ever top that.

Today, they'd gather intel. He was happy to accompany Carly to the police station. He needed to know what the hell the cops were doing about Luke and what their next steps were. If he didn't think they were adequate, he and his team, including Baker Rawlins, would take matters into their own hands. He had no idea what that would entail, but he'd do whatever it took to free Carly from the threat still hanging over her head.

CHAPTER FOUR

Carly sat next to Jag in his Jetta and tried not to panic. She didn't like being outside. Not in a car. Not at work. Not anywhere. She hated that Shawn and Luke had done that to her. Made her terrified to go about her everyday business.

As if Jag knew what she was thinking, he reached out and took one of her hands in his. He rested their clasped hands on the console between them.

It was crazy how he could make her feel protected with such a simple gesture. She wasn't safe, she knew that. Luke could just as easily take Jag out as he could her. But somehow, Jag's confidence and the way his eyes constantly scanned his surroundings made her feel as if she at least might have a chance.

"So...Baker?" she asked after a moment.

Jag glanced at her, then back at the road in front of him. "What do you want to know?"

"I heard Kenna talking about him at the wedding, bummed that he wasn't there. Who is he?"

"Baker Rawlins is a former SEAL who lives up on the North Shore. He spends his free time surfing."

When Jag didn't say anything else, Carly asked, "And? There has to be more to him than that."

His lips twitched. "Well, if you ask the girls, they'll all tell you how hot he is."

Carly's brows lowered in surprise. "Really? But they're...not single," she finished lamely.

"Well, they claim they're allowed to look, and that there's nothing wrong with saying someone is good-looking."

"That's true," she admitted. "And that's it? He's a good-looking former SEAL who likes to surf? And that somehow makes you and your friends want him involved in finding Luke?"

"No," Jag said, all teasing gone from his tone now. "He's deadly as hell. Not a man I'd want to piss off, but who I absolutely want on my side when I'm trying to track down someone who doesn't want to be found. He's intense, a little scary, but an honorable man. He was pissed when Kenna was taken hostage. Vowed to find Luke. I'm guessing the fact that he hasn't yet makes him very much *not* happy. What do you know about what happened to Monica?"

Carly blinked at the seemingly abrupt change of topic. She wanted to mention that if *Jag* thought Baker was scary, she absolutely did not want to meet him—because in reality, he was probably terrifying. Instead, she shrugged and said, "Nothing."

"She was kidnapped by a man who used her as bait to lure Baker to the Big Island. The guy used to be on Baker's SEAL team and was kicked off for being mentally unstable. His plan was for both Monica and Baker to be burned alive by Kailua's lava flow, but he underestimated his former team leader."

"Holy shit," Carly breathed, squeezing Jag's hand. "They're all okay?"

"If you mean Monica and Baker, yes. The other guy, not so much. He got a dose of his own medicine. My point is, Baker didn't hesitate to do what needed to be done to make sure Monica was safe. He also flew to New York to meet with frickin' mobsters to make sure *Elodie* would be safe from any retribution from a certain family. He should be relaxing in his retirement and worrying about nothing more than surf forecasts, but he's not. He's as much a part of our team as the rest of us, even if he's not active duty anymore."

"So, he wants to make sure Kenna's safe," Carly said softly.

"Yes," Jag said without hesitation.

For some reason, his answer made Carly's chest tighten.

"But also, he wants to mitigate the danger to *you*, angel," Jag continued.

Carly looked over at him, skeptical. "But this Baker guy doesn't even know me."

"Doesn't matter. He knows you're important to *me*, and that until Luke is neutralized, no one is safe."

She licked her lips. "Important to you?" She blurted the question without thought. Carly immediately wished she could take it back.

"Yes," Jag said, seemingly unconcerned. "I've spent every minute of my free time checking up on you and bugging him ceaselessly about what he might've found out."

Carly honestly wasn't sure what to say about that. She only knew how his words made her feel. Like she mattered. Like she wasn't invisible. Like someone cared if she lived or died. All of it made her want to cry.

As if he realized she needed a moment, he kept talking.

"After we meet with the detective, how would you feel about going over to see Kenna? I know she'd love to see *you*."

Carly *wanted* to say no. Being around Kenna felt...weird now. It was Carly's fault her friend had been taken hostage and almost blown to pieces.

"Okay," she whispered instead, after a long moment.

"If you need more time, that's all right, but I know for a fact she misses you terribly," Jag said gently. "Aleck said she talks about you all the time and complains that work isn't as much fun as it used to be because you aren't there. If you aren't ready to see her, maybe we could go down to Barbers Point and see if Lexie, Elodie, and Ashlyn need any help at Food For All."

A pang of longing hit Carly. She wanted to. She *really* wanted to. But the thought of being out in the open for so long made her heart rate spike. And if she brought attention to her friends, led Luke to any of them, she'd never forgive herself.

"Look at me, angel," Jag said in a low tone Carly couldn't ignore.

She hated being like this. She missed the outgoing person she used to be. She looked over at Jag and saw him splitting his attention between her and the road.

"I'm pushing you hard. I know that. But you aren't alone. You've got people who love and care about you. You said you wanted to take your life back, and I want to help you do that. As much as I want to be by your side every minute of every day, I can't. The last thing I want is you hiding out at my place just as you were in yours."

"You think *I* want that?" Carly asked almost angrily. "I hate feeling scared to step foot outside. I hate being bored out of my mind sitting at home. I miss my friends!"

"Then let me help you find the old Carly," Jag said, not upset by her outburst in the least.

"What if you can't? What if she's gone?" Carly whispered.

"She isn't," he said firmly. "She might be changed, but she's not gone. You're gonna get through this. Want to know how I know?"

Carly nodded.

"Because you want to. That seems simplistic, but when I look into your eyes, I see determination. And anger. And a desire to take back your life. And believe me when I say that many people who go through a trauma don't have that. They sometimes lose themselves. But not you. You can do this, Carly. It won't be easy. God, I wish I could tell you that it's just a matter of thinking positive, but it's so much more than that. It's struggling every day to overcome the demons in your head that are trying to tell you it's safer to hide out. It's forcing yourself to do things that scare you. It's leaning on your friends when you think you can't continue by yourself. You *can* do this, angel. I believe in you."

Carly swallowed hard and let his words sink into her psyche. She needed to hear that. Well, not the part about things being hard, but the rest of it.

And something else struck her right then...

Jag spoke as if he knew firsthand what he was talking about. As if he'd gone through something similar.

But that couldn't be right. He was the strongest person she knew. What could he have experienced that was anywhere near what she'd gone through? She didn't think being targeted by someone who wanted to kill him was it; being a SEAL made him a target every time he went on a mission, didn't it? Had he been a POW? Tortured?

42

Carly realized at that moment that she didn't *really* know Jag. She knew he was trustworthy, that he'd been there when she needed him. But she didn't know even the basic stuff about him. Where he grew up. If he had siblings. Why he'd joined the Navy in the first place.

And not knowing those things made her frown. Suddenly she wanted to know *everything* about this man. She'd relied on him over the last few months. Realizing only now how selfish she'd been. "Jag?"

"Yeah, angel?"

"I...okay."

He looked over at her in concern. "Okay?"

She nodded. "I can do this. I'm not going to let Shawn win."

"That'a girl," he said with pride.

"But can we wait and see how the visit with the detective goes before we make other plans? Can we take Operation Bring Back Carly in baby steps?"

Jag chuckled. "Yeah, angel. We can. And I'm sorry, I tend to get a little focused when there's something I want."

He glanced over at her again—and Carly stopped breathing at seeing the look of interest and intensity in his gaze. When he looked back at the road, she felt as if she could breathe again. Good Lord, Jag was lethal.

Yet, she couldn't help the spark of contentment deep inside that he'd looked at *her* that way.

Determination rose within her once again. She felt as if she was on a roller coaster with her emotions changing so much. One second she was terrified, then she was angry, then she wanted to cry...and now she was wondering how she could maybe attract Jag so he'd like her as much more than a friend.

It was confusing and tiring, but for the first time in months,

Carly felt alive. As if maybe, just maybe, she had a future. Even in death, Shawn had taken that from her for a while. But she was going to do her best to move on. Put Shawn behind her. And the first step was demanding the detective talk to her about her case. Tell her what he'd found out about Luke, if anything. What he learned would hopefully help her go forward.

Without Jag by her side, Carly had a feeling she never would've gotten up the courage to take this trip to the station. But he *was* there, and she felt stronger as a result. Squeezing his hand in gratitude, Carly did her best to relax against the seat.

Today felt like the first day of the rest of her life. She had no idea where she'd go from here, but it had to be better than cowering in a corner of her bedroom. Peeking over at Jag, she marveled again that he was with her. Holding her hand. Calling her angel.

She wanted this man for her own. He was nothing like Shawn, and she knew that down to the bottom of her soul. But she wanted to be a better woman for him. He deserved someone who wasn't scared all the time. Someone he could be proud of.

That thought alone gave her something to fight for. Jag was worth it, and she wanted to believe she was too.

Her positive thoughts lasted until she sat down in an interrogation room at the Honolulu Police Station downtown and was forced to wait for Detective Lee. The longer he made them wait, the more nervous Carly got. It didn't help that Jag was pacing back and forth impatiently. He was obviously not happy about having to wait either.

After an entire hour, the detective finally came into the room. "I'm sorry to keep you waiting."

Carly opened her mouth to say it was all right, but Jag spoke first.

"You should be. We've been here for an hour. Is this how you treat all your victims?"

She wasn't sure that was the best way to start out the conversation, but it was too late now.

To her surprise, the detective said, "You're right. And no, it isn't. I was at a scene where an eighty-seven-year-old man was mugged, probably for drug money. They got ten bucks, and the old man is now in the hospital trying to get his head sewn back together."

Carly grimaced.

Jag ran a hand through his hair. "Sorry, man."

The man sighed. "No, I'm sorry. That wasn't fair of me. And someone should've told you that I wasn't here. I'll figure out where the communication breakdown occurred and will make sure it doesn't happen again," Detective Lee said. "How about we start over?"

Jag nodded.

"I'm Detective Makanui Lee. Most people call me Mack. Or Detective." He held his hand out to Jag.

"Jagger Bennett. I'm a friend of Carly's. A close friend. And I'm a SEAL stationed at the Naval base. My friends and I have been trying to locate Luke, without any luck, so I'm very interested in what you've found out."

Carly saw respect creep into the detective's gaze. She hadn't expected Jag to come right out and tell the man he was a SEAL, but she figured the admission had done what he'd wanted it to—elevated Mack's opinion of him.

Mack turned to her. "You doing okay, Carly?"

She shrugged. "Yeah."

It seemed she wasn't a very good liar, because Mack immediately frowned, but he didn't comment on her blatant attempt to cover how she was really doing. "Thank you for coming down here today. I know you've already told me what you remember about that night, and the days that led up to it, but do you think we could go over it again? You might remember something new this time."

Carly sighed. She didn't remember anything else that might help the detective find Luke. She hadn't seen anything out of the ordinary prior to that day, and if she'd had any inkling that Shawn was about to do what he did, she would've said something. But she folded her hands in her lap and dutifully went back over the night of the attack. No, she hadn't seen Shawn at all that day, or in the days leading up to him coming to the restaurant. The last time had been months before, the night she'd met Jag for the first time, at Duke's. Yes, she'd seen Luke on the beach the day Shawn died, but he hadn't attempted to speak to her at all.

When she was done, she waited for the detective to ask her more questions, but he simply sighed and leaned back in his chair.

"Right, so here's the thing...we've talked to Luke Keyes, and there's absolutely no evidence that he was involved in the kidnapping attempt of Ms. Madigan."

"Wait—what?" Jag asked incredulously. "You've talked to him? In person?"

"Yes. He knew we were looking for him and he came in voluntarily."

"Fuck," Jag said, standing up and pacing again in agitation.

"How come Carly didn't know this? Carly, *did* you know they'd found him?"

She shook her head. She was in as much shock as Jag.

"We checked his alibi and it came back clear. He said he was with his girlfriend and she verified his story."

"She could be lying," Jag said.

The detective pressed his lips together for a moment, then said, "It's possible, but I've interviewed a lot of persons of interest, and they both came across as believable."

Carly could tell Jag was on the verge of losing it. When he paced by her the next time, she reached out and put her hand on his thigh. He stopped in his tracks immediately.

He took a deep breath, as if trying to calm himself, then said, "A friend of mine has been looking for Luke since this happened and hasn't had any luck. And my friend is *good* at what he does. Where is Luke now?"

"You know I can't disclose that information," the detective said. "But he apparently has a lot of friends who are doing their best to hide him."

"Isn't that illegal?" Carly managed to ask.

"Not when he hasn't been charged with anything," Mack said. "He's also lawyered up. He came in once to give us his statement, but said any more questions would have to go through his lawyer."

"So, if you don't think it's Luke, what *have* you found out about who was working with her ex?" Jag asked, his irritation easy to hear in his tone.

Carly hated confrontation. It made her extremely uncomfortable. She would much rather people get along than argue. But she was still glad Jag was with her today. He was asking all

the questions she wanted answers to, but knew she probably wouldn't have had the courage to bring up.

Detective Lee looked uneasy. He pulled over the notebook he'd been jotting notes in and flipped a page.

"We've interviewed all the people Ms. Stewart told us she thought could be involved. Jamie Redmon, Shawn's boss at the Coca-Cola bottling plant; Eddie Evans, Shawn's neighbor; Kelly Gregory, the woman Shawn was seeing before Carly; Wes Schell, Shawn's landlord; Luke and his girlfriend, Rebecca Nelson; and Shawn's three best friends, Beau Langford, Gideon Sparks, and Jeremiah Barrowman. There's no evidence that *any* of them were working with Shawn."

Carly shivered at hearing the list of names. Each and every one of them were tight with Shawn, except Kelly, and she wouldn't be surprised if one or more of the others had conspired with her ex to hurt her.

"How many own boats?" Jag asked.

"Three. Jamie, Eddie, and Beau."

"And did you check the marinas where their boats are kept?"

"Yes."

Jag kept firing questions at the detective, and to the man's credit, he didn't shy away from answering.

This meeting hadn't gone at all like Carly had thought it might. She'd been hoping to get concrete evidence that Luke had been working with his father and reassurance that it was only a matter of time before he'd be charged and behind bars. But that obviously wasn't going to happen. In fact, it seemed as if the man she'd thought was the biggest danger to her might not be the person she should be afraid of after all.

It seemed the investigation had stalled. The detective hadn't

found any information that would lead him to believe anyone was working with Shawn.

"You know as well as we do that Shawn had an accomplice," Jag said. He hadn't moved from where he was standing next to her while he'd asked his questions. Carly still had her hand on his leg, she was actually gripping his pants leg now, feeling numb after everything she'd heard.

"From what Kenna Madigan said, Shawn was out of his mind that night," Detective Lee shared. "It's entirely possible he *thought* someone was coming to pick him up, but no one actually was. The storm that night was the worst the area's seen in years. It would've been next to impossible for someone to actually navigate in the wind, rain, and near-zero visibility."

"So, what, that's it?" Jag bit out. "The investigation is over? Closed?"

"I didn't say that," the detective hedged. He turned to look at Carly. "Is there anyone else you can think of who might've been working with your ex?"

"No," Jag said, once more speaking up before Carly could answer.

She glanced up in confusion. He wasn't looking at her though, he was shooting daggers out of his eyes at Detective Lee. "It isn't Carly's responsibility to give you suspects. It's *your* duty as a detective to do your job and figure it out yourself."

"It's okay," she said softly, unconsciously petting Jag's leg.

"It's not," he said with a shake of his head.

"We've looked into the people Shawn worked with, talked to most of them either in person or on the phone," Detective Lee said. "Their alibis check out. Most were home with their families and extended families. We've spent hundreds of hours interviewing, and almost every single person was shocked at what

happened. Some didn't even know Carly, hadn't ever met her, and had no motive to help Shawn.

"We haven't closed the case, but we literally have no proof anyone was on the water that night, waiting to ferry Shawn and his hostage out of the area. We've scoured the videos from the marinas near Waikiki and haven't found anything out of the ordinary. Unless Carly can think of someone else who might've assisted Shawn, or until more evidence comes to light, there's not much else we can do right now."

Carly swallowed hard. She wasn't sure how to feel. Should she be relieved that all the people she'd told the detective to look into had essentially been cleared? Should she feel even *more* paranoid?

Without a word, Jag reached down and caught Carly's hand in his. He pulled her to her feet and immediately wrapped an arm around her waist, holding her close. It was a good thing... because Carly had a feeling if she wasn't leaning on him, she would've fallen flat on her face.

"You'll be in touch if you find out any more information, yeah?" Jag asked.

"Of course," Detective Lee said. "I'm very sorry I didn't have better news for you today. If it helps, because it's been so long since the incident, I think you're safe. Mr. Keyes was obviously the mastermind of his plot and if someone *was* working with him, his death has clearly made them back off."

Jag didn't respond, but Carly, not wanting to be rude, said, "Thank you."

She walked through the station hand-in-hand with Jag and when people saw him coming, they quickly got out of his way. He wasn't a very tall man—except compared to her—but he was

obviously throwing off enough angry vibes that no one dared mess with him.

They walked out into the warm afternoon air and he didn't slow down as he headed for the parking garage. As usual, the moment Carly stepped outside, the hair on the back of her neck stood up. She couldn't help but feel as if she was being watched. It was part of the reason she'd hidden away for so long.

Even though Detective Lee had told her he thought she was likely safe, she didn't feel that way. Glancing up at Jag made her feel marginally better. His head was on a constant swivel, watching for anyone or anything out of place.

Jag opened the passenger door without a word and Carly got in. She kept her eyes on him as he walked around to his side. After closing his door, Jag gripped the steering wheel tightly and stared straight ahead.

"Jag?" Carly asked softly.

"Give me a minute," he replied between clenched teeth.

Seeing him so upset unsettled her. In all the time she'd known him, he'd been even-keeled. But right now, it seemed as if he was on the verge of completely losing it.

Carly swallowed hard and stayed as quiet as she could. She barely breathed, not wanting to do anything that might make him even more upset than he obviously already was. But she wasn't scared of him. Not like she'd been of Shawn when he'd gotten overwhelmed with anger. No, Jag would never hurt her. He wasn't mad at her, just obviously frustrated with the situation and all the unanswered questions talking with the detective had brought up.

She reached over and put her hand on his arm, and he immediately turned toward her. He shifted and took her hand in his

and brought it up to his lips. He kissed her fingers gently and sighed.

"I'm sorry. I'm being an ass," he said.

"It's okay," Carly said immediately.

"It's not. I usually have better control over my emotions. But I'm not happy about the fact the cops don't have any persons of interest. And that they're thinking no one was working with Shawn in the first place."

"Maybe there wasn't," Carly said with a shrug.

He looked at her. "There *was*," he said firmly.

"How do you know? Maybe I'm just paranoid."

"You aren't. I know that without a doubt. There've been many missions where we've gotten a sixth sense that something wasn't right. Call it foresight or whatever you want, but I've been trained never to discount those feelings. And you haven't been hiding away from the world for nothing. If you've sensed someone is watching you, someone is watching you." He paused for a moment. "Did I scare you?"

Carly blinked. "Scare me?"

"I never want to do anything that might remind you of that asshole you dated. I'll *never* hurt you physically, and I will try damn hard not to hurt you emotionally. If I need time to process something, you shouldn't be afraid I'll take whatever is going on out on you. Okay?"

"Okay," Carly said immediately.

He kissed her fingers again, then lowered her hand so it was resting on his thigh, his hand still clutching hers. "The detective might think this is over, but I won't be satisfied until Baker talks to each and every one of Shawn's acquaintances and friends himself. And until that happens, and *Baker* tells me he's cleared them, I want you to stay with me."

The emotion swirling in his chocolate-brown eyes nearly hypnotized Carly, freezing her in place. "All right."

What else could she say? She certainly didn't want to go back to her apartment, especially not after learning the police weren't actively looking at anyone at the moment.

It finally sank in that they truly didn't believe Luke was involved. She'd given Detective Lee all those names because he'd insisted on knowing about anyone Shawn was friendly with, but she'd never really believed any of them had anything to do with his insane plot to kidnap and torture her.

But if Luke wasn't the person waiting in the ocean, ready to pick up his father...who could it have been? Were the police right? Was Shawn delusional and only *thought* someone would be coming for him? It didn't seem likely.

"Stop," Jag said, untangling their fingers and gently wrapping his hand around the back of her neck. He wasn't squeezing, wasn't hurting her, but his touch pulled her back from the panic attack that had begun to creep in. "Take a breath, angel."

She did.

"Good. Another."

Carly inhaled deeply, hating the feeling of vulnerability that washed over her.

"I'm gonna talk to Baker, let him know what the detective said. He's not going to just blindly trust him; the man doesn't trust anyone. He'll find Luke and talk to him. He'll also track down all the others the detective mentioned as well. If one of them was working with Shawn, he'll find out."

"Is he gonna...torture them?"

Jag looked surprised for a moment, then surprisingly, he grinned. Some of the emotion in his expression faded. "No. He's

a badass, but he won't go that far. He won't need to. He's got a way of making people be honest with him."

Carly tried to relax her hunched shoulders and the rest of her muscles. "All right."

"You were right in asking me to wait until after the meeting to decide what our plans would be for the rest of the day. I have no desire to be social right now. You?"

She shook her head.

"Good. So how about a walk on the beach?"

The effort she'd made to relax her muscles was wasted as she immediately tensed once more.

"A short one," Jag said. "Over at Barbers Point."

"I can't," Carly said, her voice trembling.

"You think I'm gonna let anything happen to you?" Jag asked with a tilt of his head.

Carly's breathing had sped up at the thought of walking on a public beach, out in the open. "I'm not ready," she told him, avoiding answering his question.

"You are," he insisted. "You're not fighting by yourself anymore, angel. I'm right here."

Carly closed her eyes and felt Jag's thumb brushing against the sensitive skin on her neck. She wanted to insist that he bring her back to her apartment, where she could lock herself in once more and try to process everything the detective had told her. But that would be cowardly. A step backward. She wanted to believe no one was gunning for her. That no one was out there, biding their time...but it wasn't that easy.

Hating her rolling emotions, Carly tried to bring forth the anger she'd felt earlier. "Okay," she whispered.

"There she is," Jag said.

Carly opened her eyes and met his gaze.

"My brave angel. We'll make it a short walk. Then we'll grab some takeout on the way home and I'll call Baker."

His hand began to slide away, and Carly reached up and grabbed his wrist. He stilled.

"Thank you, Jag. For everything. I'm trying, but I can't shake that feeling of being watched."

He immediately turned his head to look out the window on her side, then to his own. Only when he was sure no one was lurking around their car did he look at her. "Let him watch," he said firmly. "He'll know you're no longer alone. If he tries anything, he'll regret it."

Carly wasn't sure she liked the sound of that, but Jag had already turned to start the engine. He pulled out of the parking spot and they headed out of the city.

CHAPTER FIVE

The rest of the late afternoon had gone fairly smoothly. Carly was tense and obviously on edge while they walked on the beach, but Jag had done his best to put her at ease. After a short fifteen-minute stroll, they were back in his car, headed for his apartment complex.

He picked up some Italian food on the way home, and he hadn't missed the way Carly's shoulders slumped in relief as soon as the door shut and locked behind them. He hated that she felt so vulnerable and scared when she was out in public, but he honestly couldn't really blame her.

Hearing the detective say that the investigation had essentially hit a brick wall, that he hadn't found any evidence anyone was working with Carly's ex, made him furious. *Someone* had plotted with Shawn. *Someone* had willingly gone along with his plan to kidnap and torture Carly. Just because the detective hadn't figured out who or someone was possibly an expert liar, didn't mean the threat to Carly was over.

It had been a mistake to let as much time pass as it had before acting. Carly had suffered needlessly, alone in that apartment, and Jag wouldn't soon forgive himself for that.

Jag was glad he'd at least been able to convince Carly to call Kenna on the way home. She'd seemed buoyed after the short conversation.

It was only a matter of time before she rekindled the close friendship she had with the other woman, before she was sucked back into the girl tribe. He had no doubt she and Monica would get along when they got to know each other. Monica was a bit standoffish, and that would probably endear her to Carly even more. Yes, Carly was previously outgoing and gregarious, but after the last couple of months, she certainly understood the appeal of keeping to herself. She'd respect that aspect of Monica's personality.

He'd sent a text to Mustang letting him know that they needed to talk, but later, when he didn't have to watch what he said around Carly. It wasn't that he wanted to keep secrets from her, but he did want to shield her from any more of his anger over the situation. He'd been an asshole earlier, letting her see his frustration after talking with the detective. He didn't want to give her any reason to compare him to Shawn.

But Jag was definitely furious about the situation. At the police. At himself for not bringing her here sooner. At whoever was out there in the shadows, watching and waiting.

Carly said she felt as if she was being watched, and Jag had no doubt that the mysterious accomplice *was* out there. There was a reason she'd hidden herself away in her apartment, and feeling as if someone was watching her every move was a damn good one.

"Why don't you head to bed?" Jag suggested after it had

gotten dark outside. Since dinner, Carly had been reading a book on her phone, or at least trying to. Her eyes kept closing involuntarily. She reminded him of a kid in school who fell asleep in class. Her head bobbed down, waking her up before she did her best to concentrate on her book. But inevitably her eyes would close and her head would droop once more. She had more sleep to catch up on.

She stared at him, and he could read the question in her eyes. Jag had done his best to give her space. Had longed to sit right next to her on his couch and pull her against him, but he'd resisted. He'd moved fast enough as it was. The last thing he wanted was to make her uncomfortable with their living situation.

Jag liked having her here. He'd spent too many nights worrying about her. Wondering if she was eating, sleeping all right, if she was scared. Having her here went a long way toward soothing the part of him that wanted to take care of her. Make sure she was all right.

"Um, okay. But..." Her voice trailed off.

"What, Carly? You can ask me anything. Tell me anything."

"You only have one bedroom," she blurted. "I thought I'd sleep out here."

"No." His response was firm and nonnegotiable. "If anyone's sleeping on my couch, it'll be me."

"I can't take your bed," she protested.

"Why not?"

"Because," she said.

"That's not an answer," he teased. "Look, it's a king-size bed. There's plenty of room for both of us. I swear on my honor as a SEAL, I will *not* touch you or do anything to make you uncomfortable. You're safe, angel. From anyone who might want to get

their hands on you, and from me. But if you don't feel comfortable with me sleeping in there, I'll stay out here. It's fine. This couch is comfortable, I've fallen asleep on it plenty of times while watching TV. Besides, I've slept in way worse places in my lifetime. The only thing I care about is you, about you feeling safe."

Carly stared at him for a long moment. He couldn't read the emotions swirling in her eyes, which bothered him. A lot.

"Okay."

He relaxed a fraction at her answer, but still grinned and echoed, "Okay what? You want me to stay out here, or in the bedroom with you?" He held his breath as he waited for her answer. Mostly because he wanted to sleep next to her *more* than he wanted to breathe.

Last night had been a dream come true. Her presence calmed the demons swirling around in his head, which seemed like a minor miracle, since he'd lived with them for so long. But he'd do whatever she needed him to do, and would simply be grateful she was sharing his space.

"I have one question," she said.

"Shoot."

"Which side of the bed do you like? Because I like the right, and I'm not sure I can sleep on the left." Her lips twitched as she waited for his response.

Jag chuckled. "You can have the right."

"Jag?"

"Yeah, angel?"

"I can't thank you enough for—"

"No." He totally interrupted her, but didn't care.

"You don't even know what I was going to say," she protested.

"I do, and the last thing I want is your gratitude," he said

honestly. "I'm already kicking myself for not acting sooner. The thought of you huddled in your apartment, scared out of your mind, is..." He shuddered. It hit too close to home, is what it did. But he didn't say that. "You're here because I care about you. Because I hate the thought of you not living your life. So no more talk of gratitude, okay?"

"I'll try," she said.

"Good. I'll be in a bit later."

Carly stared at him for a beat before nodding and standing. She headed down the hall and he heard the bedroom door shut.

Taking a deep breath, Jag stood and grabbed his phone. He'd been itching to call Baker all afternoon. The man wasn't going to take what he had to say well, but he didn't want to wait another second.

Keeping one ear open for Carly coming out of the bedroom, he impatiently paced as the phone rang in his ear.

"Baker."

"It's Jag. I have info."

"Hit me."

And he did. Jag told Baker all about the detective speaking with Luke in person, and how they believed his alibi. He went on to detail the other people Carly had mentioned, explaining that the police didn't believe any of them were involved.

When he was done, there was silence on the other end of the phone line.

"Baker? You still there."

"I'm here," he said. "It's obvious I haven't been putting enough effort into this. That's gonna change right now."

Feeling a little concerned about the lack of emotion in Baker's tone, and knowing that didn't bode well for Luke Keyes or anyone else, Jag said, "Carly's safe. She's here with me."

"About time," he bit out.

Jag wanted to laugh. It hadn't been that long since he'd first met Carly. Only someone in their circle would think too much time had gone by before he'd moved her in. The only person moving slower was Slate. "Keep me in the loop," Jag ordered. "I want to know what you've learned the second you touch base with any person of interest."

"I work alone," Baker reminded him.

"Not in this you don't," Jag insisted. "I don't know your story, but SEALs work together. And you might not be active duty anymore, but you're still a fucking SEAL. Not to mention, this is my woman we're talking about. This is Carly's life at stake, and if I'm going to keep her safe, I have to fucking know what the hell is going on. Got it?"

Baker hesitated for a beat before Jag heard a rusty chuckle across the phone line. "Shit, man, I don't think I've heard you talk so much in one breath before."

"Fuck off," Jag griped.

"You believe the detective?" Baker asked, abruptly switching topics.

"Yes and no. Obviously I don't think all the suspects are guilty, but I absolutely believe one of them is. *Someone* was out there in the ocean waiting for some sort of signal from Shawn to come and get him."

"You think he, or she, will try to finish what Shawn started?" Baker asked.

Jag was getting annoyed. The man already knew the answer to that question. "Yes. If they were crazy enough to agree to the scheme in the first place, they're invested. Maybe invested enough to see Shawn's plan through."

"Exactly. I'll do some digging. Then I'll be in touch." Baker

hung up without another word.

Jag felt edgy. Keyed up. He wanted to be *doing* something. Hunting down the suspects and interrogating them himself. But as an active-duty SEAL, he had to tread lightly. It was better that Baker did the legwork, but that didn't mean Jag liked it.

Without hesitating, Jag spun around and stalked down the hall toward his room. It was earlier than he usually turned in, but then again, he didn't normally have Carly waiting for him.

He slowly pushed open the bedroom door, and stared at the woman in his bed. She'd left the bathroom light on, giving him more than enough light to see. She was on the right, on her side, curled into a ball. He hated her defensive position.

He grabbed a pair of sweats and headed for the bathroom. Within a minute or so he was done and heading for the left side of his king-size bed. He'd left the bathroom light on, not wanting Carly to wake up and forget where she was.

He'd hadn't lied earlier. He didn't mind if Carly took the right side of the bed...because he usually slept in the middle. It made it harder for someone to sneak up on him in the dark hours of the night if he was smack dab in the center of the large mattress. He scooted over to his usual spot and couldn't help but smile when Carly immediately turned and snuggled into him.

So much for not touching while they slept.

But a part of Jag knew this would happen. There was no way he'd be able to keep his distance. Not after he'd held her in his arms last night. He wanted the right to touch her, and not just in bed.

That was very new. He'd never been fixated on sex. Ever. And it was disconcerting to be thinking about it so often now. Sex with Carly would change his life, he knew that without a doubt in his mind.

He wasn't ready for that step yet. He wanted to be sure. Wanted *her* to be sure. Wanted her to be with him because of who he was, not because he was keeping her safe. It was a dangerous line to walk because he had no idea if she'd ever be able to separate the two.

He was a SEAL, keeping people safe was what he did. Well, it wasn't *all* he did, but it was a large part of who he was. He'd made it his mission in life early on to champion those who couldn't protect themselves. The vulnerable and weak. Not that Carly was weak; far from it. Maybe he should be more worried about himself; about separating Carly from his own past.

Memories threatened to pull him into a dark place, and Jag did his best to push them back. He inhaled, bringing the slightly sweet smell of her lotion into his nose. He's seen her bottle on his bathroom sink. Cherry blossom. He'd never smell it again without thinking of her.

"What time is it?" she mumbled.

"Shhhh," Jag whispered. "Late."

It wasn't really that late, but he didn't want her to fully wake up and feel weird about being snuggled next to him and turn away, putting space between them once more.

"'Kay."

He held his breath until he felt puffs of air from her long, deep breaths waft over his skin. There were a million and one things Jag needed to think about. Things he wanted to do to help Carly. But at the moment, all he could focus on was how right it felt to have her by his side.

Slowly, he lifted a hand and smoothed her hair away from her face. Her nose scrunched up a little at his touch, but she snuggled into him even more. Her blonde hair was spread across his pillow and he resisted the urge to bring the strands up to his

nose to inhale her scent. Her face was relaxed in sleep and she had tempting full lips he couldn't stop staring at. She was only a little bit shorter than he was, and he loved how she fit against him.

Being as attracted to her as he was, noticing every little detail about her, should've surprised him. Jag had never cared about a woman's looks, really; he was more concerned about any ulterior motives they might have.

And they always seemed to have them. Wanting to sleep with a SEAL just to say they'd done it. Wanted something from him. To use him in some way. It wasn't until Mustang hooked up with Elodie that Jag had met a woman who was completely selfless. Elodie loved his team leader unconditionally, and the sentiment was definitely returned. Then Lexie had come into Midas's life, and Jag witnessed the same thing between them.

By the time Aleck met Kenna, Jag had begun to open himself up to the possibility that maybe, just maybe, there was someone out there for him too. Monica and Pid's relationship had strengthened the idea.

And now here he was, with Carly. Oh, they weren't in a relationship. Not a romantic one, at least. But he felt much more comfortable because they'd started out as friends. He'd gotten to know her over the last few months and trust had grown.

For the first time in his life, Jag wanted a girlfriend. Wanted to share his space with someone. He even found himself wanting to open up to her, to let her in and share all his hidden secrets. But it was definitely too early for that.

In the meantime, he'd do what he could to help Carly take back her life...and if anyone tried to take it away from her again, they'd have to deal with him.

Jag fell asleep with a feeling of anticipation running through

his veins. He was ready for this. Ready to slay Carly's dragons...
and maybe have her slay his at the same time.

CHAPTER SIX

Carly fought the urge to puke. She couldn't believe she'd let Jag talk her into this.

The last week had been amazing. She almost felt like her old self again. She'd talked to Kenna almost daily on the phone and had been out of Jag's apartment at least once each day as well. Granted, he'd been at her side every time, but still.

They'd gone to the grocery store, he'd taken her to the mall to get some more odds and ends that she needed, and he'd even taken her to the beach for a picnic dinner one evening. It was funny, because others seemed to always give them a wide berth, as if they were afraid of Jag or something. But Carly had never, not once, been afraid of the large man. He made her feel less vulnerable...and she secretly liked the air of danger he seemed to exude for others.

To her, he represented safety. But that wasn't all he represented.

The more time they spent together, the harder it was to not throw herself at him.

He was constantly touching her. Small brushes of his hand against her lower back, putting their entwined hands on his thigh as they watched TV, even kissing her temple now and then. But it was at night when it was the most difficult to keep her hands to herself.

Every night, he sent her to bed first then followed later. She was usually asleep by the time he came in, but immediately woke up when he climbed into bed. She turned over and snuggled into him, knowing he'd wrap his arm around her and hold her close. For the last few months, nighttime had been the worst for her by far. She imagined she saw people lurking in the shadows all the time. She'd slept better in the week she'd been with Jag than she had in her entire life, even before her paranoia.

But being around him constantly only made her want him *more*. She was glad that he didn't want her gratitude, even though she still felt it, because she wanted him to see her as more than a charity case. She wanted what Kenna had. What Elodie, Lexie, and Monica had. She wanted the right to touch Jag how and where she wanted, when she wanted. She wanted the privilege of knowing his innermost thoughts.

But they weren't there yet. She wanted to think they were moving toward a more intimate relationship, but it would take some time.

One thing Carly *wasn't* all that thrilled about was the way Jag pushed her, hard, to talk to Alani, her manager at Duke's. Or rather, her former manager. Which brought her back to her present predicament.

Carly wasn't sure she was ready to go back to work. Leaving Jag's apartment was still incredibly stressful and difficult. And he

wanted her to put herself out there, maybe even in danger, by going back to work?

"I still don't understand why you're insisting on this," she said as they sat in his car in a parking garage in Waikiki, not far from Duke's. She'd agreed to come down and talk to Alani, but now that she was actually here, she wanted to insist Jag take her back to his apartment.

"What did you like about being a waitress?" he asked, instead of acknowledging her statement.

She sighed. "Hanging out with Kenna. And Paulo and Kaleen. I liked seeing people's faces when they tried the hula pie. I enjoyed when groups came in to celebrate something... birthdays, anniversaries, weddings. And I'd be lying if I didn't say I liked the money."

"It's not lost on me that you listed the friendships you made first," Jag said. "Carly, you're a lot like Kenna in that you thrive when you're around other people. They make you happy. You need that."

"But being around people means Luke, or whoever was working with Shawn, can get to me," Carly protested.

Jag reached for her hand and clasped it between both of his own. "I wish I could sit here and tell you that won't happen. But I can't. I'm not exactly thrilled that the police haven't found any connection between Shawn's plan and his acquaintances, but I think your need to be around your friends outweighs my desire to lock you away until we figure out who Shawn recruited to help him."

Carly's respect for Jag increased. She needed him to be real with her, even when it upset her, and this was about as real as it could get.

"I've talked to Aleck, and he's hired a car service to bring

Kenna to work each day, then he picks her up himself after her shifts. He said it wouldn't be a problem to add you to the pickup schedule. I think if you can work the same shifts as Kenna, you'd feel a lot more comfortable. And you told me yourself that when you had that protective order out against Shawn, you were hyper alert at work, as were the bartenders and other servers. Kenna also said there's now a security guard at the restaurant at all times when they're open. You can do this, Carly, I know you can."

His belief in her made Carly want to cry. He had more confidence in her than she did. "I'm scared, Jag," she admitted. It wasn't as if he didn't already know how frightened she was to leave his apartment. He'd seen her mini panic attacks every time he convinced her to go with him on one errand or another. He'd seen how she was constantly on the lookout for anyone who seemed like they might want to try to snatch her.

"I know," he said softly, moving one of his hands to the side of her face.

Carly closed her eyes and leaned against his palm.

"But I also know that you need this."

Carly wanted to disagree. Wanted to tell him that no, she needed to hang out at his apartment until the police, or Baker, found some concrete evidence against someone and an arrest was made. But even she knew that wasn't realistic...or brave.

"If I get kidnapped from Duke's, I'm gonna blame you," she lamely joked.

Not one ounce of humor showed on Jag's face. "I will too," he agreed. "You ready?"

Carly shook her head, but said, "Yeah, I guess."

Now his lips quirked upward. "You're amazing," he said without making a move to get out of the car.

"No, I'm really not," she protested.

Jag leaned forward—and Carly held her breath. Was he going to kiss her? Oh, God, please let him be about to kiss her.

But instead of dropping his lips on hers, he kissed her forehead.

Carly let out the breath she'd been holding—and thought she felt Jag smiling slightly—but when he pulled back, his facial expression was blank. "After you talk to Alani, how about we go visit Food For All?"

It was Saturday, and Carly knew the food pantry would be busy. Lexie, Elodie, and Ashlyn worked their asses off trying to help feed as many people as they could.

"Maybe Alani will have some food we could bring," she suggested lightly.

"Maybe," Jag agreed. "Stay put, I'll come around."

Carly nodded and watched as he climbed out his side of the vehicle and walked around the front. They'd had a talk about this, and while Carly insisted she could open her own door, she had to admit she felt better about him getting out first and checking the area. Not to mention, he'd be with her if anyone dared try something in the parking garage.

He was at her door in seconds, holding out a hand to help her out. After he shut the door, he didn't let go of her hand, and Carly didn't even think about protesting. This was a new thing in the last day or so, the constant hand-holding when they were out of the house. And she loved holding Jag's hand. It gave her more confidence. Maybe if someone was watching her, they'd realize it would be stupid to do anything with this muscular man at her side.

They headed down the stairwell to the street and turned

toward Duke's. They walked through the mall part of the hotel entrance, toward the back, where the restaurant was located.

As soon as they got close, Vera let out a high-pitched shriek and came out from behind the hostess stand, running toward them.

Carly heard Jag chuckle right before he dropped her hand. She braced, and Jag's hand at Carly's back kept her from falling backward as Vera tackle-hugged her.

"Oh my God! It's so good to see you, woman!" Vera said, her voice muffled in Carly's hair.

"Thanks," she told her.

Everyone around them was now staring, but for once, Carly didn't care. She closed her eyes and reveled in the pleasure coursing through her. Vera's reaction was genuine and heartfelt, and Carly fought to keep her tears from falling.

Vera pulled back and smiled. "Please please please tell me you're here to work and not to eat," she said.

Carly shrugged. "I'm here to talk to Alani. I'm not sure if I can get my job back or not. I did quit."

Vera waved her hand in the air breezily. "Oh, you'll get it back," she said confidently. "The most recent hires have been horrible. Always late, wanting to take longer breaks than they're allotted." The hostess linked her arm with Carly's and escorted her toward the entrance. "It really *is* wonderful to see you," Vera said.

Carly looked back and saw Jag following at a discreet distance. Having him at her back was a huge relief. For the first time in ages, she didn't feel the need to be constantly on guard. Because Jag would make sure she was safe.

Alani must've heard Vera's screech when she first saw Carly,

because as they neared the entrance, the manager came around the corner and smiled at her. She didn't make a scene like Vera did, but the look on her face was just as genuine. She hugged Carly tightly then put her hands on her shoulder and asked, "Are you okay?"

"I'm good," Carly said.

"We've all been really worried about you," Alani said. "What happened was horrible. And damn scary."

"I'm sorry I wasn't here," Carly replied, guilt threatening to overwhelm her. "Shawn came looking for *me*."

"Well, I'm not," Alani said firmly. "There's no telling what that asshole would've done if he'd gotten his hands on you."

Carly swallowed hard. This was even more difficult than she'd anticipated. But Alani didn't seem to notice her discomfort. "Come on. If I don't let a certain bartending duo see you before we talk, I'll never hear the end of it." Her former manager towed her into the restaurant toward the bar area.

There was another loud screech, then Paulo was racing toward her. Carly couldn't help but laugh. Paulo was always a little dramatic and it felt good to see that nothing had changed in the time she'd been gone.

The bartender grabbed her up and twirled her around in circles before letting her feet touch the floor once more. "Girl! You're back!"

"Well, I'm not sure I'm *back*-back, but I'm here to talk to Alani about the possibility."

"Oh, you're back," Paulo said with certainty.

Then Kaleen was there, and Carly was smothered in another hug. The two bartenders did their best to talk over each other as they tried to catch her up on months of gossip.

Carly couldn't help but laugh. "Enough, you two, jeez.

Nothing changes around here, does it? You're still like the three stooges, but there's only two of you."

They both laughed, and Alani joined in.

"I swear customers come just to listen to their banter," the manager said. "I'd schedule them on different shifts if I didn't think our patrons would complain."

"Paulo's a pain in the ass, but he's a damn good bartender," Kaleen said with a smile.

"I'm not a pain, *you're* a pain," he retorted.

"Yeah? Who was it who convinced that guy to ask you out on a date last week?" Kaleen asked. "You weren't thinking I was a pain then."

"True, and that man was f-i-n-e," Paulo said, fanning his face with his hand dramatically.

"All right, you two, back to work," Alani said. "I'll bring Carly by after we talk."

Paulo leaned forward and winked as he said, "Is that tall drink of water who hasn't taken his eyes off you for a second with *you?*"

Carly turned and saw Jag leaning against a wall not too far away. He definitely had his eyes on her, and for once, Carly was thrilled to be watched. She turned back to Paulo. "That's Jag. You've met him a few times already."

Paulo squinted then stood up straight. "Damn, it is. All the good ones are taken." Then he leaned forward and hugged Carly once more before heading back to the bar. Luckily it was early enough that it wasn't terribly busy and no one seemed to mind the short wait for their drinks.

"Come on," Alani said. "I think we'd better have our talk before the rest of the staff sees you. Otherwise, we might never

get a chance." Carly followed her toward the kitchen, and the small office that was in the back of the space.

She looked at Jag once more, relieved to see his eyes still glued to her. It felt incredible to have him watching over her. That was one of the biggest reasons she'd let him convince her to leave his apartment at all this week, because she trusted him.

She mouthed, "You okay?" before she entered the kitchen area.

Jag nodded and made a swirling motion with his finger, then pointed to where he was standing. Carly interpreted that to mean he'd be waiting for her right where he was. She nodded, and he smiled.

That smile gave her courage a boost, something she definitely needed before talking to her former boss.

CHAPTER SEVEN

Jag stayed right where he was as he waited for Carly to finish her chat with her manager. He had a good view of the bar and the beach beyond the eating area. Everywhere he looked, he saw smiling tourists and employees who seemed to be in a good mood. He could understand why Kenna and Carly enjoyed working here.

The other employees seemed nice enough, and Jag wasn't surprised with the welcome they'd given Carly. She wasn't quite as outgoing as Kenna, but she could certainly give the other woman a run for her money.

Jag didn't see anyone who looked out of place, which was a relief. He was still waiting for Baker to send pictures of the people the detective had investigated. The people who Carly had said were somewhat close to Shawn. Until he had those, he couldn't let down his guard.

His gaze wandered to the ocean. Right now, the water was

almost as smooth as glass. It was hard to believe it had been so dangerous a few months ago.

Jag had no problem waiting for as long as it took for Carly to talk to Alani, so he was surprised when the pair reappeared out of the kitchen area only twenty minutes later.

Carly hugged her boss before joining him.

"All good?" Jag asked.

"Yeah."

She didn't tell him what they'd discussed, whether she'd gotten her job back or not, and before Jag could ask, two of the servers approached.

Once again, he watched as Carly was welcomed back. She introduced them as Justin and Charlotte. As they talked...it was just as he'd expected. Carly seemed to glow from within the longer she spent around people she liked and respected.

It took another forty minutes before she finished speaking with the staff she knew, and even a few of the customers who were apparently regulars stopped her to say hello.

As he walked them back through the mall area and toward the main street that went through Waikiki, Jag took her hand in his once more.

They didn't talk as they headed toward the parking garage. There were a lot of people around, and he concentrated on weaving in and out of the many tourists. Once he'd gotten her settled in his car, and he'd locked the doors behind them, Jag turned to her and asked, "So?"

Carly gave him a small smile. "Apparently Alani never turned in the paperwork to terminate me. So she doesn't have to rehire me at all. I can start whenever I'm ready."

"That's great news, angel."

Carly took a deep breath. "Yeah, I guess it is. I wasn't all that

fired up to start working again, especially not back at Duke's where everything happened. But being there today, and seeing everyone, made me realize how much I've missed it."

Jag couldn't stop the smile from forming on his face.

Carly saw it and rolled her eyes. "Go on and say it."

"Say what?"

"I told you so."

"I'd never say that to you. I was pretty sure things would go well today, but there was always the chance you would decide this wasn't what you wanted anymore. That there were too many bad memories. It's obvious how much you're respected and liked by everyone at Duke's, that says a lot about not only the kind of waitress you are, but who you are as a person."

"I'm still scared though," Carly said earnestly.

"I'd be surprised if you weren't," Jag said.

"Alani said I could work the same shifts as Kenna for as long as I want to, which makes me feel better. I just hope Kenna won't mind."

"She won't," Jag said with confidence.

Carly looked down at her hands for a moment, then lifted her chin and met his gaze. "Do you think I'm being paranoid? Maybe Detective Lee is right and there isn't anyone out there gunning for me. It's been months. Even if there was someone working with Shawn, it's possible that they have no interest in me now that he's gone."

Jag could hear the hope in her voice, and while he didn't want to scare her any more than she already was, he couldn't in good conscience agree with her. "I don't think you're being paranoid," he said carefully. "I think you're smart to be cautious. Until we figure out exactly what Shawn had planned, and who he'd planned it with, you do need to be careful. I don't think he was

so unhinged that he hallucinated an accomplice. And your ex was obviously the mastermind behind the insane plan, but I'm not willing to ignore the possibility, no matter how small, that his partner might want to carry through, even with Shawn gone."

"Yeah. That's what I thought."

When she looked down at her hands once again, Jag put his finger under her chin and lifted her head. "But that doesn't mean that you shouldn't live your life. You just have to be a bit more cautious than you would otherwise."

Carly stared at him with emotion swirling in her blue gaze. "Can I ask you something?"

"You can ask me anything," Jag reassured her, dropping his hand.

"If you really think I could still be in danger, why aren't you insisting I stay locked away until the person is caught? I mean, I can't imagine Mustang letting Elodie keep going to work if she was in my shoes. And Aleck definitely wouldn't be happy with Kenna if she insisted on waitressing while Shawn was still on the loose."

Her question was a good one. Jag wasn't sure she was really ready to hear his answer, but he didn't want to lie to her. He never wanted to lie. "The short answer is because locking you away would kill you. Slowly but surely. You have to admit the last few months have been hell for you."

Carly nodded in acknowledgement.

"As I've already said, you aren't the kind of person who does well with solitary confinement. You need your friends. You need people. Is this ideal? No. I want this asshole caught as much as you do. But I can't lock you away. It's not what you need. And I'll tell you this right now, angel, I'll *always* do what I think is in your best interests, even if it kills me."

She stared at him with wide eyes. "Jag," she whispered.

He lifted a hand and palmed her cheek once more. God, he loved when she tilted her head and gave him some of her weight. "I don't know what you think is going on between us but...as far as I'm concerned, we're dating. We've had an unconventional relationship up till now, but I'm going with it. And you should know...I decided at Aleck's wedding that I was done giving you space. If you hadn't texted me when I got back from that mission, I wasn't going to let you hide away anymore."

"I thought you had a stubborn look in your eyes when I told you I wanted to go home after the ceremony," Carly said.

Jag smiled. "Yeah. I was happy to see a flash of anger from you, actually," he admitted.

"I *am* angry," Carly told him. "Furious that Shawn has put me in this position. I know I'm young, but I truly thought he cared about me. In the end, all he wanted was to control me. And when he couldn't, his crazy came out."

"That's exactly what happened," Jag agreed. "But none of it was your fault, you know that, right?"

"I'm trying to believe that," Carly said softly.

"You're amazing," Jag told her for what felt like the hundredth time. Maybe if he said it enough, she'd eventually believe him. "You're a great friend, funny, a hard worker, and self-less. Any problem that asshat had with you was on him, not you. And you aren't *that* young."

Carly smiled and shook her head a little.

"You have a problem dating an old man like me?" Jag asked.

"You aren't old," Carly protested.

"I've got ten years on you...although some days I feel much older."

"The truth is that I've always preferred older guys. I don't

know why. Maybe because they just seem more mature, more settled than men my age. I don't know. But to answer your question, no, I don't care that you're thirty-five. Do you care that I'm only twenty-five?"

"Fuck no," Jag said with feeling. "So...we're dating?"

She gave him a small smile and lifted a hand, covering the one still resting on her cheek. "I guess we are. Jag?"

"Yeah?"

"Since we're dating and all now...maybe you can kiss me?"

Jag felt his heart rate speed up. He couldn't speak. Couldn't find the words to tell her how much this moment meant to him. Couldn't figure out how to tell her how worried he was about her. That he might be encouraging her to get back to her normal routine, but he wasn't going to leave her vulnerable to an attack. That she was quickly becoming the most important person in his life.

Instead of speaking at all, he shifted his hand so he was holding her nape, and leaned forward. The angle was awkward with the console between them, but there was no way Jag was letting this moment go by without getting his lips on hers.

The moment they connected, Jag closed his eyes, almost overcome with emotion. The hair on the back of his neck stood up as if electrified when she shyly opened her mouth under his. Jag felt as if he was a virgin. And in many ways, he was.

His hand around her neck tightened and Carly moaned, tilting her head so she could get closer. Her tongue licked his, and it was Jag's turn to make a tortured sound in the back of his throat. What might've started out as a sweet, shy meeting of their lips instantly turned into more. Much more.

Jag couldn't get close enough. He held Carly still as he devoured her.

How long they made out, Jag had no clue. When he finally pulled back, he was panting as if he'd just finished a ten-mile run on the beach with his thirty-pound pack on his back. He stared at Carly in reverence. He felt as if he'd smashed through a brick wall he hadn't even known he'd built in his mind.

Never in his thirty-five years had he ever wanted a woman so much. His cock was throbbing in his pants and for the first time in his life, he understood why men got crazy over a woman.

"Um...wow," Carly said, licking her lips.

He hadn't taken his hand from her nape and his fingers tightened involuntarily at her breathless comment.

"Yeah," he agreed, finding it hard to take his eyes from her lips. He had a vision of her on her knees, those lips around his cock as she looked up at him with her smoky blue eyes. It was so carnal. Jag couldn't stop thinking about it.

"There are a lot of things that scare me," Carly said as she tightened her hold around his wrist. "But you aren't one of them."

Fuck. She was killing him.

Jag forced his hand to loosen. He didn't even realize that he'd latched onto her so tightly. "Good. The last thing I ever want to do is scare you," he said.

Carly's gaze bored into his own, and she said with uncanny insight, "I feel the same way about you."

For a nano-second, Jag panicked. Had she guessed? Had she figured out he was out of his depth when it came to being intimate with a woman? He wasn't a virgin—the thought almost made him snort out loud—but in all the ways that mattered, he might as well have been. Everything seemed different with her. Natural. Right. The way it always should be between two people.

Taking a deep breath, and inhaling Carly's sweet cherry

blossom scent, Jag pulled her toward him once more and gave her a quick kiss. He wanted to linger, wanted to explore their connection, but this wasn't the time or place. Reluctantly, he let go of her as he sat back. "You still up for going to Food For All?"

It took a moment for Carly to get her bearings, and Jag couldn't help but be flattered. He liked keeping her off balance. At least at the moment she was thinking about him and not about being scared that she wasn't inside his apartment, where she felt safe.

She slowly nodded. "Yeah, I think so."

"Good."

"Although I forgot to ask Alani if there was any extra food I could bring."

"You'll have plenty of time in the future for that," Jag reassured her. He reached for the keys in the ignition and felt Carly's hand on his arm.

He turned to her.

"I...thank you, Jag. For everything. If it was up to me, I'd still be sitting in a corner of my apartment, hearing and seeing monsters everywhere. I'm not saying I'm ready to skip around town without a care in the world, but it feels good to at least be starting to try to take control of my life again."

"You're welcome, angel. And no one's saying you have to immediately forget about all your fears. I happen to think some level of caution is a good thing. You'll get back to your old self, I know it." He didn't add that he hoped she'd still want him in her life when she did.

Not even wanting to think about the possibility of her outgrowing her need for his protection, Jag backed out of the parking space.

He was confident when it came to his SEAL abilities. On a

mission, he was unbeatable. He didn't accept defeat and would do whatever it took to be successful. But on a personal level, things were much different. Jag hated that about himself. He wanted to be the self-assured Navy SEAL all the time. But the truth was, he was too damaged to be able to carry that confidence over into his personal life. He could kill without a second thought, but thinking about being with a woman made him break out in hives.

Until Carly.

She was different. Special.

But could she deal with his quirks when it came to intimacy? He wasn't sure. It was nothing against her, but he had some pretty fucking big issues.

Not wanting to think about how or why he was the way he was when it came to women, Jag concentrated on driving. He checked the rearview mirror and didn't see anyone or anything to be concerned about. But he had to stay on his toes. Carly's life might depend on it, and if he let her down, he would never recover.

The man in the shadows of the parking garage scowled. He just happened to be in the right place at the right time to see the bitch walking along Kalakaua Avenue, as if she didn't have a care in the world. The last he knew, she was still cowering in her apartment.

As if it was meant to be, a car pulled out of a parking space on the street right after he'd seen Carly, so he'd pulled in and followed her to Duke's. He had no idea who the man with her was...but he didn't like the way the guy constantly scanned their

surroundings. He was much more aware of who was around than the bitch ever was, which wasn't good for his plans.

He called and let his boss know he was going to be late getting back to work, lying about having car trouble. He was a model employee though; no one would question his word. It was more important to try to find out what was happening with Carly.

He watched from a distance as she was welcomed back at Duke's with open arms and laughter. The longer he watched, the more upset he became. He'd been glad when she quit. He wanted her isolated and scared out of her mind. He'd had her right where he wanted her and was getting ready to make his move.

But now something had changed.

It was the man with her. He knew it.

And it pissed him off.

Nothing would keep him from carrying out the plan. Shawn might be dead, but he'd complete what they discussed if it was the last thing he ever did. He owed it to the man.

Shawn had taken him under his wing. He'd never been able to make friends easily...people thought he was weird or awkward. He never said the right thing, laughed at inappropriate times. But Shawn had accepted him. Taught him how to be a *real* man, including how to take charge of his woman. They'd gone to bars, watched football, and generally hung out a lot. Shawn was a true friend. His only friend. And with Shawn's help and expertise, he'd been laying the groundwork for a special someone of his own.

The fact that his mentor had done everything for Carly, and she'd dismissed him so easily, enraged him. She'd been *lucky* to have Shawn.

It was up to him to avenge his friend.

He and Shawn had talked long and often about how they would make Carly pay for her disrespect and disobedience. For thinking she could just walk away. Their friendship deepening as they planned her downfall.

And when everything went to shit, he felt as if a part of him had been irrevocable lost. He was nothing without Shawn. He was back to being the weird guy no one really wanted to make eye contact with. Especially women.

More than an hour later, the man watched Carly leave Duke's with a huge smile on her face. It was easy to blend in with the tourists as they returned to the parking garage. Needing to know what kind of car the man drove, he snuck into the garage and watched from a stairwell.

When they kissed, the man's hands clenched into shaking fists.

No! She wasn't allowed to suck another man into her fucking trap! She didn't deserve to be happy, not after she'd ruined Shawn's life!

As he memorized the license plate, new ideas began to swirl in the man's head. He needed to go about this differently, now that another man was in the picture. Let her think she was safe. That there was no threat lurking in the darkness.

Yes, his new plan was much better. The cops had talked to him, and he'd easily deflected all suspicions. He could do the same with Carly.

Chuckling to himself and thrilled with the scheme taking shape in his mind, the man walked back down the stairs and into the hot afternoon. He didn't get angry when someone bumped into him. He even stopped to help an obviously lost couple

figure out where they were and where they needed to go. He was all smiles.

Yes, this was going to work out just fine. Carly would still end up dead, Shawn would be avenged, and he'd never be suspected.

Whistling, the man headed for his car.

"I'm comin' for you, Carly," he said under his breath. "When you least expect it, retribution will be mine."

CHAPTER EIGHT

Carly was still tingling by the time Jag neared Barbers Point. She couldn't stop smiling either. Kissing Jag was unlike any kiss she'd ever experienced. Her nerve endings seemed to spark when their lips met, and she'd felt giddy and desperate. It was almost laughable, but at first, she'd actually thought he was shy. She made the first move to deepen the chaste kiss. But when she'd touched her tongue to his lips, he'd finally taken control.

She didn't mind taking the lead with a guy now and then, but Carly preferred the guy to be in charge. It excited her. And Lord, did Jag end up checking all the boxes in that sense. He probably just took it slow to make sure he didn't scare her.

Jag definitely didn't scare her.

Carly wasn't an idiot. She knew what he did for a living. It wasn't as if he was running around foreign countries talking the bad guys into giving up. No, he was a deadly fighting machine, there was no doubt. But she had to admit, she liked the sweeter side he'd shown her.

The man was as complex as anyone she'd ever met. A badass Navy SEAL, yet someone who seemed a little unsure about a kiss. Pushy and stubborn when it came to getting her to do what he wanted, namely go and see Alani.

And that had worked out. Carly couldn't believe how excited everyone had been to see her. And she'd actually seen tears in Alani's eyes when Carly told her she wanted to come back. Her boss had bent over backward when she'd agreed, promising she could have any shift she wanted, including the same as Kenna.

Shawn's actions had changed Carly, had made her wary and uncomfortable being back at Duke's. Kenna had almost died because of her, and Carly had been scared that her coworkers would blame her. It had been *her* ex, after all, who'd gone all psycho. But she hadn't seen censure in anyone's eyes. They'd all been welcoming and excited to hear she was coming back to work.

Looking over at Jag, Carly had to admit he was right. She did need people. But how had he known that after such a short period of time? It was a testament to his observation skills.

She knew she was becoming attached to him. In the months since Shawn had taken Kenna hostage, when he couldn't get his hands on Carly, Jag had always just...been there.

He'd messaged, emailed, called, stopped by. He'd been patient and understanding. He hadn't pushed her to go to work or to call her friends. He'd listened to her when she'd needed to talk, kept her up to date on what everyone was doing, and generally had been supportive in any way she needed.

When he'd finally had enough of babying her, it was a good thing Carly was on the same page, tired of being the scared and pathetic person she'd become. She'd needed his encouragement. His decision to move her in with him had been the right call

too. If he'd asked instead of insisted, she would've turned him down.

Basically, Jag had done everything right, and very quickly the attraction she felt toward him was morphing into something more.

"What's that smile for?" Jag asked.

Because she was in a good mood for once, and fear wasn't pressing down on her as much as it usually did when she was out and about, Carly shared what was on her mind. "I was just thinking about how bossy and highhanded you are."

He looked surprised. "And that's making you smile?" he asked in disbelief.

"Yup."

"Most women would be pissed about something like that," he observed.

"I'm not most women," Carly told him.

"Damn straight," Jag mumbled.

Which made Carly's smile widen. Then she felt the need to say, "I should warn you, I'm usually not as amicable as I've been lately. I've let you talk me into a lot of things, but don't get used to it."

It was Jag's turn to smile. "Yeah?"

"Yeah," she said.

"Okay."

"Okay? A lot of *guys* don't like independent women who think for themselves."

Jag didn't answer right away. He pulled into the parking lot down the street from Food For All and turned off the engine, before turning to face her. "Some men do love having submissive women. But it's exhausting having to work all day, then go home and make all the decisions about a relationship or a

household. Especially in my line of work. SEALs need their women to be strong enough to not fall apart when they're sent on a mission. Throw kids in the mix and it's even more important."

Carly couldn't help but be relieved at his words. He went on.

"And you can't use that asshole Shawn as a metric," Jag went on. "Guys like him want all the control, they thrive on it. They don't want a partner. Don't want someone to share their lives with. They need to completely dominate someone to make themselves feel like they're hot shit."

"He wanted me to move in with him, but I kept putting him off," Carly admitted. "He wasn't happy. But I couldn't do it. Luke was still living at home, and it felt weird to me. I knew his son hated me, and the more Shawn tried to convince me moving in was what good girlfriends did, the more I balked."

Jag's brow furrowed. "Is this about you staying at my place?" he asked, the worry evident in his tone. "Because I am *nothing* like that fucker. If you want to go back to your apartment, you can."

"No!" Carly blurted. "That's not what I meant at all...unless," her voice got softer, "you want me to go?"

"Hell no, I don't want you to leave," Jag said. He took a deep breath and closed his eyes. "I'm screwing this up," he muttered.

Carly couldn't stop herself from reaching out. This man was such an enigma. "You aren't. I shouldn't have used that as an example," she said, resting her hand on his forearm.

Jag's eyes popped open and he looked at her. "I'm not good at relationships," he admitted. "I'm good with being a friend. I'm a great teammate, both on and off the battlefield. But man-woman stuff is completely foreign to me. I...I haven't had very good role models."

Carly stared at him, sensing he was trying to tell her something, but not sure what it was.

"I'm trying to learn from Mustang and the others by watching the way they interact with their wives and girlfriends, but it's a lot different than I expected. I said this earlier, and I'll say it again—I'll always have your best interests at heart. I might not explain myself very well, and I'll probably say stupid shit. But you're important to me, angel."

"You've had girlfriends before, right?" Carly asked.

Jag blushed. He actually *blushed*. Carly wasn't sure she'd ever seen a man truly blush when he was embarrassed before. It was one more thing that endeared him to her.

"No."

It was Carly's turn to be confused. "Never?"

"I've been with a couple women, but never had a true girlfriend."

"Jag...I just...that's just so hard to believe. You're...Look at you! You're so damn good-looking. You've got all those muscles, and you have this badass expression on your face most of the time. Yes, it scares people, I've seen it, but women *love* that shit. The bad boy thing and all that. And what about high school? Or when you were in your twenties? Don't most SEALs take advantage of the fact that women fall all over them because of what they do?" Carly knew she was babbling, but it was impossible to believe that this man hadn't had a girlfriend—ever.

"Most SEALs, yes. But not me."

Emotions swirled in his chocolate gaze, and Carly wanted to know everything he was thinking and feeling. But they were in a car, in a parking lot, and this didn't feel like the right place to have a deep conversation.

"So...you're a virgin," she teased.

He didn't even crack a smile.

"Holy crap. You're not a virgin, right?" she asked, completely shocked.

"No, I'm not a virgin," Jag said after a long pause.

"Not that it would matter if you were," she added. "I just... seriously, Jag, you're like my every fantasy come true. You're hot, smart, protective, compassionate, scary when I need you to be, and I don't care if you've been with five hundred women or none. I'm just thrilled, and nervous as hell, that you want to date *me*."

Jag reached out, palming the back of her head and bringing her forehead to his. He held her against him, and Carly gripped his forearm. She had no idea what he was thinking.

"You're mine," he said in a low, rumbly voice that seemed to zing through every nerve ending in her body. "I don't mean that in an asshole way. You're mine as much as I'm yours. I want to make you happy, see you smile. I know I'm the lucky one in this relationship, and I swear not to *purposely* do anything that will fuck it up."

"Jag—" Carly started. But he pulled back a bit so he could look her in the eyes and kept talking.

"I haven't ever minded that people sometimes cross the street rather than walk by me. I've actually cultivated that response. Believe it or not, I'm usually not even talkative. The guys give me shit about it all the time. But with you, I can't seem to keep my mouth shut."

Carly smiled. Loving that she had that kind of effect on him.

"You ready to head inside?"

It was an abrupt end to the discussion, but Carly had a suspicion Jag was feeling a bit awkward about all the touchy-feely talk. "Yeah."

"Stay there. I'll come around," Jag ordered. He brushed his knuckles against her cheek, then turned to get out of the car.

Carly took a deep breath, trying to center herself. How in the world no other woman had caught his eye, she had no clue. But she liked the idea of him being hers. Liked that he talked to her more than he did anyone else. It made her feel different. Special. And it had been a very long time since she'd felt that way.

Her door opened and Jag was there with his hand out. Carly took it, and he didn't let go as they started for the entrance to the food pantry. It wasn't a terribly long walk, but Carly shivered thinking about making it by herself. She might have said she was independent, but right now she felt anything but.

"Cut yourself some slack, angel," Jag said as if he could read her mind. "You'll get there."

She didn't get a chance to respond because they'd arrived at the door to Food For All. Carly had heard all about how the front window was broken out by Theo when he'd seen someone inside robbing the place. But looking at it now, she'd never know any damage had been done.

"Oh my God! It's Carly!" Lexie yelled out when she and Jag entered. As she headed their way, her gaze flicked to their hands before she smiled even wider. But she didn't comment and instead hugged Carly.

She was aware of Jag taking a step back, but knew he wouldn't go far.

Her reception was the same here as it had been back at Duke's. Elodie came out from the back of the store and greeted her just as warmly. And to Carly's surprise, Theo approached and briefly wrapped his arms around her as well. She'd met him a few times, but hadn't expected him to hug her, especially after he'd practically looked through her at Kenna's wedding.

"Hey, guys," Carly said.

"You look good," Lexie told her.

"It's so nice to see you," Elodie chimed in.

"Wanna see my new drawing?" Theo asked.

Everyone chuckled.

"I'd love to," Carly told him.

He reached out and grabbed her hand and started towing her toward the kitchen. Carly saw Jag take a step forward, but Elodie stopped him. "I'll go with them. She's good, Jag."

He didn't respond verbally, just nodded. Carly could feel his gaze on her as she and Theo headed for the door to Elodie's domain, the kitchen.

As they entered, Carly immediately saw the huge mural on the back wall. Theo had painted the inside of a fancy restaurant kitchen on the entire surface, which looked amazingly lifelike.

"Holy crap," Carly muttered.

"Right?" Elodie said with a smile.

"I painted Elodie a kitchen," Theo said proudly.

"Yes, you did," Carly agreed. "And it's marvelous."

She could practically see Theo's chest puff out with pride. And he *should* be proud; what he'd painted was so realistic, she expected the scowling head chef in the corner to start barking out orders any second. There were sous chefs bent over dishes, plating them in one section, and in another, a large flame was shooting up from a pan over a gas burner on a stove. He'd captured the chaos and excitement and beauty of a fancy restaurant kitchen perfectly.

"I showed him some pictures," Elodie said. "And he wanted to know all about the restaurants I'd worked at in the past. What went on and how many people were cooking, things like that. We talked about it for a week straight, then he didn't ask

any other questions. I thought it was just a passing curiosity for him. Apparently he'd talked with Lexie, and they arranged for him to come in one afternoon after I left. It took him almost all night, but when I came in the next morning, this is what I walked into."

"It's seriously amazing," Carly said with a smile.

"Yeah, it is."

"Do you miss it?" Carly blurted. The look of pleasure and longing on Elodie's face had prompted the question.

"Miss the chaos? Miss being yelled at when I did nothing wrong? Miss people sending a meal back claiming their steak wasn't cooked correctly when it certainly was? Miss the late nights and the stress? No, absolutely not. I do miss the people I worked with though."

"Yeah." Carly got that, one hundred percent.

The two women shared an understanding look.

"I'm sorry about what happened," Elodie said gently.

Carly wasn't sure she wanted to talk about that, but she straightened her shoulders. As Jag had said, and as Jack in the movie *Speed* told Annie, Shawn was the asshole here. Not her. "Thanks."

"Are you... Never mind."

"No, what?" Carly asked, curious as to what the other woman was going to ask.

"Are you back? I mean, Kenna's missed you something terrible. And Lexie and I had just started to get to know you when all that shit went down. And we've told Monica all about you, and while she doesn't talk much, she's interested in getting to know you too."

"I *want* to be back," Carly admitted. "But I'm scared. *Everything* scares me lately. The last thing in the world I want is some-

thing happening to any of you guys. I think that's why I stayed away for so long, I felt as if I was protecting you. If something had happened to Kenna..." Her voice trailed off.

But it wasn't Elodie who comforted her, it was Theo. He hadn't left and was listening to their conversation intently. He walked over to Carly and stood right next to her, in her personal space. He didn't touch her, didn't even look at her, but said, "Nothing happens on my watch."

Carly smiled and squeezed his arm. "I heard you stopped those robbers recently."

He nodded.

"Know what my favorite line from *Home Alone* is?" Carly asked.

Theo finally turned to look at her. He met her eyes for a moment, then dropped his gaze once more. "What?"

"'When I grow up and get married, I'm living alone!' Then he stomps on the floor and yells, 'I'm living alone' to the beat of his stomps."

He smiled. A huge smile that lit up his face. "That's a good one. 'I'm gonna give you to the count of ten to get your ugly, yella, no-good keister off my property before I pump your guts full of lead,'" he said in a deep voice like Gangster Johnny did in the old-time movie Kevin McCallister liked to watch in *Home Alone*.

Carly laughed. "I love that part!"

"And this one," Theo said solemnly. "'You can be too old for a lot of things, but you're never too old to be afraid.'"

Carly stared at the man next to her. Sometimes he acted as if he were seven years old, and other times, like now, he seemed to be an old soul. "That's true," she said softly.

"Are you scared a lot?" Theo asked.

He still wasn't looking at her, but Carly knew he was definitely paying attention to her every word.

"Lately? Yeah."

"Because of the bomb man?" Theo asked.

She shouldn't have been surprised that he knew what happened, and yet she still was. "Well, he can't hurt me anymore...but of whoever was working with him, yes."

"I'm scared of needles," Theo said.

Carly would've laughed, but he was completely serious.

"And cockroaches. Especially the ones that can fly," Theo added.

"They're icky."

He nodded in agreement. "Jag'll make sure no bad men hurt you. And Baker."

"What do you know about Baker?" Elodie asked.

"He's my friend," Theo said, his chin lifting a bit. "He said it was my job to watch over Food For All."

"Ah," Elodie said with a nod. "You're a big help around here for sure."

Theo nodded, and without another word, turned and left the kitchen.

"He's...interesting," Carly said after he'd gone.

"That he is. It's nice having him around though. When others are here, he doesn't say much, so him talking says a lot about how much he likes you and is comfortable with you."

That made Carly feel good.

"For the record...nothing that happened was your fault. And if Jag thinks it's okay for you to be out and about and going back to work, then it's okay."

"How do you know about me going back to work?" Carly asked in surprise. "We literally just came from Duke's just now."

Elodie blushed and shrugged. "Kenna texted us all. She's super excited."

Carly laughed. She'd sent her friend a short text on the way to Food For All, asking if it was all right if she piggybacked on her shifts for a while, and Kenna had been ecstatic. And apparently had already begun to spread the word.

"We've already packaged up the meals for people to pick up today, but do you want to help us organize the requests for tomorrow?"

"Sure. Is Ashlyn around?"

"She's still out delivering today's meals to the homebound people."

"Oh. Last I heard, Slate wasn't too keen on that idea."

Elodie nodded. "He isn't. But Ashlyn isn't about to let him tell her what she can and can't do."

"Oh, man, they're still squabbling like little kids, aren't they?" Carly asked. She loved this. Gossiping and laughing, feeling as if she'd never been gone.

"Yup. Mark my words...they're gonna end up together."

"You think?"

"Oh, yeah. There's so much tension and chemistry between them, it isn't even funny."

"That's cool."

"Yup. And speaking of which...you and Jag...?" Elodie let the question hang.

She smiled. "Yeah."

"Thought you said you weren't ready for another boyfriend?" Elodie teased.

Carly felt her cheeks heat up. "Yeah, well, it just kind of happened."

"I understand that all too well," Elodie said with a smile.

"And for the record, I think it's awesome. Doesn't say much, but he's a great guy."

Carly wanted to laugh at the "doesn't say much" part, since Jag didn't seem to have any issues talking with her. But she simply nodded and said, "Yes, he is."

"Well, come on, I'm sure Lexie's dying to talk more with you too. I've been hogging you back here long enough. And I'm guessing Jag's about ready to come check on you as well."

"Oh, I'm sure he's not—"

Her words were cut off by the man himself sticking his head into the room. "Everything okay in here?" he asked.

Carly ignored Elodie's laughter and smiled at him. "We're good. We were just coming back out."

Jag nodded and opened the door all the way, holding it for the two of them.

"Told you," Elodie whispered as she passed Carly on her way to the door.

Carly followed, but when she got to Jag, he stopped her and asked quietly, "You good?"

She nodded. "Yeah."

"Just making sure. Lexie's extra chatty today, she's busting at the seams to talk to you."

"She driving you crazy by making you talk?" Carly teased.

Jag's lips twitched. "I'm not the talkative type."

"Except with me."

"Except with you," he agreed. Then he leaned close and kissed her. It was a quick kiss, nothing deep, but she still felt tingles throughout her body at the intimate touch. She was aware that Elodie, Lexie, and Theo could clearly see them standing in the doorway, but if Jag didn't mind kissing her in front of them, Carly certainly wasn't going to complain.

"What was that for?" she whispered.

"Because I can't resist you," he said. Then he put his hand on the small of her back and urged her into the other room.

"Theo, want to take a walk around and scope out the area? Make sure it's all safe?" Jag asked the other man.

"Yes!" Theo said eagerly, as if Jag asking him to check the perimeter was akin to winning the lottery.

"We'll be back soon, and I've got eyes on the area, so don't worry," Jag said, directing his words to Carly.

She nodded at him.

The second the front door shut behind the men, Lexie said, "Giiiirl, we need more info on what's up with the two of you!"

Carly knew she was blushing, but smiled anyway. "There's not much to tell."

"Bullshit," Lexie retorted, pulling out a chair and pointing to it bossily. "There's so much chemistry crackling between the two of you we could bottle it and not have to pay electricity for a month. Now, start talking."

Carly laughed, enjoying girl time. She wished Kenna was here, and Ashlyn. And she wanted to get to know Monica. As she'd admitted to Jag, she *did* need this. A connection with her friends. Being holed up in her apartment had made her more paranoid, more terrified. She still wasn't comfortable with her situation, with the fact that someone could be out there somewhere, waiting to get to her. But with Jag's help, she knew she'd be able to start living fully again.

Thirty minutes later, Jag and Theo walked back into Food For All, accompanied by Ashlyn.

"Carly!" the other woman exclaimed, rushing forward to greet her.

Carly saw the amused grin on Jag's face before he could hide it.

They stayed another twenty minutes or so before Carly's stomach growled. She'd been so into catching up with her friends that she hadn't realized how much time had gone by or how hungry she'd gotten.

Jag ushered her out of Food For All before she had time to do more than tell the others she'd be in touch. Elodie told her that Kenna would probably have another sleepover soon, now that Carly was "back," and that she should be prepared to say yes to attending.

The thought of being isolated somewhere with the other women, who could be hurt because of her, was distressing, but Carly just smiled and nodded. Then Jag took hold of her hand and they were walking back down the sidewalk toward the small parking lot and his car. He got her settled in the passenger seat and they were on their way in less than a minute.

"I needed that. Thank you," she told Jag.

"You're welcome. I've got some chicken I can bake when we get home, if that's okay. It's nothing fancy, but while it's cooking, we can have a salad and I can roast some broccoli to tide you over until the chicken's done."

Talking about what to have for dinner seemed so...domestic. And Carly loved it. "Sounds good. Jag?"

"Yeah, angel?"

"I had a good day."

"I'm glad," he said with a small nod.

"I know you can't spend every day hauling my butt around and babysitting me, you've got a job and all, but I appreciate you giving me the kick in the ass I needed to jumpstart my life again."

"You would've gotten there without me," he said with a shrug.

"Maybe."

"No maybe about it, angel. You would've."

He had more confidence in her than she did herself. "Did things with Theo go okay?"

"Of course. He's unusual, but a good man," Jag said.

"Did you see the mural he drew in the back room?"

"Yup. Couldn't believe my eyes when I first saw it," Jag told her.

"Did you, um, see anything unusual when you were walking around?" Carly couldn't help but ask.

"Why? You feel someone watching you today?" he asked quietly.

"No, not this afternoon, actually. I was just wondering."

Jag reached out and took her hand, and just his touch made Carly feel better.

"If you feel uneasy at any time, I want you to tell me. I don't care if you think you're just being paranoid, I'd rather be safe than sorry."

"Okay."

"I've got a meeting with Baker set up in a few days. Maybe he'll have more information."

Carly shivered. She was torn between wanting to know everything and not wanting to know *anything*. There was some peace in not knowing the details about someone out there, possibly stalking her. But that would be stupid, and she didn't want to be that person.

"If it's all right with you," Jag continued, "I thought I'd sit down with Baker and the rest of the team, hear what he's found

out and discuss what our next steps should be. Then you and I can talk about it."

She sighed in relief and nodded. "I'd like that."

"Good. I want to protect you from living and breathing this shit every day. You need to keep moving forward, and constantly thinking about the case won't be good for you. Do you trust me to pass along the information I think is pertinent?"

"Yes," she said without hesitation. "But I don't want you to live and breathe this either. I don't want or need a bodyguard, Jag. I think that would irrevocably change the relationship I'd like us to have. You'll see me as helpless and someone who needs to be looked after. I don't want that for us."

"Agreed. But there's no way I'm stepping out of the investigation altogether," he warned her. "At this point, Baker's basically in charge of the information flow. He's pissed about the entire situation and is determined to figure out who might've been working with Keyes."

"I still don't really understand that, but I'm selfish enough to be okay with it," Carly replied. "Am I going to get to meet this Baker guy at some point?"

"Oh, Lord, here we go," Jag muttered.

"What?"

"You've been talking to the other women," he said.

Carly frowned in confusion. "Yeah, but we didn't talk about Baker."

"You didn't?"

"Nope. What am I missing?"

"Nothing."

Carly poked him in the side and he grunted in protest. "Tell me," she ordered, a smile on her face.

"I've already told you. They think he's hot. A silver fox."

Carly giggled.

Jag went on. "A scary, intense, they-wouldn't-want-to-be-on-his-bad-side, sexy-as-hell silver fox."

"So...kinda like you, but without the silver part," Carly said.

Jag glanced over at her, a brow raised in clear disbelief.

"You just described yourself, Jag. You can be intense, and I certainly would never want to be on your bad side, but you're definitely sexy as hell. Even without the silver part."

He rolled his eyes. "Whatever."

Her man didn't take compliments well. Carly made a mental note to make sure she told him often how great she thought he was. "Well, if the others think he's good-looking, I'm sure he is, but I'm more concerned with his investigative skills."

"He's good," Jag said simply.

Carly nodded. "So, I'll get to meet him?"

"I'll make it happen."

"Thanks."

They were silent the rest of the way to his apartment complex. But it was a comfortable silence. And for once, Carly let herself close her eyes and relax. She was with Jag, he wouldn't let anyone ambush them. It was almost scary how quickly she'd let herself trust him, but she knew without a moment of doubt that if something happened, Jag would take care of it...of *her*.

CHAPTER NINE

Almost a week later, Jag finally got a chance to sit down with Baker and find out what he'd discovered about Carly's situation. The retired SEAL had come down to the Naval base and the team had commandeered a conference room, waiting anxiously to hear what he had to say.

"Thanks for coming down," Jag told him.

"I was in the area anyway," Baker said. "I needed to speak with a couple people last night, so I figured I'd just stay down here and meet with you guys this morning."

"Where did you stay?" Mustang asked.

"With a friend," Baker said mysteriously.

"You could've stayed with us," Aleck said. "You know we have plenty of room, and Kenna would've loved the chance to catch up."

Baker raised a skeptical eyebrow.

Aleck chuckled. "Okay, she would've given you the third

degree, but still, you know you're welcome to bunk at my place anytime."

"I think that goes for all of us," Midas chimed in.

Everyone agreed.

"It's fine. I didn't get done until late, and the last thing I'd want to do is disturb anyone."

"Whatever. As if you'd disturb us," Slate said with a drawl. "You could've stayed at my house and gotten some wave time in this morning."

"Who says I didn't?" Baker asked.

Slate dipped his chin in acknowledgement. "Right."

"If we can get this started...I've got someone else to track down today before I head back up north," Baker said.

Jag leaned forward and pinned his gaze on the man. He really needed to hear some good news. That Baker had either figured out who was working with Carly's ex or that he didn't think there was a threat from anyone. His gut didn't think the latter was a possibility, but he could still hope.

"First off, is Carly in danger?" Mustang asked.

Baker hesitated—and Jag's stomach dropped.

"From what I've been able to uncover, no, but..." He trailed off.

"But?" Jag prompted after a moment.

"This entire situation stinks to high heaven," Baker said in a hard voice. "Someone's lying. Or they all are. The people I've talked to have all said the right things, but I'm not getting warm, fuzzy feelings from any of them."

"Who did you talk to and what did you find out?" Pid asked.

"I started with the son. He's a prick," Baker said bluntly. "A misogynistic asshole who doesn't have the least bit of respect for women. I'm guessing he learned that from his old man. I grilled

him pretty hard, and he stuck to the same story he told the cops. That he was with his girlfriend."

"How'd he explain the fact that Carly actually saw him on the beach near Duke's that night?" Aleck asked.

"He swore that he was there looking for his dad, to try to talk him out of doing something stupid—Luke's words, not mine," Baker said.

"You believe him?" Pid asked.

"No. But then again, if the timeline Carly gave the cops is correct, he didn't exactly have time to go from the beach to a marina, then head out to the ocean so he could pick up his dad," Baker said.

Jag clenched his teeth in frustration. He'd thought the same thing. "You think there was more than one person working with Keyes?" he asked.

Baker turned his green gaze on him and shook his head. "No. The son knew about his dad's plan—he all but admitted it by sayin' he was at Duke's to try to talk him out of something. But I don't think he was part of the plan to actually kidnap Carly. So someone else had to have known as well. Maybe Luke had a role that would come into play later, maybe he was looking forward to having a spin with Carly once his dad brought her to wherever he'd planned to take her. Or maybe he was supposed to help dispose of her body. But I don't think he was part of the actual kidnapping plan."

"Motherfucker!" Jag said, pushed up and out of his chair. He began to pace in agitation. He couldn't sit still and listen to Baker talk about Carly being assaulted.

"What I believe Luke Keyes was doing at Duke's that evening is irrelevant," Baker continued, ignoring Jag's outburst. "There simply wasn't enough time for him to drive to a marina,

get a boat, and go out into the water. Especially because I uncovered some video of him in his car, right around the time everything was going down."

"So his alibi is bullshit," Slate observed. "He said he was with his girlfriend."

"Yes," Baker agreed. "But since he was recorded driving his car at the time Keyes was standing on the beach with Kenna, he couldn't have been the pickup guy in the ocean."

"Shit. Okay, what else?" Mustang asked.

"I talked to Rebecca, the girlfriend. She tried to bullshit me with the story she and Luke had come up with, but I quickly convinced her that wasn't going to fly. She admitted Luke hadn't been with her, but she swore she didn't know anything about the plan to kidnap Carly. And honestly, she doesn't seem like the type. Very mousy, zero self-esteem, no close relatives to look after her, and Luke's alienated her from her friends. She's also young. Just turned eighteen a few months ago. I advised her that it was in her best interest to get away from Luke; that the first chance he had, he'd throw her under the bus to save his own ass."

"Like he already attempted to do," Midas said dryly. "By involving her in this shit and using her as an alibi, and getting her to lie to the police."

"Exactly," Baker said with a nod.

Jag wanted to feel bad for Luke's girlfriend, but at the moment he didn't have it in him. "Who else?" he asked, still pacing. He wanted to *do* something. Standing around talking about what had happened, and what had *almost* happened to Carly, and guessing who might still want to harm her wasn't sitting well.

"I tracked down the three friends," Baker said. "Jeremiah

Barrowman was Keyes's closest friend, best I can tell. The two did a lot together. They were thick as thieves and he's on the top of my list of suspects. Of course, Barrowman denies being involved. He told me that Keyes was always bitchin' about one thing or another, and Carly had become his latest whipping post. When they got together to play poker, he was constantly complaining about her. About how he'd worked hard to 'train' her—again, his words, not mine, Jag. Settle the fuck down."

Jag realized that his fists had clenched and he'd taken a step toward Baker as if to beat the shit out of him. That would be a mistake. Even though Baker was in his fifties, the man was definitely still in shape and could quite possibly win in a hand-to-hand encounter.

"Sorry," Jag said. "I just hate hearing anything derogatory about her."

"I get that, but I'm just relaying what these other assholes said. You want to hear this or not?"

"Yes," Jag said simply.

Baker nodded and continued. "Barrowman admitted he knew what Keyes had planned, but swears he didn't have anything to do with it. Told me that he wanted nothing to do with a kidnapping plot, even if he didn't like Carly."

"Do you believe him?" Midas asked.

"It doesn't matter if I believe him or not," Baker said. "His alibi checks out. He was at work, or at least his timecard says he was. He works at the Waialae Country Club and he didn't clock out until well after everything went down."

"That's by the coast, right?" Pid asked. "He could've gotten someone to clock him in and then taken a boat from there. It's not too far from Waikiki."

"Right," Baker agreed. "Which is why I haven't ruled him out."

"What about the others?" Jag asked. The more Baker talked, the more Jag wanted to get to Carly right this second and make sure she was all right.

"Gideon Sparks and Beau Langford are Keyes's other two close friends. I guess the four of them got together at least once a week to play poker or watch football, and drink. Sparks doesn't have an alibi. He's not married, has no kids. He's employed at the Honolulu Zoo. I guess he works with some of the bigger animals. He's kind a loner and the people I talked to who know him didn't have much to say, just that he keeps to himself. Anyway, he had that day off. Told me he was doing errands. He was able to produce a few dated receipts, but I haven't had time yet to verify his location on any of the surveillance cameras at the shops where he claims to have been. Beau Langford is the youngest of the three friends, at forty-five. The others are all in their fifties. He works at a marina."

Jag abruptly stopped pacing. "Yeah?"

"Yup. But I scoured the surveillance videos at the marina from that night and haven't found evidence that he took any of the boats out," Baker said.

Jag felt nauseous. He'd been hoping Baker would immediately solve this shit. Help them figure out the threat and neutralize it. He now realized this wasn't going to be as easy as he'd thought.

"But Langford would know where all the cameras were, since he works at the marina. He'd easily be able to go undetected if he wanted to," Baker added. "He also doesn't have anyone to back up his alibi. Says he was stuck in traffic on the interstate.

With all the rain that moved in so quickly that night, we all know how easily the interstates flood around here."

"Cell phone activity?" Slate asked.

Baker shrugged. "Langford said he dropped his phone when he was running to his car. Landed in a puddle and fucked it up."

"Convenient," Pid muttered.

"I checked into Wes Schell, Keyes's landlord, and while they seemed to be friendly enough on the surface, apparently the two men hated each other. Keyes had a bad habit of paying his rent late, which pissed off Schell. I'm ninety percent sure if he had the chance, Schell would've turned Keyes in for pretty much anything, just to get him out of his apartment complex."

"Who does that leave?" Mustang asked.

"I haven't spoken with Kelly Gregory yet, she was Keyes's most recent ex-girlfriend. I'm guessing if she was treated as badly as Carly, that she most likely wouldn't want anything to do with Keyes and his asinine plan, but I don't pretend to under-stand women. It's possible she was jealous and wanted to get back with Keyes. He broke up with *her*, as I understand it, so she might've wanted a chance to get rid of her competition, so to speak, if Keyes approached her."

Jag pressed his lips together. He wasn't willing to dismiss the woman. He'd had up-close-and-personal experience with how insane women could be. He pushed the thought away for now and concentrated on what Baker was saying.

"I also need to speak with Eddie Evans, Keyes's neighbor, and his boss, Jamie Redmon, at the Coca-Cola plant where Keyes worked."

"Any good leads with either of them?" Midas asked.

"Evans, maybe. His statement to the cops claimed that he didn't know anything. Apparently he keeps to himself, said he

minds his own business. Which I don't doubt. What the detective *hasn't* figured out yet is that the neighbor has a good reason to lay low. He's got half a dozen scams going that I'm sure he doesn't want anyone to find out about."

"What kinds of scams?" Mustang asked.

"Charity, soliciting disaster relief funds, identity theft...the man's a fuckin' genius, as far as I can tell, except he's using his smarts to scam people out of their money," Baker said, the disgust easy to hear in his tone.

"You gonna shut that down?" Pid asked.

Baker shrugged. "Not my concern. Now, if someone I know and respect fell for one of his scams, then absolutely. But right now, my plate's kind of full."

Jag didn't give a shit about the neighbor running his scams. All he cared about was Carly's safety. "And the boss?" he asked.

"Another asshole. Seems Keyes surrounded himself with people just like him. But his alibi seems solid. He was at work, making someone's life miserable by conducting their yearly evaluation. It's why I haven't made him a priority."

Jag stomped over to his chair and collapsed into it with a sigh. "So, where does this leave us?" he asked. It didn't feel as if he was any closer to finding out who might've been working with Keyes than he was a week ago.

"I'm still digging up shit," Baker said. "Someone had access to a boat. Redmon, Langford, and Evans own boats, the others don't. But that doesn't mean they didn't borrow someone else's. Half the residents on this island own a boat, or at least have access to one. The weather was so shitty that night that most of the cameras at the marinas I've checked out so far either weren't working or were useless because of the rain and wind. There are also plenty of private boat slips

on the island that don't have security cameras. But I'm not giving up."

"What do you think?" Mustang asked. "Do you think there was an accomplice crazy enough to be out on the ocean that night in the storm? Do you think Carly's still in danger, or has whoever Keyes was working with maybe slunk back into the shadows after he was killed?"

Jag waited impatiently for a response. He respected Baker. The man had an uncanny sixth sense. He knew what *he* thought, but wanted to know what the former SEAL was thinking, now that he'd been looking into the situation.

"My brain tells me that there's nothing to find," Baker said. "But my gut says differently. I can't say for sure that I'm even looking at the right people. Keyes was an asshole, but he wasn't stupid. He worked with a lot of people at the Coca-Cola plant, he could've talked any one of them into helping him. Detective Lee has done a good job interrogating the people Carly told him about, but Keyes likely had friends Carly *didn't* know about." Baker turned and met Jag's gaze. "I'm on this."

"On a scale of one to ten, how much danger do you think Carly's in?" Jag asked bluntly.

"Five," Baker said without hesitation.

Jag scowled. That wasn't helpful. Not at all.

"It's been months since that night," Baker continued. "It's obvious the accomplice is lying low. Not to mention, Carly's been hibernating—which, for the record, I don't think was a bad thing. There's a good possibility that kept any accomplice from getting to her already. I hear she's started working again."

Jag nodded. "Part-time. Started yesterday, actually."

"Right, trying to get back out there. Trying to reclaim her life. I admire that," Baker said. "One of two things could

happen...going about her regular business could light a fire under whoever Keyes was working with, set him off, make him try to finish what they started that night. Or he could slink back under the hole he came from, deciding she's not worth the trouble."

"And which do you think will happen?" Midas asked.

Baker looked at him. "I honestly have no clue."

"Fuck," Jag muttered.

"You can't keep her in a gilded cage to protect her," Mustang said quietly.

"I know," Jag said. And he did. It was why he'd encouraged her to talk to her boss. To start working again. But that didn't mean he was completely comfortable with it. "I've arranged for her to take some self-defense classes from Senior Chief Petty Officer Albertson," Jag said.

Slate whistled low under his breath.

"Good choice," Midas said. "I have to admit, she kind of scares me."

Jag nodded. Elizabeth Albertson was in the Naval security force and was damn good at her job. She wasn't a SEAL, but she'd actually gone through the training just to prove that women *could* do it. She was the perfect choice to help Carly gain some confidence that if something happened, she could defend herself.

"Any chance Elodie can tag along?" Mustang asked.

"Oh, yeah! Kenna would love to try something like that," Aleck agreed.

"Lexie too," Midas said.

"Fuck. Well, we can't leave Mo out then," Pid said.

"I'll try to convince Ashlyn to attend," Slate added. "She thinks she's invincible, and I hate that she goes to so many strangers' houses delivering food."

Jag nodded. "I'm sure Albertson wouldn't mind." He sobered and turned back to Baker. "If you were me, what would you do? Would you lock your woman away until we've got some concrete evidence, or would you encourage her to go about her normal life, albeit with a lot more caution?"

"I can't answer that," Baker said.

Jag sighed.

"If it was Monica, I'd lock her up and throw away the key," Pid said. "But then again, Mo *likes* being by herself. If I'd known she was in any danger whatsoever from that piece of shit Shane Beyer, I would've done just that."

"Carly tried that. It didn't help. It made her paranoia worse," Jag said.

"She thrives on interacting with people," Aleck said. "Like Kenna."

"We'll keep an eye on her," Mustang said. "Let her live her life...while taking precautions."

"Anything you need from us, you've got it," Pid agreed.

"You need me to stay at your place?" Slate asked. "Give you another pair of eyes?"

Jag paused. This was why he loved being a SEAL. Loved being a part of this team. He looked over at Slate. "I think we're good. No one's getting into the apartment complex without being on camera. And at the moment, Carly's not too keen on driving anywhere herself. She still doesn't feel all that safe outside."

"But she's okay working, right?" Pid asked.

"She is," Jag said. "Today's only her second shift, but so far, I think she's doing well, all things considered. The first day back she had a mini panic attack, but Kenna was with her and talked her down. Then she thought she saw Luke and panicked again.

One of the bartenders ran down to the beach when he found out what was happening, toward the guy Carly was looking at, but it turned out to be some random dude, not Shawn's son. But she didn't dwell on it after work. I'm still hoping today goes a little smoother."

His teammates all nodded.

"I'll keep you in the loop as to what I find out," Baker said. "I'm not gonna let up on this until we have some answers."

"Thanks," Jag said.

"And I'll talk to the commander," Mustang said. "I know we can't exactly schedule our missions around our personal lives, but I'll make sure he understands how serious the situation is and, if at all possible, give us some breathing room."

Jag's chest immediately tightened. "I can't leave her alone," he told his team leader. He felt bad enough that Carly had been on her own for a week and a half when they'd last been deployed. But now that they were together...it didn't sit well with him to leave her when they didn't know which of Shawn's friends might be holding a grudge.

"If you get deployed, she can come up to the North Shore and stay with me," Baker said.

Jag looked at him in surprise. "But...and don't take this the wrong way...but will that send the wrong message to Jody?"

"What do you know about Jodelle?" Baker sat straighter and glared at Jag.

He held up his hands in capitulation. "Nothing really. Just that you seem very protective of her, and the last thing I'd want is her getting the wrong idea about you and Carly."

Baker took a deep breath, and Jag could see him trying to get control of himself before responding. "Jodelle won't get the wrong idea," he finally said simply.

Jag wanted to ask more questions about the mysterious woman Baker seemed extremely protective of, but he was itching to get to Carly. He was picking her up from work, even though Aleck said he was more than happy to give her a ride when he went to get Kenna. Jag was anxious to see her for himself. To make sure she was all right. To hear how her day went. It seemed as if from the second he left her each morning, all he thought about was Carly, and looked forward to being with her again.

He'd never felt that way about anyone. And he had his reasons. But everything about Carly appealed to him. Drew him in. She was nothing like—

No. He wasn't even going to *think* that bitch's name.

She was in his past, and that was where Jag was determined to keep her.

He nodded at Baker. "Thanks."

"I'm hoping it won't come to that," Mustang said. "If necessary, I'll tell the commander that you need to be taken off the deployment list."

Jag shook his head. "No. I don't want that."

"Neither do I," Mustang argued. "You think I want to go on a mission without you? Fuck no. But most of us have learned that shit can go sideways in a blink. And our women come first...well, as much as they can when we're employed by the Navy. But let's not borrow trouble. Knock on wood, shit's been fairly quiet recently. We'll take things one day at a time."

Baker nodded at them all and stood. "I need to get going. Redmon's shift ends soon and I want to be sure to catch him before he heads home. Later."

Jag gave the other man a chin lift and the others stood up to head out as well. Slate caught him before he left.

"I was serious," Slate said. "You need me to play bodyguard, I'm more than happy to."

"I appreciate it," Jag told his friend.

"You'll let us know when you've set up the sessions with Senior Chief Petty Officer Albertson?"

"Yes. I'm hoping to get that started soon."

"Good. Thanks."

"Things okay with you and Ashlyn?" Jag ventured. He wasn't one to pry into anyone's relationship, but his friend had seemed a bit stressed recently, and he was worried about him.

"As good as they *can* be. I think she hates me most days, and she's stubborn as hell. And won't listen to me when I tell her that it's not safe to be driving all over the island, including to some of the worst neighborhoods, to deliver food."

"Maybe she *does* hear you, but instead of telling her over and over that she's making a mistake, you can try to offer alternatives or suggestions on how to do her job safer?" Jag said hesitantly.

Slate sighed. "She's driving me crazy," he admitted.

Jag couldn't help but smile. "Welcome to the club." He clapped Slate on the back.

He merely shook his head. "I'm headed down to Food For All to see if she's back from today's deliveries. I'll tell her about the self-defense classes."

"A suggestion?" Jag said. "If possible, make it seem like it's *her* idea to go. I'm guessing that'll go over better than ordering her to do anything."

Slate thought about that for a moment, then nodded. "Good point. Maybe I'll tell her that Carly's not sure about going by herself. She'll definitely volunteer to go with her then."

Jag nodded. "Exactly."

"Thanks. Hey...who do you think Baker stayed with last

night? I mean, I wasn't aware that he was all that close with anyone on this end of the island."

"I have no idea. But Baker's got connections everywhere. For all we know, he bunked in with the base admiral," Jag said dryly.

"True. It's probably better if we didn't know. I'll see you at PT tomorrow. Call if you need me," Slate said.

Jag nodded and took a moment to gather his thoughts. He wasn't sure he'd learned anything new in the meeting with Baker, but it did feel good to know his team had his and Carly's backs. Not that he'd expected anything different.

Despite that, his belly churned with anxiety. He hadn't felt like this in a very long time. Not even in the middle of a mission when things had gone completely fucking sideways. He had more to lose now. It wasn't *his* life on the line, it was Carly's. And somehow, Jag knew her ordeal wasn't over. She'd have to be strong to get through whatever was coming...and something *was* coming.

He'd learned over the years that he couldn't control other people. He could only control himself and how he responded to whatever was happening around him. The same applied to Carly. Ultimately, they might not know who was working with her ex until it was too late. All he could do was give Carly the tools to deal with whatever happened.

The thought of some asshole getting his hands on her made his skin crawl, but no matter what happened, his Carly could handle it. He had no doubt. Working with the Naval security officer would hopefully give her confidence in her own abilities against someone taller and stronger than she was. That, along with the knowledge that he'd do whatever was necessary to get to her, would hopefully get her through anything that might happen.

The hair on the back of Jag's neck stood up, and he realized he'd been standing in the conference room for too long. He needed to get moving. Get to Duke's and to Carly.

As he walked quickly out of the building and toward his Jetta, he thought about his sometimes overwhelming inner turmoil. Some men might be more positive in his shoes. Might trust the police when they said they couldn't find any evidence of a threat. But just because no one knew something was wrong, didn't mean all was well. He'd learned that firsthand when he was just eleven years old.

Trouble was coming, and just because he and Carly didn't know from which direction it might appear, didn't mean it wouldn't eventually catch up with them.

Determination rose within Jag. He had no idea if he and Carly would last as a couple, but he was going to do everything possible to make sure she not only made it through this blip in her life, but that she flourished.

That meant giving her the confidence to live her life. Baby steps. That's all she needed. And while she was learning to fly once again, he and his team would have her back, doing what they could to give her the space to thrive.

When the shit hit the fan—and it *always* seemed to hit the fan—Jag just had to be sure his woman was strong enough to withstand the storm.

CHAPTER TEN

Carly felt like a coward hiding out in the kitchen, but when one of Shawn's best friends showed up at Duke's for an early dinner, she'd started shaking and couldn't stop. He was with a group of men she'd never seen before, and just the sight of Jeremiah Barrowman had her trembling uncontrollably.

Kenna had noticed her reaction and swept her out of the public eye and into the kitchen before Carly knew what was happening. Vera sat the men at a table near the beach, and Justin was waiting on them.

"You're okay, Carly, just breathe," Kenna soothed.

Carly took a deep breath and nodded. "I'm sorry."

"Don't apologize."

"It's just that I haven't seen any of Shawn's friends since... well, you know. And Jeremiah has always given me the creeps."

"Well, you don't have to deal with him today," Kenna said firmly. "Justin's got their table and we'll stay on this side of the restaurant."

Carly nodded. "Thanks. I feel so stupid."

"Why? You shouldn't. Not at all. You want me to go out there and scope things out? Maybe I'll offer to help Justin so I can see his reaction when that asshole sees *me*. If he was working with Shawn, he's bound to react negatively to seeing me, right?"

"No!" Carly exclaimed, grabbing Kenna's arm and holding on tightly.

"Okay, okay, okay! I won't."

Carly breathed out a sigh of relief.

"But that doesn't mean Charlotte can't go over there and eavesdrop on their conversation..."

Carly shook her head in exasperation. Kenna was her best friend, but she drove her crazy sometimes. She couldn't resist leaning forward and giving her a long, hard hug.

"What's this for?" Kenna asked as she returned the embrace.

"I'm just so thankful you're in my life," Carly said.

Kenna pulled back. "Same goes for me. You know that, right?"

Carly nodded.

"Good. And best friends stick together. Let's get the salads for table three and try to ignore Jeremiah what's-his-name. He can't hurt you here."

Carly wanted to disagree. Shawn had managed to hurt Kenna there. But she let it drop.

Within ten minutes, all the servers in the restaurant knew that one of Shawn's friends was there. They all made a point to go over to the table for one reason or another. Kaleen threatened to put something in the drink he ordered, to make him shit his pants, but Carly managed to talk her out of it, not wanting to see her friend get hauled off to jail for trying to poison one of the patrons.

It took a while, but eventually Carly stopped shaking and, instead of being scared, got mad. It seemed to be a new pattern with her. Her first instinct was to cower and hide out, but then she got pissed. She was giving Jeremiah power over her, just as she'd done with Shawn. He didn't own this city, and Carly had the right to live and work there, just as he did.

She wasn't quite ready to go up and have a conversation with the man, but she did walk by the table a few times. She even met the man's eyes once—and was surprised when he looked shocked to see her. He had to know she worked here.

The next hour went by uneventfully, and Carly actually felt very proud of herself for not hiding out in the kitchen until Jeremiah left.

But when he and the rest of the people at his table got up to leave, she was unfortunately standing at the front of the restaurant, talking with Vera.

Jeremiah stopped right next to her. "Can I have a moment, Carly?"

It was actually Vera who broke Carly out of the paralyzed trance she'd fallen into. "I don't think so," the hostess said.

Carly put a hand on her friend's arm. "It's okay," she said, surprising herself.

Vera looked equally surprised, but nodded. "I'll be right here," she told her. Then looked at Jeremiah. "So don't try anything, buddy."

Carly wanted to laugh at Vera's guard dog act. She didn't exactly look very tough. She was actually a few inches shorter than Carly, but then again, weren't the smallest dogs the most vicious?

Taking a deep breath, Carly took a step to the side and waited for Jeremiah to say what he wanted to say.

"I'm sorry about what happened," he said. "Shawn was out of line."

"Out of line?" Carly couldn't help but repeat. "Coming here with a *bomb* strapped to his chest to *kidnap* me was 'out of line'?"

Jeremiah winced. "Yeah, probably a bad way to phrase it. But you have my word that I wasn't involved."

"You expect me to believe you?" Carly asked. She was quaking inside, but determined to stand her ground. "You and Shawn, along with Gideon and Beau, were always together. I know he probably told you what he'd planned."

"He did," Jeremiah admitted.

Carly stared at him with her mouth open. She couldn't believe he'd just admitted that out loud.

"I should've done something. I honestly thought he was kidding! He was always talking shit about one person or another. I never thought he would actually go through with it."

Carly didn't want to let Jeremiah off the hook. But she couldn't help but feel a little better that he'd actually owned up to the colossal mistake he'd made in not taking Shawn seriously. "He certainly did," she said lamely.

"Yeah," Jeremiah said a little guiltily.

"Yo! Let's go, Jer!" one of the men he'd eaten with yelled from nearby.

Jeremiah waved at the man then turned back to Carly. "Maybe you can tell your watchdog to back off, now that I've apologized."

"My watchdog?" Carly asked, one brow lifting.

"Yeah. I need my job, and if he stays on my case, my boss'll fire me. If there's anything he hates, it's scandal. The country club has to be completely on the up and up."

Carly had no idea who or what Jeremiah was talking about,

but she pretended she did. "If you cooperate with him, then I'm sure you'll be fine," she bluffed.

Jeremiah stared at her for a long moment, and Carly did her best to stand her ground despite the look in his eyes. He wasn't happy with her...and it showed.

"Whatever," he finally spat. Then he spun and stalked away.

Carly watched him go, slowly letting out the breath she'd been holding.

"You all right?"

The feminine voice startled Carly so badly, she jumped. She turned and saw Vera standing at her side with a concerned look on her face.

"Sorry, didn't mean to scare you."

"It's okay," Carly said.

"Did he threaten you? Do I need to call the cops?" Vera asked. "Officer Brown is around here somewhere, doing the rounds, checking to make sure all is well. I can get him back here if you need him."

"I'm good," Carly reassured her friend. The encounter with Jeremiah was unsettling, but at the same time, she was proud of how she'd handled it...at least after she'd stopped hiding in the kitchen. Honolulu was the most populated city in Hawaii, but it was actually small in a lot of ways. It was inevitable that she'd run into more friends of Shawn's. Gideon, Beau, Wes, Eddie... her ex knew a lot of people, and they were all well aware of what had happened.

It was likely most or all of them had heard Shawn ranting about her, about what a bitch she was. People heard stuff like that all the time, and no one ever thought it meant anything. Hadn't she complained to Kenna a time or two about how annoying someone was? She didn't think she'd ever wished

someone else dead, or made a bogus threat about wiping them off the face of the earth, but she could see Shawn saying that sort of thing. And not caring who he said it to. So the fact that Jeremiah hadn't believed her ex would actually try to kidnap her wasn't exactly a surprise.

"Where is he?" Kenna asked as she came running out to the front of the restaurant. "Shit, I missed him, didn't I? What'd he say? Are you all right?"

Carly was amazed to find herself smiling slightly. "He's gone. And I'm fine."

Kenna put her hands on Carly's shoulders, narrowing her eyes as she studied her friend. "You *are* okay, aren't you?"

"Yeah."

Kenna smiled. "It feels good to stand up to bullies, doesn't it?"

"It does. Although he wasn't bullying me. He actually apologized."

Kenna wrinkled her nose. "As if that lets him off the hook."

"And he told me to call off my watchdog. Said he could get fired."

"Who? Jag?"

Carly shook her head. "I don't think so. I mean, it's possible, but when he's not at work, Jag's with me."

"Baker," Kenna said with a grin.

"That's who I thought too."

"Good. Hope his ass *does* get fired. And with Baker on the case, he'll figure this shit out eventually."

"I hope so."

"Come on, table thirteen's food is ready. And we've only got thirty minutes left before our guys'll be here to get us."

Carly hooked her arm with Kenna's and let herself be led

back into the restaurant. If someone had told her she'd see Jeremiah at work today, Carly would've stayed home, too freaked out to confront any of Shawn's friends. But now that she had, she felt stronger. She didn't dread seeing other people he knew quite so much now. It wouldn't be comfortable, but she suspected she could handle it.

A spark of the old Carly lit up within her, and she smiled. She was still nervous, still cautious, but making it through the first face-to-face contact with someone from Shawn's life made her feel so much better. It didn't hurt that she didn't have to walk out to her car by herself and drive home. Knowing Jag was on his way to pick her up gave her the confidence to put the uncomfortable confrontation behind her. She'd get to see Jag...soon.

"How was work?" Jag asked once they were settled inside his Jetta and on their way to his apartment.

Carly had purposely not said anything about seeing Jeremiah until now. She didn't want Jag to lose his mind and storm back into the restaurant. There was nothing he could do now, and going all SEAL on her friends and coworkers wouldn't help anything.

"I saw Jeremiah," Carly blurted.

Every muscle in Jag's body tensed. "What?"

"He showed up with a group of men to eat. I was scared at first," Carly admitted, talking fast, wanting to get the entire story out before Jag decided to turn the car around and go hunt the man down. "But eventually I got mad. Why was I hiding in the kitchen? I had just as much right to be there as he did. I didn't wait on his table, but I did walk by it a few times. He

didn't say anything, but when he was leaving, he asked if he could talk to me. I stayed near the hostess stand out front and let him talk. He admitted that Shawn had told him about his plan, but he claimed he thought he was kidding. Just talking out his ass. He even apologized. Then he left. That's it. Oh—wait, he did ask me to call off my watchdog, and I'm assuming he meant Baker...Speaking of, you met with him today, right? What'd he say?"

Carly held her breath as she waited for Jag to respond.

"I'm trying not to freak out here," he said after a long moment.

"I know. I felt the same way. And I didn't mean to spring that on you. I mean, I was completely wigged out for at least half an hour after I saw him. But nothing happened, Jag. He barely even looked at me. I admit that the man creeps me out, but he didn't do anything."

Jag's knuckles were white around the steering wheel.

"And after thinking about it, I'm glad he was there today. I'm going to run into other friends of Shawn's, and I need to figure out how to deal with that. I never want to feel again the way I did for the months I hid out in my apartment. I was paralyzed with fear, and I don't even know what, or who, I was scared of. I mean, I thought it was Luke, but now I think it was just the fear of what *could* happen. I can't live that way. I *could* get run over tomorrow. I *could* have a heart attack. I *could* be minding my own business in the grocery store and be killed by someone holding up the pharmacy or something. But I want to *live*, Jag. Experience life. I'm rambling. Sorry."

"No, you're making complete sense. That doesn't change the fact that I hate that any of Shawn's friends got anywhere close to you."

"I know."

"I did talk to Baker today. He met with the team."

"And?" Carly asked when Jag didn't continue.

"He doesn't have anything concrete yet."

"Damn."

"But apparently, the talk he had with Barrowman had some effect."

"Yeah," Carly agreed. "Maybe stirring all this up, forcing people to talk with him, making them worry about their jobs, will make something happen. Not that I want anyone to try to kidnap me or anything, but if someone reacts enough to make a mistake, or feels guilty enough to admit they were in the ocean waiting to pick up Shawn, I can move on with my life."

"You're moving on no matter what happens," Jag countered. He peeled his hand from the steering wheel and held it out. Carly gladly latched on to him, intertwining her fingers with his.

"You want to hear more details about what Baker found out?"

Carly thought about that for a moment, then asked, "Is there anyone I should be more watchful for than others? Like, does he think Luke is more a danger than someone else?"

"No. Baker hasn't found out any concrete evidence about anyone. He's still looking into alibis and watching surveillance videos."

"Okay, then no, I don't need details. I know you'll let me know if he finds something out for sure."

"*When* he finds out, and yes, I will. And I won't wait until the end of the day either. I'll drive my ass to wherever you are and tell you in person," Jag said.

"Thanks."

"No need to thank me, angel. You're important to me. More important than just about anyone in my life at this point. I'll

never do something to put you in danger. And if that means giving you intel that might scare you, that's what I'll do."

Carly nodded.

"Oh, and I've got the self-defense training sessions all scheduled for the days you aren't working. Hope that's all right."

"It's great. Although, I'm kinda nervous about them."

"Why?"

"Well, you said the woman you were going to ask is like a female Rambo or something."

Jag chuckled. "She's pretty badass."

"She's gonna think I'm a wuss. I'm not exactly in shape, Jag. I get tired going up the stairs in the parking garage by Duke's."

"You don't have to be in shape, and she'd never think you're a wuss. Would it make you feel better if I said the other women will probably be joining you? When I told the guys about it, they all volunteered their women to come too."

"Really? That's awesome! I'd love that!" Carly said happily. Somehow it didn't feel as intimidating to have the lessons with her friends.

"Good. After we stop at Food For All and drop off those bags of food Alani gave you, you okay with going straight home?"

"Yes, why wouldn't I be?"

"I don't know. I wasn't sure if you needed to pick something up at your apartment, or at the store or something."

"I don't need anything," Carly said. "Except to hang out with you and try to forget the world exists for a while."

Jag beamed and squeezed her hand. "Same, angel. Same."

"Jag?"

"Yeah?"

"I'm really ready to move on."

"What?"

"I'm ready to move on," Carly repeated. "With my life. I've let Shawn hang out in my head for way too long. I believed the awful things he said to me and began to doubt myself. I felt better when I broke it off with him, but when he started harassing me, I admit that I had second thoughts. Why would anyone else want to be with me? Maybe I was all the things he accused me of being. Immature, stupid, ugly... but I realize now that he was trying to break me. I'm ready to put all that behind me. I know I need to be safe and watchful, but you were right to get me out of my apartment, to make me talk to Alani. I appreciate that more than I can say."

"I'm glad, angel," Jag said softly.

"I told Kenna and the others over and over that I didn't want another boyfriend. That I was done with men. Maybe not forever, but for the foreseeable future. But you've somehow stormed your way past my defenses...and I'm so happy that you have."

"Me too. You're an amazing woman, Carly. And Shawn was an asshole."

"Yup," she agreed.

They held hands in silence the rest of the way to Barbers Point. Jag parked in the lot down the street from the food pantry and they carried the bags toward Food For All. Lexie was the only one there, and she seemed a little distracted, mumbling about the increase in the number of people the place was providing food for, so Carly and Jag didn't stay long.

Carly studied the area as they walked back to the car and didn't see anyone out of the ordinary. She didn't recognize any of the men or women walking around, and they were currently the only people in the parking lot.

"You're safe," Jag said, obviously noticing the way she'd nervously checked out every passerby.

Carly nodded. "I feel safe with you."

"You'll feel safe when you *aren't* with me soon. Senior Chief Petty Officer Albertson will make sure of that. And we'll talk about some things you can look out for when you're on the road or in a parking garage. You *will* get back to your normal life, Carly. Promise."

"Senior Chief Petty Officer Albertson?" she asked. "That's quite the mouthful."

Jag chuckled. "Yup. I'm sure she'll let you use her first name."

Carly hoped so. She didn't think she could say Senior Chief Petty Officer Albertson every time she had a question for her. She let a sigh of relief when she was safely inside Jag's Jetta and he started the engine.

"Home?" he asked.

"Home," she said in satisfaction.

* * *

The man watched Carly and her boyfriend with a scowl. He hated how happy the bitch looked. He enjoyed the nervous look on her face as she glanced around, but then it quickly disappeared after the man distracted her.

She should be scared.

Terrified.

He liked her that way.

She'd killed Shawn. She hadn't been there when he'd accidentally blown himself up, but she might as well have pulled a trigger and shot him in the head.

He longed to see the terror in her eyes when she realized

who he was and what was going to happen to her. Shawn had taught him how to control women. How to make them second-guess themselves, to cower in fear, and he'd been coaching him on breaking down a woman's barriers, to make her vulnerable and dependent on her man to make decisions. He'd been preparing to put all his skills to use when Shawn died. Without his friend and mentor backing him up, he no longer had the confidence he needed to mold his own perfect partner.

That was *Carly's* fault.

He'd dated another woman years ago. Someone he thought he loved, but things had ended badly. And with Shawn's help, he now understood why. He hadn't been assertive. Hadn't broken her down before molding her into exactly what he needed. And just like Carly, she'd gone to the fucking police when he'd followed her around for her own safety. The bitch!

Just when he was beginning to try again, his friend had died.

He needed to step up his plans. That other asshole who'd come to his workplace, insisting on talking to him about Shawn, about what had happened, was too inquisitive. He'd covered his tracks well, but there was still a chance the older man would figure out *he* was the one waiting in the ocean.

If it hadn't been for that damn storm. If Carly hadn't gone home sick. There were so many "if onlys" that it almost drove him crazy. But he wasn't going to let anything get in the way next time.

Not the fucking watchdog she'd sicced on him.

Not the new boyfriend.

Nothing.

He'd gain her trust. Get her used to seeing him now and then. Use the tricks and tips Shawn had taught him to lure her in. Get her to let down her guard.

Today he was doing one of the most crucial steps in his plan. Learning her routine.

He knew what shift she'd worked the last two days, knew she sometimes brought food from Duke's to this hole-in-the-wall food pantry, and he knew where the boyfriend lived—where *she* was currently living. It wouldn't be long before he knew where she shopped, where her friends lived, what she did on her days off.

It was only a matter of time before he'd have Carly exactly where he and Shawn had wanted her.

At his mercy.

But this time, he wouldn't risk her getting away. He'd kill her and be done with it. Feed her body to the fish. She'd disappear and no one would be the wiser. No one would suspect him. He'd make sure of it.

Grinning to himself, the man straightened and headed for his car, which he'd parked a few blocks over...just in case.

CHAPTER ELEVEN

Carly winced as her muscles protested when she reached to the top shelf in the grocery aisle. Senior Chief Petty Officer Albertson—Elizabeth—had no mercy for her or the others. She'd pushed them hard, insisting that if someone tried to mug them or take them hostage—which wasn't outside the realm of possibility, since they were with decorated Navy SEALs who had many enemies—they'd need to be ready to fight for their lives.

Despite the difficulty, Carly had loved yesterday's first self-defense lesson. She'd felt extremely powerful after the hour-long session. Even though she was sore, she couldn't wait to go again. After Jag had driven them home, she'd demonstrated what she'd learned and had actually managed to escape his hold when he grabbed her from behind. Carly suspected he knew exactly what she was going to do to get away, but appreciated him letting her succeed all the same.

"Good lord, I'm sore," Kenna groaned from next to her.

Carly couldn't help but chuckle as she put a box of noodles into the cart. This was the first time she'd been out anywhere without Jag. Riding to Duke's with Kenna didn't really count, as her friend had told her the driver Aleck hired used to be a Marine, and he looked more than capable of taking care of any threat that might come their way.

Surprisingly, Carly was feeling all right about the outing. Kenna had called after lunch and asked if she wanted to go to the store with her. And while Carly had been hesitant at first, she'd straightened her spine and agreed. She needed to start getting out on her own. And being with Kenna seemed like a good compromise to start.

She'd had a small moment of panic when they'd arrived at the store, but she'd gotten control over her emotions and carried on, which she was extremely proud of. Some people might not think going to the grocery store, with a friend at that, was very impressive, but after spending months in her apartment, too scared to even go outside to check her mail, going to the grocery store seemed like a major victory.

"So...how're things between you and Jag going?" Kenna asked as they strolled down the aisles.

"Good. He's different than I thought he'd be," Carly said.

"In what way?"

"It's hard to explain. I guess when you first started going out with Aleck, I figured his friends would be kind of conceited hard-asses. But even from that first dinner at Duke's, they seemed pretty down-to-earth. You know I wasn't ready for any kind of relationship, not after Shawn, but Jag kind of snuck up on me."

Kenna chuckled. "Yeah, I know what you mean. Do you think this'll be a long-term thing?"

"I have no idea," she said with a shrug. "I mean, I'm not counting on him getting down on one knee anytime soon. And honestly? I think he's got a savior-complex thing going on. We didn't really get a chance to know each other very well before everything with Shawn happened. And since then, he's been more of a caretaker for me than anything else."

"Do you seriously think that?" Kenna asked, stopping in the middle of the aisle.

"Well, yeah," Carly admitted.

"You're wrong," her friend replied, somewhat forcefully. "Jag isn't the sort of man to spend so much time making sure you're all right simply out of the kindness of his heart. Don't get me wrong, he's a good man. But he wouldn't have done what he did in the months after Shawn lost his fucking mind if he wasn't interested in having more than a friendship with you."

Carly swallowed hard. She knew that. Somehow, deep down, she'd always known that Jag wasn't just checking up on her because his friend was dating Kenna. She'd felt a connection to him from the first moment they'd met at Duke's. She just didn't want to admit it at the time.

"I don't know what I would've done without him," Carly said softly. "How do I know my attraction toward him isn't just because of some damsel-in-distress syndrome?"

"I know a lot of people poo-poo the damsel-in-distress thing, and it pisses me off," Kenna said. She didn't seem concerned in the least that they were completely blocking the grocery aisle to have this intense conversation next to the pickles and condiments. "But here's the thing—there's nothing wrong with needing a helping hand sometimes. When, exactly, society decided that was a bad thing, I have no idea. But whatever. And even though our men are badasses, they need us just as much as

we need them. That's how relationships work, Carly. No, we probably won't be hanging out of helicopters and swooping in to save our men from red-hot lava like Pid did for Monica, but that doesn't mean we don't make their lives better, more complete. So what if you leaned on Jag recently? You shouldn't be ashamed of that. It's what couples do."

This was one of the reasons Carly loved Kenna so much. She wasn't afraid to speak her mind, and it was usually what Carly needed to hear. "Thanks," she whispered.

"Giving pep talks is what friends are for," Kenna said with a smile. "And for the record, I love having you back at work. Don't get me wrong, I like Vera, Justin, Charlotte, and the others, but having you there makes the time go by so much faster."

"I'm actually surprised by how much I missed it. I didn't think I would, and it's a little scary being out in public, but I definitely like spending time with you again."

The two friends smiled at each other, then started back down the aisle. They were in the middle of a conversation about pickles—if sweet or dill were better—when someone came around the corner and almost ran into them.

Carly froze, gaping at Luke and his girlfriend in shock.

For what seemed like a full minute, the four of them stared at each other without a word. Carly could feel her heart beating a million miles an hour. She felt paralyzed with fear. This was pretty much her worst nightmare come true. The reason she'd hidden out in her apartment for so long. She never wanted to see Shawn's son again—and now here they were, face-to-face in the damn grocery store.

Both Luke and Rebecca glared at her.

"Move," Kenna said in a low, determined tone.

Carly wanted to tell her to hush, to not make Luke angry, but her voice wouldn't work.

"*You* move," Rebecca replied in a pissy voice.

"I didn't have anything to do with what happened," Luke blurted out of the blue.

Carly was surprised he'd brought it up. She could only stare at him.

"My life's been a living hell for the last few months. I had to hire a fucking lawyer to get the cops off my back, but even still, they're following me around and digging through my trash and shit. You need to talk to them, tell them to back the fuck off," Luke said.

"If you didn't do anything wrong, then you don't have anything to worry about," Kenna retorted, taking a small step sideways so she was partially standing in front of her. "And Carly has no control over what the cops do anyway."

"You ruined my dad's life!" he seethed. His gaze was glued to Carly's, and the venom she saw there made her tremble.

But then she remembered something Elizabeth had said in their self-defense lesson. She'd said that acting as if you aren't afraid can many times throw off an attacker. They don't like confident victims. They want the people they're beating up, mugging, or intimidating to cower in fear. It gives the attacker power.

The last thing Carly wanted to do was give Luke more power over her. His father had done that long enough. So she straightened her shoulders and lifted her chin. She was still trembling from the adrenaline coursing through her body, but she forced herself to meet his gaze.

"Your father ruined his *own* life," she spat. "I didn't ask him to belittle me and treat me as if I were a moron. I didn't

deserve to be smacked around. No one does. I don't think he even liked me very much, so I have no idea why he wasn't thrilled when I finally broke up with him. All he had to do was move on, and he'd still be here to knock around some other woman. But instead, he lost his fucking mind. He tried to *kidnap* me, which I'm sure you knew all about. I have no doubt you knew every detail of his plan—and that makes you just as bad as he was."

Carly was practically sweating by the time she'd finished speaking, but it felt good to stand up to Luke. She'd tried to make the man like her for way too long, and it was freeing to finally not give a shit what he thought of her.

Luke took a step toward her, and Kenna said, "Do it, asshole. I dare you." She was holding her phone up, obviously filming.

He glared at them both and scowled. "You aren't worth the effort," he said.

"Come on," Rebecca said, tugging on his arm.

"I'm guessing he treats you like shit," Carly said in a slightly more subdued tone. "Get out now while you can. Before he ruins your life."

"Shut up, bitch!" Luke growled. He turned to his girlfriend and pushed her hard enough to make her stumble. "Come on, let's get out of here."

He left his cart right there at the end of the aisle as he stomped off, with Rebecca protesting about leaving their groceries.

"What a fucking dickhead," Kenna said, lowering her phone.

Carly couldn't stop herself from throwing her arms around her friend. She wanted to thank her for standing up for her. For being there. For being smart enough to film their encounter, thus making Luke think twice about whatever he might have

done to her. She also needed Kenna's support so she didn't fall into a puddle right there in the middle of the store.

"You're okay," Kenna soothed, holding onto her tightly. She obviously felt her shaking. They stood there in each other's arms for at least a minute before Carly felt as if she wouldn't fall on her face if she let go.

Taking a deep breath, she did her best to get control over her emotions. "That was kind of fun."

Kenna grinned. "It was, wasn't it?"

"And Elizabeth was right, pretending you aren't scared does kind of work."

"You were amazing," Kenna praised. "I bet it felt good too, didn't it?"

"It totally did," Carly agreed. "I used to tiptoe around him because I so desperately wanted him to like me. And getting along with him made Shawn happy. Well, not happy, but you know what I mean. Not worrying about what Luke thought of me and saying what I was thinking felt awesome."

"He's a dick," Kenna said.

"Yup. It's gonna suck having to tell Jag about this. I'm sure he's going to want me to call Detective Lee too."

"Which will probably mean the attention Luke's getting from the cops will increase, which in turn will piss him off more," Kenna said.

"No doubt," Carly agreed. Then she shook her head in amazement. "I can't believe I'm not a complete basket case right now. If this happened even a few weeks ago, I would've probably needed to be carted away and sedated."

"Would it be weird for me to tell you how much I love you right now?" Kenna asked.

Carly grinned. "Nope."

"Good. I love you, Carly. You're amazing."

"I think the same about you," Carly told her. They smiled at each other.

"Come on, let's finish up shopping and get you home. You need to get on with seducing Jag."

Carly almost choked. "Um, what?"

"You guys have been tiptoeing around each other for months. You need to get on with things already."

"How do you know we haven't?" Carly asked.

"Because you would've told me about it by now," Kenna said as they headed up another aisle.

Carly wrinkled her nose. Her friend was probably right. "You don't think it's too fast?"

Kenna raised both brows and looked at her incredulously.

Laughing, Carly said, "Right, little miss, 'I married my man two-point-three seconds after I met him.'"

Kenna giggled. "It wasn't quite that bad."

It was Carly's turn to look incredulous now.

"But seriously...our SEALs move fast when they find the woman they want to spend the rest of their lives with, because they know how short our time on earth really is. As much as I hate to even think about it, what they do is crazy dangerous. They could die on any of their missions. They don't fuck around when it comes to tying their women to them permanently. So no, you aren't moving too fast at all. If anything, I'd say you and Jag have moved slowly. You were actually friends before anything else."

She was right. Carly felt as if Jag had gotten to know her pretty well over the previous months, but she didn't feel as if she knew *him* all that well. She knew he was dependable, protective, a little bossy. Knew he smelled absolutely amazing and that

sleeping next to him every night made her feel safe and secure. He liked pizza and sushi, but hated pineapples and mangos... which was amusing, since he lived in Hawaii.

"Yeah," Carly said after realizing she hadn't responded to Kenna's last comment.

Her friend just chuckled. "There's no timetable on love," she said after a moment. "Everyone's relationship is different. I want you to be happy, Carly, and I think Jag does that for you."

"He does," Carly agreed.

"So just go with the flow. I'm not surprised Jag moved you in. It seems to be a pattern with the guys on his team. But if you want to just be friends with him, that's okay. You have to do what's right for you."

"I don't want that," Carly said without hesitation. "I just...I don't want him to be with me because he feels responsible for me."

"Talk to him," Kenna urged. "There's been a lot going on with your life, and with his, recently. My suggestion is to tell him what you want. Open up. You want sex? I think you're going to have to make the first move. He's been in this weird friendship role for a while now, and he probably doesn't know exactly how to change the status quo. It's obvious he wants you, the chemistry between you is off the charts. You just need to give him the green light to move forward."

Just the thought of Jag doing more than holding her at night made Carly squirm. She wanted that. A lot. And Kenna was probably right. Jag had been her friend, her lifeline, for so long, he was probably leery of doing something that might scare her. She'd even had to initiate their first kiss. "You're right," she said.

"I know," Kenna said smugly. "Come on, let's finish up here. I'm guessing Luke and his girlfriend are probably gone, but I'm

not all that keen on having another confrontation with them anytime soon."

Carly shivered. She wasn't either.

They finished the rest of their shopping and checked out. There was no sign of Luke, thank goodness. But when they were putting the grocery bags into Kenna's Chevy Malibu, Carly glanced to her right—and was shocked to see Beau Langford. Another one of Shawn's best friends.

"Holy shit, I can't believe this," she muttered.

"What?" Kenna asked.

"Over there, to our right," Carly said, gesturing in Beau's direction with her head.

"Who? What? The guy over there at the over-the-top sports car? What is that, a Corvette?"

"I guess. And yes. That's Beau Langford."

"Am I supposed to know who that is?" Kenna asked.

"Yes!" Carly hissed. "I mean *no*." She took a breath. "That's one of Shawn's friends. One of the men I told the detective might be involved in Shawn's kidnapping plot."

"Holy shit. I can't believe this. What are the odds of running into two suspects on the same day, in the same place?" Kenna asked. "Get in the car," she ordered.

"But we have to take the cart back," Carly protested.

"I'll do it. Get in."

Carly did as her friend ordered. She felt like a coward, but standing up to Luke was all she could manage for one day. She kept her eye on Beau, but he didn't even look in her direction. He put his own groceries into his trunk, then shut it. Carly hadn't even seen him in the store, but it was obvious he'd been there.

By the time Kenna opened her door and climbed in, Beau

was backing out of his parking spot. Just when Carly thought he'd been totally oblivious to her presence, he turned his head and met her gaze.

Time seemed to stop as they stared at each other. For a second, Beau looked as if he didn't recognize her. Then his lip curled into a scowl, and he put his car in drive and drove away as fast as he could.

"Okay, I know the island is small, but this is ridiculous," Kenna bitched as she started the engine.

Carly didn't know whether to laugh or cry, so she settled on simply shaking her head. "Right? This feels like some sort of immersion therapy or something. Who's next? Wes? Shawn's landlord? His ex?"

"No. Next is *no one*," Kenna said. "Next is you going home, telling Jag about your tough day—and how amazing you did being out and about by yourself—then putting it all behind you and telling your man that you want to jump his bones."

Carly burst out laughing. God, Kenna always seemed to know just what to say. "Right," she said sarcastically.

"I'm serious," Kenna protested.

"I want him, I can't lie about that, but I kinda like how things are between us right now. They're...comfortable."

"There's more to life than being comfortable," Kenna said.

"I know, but for now, it's what I need," Carly told her friend.

"Okay. But when you're ready to get out of that comfort zone, I'm sure he'll be ready too."

Carly nodded. Kenna had more experience when it came to relationships than she did, but because she'd been such a bad judge of character in the past, she was liking the way things were with her and Jag right now. "And...for the record...I'm not out and about by myself today."

"You know what I meant," Kenna said, waving her hand dismissively. "Without Jag by your side. I know firsthand how our men can be a crutch. It's hard to worry about anything when they're with us. And you coming out with me today, and trusting me to have your back, means the world."

She smiled at her friend. She knew exactly what Kenna meant about their men being crutches. It was part of the reason she'd forced herself to say yes when Kenna asked her to go to the store. It was scary, but Carly didn't want to cower in her apartment anymore.

The ride back to Jag's complex didn't take very long and, to her relief, she didn't see any more of Shawn's buddies. Kenna parked and helped Carly carry her bags up to Jag's apartment. He lived on the sixth floor, and his building was much safer than hers.

"I'll see you tomorrow?" Kenna asked.

"Same time?"

"Yup. Mark and I'll be here around noon."

Mark was the former Marine and all-around badass who drove them to work. "Sounds good," Carly said.

"Talk to Jag," Kenna ordered.

"I will."

"Good. See you tomorrow."

Carly watched out the window facing the parking lot until Kenna got into her car and drove off, then began putting away the groceries she'd bought. It felt good having money in her bank account again. It wasn't much, but it was a start. She didn't want to mooch off Jag, though he'd said he had no problem paying for food, since he had to eat too.

Sitting on the couch after she was done, Carly stared off into space as she thought about the day. Seeing Luke, and Beau, had

been stressful...but she was beginning to think she'd overreacted.

She used to believe that someone *had* to be waiting to pick up Shawn from the beach. Of course he had to have an escape plan. But Detective Lee had worked his ass off to try to come up with leads on someone, anyone, with no luck. Even the amazing Baker, who Carly still hadn't met, hadn't found any concrete evidence against anyone yet.

It really was beginning to look like she'd overreacted. All those months of hiding out, of feeling like she was being watched, of feeling her skin crawl when she left her apartment, just might've been her imagination.

Carly wasn't going to be like one of those stupid women in horror movies who recklessly put herself in danger, but she felt some of the dread that had lingered within her for months slowly begin to slip away.

She wanted the old Carly back. The woman she'd been before Shawn had started trying to beat her down. She resolved to purge him from her life and mind once and for all. She wasn't the stupid, useless person he'd tried to make her into. She was Carly Stewart. Smart, funny, and a damn good catch for someone.

And she wanted that someone to be Jag.

Smiling, she rested her head on the back of the couch and hugged a throw pillow to her chest. Jag was her friend. He'd said they were dating, but she didn't really *feel* like they were quite yet. They'd kissed that one day, but never since. Yes, he touched her all the time, and they held hands when they went anywhere... but she practically did that with Kenna.

She wanted more, even if she didn't want to just jump into bed with him.

Which was somewhat amusing, since she'd done that already. Sleeping with him every night was one of the highlights of her life right now. But she didn't want to ruin what they had by throwing sex into the mix prematurely.

Kenna was right. She needed to talk to Jag. Get to know him better. When the time was right, they'd make love, she had no doubt. But until that moment, Carly vowed to be a better girlfriend. To talk to her man.

CHAPTER TWELVE

Jag smiled the second he entered his apartment. Carly was in the kitchen, leaning over to put a pan into the oven.

She stood up and turned, gifting him with a huge smile of her own.

His breath hitched. She was so damn pretty. He'd been told all his life that he was handsome, but inside, he never really felt as if he was anything special. He even sometimes wished that he looked different...fatter, uglier...maybe if he did, his life would've been different. He'd never cared about physical looks, his or anyone else's. Just because someone was pleasing to the eye didn't mean they were a good person.

But the longer he knew Carly, the more in awe he became. Her blonde hair fell in waves around her shoulders and her blue eyes seemed to sparkle. She was wearing a pair of leggings that showed off her curvy legs and an oversized T-shirt. He hadn't ever seen her look so...relaxed.

"Jag! You're home," she said happily.

He strode toward the kitchen, drawn to her like a moth to a flame. He couldn't stay away. Told himself not to alarm her, to go easy—when all he really wanted to do was take her in his arms and kiss the hell out of her. He couldn't forget that first kiss in his car. It had blown him away...and frankly, scared him a bit. Being horny and lusting after a woman wasn't like him.

"It smells great in here," he said as he reached for her.

Carly snuggled into him without hesitation, and Jag's heart swelled. He bent his head and inhaled her cherry blossom scent and smiled. God, he loved that. It made him think of dark nights and holding her against him as she slept.

"I made lasagna," she said, pulling back and looking up at him. "But I have no idea if it'll be good or not. I found the recipe online."

"Did we have all the stuff to make lasagna?" Jag asked, his brow furrowing.

"Nope. But Kenna and I went shopping."

Jag blinked at her. She hadn't stepped away from him, and he had his hands looped together at the small of her back. He loved how perfectly she fit against him. He'd never been the tallest guy, but her five-foot-five frame perfectly matched his five-nine. "You went shopping?" he asked.

"Yeah. I didn't want to, but I needed to, if that makes sense."

Jag was proud of her, even though he had to admit, he was a little freaked out at the same time. "It does," he managed to say.

"And before you hear about what happened from Aleck or one of the other guys, because I have no doubt Kenna's gonna tell her husband, who will probably blab to the rest of your team...You guys are the biggest gossips in the world. I swear no one can do anything without the rest of you hearing about it within hours."

She was babbling, which he knew was a sign of nervousness. And Jag needed her to tell him what had happened to cause those nerves. "Angel, what happened?" he asked gruffly.

"We ran into Luke and his girlfriend."

Jag inhaled sharply. That was her worst nightmare. The thing he knew she was terrified about the most. But before he could say anything, she continued.

"And he was a jerk, but it was okay. I mean, not him being a jerk, but seeing him. I was scared, I can't lie about that. But Kenna was right there and something in me kind of snapped when he said something about me ruining his dad's life. I thought about what Elizabeth said...sorry, Senior Chief Petty Officer Albertson, to you. She said that sometimes pretending to be brave actually makes you feel a bit more courageous in stressful situations, and can throw off your attacker. So I told him to go fuck himself. Okay, I didn't really say that, but that's the point I was trying to get across. He wasn't happy, but Kenna was filming him, so if he did anything or said anything, he knew he'd be in deep shit. So he grabbed his girlfriend and left."

Jag stared down at the woman in his arms. There was so much he was feeling at that moment. Fury that Luke Keyes dared to infer Carly had ruined his dad's life. What a fucking joke. Pride that Carly had stuck up for herself. Gratitude that Kenna knew just what to do to deescalate the situation. And regret that he hadn't been there to shield Carly from the vitriol Keyes had spewed.

"Jag?" she asked, her brows furrowing as she flattened her palms on his chest. "Say something. You're kind of worrying me here."

"I'm having a hard time coming up with the right words to tell you how impressed I am," Jag admitted. "I know being

outside the apartment is still hard for you. And seeing Like had to be difficult. I hate that I wasn't with you, but it sounds as if you handled the situation perfectly."

She smiled up at him. "I don't know about that, but I have to admit it felt good. After I stopped shaking, that is. There's something else."

Jag braced. "What?"

"I saw Beau in the parking lot."

"What the fuck?" he barked, loosening his hands. He needed to move. To let out some of the pent-up anger simmering over the fact that his woman had finally ventured into the world she'd been fearful of for so long, only to run into *two* people who scared her just as much...and he hadn't been there to protect her.

Carly watched him with an anxious expression on her face. "He didn't say anything to me. I don't think he even knew I was there until he was about to leave. He was literally inside his car, about to drive away, when he happened to turn his head and see me inside Kenna's Malibu. He didn't look happy to see me, but left without doing anything."

Jag forced himself to take a deep breath. Then another. Then he stopped abruptly and said, "You need to call Detective Lee."

"I already did," Carly said.

That stopped him in his tracks. "And what'd he say?"

"Well, not much. I mean, with Beau, there wasn't even any interaction between us. And he's not under arrest or anything, and there's no law about grocery shopping. He was more interested in what Luke said, but again, he didn't break the law. He did say he'd pass along the info to the detectives who are keeping an eye on him though. The altercation with me might be enough to make him do something stupid."

"I'd love for him to try," Jag muttered.

To his surprise, Carly giggled.

He looked at her then—*really* looked at her. He would've expected her to be tense, maybe even have reverted to the scared woman he'd whisked out of her apartment. But instead she looked...calm. Too calm? He couldn't tell. And that bothered him.

She stepped toward him and put her hands back on his chest. "I'm okay, Jag. I promise. I can't deny that the last person I wanted to see, or talk to, was Luke, but it wasn't as bad as I'd feared it would be. I think I'd built up all these scenarios in my head where I'd see him and he'd attack me, and when that didn't happen, I finally realized that I was giving him way too much power over me."

"You can't let down your guard," Jag warned.

"I won't," she said immediately. "I mean, it's not like I want to invite him over so we can have a heart-to-heart chat or anything. But I need to stop obsessing over him. And about what happened. I'll always feel guilty that Kenna almost got hurt instead of me, but like you told me once, Shawn's the asshole here. *He's* the one who was mentally unbalanced. Not me."

"Fuck, you're amazing," Jag whispered.

"It's because of you," she said, leaning into him.

Jag's arms went around her once more, and if he held her a bit too tight, she didn't complain. "I didn't do anything," Jag said with a shake of his head. "If anything, I didn't do enough."

"You did. You talked to me. Texted me. Called. Kept me from completely losing myself. You forced me to get out of my own head. You brought me here, which was the best thing you could've done. My apartment had become my prison. You gave me Kenna back. You convinced me to go back to the job I realized I actually love. I have money in my bank account again. Not

a lot, but it's better than none. You've given me the courage to *live*, Jag. It's going to be a while before I'm ready to go anywhere on my own, but if it wasn't for everything you've done, and for hooking me up with Elizabeth, I wouldn't have been able to face Luke today."

"Yes, you would've. I have a feeling you can do anything you set your mind to."

"But that's just it. I wouldn't have set my mind to it without you pushing me. Without you being there for me. And I feel awful, because I've given you nothing in return. I've been like a parasite, taking but not giving you anything."

"You being here is enough," he said.

"It's not," she insisted. "From here on out, things are going to be different."

Jag couldn't help but smile at that.

"I'm serious," she insisted. "I'm gonna be a better friend. A better girlfriend. I want this to be a two-way relationship, and not just you being amazing and me being lame."

"Okay."

"Okay?" she asked with a tilt of her head.

"Yeah. I haven't done anything I haven't wanted to do. I like being needed, if I'm being honest, but since I want this relationship to work, more than I've wanted just about anything in my life, including Hell Week to be over when I was in SEAL training, I'll agree to just about anything you suggest."

"Well, I certainly hope being with me is nothing like Hell Week. I've read some stuff about what you probably went through, and it definitely doesn't sound fun."

"It wasn't."

"Right, so...starting now, I'm gonna ask you more questions. I want to know everything about you. Your childhood, what

kind of kid you were in high school, what your first job was, why you decided to join the Navy and...well, everything."

Jag felt a pang of apprehension move through him at her announcement. "I'm not that interesting."

"Nope," she said with a shake of her head. "You don't get to decide that. You have to tell me everything and I'll decide. And for the record...you have nothing to worry about, I'm fascinated by you already."

"I'd rather talk about you. I don't know that much about you either. Where you grew up, if you were a shy kid, how you ended up out here in Hawaii."

Carly smiled. "And I'm happy to tell you all of that. I just... I've gotten too comfortable here, Jag."

"What does that mean? You want to leave?" he asked in alarm.

"No!" she exclaimed.

Jag relaxed a fraction. "Good, because I like having you here."

"I like being here. I like being your friend, Jag...but I want more. And I feel as if we've already fallen into a routine. You... you haven't even kissed me since that one day."

Jag's arms tightened. He was well aware that he hadn't kissed her again. He wanted to, always, but the truth was, that first kiss had knocked him on his ass. He'd also wanted to make sure he didn't pressure Carly in any way when it came to being intimate.

"What are you thinking about so hard?" she asked gently. "You do that all the time, go into your head, and I can't help but wonder what you're thinking about."

"Nothing important," Jag said.

Carly frowned.

"I'm sorry," he apologized, knowing he was trivializing some-

thing that was obviously important to *her*. "I'm not used to talking about my feelings. I guess I'm a typical guy in that sense."

"That's okay. But, Jag, you can talk to me about anything."

Jag nodded. He actually knew that, and a part of him was desperate to tell her his deepest, darkest secret, but he'd kept it to himself for so long, he wasn't sure he *could* talk about it now.

Forcing his thoughts away from that dark place within him, he growled quietly, "You want more kisses, angel?"

Shyly, she nodded.

"You like me touching you?"

She nodded again.

"Holding you at night?"

"Yes."

"You want more, all you have to do is tell me, or show me, whichever is more comfortable for you. I haven't touched you more intimately because I never want to pressure you. If at any point you don't like what I'm doing, or how I'm touching you, all you have to do is tell me no. I'll honor that. I swear."

"I know you will," Carly said, licking her lips as she stared up at him.

"How long does the lasagna need to cook?"

"At least for another thirty minutes," she told him.

Without a word, Jag loosened his hold on her and grabbed one of her hands. He immediately headed for the couch in the other room.

Carly giggled as she followed.

Jag knew he should be on the phone calling the detective, or Baker, or something. He wasn't thrilled with the fact that Carly ran into both Luke and Beau today. It was as if seeing Jeremiah at Duke's the other day had somehow opened some Karmic

wormhole. He wouldn't be at all surprised if she started seeing even more people associated with her ex now. That always seemed to be how these things worked.

But at the moment, all he could think of was the fact that Carly wanted more kisses. He was eager to give her exactly what she wanted. And to confirm the chemistry they'd felt with that first kiss wasn't a fluke.

He fell onto the couch and pulled Carly with him, then eased her to her back, hovering over her. Carly smiled at him.

"This okay?" he asked.

"It'd be better if you were actually kissing me," she teased.

Jag took a moment to visually drink her in. Her hair was spread around her head like a halo. Her lips were bare of makeup, but still a rosy pink. As he stared, she licked her lips once more. Then her hand moved to the back of his neck and she gently tugged him downward.

He let her take the lead...and the second her lips touched his, Jag knew he was a goner. He'd never felt this way before, like if he stopped touching her, he'd die. It was a melodramatic thought, and so strange for him, but not unwelcome.

Carly was so different. Jag knew that down to the marrow of his bones. He'd kill anyone who dared to fucking touch one hair on her head. It was a vicious sentiment, considering what they were doing right that second, devouring each other as if they'd never get enough. But Jag knew it was true.

The woman beneath him was precious. She was *his*. He'd bend over backward to be the man she needed him to be. The problem was, Jag knew she could do so much better than him. On the outside, he seemed like a catch. Inside, he knew otherwise.

For now, he planned to make sure Carly knew what an

incredible, desirable woman she was. But when the day came that she realized how broken *he* was, he'd give her up without a fuss, if necessary. He only wanted her to be happy, and if that meant watching her walk away, so be it.

In this moment, he was going to be selfish.

Time had no meaning as they made out on his couch. Jag lost himself in her. Her soft body under his hard one, her tongue twining with his, the feel of her breasts against his chest, her soft moans...she was perfect.

The annoying sound of a buzzer in the distance made his brows furrow as he finally managed to peel his lips off Carly's.

"The lasagna," she said in a shaky voice.

Jag felt as off-kilter as she sounded. He brought a hand up and smoothed her hair off her forehead. Her lips were now slightly swollen and a deeper pink than they'd been before. Glancing down, he saw her tight nipples even through her bra and the material of her T-shirt. Some men might be turned off by the oversized top she was wearing, but not Jag. He knew it was one of *his* shirts—which made her even sexier to him.

"You good?" he couldn't help but ask. "Not too much?"

"Not too much," she breathed, eyeing him. "You can definitely do that whenever you want. I won't ever complain about being kissed stupid."

"I've never been that into kissing," Jag admitted.

"No?" she asked. "But you're so good at it."

"Only with you," he said.

"Flatterer," she teased.

He was being serious, but if she thought he was giving her a line, he wasn't going to correct her. He wasn't hungry in the least, would prefer to lie on his couch and make out with Carly all night, but she needed to eat. He couldn't help but remember

how bare her own cabinets had been back at her apartment, how she'd been eating ramen because it was cheap and she was too scared to go to the store.

He sat up and pulled her into a sitting position next to him. "Come on, let's rescue dinner. You worked hard on it and it smells delicious."

"It wasn't *that* hard," she protested, but blushed a little at the same time.

Damn, Jag loved the effect when he complimented her. He pulled her to her feet and kept hold of her hand as they headed for the kitchen. He was still wearing his uniform, but didn't want to let go of her long enough to change. He'd put on a pair of sweats or something after they ate.

She grabbed some plates and he dished up a huge slice of the ooey-gooey pasta dish on each. She poured them glasses of lemonade and they headed to the table to eat.

"Carly?" Jag said after they'd sat down.

"Yeah?"

"I'm so proud of you."

"Thanks," she said. "I'm proud of myself."

And that right there was one of the many reasons Jag loved her.

Wait, shit...*did* he love her?

He thought about it for two-point-two seconds...then admitted that yes, what he felt for her was definitely love. She'd changed his life, and in return, he'd do everything in his power to give her back the confidence Shawn Keyes had stolen from her.

What was the saying, if you loved someone, set them free? If it was meant to be, they'll come back to you? That was how he felt. That was how he knew this was love. Whatever Carly needed, he'd give to her. Even if it broke his own heart.

"There you go thinking again," Carly teased.

"All good things, promise," Jag told her. He'd taken the seat next to hers, instead of sitting across the table, and he was very glad for that now, as he leaned in and kissed her hard and fast on the lips. "Eat," he ordered, nodding to her plate.

"Yes, sir," she quipped. "And I have to admit," she added under her breath, "I'm loving the kissing thing."

Smirking, Jag said, "Me too, angel, me too. You can probably expect a lot more of that, now that I know you're okay with it."

The smile she aimed at him made Jag's heart beat faster. He loved her like this. Happy and joking around with him. It was something he wasn't sure he'd see from her for a long while, and he was thrilled with how quickly it had happened.

He knew he had a goofy smile on his own face as he ate, but didn't even care. Around Carly, he wasn't the quiet but deadly Navy SEAL, he was simply Jag. And he liked that. A lot.

CHAPTER THIRTEEN

It had been a week since the shift in their relationship, since Carly had seen Luke at the grocery store. Jag's guess had been right; it seemed as if she saw people related to her old life with Shawn all the time now. He was proud that, each time she did, it affected her less and less.

Gideon Sparks, Shawn's other best friend, the guy who worked at the Honolulu Zoo, had seen her and Kenna in an ABC Store near Duke's, when they'd gone there to grab a snack on one of their breaks. Carly had wanted some Maui Onion potato chips—she was addicted to the things—and Gideon had walked in just as they were checking out. According to Carly, he'd merely muttered hello and walked past them, but it had still weirded her out a little bit.

She hadn't seen Luke again, thank goodness, but Wes, Shawn's landlord, had somehow found her phone number and called. He'd left a message telling Carly that when Luke had cleaned out his dad's apartment, he'd left some of her things to

be carted off with the trash. Wes had wanted to know if Carly had any interest in claiming her belongings.

She'd also seen Beau at the grocery store again—and Jag had put his foot down and told her that she had to find a new place to shop.

But he'd still been proud that none of the encounters seemed to faze her. At least not for long. He was torn though; he wasn't sure if her getting used to seeing her ex's friends was a good thing or not. If one of them had plotted with Shawn, Jag didn't want them anywhere near Carly. In the end, he decided that he would rather her not have a panic attack anytime she went outside and definitely didn't want her to be paranoid to go anywhere.

They were currently lying on his couch, and Carly was curled into him. The TV was on, but Jag had no idea what was playing. His attention was fixed on the woman in his arms.

"Are you close with your dad?" Carly asked.

She'd also done exactly what she said she would, doing her best to get to know everything about him. Every night, they played twenty questions as they learned as much as they could about each other. Jag had been uncomfortable with it at first, but had actually found himself enjoying their nightly talks

He shrugged in response to her question. "Not really. I mean, I call him on his birthday and Christmas every year, but otherwise, we don't really talk."

Carly had a hand on his chest, and every now and then she would trace circles with her fingers. He loved her casual touches, craved them.

"Hmmm."

"No comment on how that's sad? Or that I should make more of an effort to talk to him?" Jag asked. He didn't mean the

162

question to come out as harsh as it sounded, but he'd had plenty of people in the past try to make him feel guilty for not being closer to his only parent.

Carly lifted her head and propped her chin on his arm as she looked at him. "No. I'm not all that close with my parents either, so I'd be the last one to judge. Besides, familial relationships can be tricky. Fraught with triggers for people. If you don't get along with your dad, I'm sure you have a good reason."

Jag pressed his lips together for a moment. "We're just very different people."

"I get that. My mom wanted me to be exactly like she was as a kid. Wanted me to be in a gazillion sports, have tons of friends, and be part of the popular cliques. She never said it, but I know she was disappointed when I turned up my nose at most of that. I mean, I've always been outgoing, and I was on my high school swim team, but the people I hung out with were on the fringes of what was deemed 'cool' in high school. Band geeks, the drama kids. I even dated a guy who was president of the robotics club." Carly chuckled, and Jag couldn't help but smile too.

"And your dad?"

"He was gone a lot. He worked long hours and he spent most of his free time with his poker buddies," Carly said with a shrug. "I have to admit that really bothered me about Shawn...the amount of time he spent with his friends. He'd sometimes invite them over even when I was there. Many times I ended up leaving and going back to my apartment, and he'd call me later and ask when I'd left. It was pretty telling that he didn't even notice me leaving."

Jag brought a hand up and smoothed it over her head. She rested her cheek on his shoulder and began to play with the buttons on his shirt.

"My mom left when I was young," Jag said. "I don't even remember her, and Dad never talked about her. I remember asking why I didn't have a mother once, and he got really upset, so I never asked about her again. But my dad was a guy's guy... you know the type. Really into cars and football, always telling me boys shouldn't cry. Had a new girlfriend every other month, and he drank a lot of beer. He was always telling me to man-up, to stop being a pussy, things like that.

"I tried my best to be just like him, but I always seemed to fall short. I didn't love the things he did, and it took a toll on me, constantly trying to impress him. It was exhausting."

"I know how that feels," Carly said softly.

"Yeah. I was on the football team in high school, and my ol' man was so proud. But I wasn't really very good. I wasn't big enough to be a good linebacker. I was a fast runner, so the coach tried to turn me into a wide receiver, but I couldn't catch the ball worth shit, so that didn't last long. Interestingly enough, though I couldn't catch, I could throw. So eventually I settled into the quarterback position."

"Really?" Carly asked, sitting up so she could see Jag's face more clearly. "You were the freaking quarterback? Jeez, Jag, that's like being high school royalty."

His lips twitched and he shook his head. "It would be if I actually got any field time. I was the backup to the backup quarterback. I spent most of my time standing on the sidelines during games. I think I played about ten minutes in my entire four years."

"Oh," Carly said, lying back down. "I'm sure you were great during those ten minutes," she told him.

Jag loved how supportive she was, but he didn't want to

mislead her. "I had two interceptions, ten missed passes, and a grand total of thirty-seven yards gained."

"Well, that's thirty-seven more yards than I had," she said with a goofy grin.

He shook his head. "My point is, I was always a disappointment to my dad. I didn't go to my junior or senior prom and wasn't that interested in girls." Jag's heart rate sped up. He was getting dangerously close to thinking about a time in his life that he really just wanted to forget.

"He has to be proud of the fact that you're a SEAL," Carly said after a moment.

Jag relaxed a fraction, now that they were veering away from his childhood. He shrugged. "I guess."

"You guess?" Carly asked in disbelief. "Jag, you're the best of the best in the Navy. You're doing amazing things for our country. You put your life on the line constantly, even though no one knows exactly what you do. And if your dad wanted a son who was a 'man's man,' you are the epitome of that."

He liked the defensiveness in her tone a little too much. He hadn't had anyone who'd really stood up for him growing up. If something happened at school, his dad had just told him to suck it up and deal.

"He wanted me to go into the Marines," Jag said. "His father was a Marine, and to him, that's the best branch of the Armed Forces. He told me more than once that the Navy was for wimps."

"Oh, good Lord," Carly said with a shake of her head. "He's an idiot."

Jag couldn't help but chuckle.

"I'm serious," she huffed. "For the record, Jag, I think you're incredible. And you're more of a man's man than anyone I've

ever met. It has nothing to do with guzzling beer and sitting on a couch and watching football. It's about more important things. You're protective and bossy, which are both traits I associate with men—sorry, but it's true. More than that, you pay attention and listen to what's going on around you. You take everything in, then act if needed.

"Like when you dropped me off at Food For All last week, and Lexie was carrying on about the spiderwebs in the corners of the ceiling, complaining that she couldn't reach them and was genuinely afraid to walk under them because she thought a spider was going to fall on her head. Elodie and Ashlyn made fun of her, and even I thought it was a little funny. But when you came back to pick me up, you brought a *ladder* and you cleared every single spiderweb.

"Every time we walk from the parking lot to Food For All, you take the outside of the sidewalk. You make me stay in the car while you come around and open my door. And I know that's not just you being polite; you're checking out the area, looking for anyone or anything you think might be a danger to me. You texted me almost every day when I was too scared to leave my apartment, and you came over when I needed you.

"To me, *that's* being a man's man. Being helpful. Protective. Considerate. Perceptive. Most men wouldn't have stuck with me for so long when I was hiding out. Not only that, but you haven't pushed yourself on me sexually. Haven't asked for more than I'm ready to give. Not once have you made me feel as if I'm just another notch on your bedpost. I know what society believes is appropriate behavior for a guy, but I'm very happy that you're exactly the way you are."

Jag couldn't take his gaze from the woman staring back at him with wide eyes. She was practically winded by the time she'd

finished having her say, and Jag knew he'd remember this moment for the rest of his life.

He'd worked hard to be the man he was now. It wasn't always easy, especially with his father constantly judging every decision he made, but Carly's words made everything he'd done in his life worthwhile.

"Sorry," she said, wrinkling her nose. "I just think it's ridiculous that you somehow think you don't measure up to anyone's idea of what's masculine and what isn't."

"I..." Jag stopped and cleared his throat before he could continue. "Thank you."

She nodded and snuggled closer. "Besides, you're also a hell of a good kisser. That has to count toward manliness too."

Jag couldn't stop the bark of laughter that burst out of him.

Carly grinned. "I like you smiling and laughing a lot more than you being all introspective and finding yourself wanting," she told him.

"Me too," he agreed. "Tell me more about yourself," he ordered.

"What do you want to know?"

"Everything."

She laughed once more. "Can you maybe narrow it down a bit?"

"How'd you end up in Hawaii?" he asked with a small grin.

"After I got my associate degree, I didn't really want to spend another two years in school. I wasn't a great student, got mostly B's and C's, and decided I wanted to do something different. Something exciting. At least more exciting than staying in my hometown in Illinois. I remembered the pictures one of my friends in high school showed me of a vacation she took out here, and I was so jealous. So on a whim, I bought a one-way

ticket to Honolulu. I was young, and kinda dumb, and came out here without a plan. I had a thousand bucks that I'd saved up and was full of hopes and dreams.

"The first two years were great. I stayed in a hostel downtown at first, met some cool people, couch surfed for a while before settling down in a very crappy studio apartment." Carly chuckled. "I can't believe how great I thought it was. I worked a few waitressing jobs, then got the gig at Duke's. I made enough to trade in the studio apartment for the one I currently have."

She got quiet, and Jag knew what was coming next. "Then you met Shawn."

"Yeah. He wasn't always an asshole," she said a little defensively. "At first he was kind, and quite the gentleman. He definitely wooed me. I was leery at first, because he was *so* much older than me...and I'd dated some older guys. But eventually he won me over. Then he slowly began to change, and I didn't realize it at first. It was little things here and there, that I could easily blow off because everything else about him seemed so great.

"I feel so stupid for staying with him after the first time he manhandled me. He apologized profusely and said it would never happen again. Said that if I tried harder not to make him mad, he'd be able to control himself in the future. He made me think it was *my* fault he'd shoved me against the wall so hard, I knocked my head against the plaster and had a headache for three days."

Jag growled low in his throat. "What a guy decides to do is never a woman's fault. We all have free will. One thing I hate hearing is when someone blames a woman for being assaulted because of the clothes she wore, or because of something she said, or the way she acted. A guy doesn't get a free pass

because he can't control his own lust or anger around a woman."

"Yeah," Carly agreed. "Shawn had already begun to belittle me, made me feel incredibly naïve and stupid compared to him. Thank goodness I never moved in with him. I totally get why people stay with abusive partners though. It was incredibly hard to break up with him, even though I had my own bank account and place to live. If I had no place to go and no money to move, or if we had children, I can imagine it would've been next to impossible."

Jag nodded. "That's one of the reasons I wholeheartedly support Food For All. A number of their patrons are single parents who've left abusive relationships."

"Same. Speaking of which, there's a big catered thing tomorrow at Duke's. Some company is bringing in all their employees. They rented out the entire restaurant for two hours. I assume there's going to be a lot of leftover food, so I volunteered us to bring it to Food For All. I hope that's okay."

"Of course it is," Jag told her. Then he asked something that had been nagging at him. "Now that you've been here a while... you ever think about moving back to the mainland?"

"No way," Carly said. "Yes, there are a lot of bad memories here, not to mention I keep running into Shawn's friends and that sucks, but I love Hawaii. I love the energy, the sunshine, the people. I can't imagine going back to Illinois and the cold winters. What about you? Will the Navy be moving you anytime soon?"

He could hear the concern in her voice.

"It's always a possibility," he said honestly. "The government can do whatever they want, no matter what they've promised. But when the team agreed to come out here, one of the stipula-

tions was that we'd be here for at least five years. That's an eternity in the military."

"Good," Carly said.

"Not to change the subject, but how are you doing with everything, angel?" Jag asked. "Honestly. There have been a lot of changes in your life recently, and it has to be a little overwhelming."

Carly sighed. "It is. But I'm actually surprised at how well I'm coping. I mean, at first, stepping foot outside my apartment seemed like the hardest thing in the world, and now I'm working again, and even seeing Shawn's friends hasn't sent me back to the terrified blob I was not too long ago." She looked up at him. "I have you to thank."

Jag shook his head. "No, you don't. It's all you."

She laughed in disbelief. "Um, no. If it was up to me, I'd still be cowering in my apartment. You make me feel braver, Jag. Just by being here. Sometimes when I get scared, I think about what you'd tell me to do, and it gives me the courage to get through whatever it is I'm struggling with."

"I think you're giving me more credit than you should," Jag told her. "But I'll take it if it means you'll continue to blossom like you have."

Her cheeks turned pink. "Did Elizabeth really make it through SEAL Hell Week?"

"Yes."

"She's amazing. And kind of scary," Carly admitted. "But she's inspiring and has really given me a lot to think about when it comes to personal safety. Now when I'm out at the store, or even in the car with Kenna headed to Duke's, I think about what I'd do if something happened. I'm more aware of my surroundings."

"That's great, angel. That's exactly what I wanted you to get out of the sessions with her. Yes, knowing how to break a hold or where to punch and hit someone so you can get away from them is important, but it's also just as vital to be able to recognize danger before it can touch you."

"I didn't notice it as much before, but now I can see that's what you do all the time. You're constantly on the lookout for trouble."

"Does that bother you?" Jag asked.

"Not at all. It makes me feel even more safe when I'm with you."

Jag stretched out and rolled them until Carly was under him. He propped himself up on an elbow so he didn't crush her. "You will always be safe with me. You can also talk to me about anything. *Anything*, Carly. If you're scared, nervous, happy, excited, or any other emotion. I will listen without judgement. Okay?"

Carly stared up at him and nodded. "All right. And you know the same applies to me, right? I know you can't talk about specifics with your job, but if you're having trouble dealing with something that happened on a mission, I'll listen. I won't judge you for anything that you've done, or not done."

Her words sank into his soul, filling in the cracks that had formed so long ago. He'd never in his life felt as if he had someone he could be completely honest with. Not his judgmental father, not his classmates, not even his SEAL teammates. And not because he didn't trust them with his life, but because he didn't think they'd understand what he'd survived.

But Carly would. She wouldn't judge him, would probably get extremely pissed off on his behalf.

"What's that smile for?" she asked.

Jag hadn't even realized he'd grinned while thinking about Carly being defensive on his behalf. "Nothing. But thank you. Knowing I've got you to talk to means the world to me."

"Good."

"One more thing before we find more interesting and fun things to do," Jag said. His hands itched to touch her. He wanted nothing more than to lose himself in her kisses. But this was important.

Carly smiled coyly as she ran her hands up his chest. "Interesting and fun sounds good."

Jag caught a roaming hand with his free one and brought it up to his mouth and kissed her fingers. "I'm not thrilled about Shawn's cronies suddenly showing up everywhere you are. Baker hasn't found anything incriminating on anyone, much to his frustration, but that doesn't mean someone isn't still out there who wants to finish what Shawn started."

Carly sighed. "I know."

"I just need you to be careful, angel. Remember what you're learning in your self-defense classes. I don't want you to go back to being terrified of people, but I need you to be aware of your surroundings at all times."

"I am. I will," she said. "If something happens...you'll come find me, right?"

"Nothing in this world would stop me from not only finding you, but making whoever dared fucking touch what's mine pay." Jag knew he sounded a bit bloodthirsty, but Carly didn't even blink.

"Okay."

"You can't ever give up fighting though, angel."

"I won't."

"I mean it. No matter how bleak things seem, don't lose hope

in me. Or my team. Or Baker. Or your friends. I will turn over every single damn rock on this island to get to you, but you can't ever give up, understand?"

She nodded, then got a thoughtful look on her face.

"What? What's going through your head right now?" Jag asked.

"Most guys would probably tell me not to think like that at all. Would tell me nothing's going to happen, that I'll be fine."

"First, I'm not most men. Second, I wish to God I could tell you that you'll be fine. That I'll keep you safe. But I've learned that what we want to happen isn't always what *does* happen. I want you to be prepared for anything, and if I sit here and tell you that all is well, that you're safe, that nothing bad will ever happen to you, I'm doing you a disservice.

"Life is fucking hard. It's not all birthday parties, doughnuts, and pretty pictures on Instagram. It's falling down and skinning your knees, it's losing people before they've gotten to live out their lives, it's cancer, chronic diseases, and bullies getting away with being assholes. I need you to be strong enough to weather those storms, both with me by your side and when you're on your own. As a couple, we're only as strong as we are individually. I can't be with you every minute of every day, no matter how much I want to. If shit happens, I need you to fight, angel. Fight for yourself. Fight for me. Fight for *us*."

Tears formed in Carly's eyes as she stared up at him. "I will."

"Promise?"

"Promise. I know you go into horrible situations on missions. Dangerous ones. With bullets flying and stuff. I need you to promise the same thing. If you get captured, or shot, or whatever, please hold on until you're rescued or see a doctor."

"I promise," Jag said. This conversation felt like they were

taking vows. And in a way, they were. He cleared his throat once again. They'd had some pretty emotional conversations tonight, and he was ready to move things into more pleasurable territory.

"You good?" he asked.

"Yeah. You?"

"Yup. You want to watch TV? I could put on a movie. Make us some popcorn or some other snack," he suggested.

"Or...?"

"You have something else in mind? A card game or something?" he teased.

She laughed. "Or something." Carly reached up and palmed the back of his head and did her best to force him closer.

Jag smiled, resisting. "You want something, angel?"

"Yes. You," she said simply.

"I'm yours," Jag told her, then let her lower his head.

They made out on the couch for what seemed like hours. When Jag was with Carly, nothing else mattered. Not his past, not the present, and definitely not what might await them in the future. It was only the two of them, lost in passion, in each other.

When Jag's hand eventually slipped under the baggy T-shirt she was wearing—he'd never get enough of seeing her wearing his clothes—he stilled when she stiffened beneath him. He stopped immediately, lifting his head to stare down at her.

"I'm sorry, I just...I like your hands on me, Jag."

"But?" he asked, sliding his hand back out from under her shirt. The brief touch of her warm skin made his palm tingle, but he'd rather cut off his hand than make her uncomfortable even for a moment.

"I keep thinking about how fast we're moving, now that

we've decided we're more than friends. I jumped into things with Shawn and that didn't turn out so well."

Jag didn't take offense. He understood how she felt better than anyone. "It's okay," he soothed, shifting them so he was on his back once more, and she was plastered to his side.

"It's stupid. I mean, we sleep together every night," she grumbled.

"I told you once and I'll say it again as many times as you need to hear it," Jag said. "We don't have to rush anything."

"I want you," she said softly. "I'm just...scared." She let out a long breath of air. "I'm sick of being scared," she muttered. "Seriously, I'm so pathetic."

"You aren't," Jag reassured her. "And I'd be upset if you did something you weren't comfortable with or ready for. Is sleeping in the same bed as me awkward? I can—"

"No!" she exclaimed, quickly interrupting him. Her voice lowered as she said, "I like being next to you at night. It calms me. My subconscious knows you'll never let anyone come in and steal me away if you're there with me."

"Damn straight," Jag muttered. She giggled, and the sound made his muscles relax. "We *are* moving fast, but you should know, I've had a crush on you for months," he admitted.

Carly smiled up at him. "Yeah?"

"Yup. Ever since we all accompanied Aleck to Duke's to meet Kenna."

"I can't believe you didn't run in the other direction when I went a little spastic after Shawn's kidnapping attempt," she said.

Jag rolled his eyes. "Spastic? Please. You were trying to protect yourself the best way you knew how. And protect your friends."

"Yeah. I guess I was."

"I don't...do this," Jag admitted.

"Do what?"

"Fall for someone like I have you," he said plainly. "So you take as much time as you want to feel comfortable with me. I'll be right here when you're ready."

"You've fallen for me?"

"Head over fucking heels," Jag said quietly with a straight face.

"A girl could use that to her advantage...if she was a bitch."

"Yup. But you won't and you aren't."

"You sound sure of that," Carly said.

"I am. How about I get up and make us a snack after all?" Jag asked.

Carly sighed. "It's probably for the best. Jag?"

"Yeah, angel?"

"I'm falling for you too."

He grinned. "Good." Then he shifted, climbed over her, and stood. He leaned over and kissed her on the forehead. "Keep my spot warm," he ordered, as he turned and headed for the kitchen.

CHAPTER FOURTEEN

Jag liked the routine he and Carly had fallen into, and he was as proud of the way she was handling everything thrown at her. Not even a month ago, she'd have a panic attack if she so much as stepped outside. Yesterday, while he'd been at work, she'd gone to the grocery store by herself.

Some people wouldn't think that was a big deal, but Jag knew how much of a huge step it was. The self-defense sessions she was attending had done wonders for her self-esteem and confidence. He could see Carly incorporating everything she was learning about being aware of her surroundings at all times, when they were out together.

To all of their frustration, Baker was still coming up with nothing in regard to who might've been working with Carly's ex. Jag still wasn't ready to believe Shawn had been working alone. He had an accomplice, Jag would bet his SEAL career on it.

While Jag, and everyone else on the team, was frustrated, he knew Baker wouldn't give up until he'd found *something*.

In the meantime, he and Carly were trying to live their lives as normally as possible. Kenna had decided they were having another girls' night in next weekend, and Jag was pleased to see that Carly was honestly looking forward to it.

He pulled into the parking garage, making sure to find a space near the stairwell. Even though they hadn't discovered who was working with Keyes, he wasn't going to take any chances by having to walk through a garage any farther than they needed to. Sometimes he found a parking spot on the street, and he used a few different parking garages, making sure to change up his route to Duke's every so often just in case someone was watching Carly. He headed down the stairs and onto the crowded sidewalks of Waikiki.

He kept his eye out for anything or anyone who looked out of place, who could be a danger. All he saw were tourists...until he happened to glance down the alley that housed the international market. It used to be an entire block wide, but after a developer bought the space to build a high-rise, the vendors were forced into the narrow alleyway.

A man was leaning against a wall smoking a cigarette. He wasn't holding a shopping bag, and his gaze was locked on the Outrigger Waikiki Beach Resort across the street. Which was the hotel where Duke's was located.

But it wasn't just any man. Jag had studied the pictures of the people Baker was investigating, and he knew without a doubt the man attempting to blend in with the tourists, and failing, was none other than Eddie Evans. Shawn's neighbor.

Scowling, Jag turned in Eddie's direction, but at that moment, the man finished his cigarette, tossed it to the ground, stepped on it, then turned and strolled away, disappearing into the international market. Jag followed, intent on finding out if

the man was watching Carly, or if it was simply a coincidence he was outside her workplace. But as soon as he entered the market, he knew searching for the man would be hopeless. Even though the alleyway wasn't very large, the number of kiosks set up with tarps and tables filled with tchotchkes provided way too many hiding places for Eddie, and too many places for him to slip away undetected.

Frustrated, but not willing to spend his time on a wild goose chase, possibly giving Eddie a chance to circle around and get to Carly, Jag headed for Duke's.

Seeing the man was a good reminder that none of them could let their guard down.

Jag walked through the shops on the bottom floor of the hotel and felt a tiny bit better when he didn't see anyone he recognized as he approached Vera, who was standing at the hostess station.

"Hey," he said as he approached.

"Hi, Jag!" she replied cheerfully.

He nodded at the perky hostess and headed inside. He'd been here enough now that no one blinked at him walking into the place as if he worked there. He glanced into the dining area and didn't see Carly or Kenna, so he continued to the kitchen.

He stood silently against the wall just outside, watching Carly without her knowing he was there for just a moment. She looked tired, as if the shift had been a tough one. Her hair was falling out of the ponytail she usually wore it in when she worked, wisps brushing against her cheeks. Her shoulders were slumped as if she was exhausted. She'd been sleeping all right— he should know—so that had to mean she'd had an incredibly busy day.

Kenna looked just as frazzled, and it made Jag worry about

them both. Aleck would be there any minute to pick up his wife, and it looked like they both needed a relaxing night. Without wasting any more time, Jag headed in their direction.

"Jag!" Carly gave him a smile as he neared.

"Hey," he said, reaching out to pull her into him. She came willingly and smiled wider as he lowered his head. He gave her a chaste kiss. He longed to deepen it, but this was her workplace, and the last thing he wanted to do was disrespect her in front of her peers and friends.

For just a moment, Carly leaned into him, giving him her weight. It was another clue that she'd had a tough shift.

"Long day?" he asked.

Carly nodded. "Oh, yeah," she said with a sigh. "There's an ironman marathon in town and I swear every athlete, trainer, and family member decided to carbo load here this afternoon. We've been slammed from the moment I got here."

Jag had noticed the large number of people waiting for tables, but he'd been so focused on getting eyes on Carly that it hadn't really registered.

"I'm sorry I didn't bring this up earlier," Kenna said to both of them. "I know it's my turn to bring leftovers to Food For All, but Robert—you know, the concierge at Coral Springs?—is in the hospital, and I was going to ask Marshall if we could stop by for a quick visit before we head home."

"Is he all right?" Carly asked in concern, turning to her friend.

Jag kept his hand on her waist as she talked with Kenna, feeling much better now that he saw for himself that she was okay. He had no idea what Eddie was doing down here in Waikiki. It might have been a coincidence that he was hanging out across the street from Duke's. Making a mental note to talk

to Baker tonight about what he'd seen, and find out if Baker could have the man followed just in case, he focused back on the conversation.

"He's okay. It was some kind of hernia repair surgery. He should be coming home tomorrow, but I thought it would be nice to visit him before he leaves. I'm bringing a hula pie. I figure he can share it with the nurses on his floor."

"That's awesome. And of course we can stop by Food For All, right?" Carly said, looking up at Jag.

"It's not a problem," he reassured her.

Carly gifted him with another wide smile before turning back to Kenna. "I'll take care of it."

"I appreciate it."

Aleck walked into the kitchen, and Jag saw him immediately recognize that the women were unusually tired.

"Tough day?" he asked.

Carly and Kenna giggled.

"What?" he asked in confusion.

"That's almost exactly what Jag said when he saw us," Kenna replied, snuggling into her husband's side.

"Well, we do share a brain, you know," Aleck quipped.

The women laughed again.

"Right, if you thought *that* was that funny, I know you're beat," Aleck said. "You ready to go?"

"Just about. Carly and Jag said they'd drop by Food For All so we could go visit Robert."

"Thanks, man," Aleck said, giving Jag a chin lift.

"Of course. I'll see you in the morning."

While Kenna gathered her things, Jag and Carly went to the back of the kitchen, where the extra food was stored. He blinked at the number of containers.

"Told you we were busy today," Carly told him.

Jag hadn't thought much about leftover food from restaurants before he'd met Carly and Kenna. He'd been shocked at how much of it got wasted every day. He was pleased that the management and owners at Duke's were doing their best to let as little food as possible get thrown away. The uneaten leftovers and table scraps from a customer's meal were always disposed of. But raw ingredients—all of the excess fruit and vegetables— could be donated, as could day-old bread that was never served. Even some individual components of dishes, like sauces that were unserved by the end of the day, could be brought to Food For All.

Alani had planned for the influx of customers with the marathon coming to town, but even with preparation, it was hard to predict what diners might want to eat. Therefore, there was always too much of one thing and not enough of another. Instead of simply throwing away the extra lettuce or the bread that didn't get eaten, it was a win-win situation for everyone to donate the food. Many pantries might turn away a lot of the leftovers, but since Elodie had started volunteering at Food For All, they'd started accepting more and more donations.

Elodie's background as a chef, and her creativeness, meant that she could repurpose just about anything that was donated and turn it into gourmet meals for their clients.

"It's gonna take more than one trip to get all this to my car," Jag said. "How about if you stay here and I'll pull up out on the street. I'll text when I'm there, and maybe you can get Justin or someone to help you carry it out?"

"Sounds good," Carly said. "Are you okay?"

Jag looked at her in surprise. "Yes, why?"

"I don't know, you look...hyped up? That's not exactly the right term, but you're different today."

"We can talk about it later," Jag said, not wanting to worry Carly before they were on their way.

She frowned. "Is everyone all right? No one's hurt or anything?"

"No, nothing like that," Jag reassured her.

"Baker found Shawn's accomplice?" she whispered.

"No," Jag said, hating that he had no new information about that situation.

She stared at him for a beat before taking a deep breath and nodding. "Okay."

It was one of a million reasons why he loved this woman. She was resilient and trusting. "Give me about five minutes and I'll be out front," he told her, before kissing her once more. This kiss was a little longer and a little more intimate, since they were alone in the back room in the kitchen. He wanted to linger, but his desire to get her home where he could pamper her was more pressing at the moment.

He brushed the backs of his fingers over her flushed cheek before he turned and headed out of the kitchen.

Within ten minutes, he had Carly and all the food loaded in his Jetta and they were on their way to Barbers Point. Carly had texted Lexie to let her know they were on the way so she'd be ready for them.

"Okay, what's up?" she asked, turning a little in her seat to look at Jag while he was driving.

"I saw Eddie Evans in the international market," he said, not wanting to draw this out.

"Shawn's neighbor?" Carly asked.

"Yeah."

"What was he doing?"

"Smoking a cigarette and looking shady as hell," Jag said. "I don't think he saw me, but just as I was going to go and find out what the hell he was doing there, he ducked into the market and I lost him amongst all the vendor tables and kiosks."

"And?"

"And what?" Jag asked.

"Did he do something else?"

"No, I told you, I lost sight of him."

"Okay."

"Okay?" Jag asked, surprised by her reaction.

Carly nodded and shifted so she was facing forward again. She rested her head against the back of the seat and closed her eyes. "Yeah. I'm not happy that he was so close to Duke's, but I can't control people's comings and goings, and there could be a hundred reasons he was there."

"Name one," Jag blurted, having a hard time believing she was truly so nonchalant about this. He was proud of how well Carly had been doing recently. She'd come a long way from the terrified woman who hid in her apartment all day. But at the same time, he was a little worried that now she was maybe being too nonchalant about her safety.

"A drug deal? Meeting with a tourist about a new scam? I don't know."

Jag knew she had a good point. Eddie Evans wasn't exactly an upstanding citizen, but he did own a boat, and if Shawn had offered him enough money to come and pick him up, he might've been all too eager to get involved in a kidnapping plot.

"Besides, he can stand across the street and stare at the hotel all he wants, he can't hurt me from over there. If he'd been inside the *hotel*, or if he'd tried to get into Duke's or talk to me, he

wouldn't have gotten far. I swear I've got more people looking out for me now than I ever would've thought. Vera's like a damn guard dog, which, don't get me wrong, I like. And Justin and the other servers all know what Luke looks like, and the pictures of the other possible accomplices are posted in the kitchen of Duke's...you know the ones Baker sent over? And don't get me started on Kaleen and Paulo. They're still upset they didn't do more when Shawn came into the restaurant and took Kenna. I have no doubt if anyone tried any shit with me, they'd lose their freaking minds."

Carly's voice was level and she didn't sound particularly stressed out, which Jag liked, but again...it also kind of concerned him. He didn't want her freaked out, but he *did* want to make sure she was still taking the situation seriously. He opened his mouth to tell her just that, but she kept talking.

"If I had to walk to the parking garage by myself, then yes, I'd probably have a very different reaction to the fact that Eddie was anywhere near Duke's. But since you've offered to continue to pick me up for the foreseeable future, and I know without a doubt you'd never let anyone get near me, I don't want to spend energy panicking about this."

She turned her head without lifting it to look at him. "I hate that we haven't figured this out, but I refuse to let my past dictate my present or future anymore. Maybe Eddie was there to spy on me. Maybe he was trying to figure out the best way to get to me. I don't know. But sitting here stressing about it isn't going to change anything. And I'm trying not to get all wigged out about something I have no control over, Jag.

"I had a long day, I'm exhausted, but I feel really good about how things went today. It was busier than it's been since I started back, and even though my feet hurt, it's nice to return to

a semblance of my normal routine. I also made a ton of great tips, which helps make the tiredness worth it. After we drop this food off, we're gonna go home, maybe you'll let me take a bath while you make us something to eat, then I get to snuggle with you. All of that is much more appealing than trying to figure out what Eddie was doing in the international market."

Jag's respect for her bloomed. She was right. He'd tell Baker and Detective Lee that he'd seen Evans in Waikiki and let them try to figure out why he was there. All he could do was make sure his woman relaxed and recovered from her day. And maybe help her celebrate another step toward getting back to the woman she used to be.

"You're right," he said simply.

Carly smiled and closed her eyes again. "I know."

"And humble," he teased.

Her smile grew. "I learned that from my boyfriend."

Jag couldn't keep the smile from his own face. "Anyone I know?" he quipped.

"Maybe. He's amazing. Tall, muscular, so good-looking you want to weep when you look at him, smart, caring, and he smells delicious."

It thrilled him to hear her describe him that way. "Nothing beats your cherry blossom lotion," he murmured.

Carly laughed. "You have an obsession with that stuff."

"Yup," Jag agreed.

They were quiet for a few minutes, then Carly spoke again. "I'm not taking my safety lightly," she said in a serious tone. "I'm not thrilled Eddie was there, but I'm trying not to let him, or anyone else, get to me again. I lost myself for a while and it didn't make me feel good. And you know that I've been seeing Shawn's cronies everywhere recently. If I freaked out every time

I saw Jeremiah, Beau, Gideon, Jamie, or even Luke, I'd have to be hospitalized. It's been months, Jag...and I'm sick of being scared."

"I know. I hate that you have to see any of those assholes. If I had my way, they'd all move off the island so you'd never have to be reminded of that fucker you dated."

Carly chuckled. "Ditto."

"Just stay aware of your surroundings at all times," Jag pleaded. "Just because it's been months doesn't mean the danger is gone. I agree that as time goes by, in theory, the threat to you lessens, but I've learned the hard way that when someone has hate in their heart, no amount of time is too long for them to act on it. Many times that hate festers inside them until they can't contain it anymore and they have to do something."

Carly nodded. "I will," she reassured him.

She rested her arm on the console and Jag immediately reached for her hand. She closed her eyes once more and sighed. "I needed this. You, holding my hand, being a solid presence next to me."

"Same," he agreed.

The rest of the trip to Barbers Point was uneventful, besides the hellish traffic. Jag pulled into the parking lot down the street from Food For All. "Stay put," he said, as usual. She gave him a small smile and grinned. She knew the routine by now, and he was relieved when she didn't complain.

Jag got out and checked the immediate area. The parking lot was pretty full, which wasn't a surprise. This area had gotten more and more popular as small businesses flourished and moved into the empty spaces in the neighborhood.

He gave Theo a chin lift. The formerly homeless man was sitting on the sidewalk across the street. He was in the shadows,

tucked between a decorative brick column outside a small Korean restaurant and a sign the owners had placed outside advertising their daily specials. If Jag hadn't looked right at him, he might've missed him.

Theo might have a roof over his head now, thanks to Lexie and Midas, but he still liked to be outside as much as possible. He had also taken it upon himself to be a sort of one-man neighborhood watch patrol. Even though he had some mental difficulties, he was pretty damn observant. He smiled at Jag and waved, but the other man didn't get up from his spot, obviously too comfortable and content to move.

There were a few people milling around, but no one Jag recognized. He opened Carly's door and she smiled up at him. Even tired from her long day, with her clothes wrinkled and her hair a mess, she was still the most beautiful woman he'd ever seen.

They walked to the back of his car and he opened his trunk. He grabbed a heavy box filled to the top with dented cans and various other food stuff, and Carly picked up three bags. There was another box in the trunk and a few more bags, so they'd definitely have to make two trips. Carly shut the trunk and they turned to head down the street to the food pantry.

They both stopped in their tracks when they caught sight of the man down the sidewalk.

"Fuck. *Again?*" Jag murmured.

"Hello," Gideon Sparks said as he walked toward them.

"What are you doing here?" Carly asked, her voice hard.

Gideon looked surprised. He had on a pair of brown overalls with the zoo logo on a patch on his chest. His brown hair had streaks of white and he was growing a beard, which was new

since the last picture Jag had seen of the man. He had quite a belly on him and was around his height.

He stopped a respectful distance from them. "I just brought some food the zoo was going to throw away," he said. "I tried to bring it to the downtown location, but they were already closed. The sign on the door said this location takes donations until seven o'clock. I read an article in the paper recently about Honolulu's homeless population and how much food went to waste every day, and had a talk with the kitchen manager at the zoo. He agreed that it would be a good thing to see about donating what we could. And I suddenly found myself in charge of dispersing it." Gideon smiled slightly and shrugged. "But I feel blessed to have what I do, so it's not a hardship."

Jag studied the man and didn't see any sign of deceit in his expression or his eyes. That didn't mean he wasn't up to no good, but at the moment, he seemed to be exactly what he said he was...someone who was doing a good deed.

"You work with the lions, right?" Carly asked.

Jag wanted to tell her not to engage, but it was too late. She was being exactly who *she* was. Or really, who the old Carly was, friendly and outgoing. Even if this was one of her ex's friends, she was doing her best to move on with her life. He admired her for that, even if it made him uneasy at the same time.

Gideon smiled and put his hands in his pockets. "Yeah. Been there about twenty years now. Started out shoveling shit and now I'm in charge of their health and welfare. It's my dream job."

Carly nodded.

"I haven't had a chance to say this before now, and it might not be the time or place, but I wanted to tell you I'm so sorry about everything that happened. Shawn was my friend, but he

was kind of an asshole. I knew that, and I regret not saying anything when he talked shit about you," Gideon said.

He sounded sincere, but again, Jag didn't trust him. "The police said Shawn told you and a few others what he'd planned."

Gideon winced and looked down at the sidewalk. He seemed repentant. "I'm ashamed to say I thought he was just talking shit. You know, how you say you want to kill someone, but don't *really* mean it? He was always saying that kind of thing, saying the governor should die, or wishing the person in the car in front of him would crash and get out of his way. He really was a dick. I'm a little embarrassed that I was even his friend."

"Why were you?" Carly asked softly. "I mean, if he was that awful, why bother coming over every week to hang out?"

Gideon shrugged. "I guess because I was lonely. I'm fifty-two, single, and I spend most of my time with four-legged animals who don't talk back when I try to have a conversation with them. And maybe just...routine. I'd been playing poker with him for years, and it was just something I did every week. I know it sounds stupid, and you have no idea how much I regret everything that happened."

Jag continued to study him carefully. The man sounded sincere, but people frequently lied convincingly. He'd seen it time and time again in his line of work.

"I appreciate that," Carly told him. "If you'll excuse me, it's been a very long day and I want to bring this stuff in and get home."

"Of course," Gideon said immediately. "I apologize for taking up your time."

"It's fine," Carly told him.

Gideon nodded, giving them a wide berth as he headed toward a white pickup truck with the logo for the Honolulu Zoo

on the doors. He drove away as Jag and Carly continued down the sidewalk.

"That was interesting," Carly said.

Jag grunted.

"You don't believe him?" she asked.

He heard the stress in her voice and didn't want to add any more angst to her already very long and tiring day. "I'm just wondering who else we're going to see today. Maybe Luke and his girlfriend are eating at the Korean place across the street. Or maybe Jeremiah and Beau will pop out of the surf shop down the road. Oh, I know, maybe Jamie's inside Food For All, donating Coca-Cola from the bottling plant."

Carly giggled.

Jag's heart eased at hearing the sound.

"I told you. It's as if the floodgates have opened. I don't know what to think about seeing all of Shawn's buddies everywhere I go."

"Me either. I knew Oahu was small, but this is kind of ridiculous."

"Agree," Carly said. She walked closer to him and bumped her elbow against his arm. Both their hands were full so they couldn't hold hands or touch any other way. "I'm glad you were here."

"Me too."

"Maybe I'll stay inside and talk with Lexie while you go back to the car and get the other stuff?" It was a statement and question all at the same time.

"Good idea."

"You don't mind?" she asked.

"Of course not. Mustang would kick my ass if I complained about walking back and forth to my car three times. He'd prob-

ably make me do burpees for an hour straight while wearing my pack, *after* running a half marathon on the beach in the deep sand."

Carly laughed again. "He wouldn't do that. He's too nice."

Jag lifted a brow. His team leader definitely wasn't nice when it came to working out and making sure his team was in shape.

He'd unload the rest of the donations quickly and looked forward to his evening with Carly. Jag never thought he'd get to a place in his life when he'd be comfortable having a woman in his space. But Carly seemed to be able to banish his demons without even trying. Though...they hadn't had sex yet. He couldn't help but worry about that. He couldn't lose Carly, and therefore would do whatever it took to make sure she didn't realize how nervous he was about making love.

The problem was him, not her, but he was smart enough to know women didn't like it when men said that.

For tonight, he'd do his best to spoil his woman. She could stay in the bath as long as she wanted, and he'd make dinner. He'd even watch *The Voice* without complaining. He secretly enjoyed the show, but they both got a kick out of his bitching about it.

It was a weird thing to both dread and crave the moment when they'd move their relationship to the next level. That time was coming soon, Jag felt it in his bones. Their make-out sessions had gotten more and more intense, and it was only a matter of time before neither could hold back any longer.

"What's that smile for?" Carly asked as they reached the door to Food For All.

Jag hadn't realized he was grinning, but it didn't surprise him. Anytime he thought about being with Carly, he was happy.

Pushing the sliver of nervousness out of his mind, Jag said, "I was thinking about you."

Carly smiled. "Yeah?"

"Yeah," he confirmed. "Come on, let's get this done so I can get you home."

"Sounds good."

* * *

Shawn's accomplice was getting impatient. He'd planned on watching and waiting longer, to wait until the bitch had gotten truly complacent, but he had to take action soon. That asshole she was living with was going to be a problem. He knew it. He'd have to make his move when the boyfriend wasn't around.

Except Carly was stupidly weak. She never went anywhere alone. Getting to her at Duke's wasn't a viable option. He'd scoped the place out and it was obvious everyone there was still on edge. Not to mention the increased security presence the managers had hired.

He'd had dreams of snatching her from the same place Shawn had tried to, as a way to honor his friend. Now, he knew that wasn't going to work.

So he'd have to move to plan B. But first, Carly had to stop being a fucking wuss and taking a babysitter everywhere she went.

His time was coming. He just had to be patient for a little while longer.

Visions of how shocked and terrified Carly was going to be ran through his head. He couldn't wait to see her crying, begging for her life. He'd make her understand exactly how pathetic she was, how she wasn't worth the dirt on Shawn's shoes.

The man smiled, the anticipation heady. She had no idea what was coming, and it excited him beyond measure.

"Just a little longer," he said softly, giving himself a pep talk. "The safer she feels, the more she'll let down her guard."

He just had to avoid the fucking detective and the asshole who was sticking his nose in where it didn't belong. They'd *never* figure out the connection between him and the boat he'd used. Just thinking about that night was enough to make his blood boil. He'd done his best to get to Shawn through the storm, but the fucking boat had nearly capsized. It had taken all his skill just to get back to the private dock that housed the boat.

"Patience," he said out loud once more. "You're smarter than all of them. Piece of cake."

Adrenaline coursed through his veins at the thought of Carly realizing it had been him all along. He'd relish her reaction, but briefly. Then he'd kill her. Dump her in the ocean where no one would ever find the body. The sharks and fish would take care of that for him.

Satisfied that it wouldn't be long now, the man smiled. He hadn't been this excited in years. "Enjoy your life while you can," he said out loud. "Because I'm coming for you."

CHAPTER FIFTEEN

Carly was happy to realize she hadn't thought about Shawn or Luke—or anyone else who might not like her—since she'd arrived at Kenna's condo. She'd been here for two hours now... and had done nothing but laugh and enjoy spending time with all the other women.

Apparently, these sleepovers were now a thing and Aleck had gotten used to being kicked out of his own condo so the girls could hang out. When she said something about that to Kenna, she'd just laughed and said her husband was more than happy to leave because he'd much rather them gather there, where everyone knew they were safe, and none of them would have to drive or deal with anyone harassing them. She also said the guys liked getting together at Slate's place for some "man time."

They'd already eaten dinner—Aleck had picked it up from Helena's, one of the best restaurants on the island for authentic Hawaiian food—and dessert, malasadas Elodie had brought from

Leonard's Bakery. And of course, there had been lots of margaritas poured over the last couple of hours.

Carly was feeling mellow and happy. It was great to spend time with her friends. She felt...normal. And after all she'd heard about Monica, she was glad to finally get to know the other woman.

She was quiet, as Kenna had said. But she was still fully present in what was going on around her. She wasn't aloof and didn't look bored...she just didn't say much, which was all right, since the others seemed to have more than enough to talk about.

"So..." Kenna drawled with a knowing look on her face. "You got anything to tell us, Mo?"

Monica looked surprised. "Um, no?"

"Whatever!" Kenna scoffed. She and Carly were sitting on the couch, both with their legs crossed. Elodie was in a huge beanbag in the corner, Lexie was on the floor, a pillow under her ass, leaning against the sofa, and Ashlyn was currently in the kitchen, mixing up another batch of drinks. That left Monica in the recliner.

"You can tell us. We're your besties!" Kenna said. She was drunk, but she always got happy when she had alcohol in her system, and tonight was no different. Her cheeks were flushed and she'd been telling hilarious stories about some of the customers she'd dealt with all night.

"I'm not sure what you want me to say," Monica replied.

Kenna leaned forward. "You've peed a hundred times tonight, and when Pid dropped you off, you two were super lovey-dovey. Even more than usual. Which, you know, is cool and all. I had my way with Aleck before you all arrived. But Pid seemed extra...*protective* today."

Carly looked at Monica and saw her new friend blushing. She looked down and began to pick at a thread on the pillow she'd placed in her lap.

"Maybe she doesn't want to talk," Carly said, giving her an out.

"She does. I mean, if she can't talk to us, who *can* she talk to?" Kenna insisted. "And I'll get to you in a second," she told Carly, shaking a finger at her.

Carly rolled her eyes.

"Kenna's right, you *can* tell us anything," Elodie told Monica.

"Right. Well...we weren't going to say anything for a bit longer, but you guys are worse than a dog with a bone. I'm pregnant, okay?"

There was silence in the room after her pronouncement, then everyone began shouting at once.

"Oh my God! Congratulations!"

"That's awesome!"

"Wow!"

"The first SEAL baby!"

"I knew it," Kenna said smugly, sitting back with a huge smile on her face.

"How?" Monica asked. "I don't drink alcohol anyway, so me not drinking wasn't exactly a clue. And it's not like I'm showing. I'm still in the first trimester."

"You keep resting your hand on your belly, which you don't usually do."

Monica smiled and shook her head. "You're good."

"I know," Kenna said. Then she leaned over and held her hand out, palm up. Monica took it. The two women held hands for a moment. "I'm happy for you."

"Thanks. I...we didn't exactly plan this. I mean, we both want kids, but we'd planned to wait at least a year, give us time to enjoy being a couple." Monica shook her head. "But I guess we weren't careful enough."

"Our guys'll do that. It's hard to think about protection when you're horny as hell and they're looking at you with those fuck-me eyes," Elodie stated.

Everyone burst out laughing.

"So true!" Lexie said with a wicked grin on her face.

Ashlyn came back into the living room with a tray of drinks. It was amazing that she didn't spill any, as she was definitely not sober. She placed the tray on the coffee table and gestured to it. "An announcement like that deserves a toast! Monica, the one on the end is yours...it's straight orange juice."

"Thanks," Monica said.

Carly was relieved that no one seemed to care the other woman wasn't a drinker, pregnancy or no. She'd had a few friends over the years who made snide comments when someone didn't feel like getting shitfaced. It was nice to be with women who seemed to truly respect and like each other exactly how they were.

"To Monica and Pid's baby!" Ashlyn said, holding up a glass.

Everyone leaned forward and grabbed a drink and held it up.

"To Mo!"

"To babies!"

"To fertility and stubborn sperm!"

Carly almost spit her drink out at Kenna's toast.

"To not having to wear a condom for the near future!" Elodie added.

"Oh, man, I'm so jealous!" Lexie moaned.

After Ashlyn settled on the floor next to Lexie, Kenna turned to look at Carly. She braced herself.

"So...how're things going with you and Jag?"

"They're good," Carly said.

Elodie shook her head. "Nope. We need more than that. Talk, woman."

Carly grinned. Elodie trying to be a hard-ass was pretty amusing. But since Carly really needed some advice, she wasn't upset. "I mean, he's amazing. Attentive, supportive, and not once have I been afraid of him."

The other women all frowned. Carly went on quickly. "You guys know my relationship with Shawn wasn't good. I mean, it was at first, but then he started making me feel like shit and manhandling me. It got to a point where I was very careful about what I said around him so I wouldn't set him off."

"Jag's not like that," Elodie said firmly. "None of the guys are."

"I know," Carly agreed. "It's nice. I actually *want* him to come home. I look forward to seeing him and it's hard to say goodbye in the morning when he goes to work."

"I'm not surprised he moved you in," Lexie said. "It seems that's a pattern with our guys."

"Any plans to go back to your apartment?" Kenna asked.

Carly shrugged. "No?"

"Was that a statement or a question?" Lexie asked.

"Both, I think. I don't want to go back to my place. I *like* living with Jag. He's easy to be with. I know things are still fairly new with us but still."

"They aren't *that* new," Kenna protested. "Like Lexie said, our guys have a pattern. They fall hard and fast and they don't fuck around in moving forward with their relationships."

"I guess that's why I'm kinda confused," Carly admitted.

"About what?" Elodie asked gently.

"I'm attracted to him. And I think he likes me too."

"He does," Monica interjected.

Carly looked over at her. The reassurance somehow felt like it meant more coming from the usually quiet woman, than if it had come from Kenna or one of the others.

"Once or twice, I was the one who stopped him when things got too intimate. But I feel as if, had I not...he would've. He's said a few things here and there that make me feel as if he's not sure he wants to be intimate," Carly admitted. She couldn't believe she was talking about this, but she really needed some advice. "He gets hard, so I know he wants me, but he never pushes me for more. And I kind of want him too, now. But he seems content to just kiss and cuddle."

"He probably isn't sure if *you're* ready for more," Elodie suggested.

"He's told me over and over again that he won't move faster than I'm comfortable with," Carly said. "But now that I'm sure I'm ready for more, I'm not sure *he* is." She took a large sip of her drink, needing the liquid courage to continue. "I'm afraid he doesn't *want* to do anything more."

"I doubt that's true," Lexie said with a frown. "Maybe he's trying to wait until your situation is resolved?"

"Well, shit, if that's the case, we might be waiting forever," Carly grumbled.

"Have you told him you want to have sex?" Kenna asked. "Sometimes guys are clueless. Especially ours. They're super observant about what's going on around them when they're in SEAL mode, but when it comes to women...sometimes not so much."

"I haven't come right out and said anything like, 'Fuck me, Jag, I'm ready,'" Carly said, knowing she was blushing.

"Maybe you should," Kenna added with a shrug.

"That's not me," Carly protested. "I mean, heroines in books and movies say that stuff, but it just sounds so awkward in real life."

"Then maybe you need to *show* him that you're ready," Lexie suggested.

"Yeah," Elodie said, nodding. "Like strip off all your clothes and walk into the living room while he's cooking and spread yourself on the table. He'll get the hint then."

Everyone laughed.

"I'm guessing that worked really well for you at some point?" Lexie teased the other woman.

Elodie blushed but nodded. "Oh, yeah," she said dreamily. "It worked out very well for me."

"We haven't been naked with each other yet. There's no way I could just nonchalantly walk around the apartment without any clothes on," Carly said.

"You guys are sleeping together every night though, right?" Kenna asked.

Carly nodded. She'd confessed as much to Kenna recently. "Yeah. We usually have dinner, hang out and talk for a while, make out. Then we cuddle on the couch, I go to bed, and he comes in later."

"You need to change that up," Kenna told her. "Maybe invite him to come to bed at the same time you do. Yeah, the bathroom thing can be awkward...you know, peeing, brushing your teeth, changing. But maybe seeing you take off your clothes and putting on the T-shirt you stole from him to sleep in will give him a nudge in the right direction."

"Or you could go down on him when he gets in bed," Lexie suggested. "Guys love that."

"I've never...I'm not sure I want to do that our first time," Carly said awkwardly.

"What if you straddled him?" Kenna asked. "You said he pulls you close when he gets into bed, so why not just keep going, throw a leg over him? When you're on top, look him in the eye and tell him you're ready. That you want him."

Carly blushed just thinking about doing that, but the more she considered it, the more she liked the idea. Jag had always been very careful not to push her too hard, but maybe if she made the first move, he'd feel more comfortable. He'd finally understand she truly was ready to make love with him.

"You guys are really good together," Ashlyn said. "Anyone can see that you're crazy about each other. Sometimes it's just a matter of going after what you want."

Carly nodded.

"So when are *you* going to go after what you want?" Lexie asked the other woman.

Ashlyn looked surprised. "Me?"

"Yeah, you," Lexie said. "You said it was obvious that Carly and Jag are crazy about each other, and the same goes for you and Slate."

Ashlyn blew out a long breath, shaking her head. "We can't stand to be around each other most of the time," she protested.

"Which usually just means you're denying the obvious," Elodie said.

"Don't go thinking me and Slate are gonna end up married or anything," Ashlyn said.

"Who said anything about getting married?" Kenna asked. "There's nothing wrong with good ol' fashioned fucking."

Everyone burst out laughing again. Leave it to Kenna to be blunt.

"I'm serious," she said, when everyone had themselves under control. "Women have casual relationships all the time. There's nothing wrong with having sex with someone you have chemistry with. And, Ash, you and Slate have a shitload of chemistry," Kenna said.

Carly nodded along with the other women.

"I'm pretty sure I annoy the hell out of him," Ashlyn said with a shrug. "And the feeling's mutual. He's too bossy. Too protective. I'd never be able to deal with a boyfriend like that."

"What about a lover?" Kenna pressed.

Ashlyn wrinkled her nose. "I'm not sure that would be any better."

"But think about all that testosterone in bed with you," Elodie said softly. "I can tell you with confidence...it's a hell of an experience."

Lexie, Kenna, and Monica all nodded in agreement.

Carly felt a pang of jealousy shoot through her—followed by determination. She wanted what her friends had. She had little doubt Jag would be amazing in bed. He claimed he didn't have a lot of experience, but she didn't know if he was just trying to make her feel better or if he was actually serious.

"I'm not going to hook up with Slate," Ashlyn continued. "You guys just need to deal with that."

"So if he met someone else, you wouldn't be upset?" Monica asked. "If that woman started hanging out with us, talking about how good her man is in bed, like we do now, it wouldn't piss you off?"

"No," Ashlyn said firmly.

Carly might've believed her if she hadn't followed that state-

ment with a gulp of her drink, nearly draining the glass. The thought of Slate with someone else clearly bothered her, but she wasn't at a place where she could admit it.

"Think about it," Lexie said gently. "Slate's awesome. But he's impatient as hell, everyone knows that. There might come a time when he decides he should move on."

Everyone was quiet for a moment, before Monica broke the silence by saying, "I have to pee again."

Carly studied Ashlyn as everyone laughed. The other woman looked almost stricken, but as quickly as the expression formed on her face, it was gone.

"Come on," Elodie said, standing up and holding out her hand. "I'll go with you."

"You know we aren't at a bar, you don't have to go in pairs," Kenna said.

"I know, but it's the girl code," Elodie insisted.

"How about we move the party to the balcony?" Lexie suggested.

"Awesome idea. I'll get some blankets," Kenna said, jumping up from the couch.

"And I'll grab the rest of the malasadas we didn't eat earlier," Carly said.

Hours later, as Carly lay on the couch and prayed the room stopped spinning so she could get some sleep, she couldn't stop smiling. Tonight had been fun. She'd missed hanging with Kenna and the others. Shawn had taken so much from her, and he'd almost taken this away too.

She vowed to herself, listening to Elodie snore from the large beanbag in the corner of the room, to never let anyone come between her and her friends again. She also began to plot. She wanted what the others had. She wanted Jag. Wanted him to

know how much he meant to her. And since she knew she was too chicken to come right out and say the words, she'd have to show him.

She didn't know when, but she figured she'd know when the time was right. And that time was coming. She couldn't wait.

CHAPTER SIXTEEN

"You're seriously not going to tell me where we're going today?" Carly cajoled.

The days were going by surprisingly fast, and while both she and Jag were frustrated at the lack of new information about her situation, Carly wasn't really dwelling on it anymore. Easier said than done, of course, but she was pretty proud of how well she was doing. She'd even gone down to the grocery store for the second time by herself the other day. Jag was working, and Carly felt stupid calling Kenna or someone else to come and hold her hand while she grabbed some butter. They'd run out, and she wanted to bake cookies to surprise Jag.

Jag and Slate had gone to her apartment and brought her car, an older model Ford Escape, to his complex a while ago. The trip to the store wasn't as difficult as she thought it might be, going out the first time by herself. She kept her eye out for anyone who might be following, just as Elizabeth had taught her. Instead of looking down, or at her phone, Carly kept her chin up

and met the eyes of the people she passed. It gave her the confidence she needed to get through the short trip.

It was her biggest baby step by far, and Jag had complimented her profusely. Carly knew he wasn't happy that Shawn's mysterious accomplice was still a viable threat, but as for herself...she was slowly coming to terms with the fact that they might never know. She couldn't live her life hiding away, in that case. She was proud of herself for how far she'd come, though she knew without Jag by her side, pushing and being her cheerleader, she wouldn't be where she was today.

He'd told her last night that he had a surprise for her today, but refused to tell her where they were going. His only clue was for her to wear closed-toe shoes.

"Are we ziplining?" she asked.

"Not telling. It's a surprise," Jag said with a smile. "But I think you're gonna like it."

Things with Jag were also going amazingly well. Yes, she was grateful for all he'd done to help her, but her feelings ran so much deeper. She enjoyed being around him more every day. He was funny, sweet, and even when they weren't talking, just existing in the same place, she was comfortable and happy.

They still spent their nights cuddled together in his bed, their physical attraction as intense as ever. Their make-out sessions had gotten more intimate...but now that she was ready to take things to the next level, it seemed as if Jag was still holding back. Carly had no idea why.

She was ready for more. Ready to make love with Jag. But every time she tried to get up the nerve to make the first move, as her friends had suggested, something stopped her. Jag didn't seem to be all that interested in having sex, and it was concerning. With every day that passed, Carly's desire grew. She didn't

think he'd changed his mind about wanting to be with her, about dating, but in the evenings when they kissed, he backed off first. It was confusing...and frustrating.

"Carly?" he asked.

She realized she'd been staring into space while she was thinking. She turned to look at him. "Yeah?"

"You okay? You seem...introspective today."

"I guess I am. But I'm good. I mean, sometimes I feel as if I'm on a roller coaster. Some days I feel like my old self, and other days I struggle to do so."

"I think that's normal. But I'm extremely proud of you."

"Thanks. I'm proud of me too."

Jag lifted their clasped hands and kissed the back of hers, sending goose bumps down Carly's arm.

She noticed they were driving to the east side of the island, but still hadn't guessed where they were going. She hadn't spent a lot of time out here, had no idea what there was to do in the area. The road turned north and Carly could see the ocean.

"It's so pretty," she mused.

"I'd never even seen the ocean before I joined the Navy," Jag said.

Carly stared at him in disbelief. "Seriously?"

"Yup. Not a lot of ocean in Oklahoma."

"I guess not. But you're a good swimmer, right?"

He laughed. "I'm a SEAL."

"Which means you're a good swimmer," Carly said. "Sorry, stupid question."

"No question you ask is stupid," he reassured her.

"Remind me never to challenge you to a race," she joked. "I mean, I'm a good swimmer, I can hold my own, but I never made State or anything. I've been mediocre my entire life."

"You are not mediocre," Jag said forcefully.

"I didn't mean that in a derogatory way," Carly soothed. "I just...I've been average in everything I've done. I think that's what frustrated my parents. They wanted me to be the best at *something*, but I never stood out, no matter what activity I tried."

"That's not a bad thing," Jag said.

"I didn't care so much when I was in high school. I had friends and my life was pretty carefree. As long as I was having fun, I didn't care if I didn't win or didn't have the highest test score. But when I was taking classes at the community college, I started to feel as if nobody really *saw* me. I was *too* average."

"I saw you," Jag said simply.

The three words shot straight to Carly's heart. "After Shawn, I didn't think I wanted to get into another relationship for a very long time. But somehow you snuck under my defenses. Now I can't imagine *not* being with you."

Jag grinned at her and squeezed her hand. "Ditto." Then he said, "Look, there's Mokoli'i. Many people call it the Chinaman's Island, since it looks like a conical hat, but I think the Hawaiian name is much more beautiful."

Carly stared at the island not too far from shore as they drove past. "There are a ton of small islands around Oahu, aren't there?" she mused.

"The state recognizes one hundred and thirty-seven islands, give or take a few," Jag said.

Carly looked at him in surprise. "Really?"

"Yup. But in actuality there are upward of a hundred and fifty or more, if you include the smaller and mostly uninhabited islets, coral reefs, and atolls."

"Wow, I had no idea."

Carly listened as Jag went on about how the islands were

formed by volcanic activity and were actually the exposed peaks of an undersea mountain range. It was interesting to think that they were all living on the very top of a mountain, and about what it might look like without the ocean there.

Jag slowed down and flipped on his blinker. Looking to their left, Carly saw a sign that welcomed them to the Kualoa Ranch.

"I've heard of this place!" Carly said excitedly. "This is the *Jurassic Park* place, right?"

Jag chuckled. "Yup. It's actually a nature preserve and cattle ranch, but the Ka'a'awa Valley is where many scenes from the movies were filmed. Along with *Hawaii Five-O*, that TV show *Lost*, and others as well. It also had an underground bunker for residents to escape to during World War II."

"Cool," Carly breathed.

"And...in case you were worried about being out here and feeling vulnerable...I've got another surprise," Jag said after he'd pulled into a parking spot.

Carly was shocked that she hadn't even *thought* of worrying about someone following her. But Jag was right, being out in a remote valley might be the best opportunity for someone to try to snatch her, or even shoot at them. But before she could say anything, he continued.

"Everyone's meeting us here."

"Everyone?" Carly asked.

"Yup. And even Baker agreed to come."

"Oh my gosh, this is gonna be amazing. Thank you!"

"Anything to see you smiling," Jag said.

Carly couldn't stop herself from throwing her arms around Jag. It was awkward with the console between them, but she heard him chuckling as he caught her. Carly kissed him. Hard.

She couldn't remember being this excited about something in a very long time.

She pulled away and sat back in her seat. "Well? Let's go!" she said.

"Keep your pants on, angel," Jag said with a chuckle. "I'll come around."

Carly practically bounced in her seat as Jag got out. Even in her excitement, she hadn't made a move to get out. She and Jag had a routine and she was more than all right with it. Anyone who didn't know the reason for their caution might think he was being chivalrous, or even over-the-top macho, but honestly, Carly wouldn't feel comfortable getting out without Jag checking the area. That had been the hardest part about driving to the grocery story on her own...getting out of the car.

The second he opened the door, Carly leaped out and hugged him again. "If I forget to tell you later, I had an amazing time today."

He chuckled, and the sound reverberated through Carly. "You're welcome."

Then something else he said finally registered. "You said Baker's coming too?"

"Yup."

"Holy shit, I don't know if I'm ready to meet him," Carly mused, some of her excitement dimming. She remembered everything the other women had said about him, and now she wasn't so sure she wanted to come face-to-face with the man.

"You are," Jag said. "Come on, let's go see if the others are here."

He took her hand and they walked toward the stairs that led into one of the buildings at the ranch. There was a huge porch that lined the front. Picnic tables were set up for people to eat

lunch, wait for their tour to start, or just to relax. Jag held open the door for her, and Carly entered into a massive gift shop. She itched to browse, to find some cool dinosaur souvenirs. But as if Jag could read her mind, he leaned down and said, "After the tour."

Carly mock-pouted, but she wasn't really upset. How could she be?

With his hand at the small of her back, Jag guided her through the surprisingly crowded shop. It was still early, but it was obvious the Kualoa Ranch was a very popular spot for tourists and locals alike. They exited out the back door into a kind of courtyard. The towering, lush green mountains in the distance made Carly inhale sharply.

"It's so beautiful," she sighed.

"Yes," Jag said softly.

When Carly turned, she found him staring at her, not the amazing view in front of them. "The mountains," she clarified.

"Them too," he told her.

Carly couldn't help but shake her head. She knew she was blushing, but she loved getting compliments from Jag.

"They're here!" a voice called out from their right.

Turning, Carly saw Kenna waving at them. It looked as if she and Jag were the last ones to arrive. "Did everyone else know about today?" she asked Jag.

"Nope. The guys decided to keep it a secret."

"I figured. Because Kenna can't keep a secret to save her life."

Jag grinned. "That's what Aleck said."

They walked over to the large group and Carly hugged everyone as if she hadn't seen them in months.

"They're gonna split us up into two groups," Mustang said. "Lexie, Midas, Ashlyn, Baker, and Slate will be in one group, and

Kenna, Aleck, Me, Elodie, and you two will be in the other. If that's okay."

Carly had forgotten all about Baker already. She tuned out Mustang and Jag talking logistics and turned to the only person in the group she hadn't met yet. He was standing off to the side, his arms crossed, and he was studying her intently.

Telling herself that she was now brave-Carly, and not cowardly-Carly, she took a deep breath and stepped toward the man. The moment he saw her move, he approached.

"You must be Carly," he said in a low, rumbly voice.

"And you must be Baker," she returned, holding out her hand.

Baker took it in his, and Carly held her breath. This man was...it was hard to come up with the right adjectives. She'd heard all about him from the others, but it hadn't really prepared her for meeting him.

It felt as if he had an aura of danger surrounding him. She could practically see it. Like if anyone made even one wrong move, he'd pounce. He reminded her of a panther, beautiful and deadly at the same time. She gaped at him, not sure if she wanted to run or if that would somehow make him attack.

She felt Jag's presence before his hand pressed on the small of her back. She couldn't help but take a step back so she was leaning into him.

"Baker," Jag said. "Good to see you."

"Same," Baker said with a small tilt of his chin.

"Anything new?"

"No."

His answer was short, and he obviously wasn't happy about it. Carly knew they were talking about her situation. She suddenly felt bad for thinking Baker was anything other than what he was...a friend doing everything in his power to help her

out. He didn't have to. He didn't know her, wasn't even an active-duty SEAL anymore. But according to Jag, and despite a frustrating lack of progress, he was still working long hours to try to figure out who'd been helping Shawn. Including spending a lot of time away from his house up at the North Shore, following Shawn's friends, trying to find something, anything, that would tie them to what had happened.

At the sleepover the other night, Carly had found out more details about Monica's kidnapping, and how Baker had put himself in danger to save her. No matter how gruff and deadly he seemed...he was a good man.

Before she could overthink it, Carly took a step forward and wrapped her arms around Baker.

He tensed in her embrace, but Carly didn't let go. He was taller than Jag, making her feel even shorter than normal, but she held on. "Thank you," she said softly. "I appreciate you trying to help me. And for what you did for Monica. And Elodie. Hell, all of us." She looked up at him. "Free food for life," she declared recklessly.

"What?" he asked, looking somewhat flustered. He hadn't hugged her back. He was holding his arms slightly out at his sides, as if he wasn't sure what to do with them.

"At Duke's, free food for life. If you're ever in Waikiki and you're hungry, you can eat there for free."

"Hey, *I* don't even get that!" Carly heard Aleck say, but she kept her gaze locked on Baker's. "I know, you probably aren't down there very often, but still. I don't have anything else to offer."

If she wasn't staring right at him, Carly might've missed the way his eyes softened. He lost some of the deadly vibe he carried

around him like a cloak. But he shored up his defenses again immediately.

"Did I ask for anything?" he asked.

Carly refused to be intimidated. "No. But you're getting it anyway."

"Just say thank you," Jag said, humor easy to hear in his words.

"Thank you," Baker said without any inflection in his tone.

"Shit, he's about as hard to thank as Tex," Mustang muttered.

Carly had no idea who Tex was, so she ignored the comment. Then, feeling awkward because she was still squeezing Baker for dear life, she let him go and backed up, running into Jag, who immediately steadied her by putting a hand around her waist.

"You're welcome," Carly said. "Though, I've decided it doesn't matter if we ever find out who was working with Shawn. I'm putting him out of my mind and putting everything about that time in my life behind me. I'm moving on."

Baker's eyes bored into her own as if he knew she was lying. She was *trying* to put Shawn behind her, but it wasn't quite as easy as she'd hoped. Then she realized that she might sound a little ungrateful for all Baker was doing for her. "I mean, I'm still being careful," she added. "Not taking any chances, but I'm trying not to be as scared as I was before."

Baker looked over her head, obviously at Jag, and said, "I see the sessions with Senior Chief Petty Officer Albertson have done some good."

Carly could hear Kenna chuckling behind them. It was hilarious how the guys couldn't call their instructor Elizabeth. But it was a respect thing for them. The woman had worked hard to earn her rank, and they were honoring her by using her full title when talking about her.

"Yeah," Jag agreed.

Baker looked back at her. "Good. Although a little fear isn't a bad thing. Keeps you on your toes. If you get too complacent, bad shit happens."

"Ain't that the truth," Lexie muttered.

Feeling as if she needed to say something to everyone standing around her—all of Jag's SEAL team members and her friends—Carly turned. "If something does happen, it's no one's fault," she said, a little more forcefully than she'd intended. "Sometimes whatever's gonna happen is gonna happen, no matter what we do to prevent it. If it does, I'm going to try to be like Elodie. And Lexie, Kenna, and Monica. I'm not going to freak out—at least I'll *try* not to—and I'm gonna let you guys do your thing and figure out where I am and nail the bastard who did it."

"Fuck," Mustang sighed, running a hand through his hair.

Midas and Aleck looked like they wanted to seriously hurt someone.

Pid's lips were pressed together tightly, and he pulled Monica into his side as if that would somehow protect her from whatever danger might be lurking out in the world.

Slate made a noise low in his throat and looked away. Carly saw Ashlyn glance at him in concern.

When she turned back to Baker, he had absolutely no expression on his face, which was somehow his scariest look yet.

Lastly, she looked up at Jag. His jaw was clenched, but even as she watched, he took a deep breath and got control over his emotions. Then he simply leaned forward and kissed her temple gently.

Carly closed her eyes and leaned into him.

"Are you all ready to go?" a cheerful voice asked from nearby, making Carly jerk in Jag's arms.

"Easy, angel," he murmured.

Feeling stupid, Carly turned to see two employees from the ranch standing near the group. They wore khaki pants, and T-shirts with "Kualoa Ranch" and a picture of a giant Tyrannosaurus rex on the front.

Mustang nodded and stepped forward. "We've broken ourselves into two groups like you asked," he told the college-aged kids.

"Wait, what about Monica and Pid?" Carly asked. She just realized their names hadn't been mentioned when they'd talked about breaking into groups.

"We're gonna stay here," Pid said easily.

"Oh, but—" Carly started, and Monica interrupted.

"It's fine. Pid doesn't want to risk anything happening with the baby."

Carly wasn't sure why they'd come all the way out to the ranch if they weren't going to do the tour, but figured maybe she and Pid wanted to visit with Baker, since they didn't get to see him very often.

"It's fine," Monica said gently at seeing the sad look on Carly's face. "Honest."

"Okay, but I'll take a gazillion pictures so you can see everything when we get back."

"Thanks."

It wasn't long before Carly found herself perched on an ATV. She had on a helmet and gloves and couldn't believe how excited she was. At first she was nervous about driving the ATV, but she quickly got the hang of it and before she knew it, their group was off. They rode single file, so it was impossible to talk to

anyone. They headed up a dirt-packed road and the views of the ocean were breathtaking.

Their guide eventually stopped and they all got off. He took a picture of their group with the ocean in the background, then led them into an old World War II bunker. It was built in 1943 and at one time, there were two cannons strategically located at the entrance and exit to protect the island from invasion. He stopped at a blueprint of the underground space, and Carly was amazed at how big the bunker really was.

They walked through, seeing posters of many of the shows and movies that were filmed at the ranch. Everything from the *Jurassic Park* movies—which Carly knew about—to *50 First Dates*, *George of the Jungle*, *Mighty Joe Young*, and the most recent *Jumanji* movie. There were relics from the forties, as well as cheesy electronic dinosaurs. They probably spent close to an hour exploring the bunker, and Carly loved every second.

When they were finished touring the bunker, they continued around the mountain, and as they rode, their guide pointed at different things they passed. Carly would've liked to have stopped and learned more about certain items, but their guide looked as if he had a specific destination in mind. After crossing a small stream and going up a rather steep hill, he stopped in front of a tree lying on its side, with a *Jurassic Park* sign in front of it.

"Who knows what this is?" he asked once they were all stopped.

"A log," Elodie quipped.

"Ten points to the lady," the young man said without missing a beat. "But more specifically, it's the tree Alan and the kids hid behind in the first *Jurassic Park* movie. You know, when they

were trying to get out of the way of the stampede of Gallimimus?"

"Yes!" Elodie exclaimed. "Cool! Can we get off and look at it?"

"You can do more than that," the guide said with a smile. "How good are your acting skills?"

Before Carly could blink, she, Elodie, and Kenna were standing twenty feet from the log. The guys refused to participate, but were watching with amused grins on their faces. The other group was nowhere in sight, so Carly assumed maybe they'd already been by the log.

"Okay, on the count of three, run toward the tree, but pretend there are huge dinosaurs behind you and you're running for your life," the guide told them. "Ready? One, two, *three!*"

Still laughing, but trying to control themselves, the three women took off toward the tree. Kenna jokingly pushed Carly back, so she was ahead of her, and ran for safety. Elodie really got into the spirit of the thing and kept looking behind her with a terrified expression on her face. Carly was laughing so hard it was almost impossible to run and she fell behind. Elodie and Kenna got to the tree first and leaped behind it.

Carly was a few seconds behind. She could hear their guys laughing hysterically now, and she vaguely wondered why. She was sure they looked funny, pretending there was a huge predator behind them, but did they really look *that* hilarious?

It wasn't long before she realized why they were laughing so hard. Apparently, when the guide started filming with Elodie's phone, he'd pulled out a hand puppet of a dinosaur head and it peeked into the left side of the frame while he was filming them.

When he played the video back in slow motion, it looked as if a dinosaur really was chasing them. And at the end, since she

was last, Carly was "eaten" by the creature. Obviously, it was something the guide did for every group, but watching the video made Carly and the other women laugh until they were crying.

Afterward, they all posed on the tree for pictures, even the guys. And when the guide told them all to look to the left and pretend there was a dinosaur, Carly had a feeling the hand puppet would be coming into play again.

She was right. Once again, everyone laughed at the pictures of them all looking terrified at the dinosaur head, which was looming over them.

Carly's stomach hurt from laughing so hard, and she couldn't remember when she'd had a better time. It was even more fun when the guys joined in.

They all climbed back onto the ATVs, with Mustang right behind the guide, then the three women, and the rest of the guys bringing up the rear. As they continued with the tour, Carly didn't even try to keep an eye out for anything out of the ordinary. Everything around them was so beautiful, and she knew Jag would keep her safe should any boogeymen be lurking.

They rode for another twenty minutes through the valley before they began to slow once more. Carly could see a structure in the distance, but the guide stopped before she could figure out what it was.

"You might recognize the pavilion ahead of us. It was the platform in *Jurassic World*, where Zach and Gray, the young brothers in the movie, got into the gyrosphere."

"Oh my gosh!" Carly exclaimed, her eyes glued to the structure. "I remember that part. How fun would it have been to be an extra?"

"Probably not too much fun, since standing out in the sun

while they filmed the scene over and over again had to suck," their guide quipped.

Carly laughed. She didn't care, she still thought it would've been amazing to be here with all the actors, to be involved with one of her favorite movies.

"Why don't you guys ride on up? I'll be there in a moment."

Not even thinking twice about why their guide would send them ahead, Carly started her ATV and headed toward the pavilion.

When they got close, she frowned in confusion. It looked like there was some sort of...party or something going on? For a second she was disappointed, thinking she wasn't going to get a chance to see the movie prop up close. Then she blinked in surprise.

"Is that...Monica?" she asked. "And Pid?"

Their group parked their ATVs next to another row of vehicles, and she saw Ashlyn, Slate, and the others waving from the deck above them. Carly looked at Jag in confusion. She felt a little better when she heard both Kenna and Elodie ask what was going on.

"They wanted it to be a surprise," Jag told her softly, unbuckling the latch of her helmet and taking it off her head.

"Wanted what to be a surprise?" Carly asked.

"Their wedding."

Carly inhaled sharply and looked back at the platform, then again to Jag, before laughing with joy and dashing to the right, where the ground sloped up to the platform.

Elodie and Kenna joined her, and the three of them ran up together, then stopped suddenly when they had a clear view of the entire platform.

Monica had changed into a simple white sundress, a pair of

white tennis shoes peeking out from under the hem. Pid had a black collared shirt with the same khaki shorts he'd worn earlier. There were brightly colored flowers hanging from the railing, filling the air with the most breathtaking scent.

Ashlyn and Lexie were beaming as they hurried over to the girls.

"Isn't this cool?" Lexie asked. "I know I told Midas I wanted a beach wedding, but I think I've changed my mind."

"We had no idea either," Ashlyn assured them. "We drove up just like you did, totally clueless."

The five women hurried over to Monica, who had a small smile on her face. She was holding a small bouquet of orchids and had a lei around her neck. "Are you mad that we didn't tell you?" she asked.

"No way!" all five of the friends said at once.

"This is awesome!" Elodie reassured her.

"I'm so happy for you guys," Kenna added.

Carly could only stand there and smile. She was almost overcome with happiness for her friends.

"I wanted to wait, but Stuart wasn't having it," Monica explained, glancing over at her soon-to-be-husband with a shy smile. "The plan was to wait a few months, get married, *then* try for a baby. But as you all know, the pregnancy thing just kinda happened. I still wouldn't have minded waiting, but Stuart insisted now was the right time to get married."

"I'm thrilled for you," Lexie said.

"Best tour *ever*!" Ashlyn exclaimed.

Everyone laughed.

"Is everyone here?" a man asked. He'd been standing next to the railing and was obviously going to marry the couple.

"Yes. Let's get this done," Pid said impatiently.

There were no chairs on the platform, but no one seemed to mind. Carly leaned her back against Jag's front as they watched their friends get married. Her gaze wandered past the happy couple exchanging their vows, to the absolutely gorgeous backdrop of the mountains directly behind them and the ocean off to the left. It was hard to believe she was standing right where movie stars had stood, attending a wedding.

And she wouldn't be here if it wasn't for Jag. If he hadn't helped her get back to living again. She squeezed his hands, which were clasped against her belly. He leaned in and rested his chin on her shoulder, holding her tighter.

The ceremony didn't last long, it was short and very romantic. Pid looked so happy he could burst. After the officiant said, "I now pronounce you husband and wife," everyone cheered and clapped as the newly married couple kissed.

The guys all went up and clapped their teammate on the back, congratulating him, while the girls hugged Monica. The guides both took what seemed like a million pictures, and then it was time to continue the tour.

One of the employees came and picked up Monica and Pid in a four-wheel vehicle to take them back to the ranch. They were leaving immediately to spend a few days at Tiki Moon Villas. They were located just north of the ranch, the bungalows right on the water.

"You good?" Jag asked quietly as they were getting ready to get back on the ATVs. He'd just placed her helmet back on her head and was buckling it up when he said, "You've been quiet."

"I'm just so happy for them," Carly said. "And very thankful I was here today. I would've been devastated to miss this. Even though I just met Monica recently, I feel as if we've been friends forever."

Jag nodded. "You want to get married?"

Carly's heart just about stopped beating. "Um, like ever? Or right this second?"

Jag chuckled. "Someday."

Carly shrugged. Glancing at the others, she knew they didn't have much time. She wasn't sure this was the right moment to be talking about this, even if it *did* make her heart speed up to know that Jag wanted her thoughts on the topic.

He put a finger under her chin and turned her head back so she had no choice but to look at him.

"Honestly?" she said. "I haven't thought about it much. I mean, if you're asking if I want to settle down with someone and live happily ever after, then the answer is yes. Absolutely. But I've never felt a bone-deep need to be married. As long as I'm with someone who loves me as much as I love him, I'll be happy."

Jag stared at her so long, Carly got a little worried. Was her answer not what he wanted to hear?

"We're perfect for each other," he finally said softly. "I have nothing against marriage, but I've seen my fair share of disastrous unions."

Carly smiled. "Is it horrible that we're talking about not wanting to get married at our friends' wedding ceremony?" she asked, only half kidding.

"No," Jag said firmly. "It's a part of getting to know each other. Of learning what makes each other tick."

"Like making love."

The words just kind of popped out, and she cringed the second she said them. But it was too late to erase them now.

"Yeah. Like making love," Jag agreed. Then he leaned down and kissed her. It wasn't a chaste or short kiss either. It was

almost desperate. By the time he pulled back, they were both out of breath—and their friends were all clapping and whistling.

"Get a room!" Mustang joked.

"If you guys are done making out, can we get on with the tour?" Aleck teased.

"Fuck off," Jag told his friends.

Carly couldn't help but smile. She loved the guys' banter. It was all in good fun and never malicious.

Elodie smiled at Carly, and Kenna gave her a thumbs up before they once again set off in single file to finish the tour.

By the time they got back to the ranch building, Carly was thirsty as hell, starving, and her face hurt from wind burn, the sun, and smiling so much. This was definitely an amazing day she wouldn't forget anytime soon.

She and the other girls spent way too long at the souvenir shop. Carly finally decided on two T-shirts and a dinosaur bobblehead. The guys were patiently waiting for them out on the porch, and the second Carly got within reach, Jag snagged her around the waist.

"Did you leave anything for the other shoppers?" he teased.

Carly rolled her eyes and held up her bag. "Only one bag, see? I controlled myself."

"No need, I was only kidding," Jag said with a small frown. "If there's something else you want, you should get it."

"I've got everything I need already," she said, not even caring how cheesy that sounded. "A great boyfriend and amazing friends. And memories of Monica and Pid's wedding. And I got to stand right where famous people did," she added.

Jag chuckled. "Which I can see was probably the highlight of the day."

"Thank you for an amazing time," she said, hugging Jag

tightly. And that reminded her of Baker. She drew back and looked around. "Where'd Baker go?"

"He left," Midas said. "Said he had stuff to do."

"I wanted to talk to him more," Carly said with a pout.

"Get used to it. That's usually how he is," Elodie said. "Here one second, then *poof*, gone the next."

"I'm impressed he came at all," Kenna said. "I mean, we invited him to our wedding, but as you all know, he didn't show."

"I'm sure it wasn't because he didn't want to be there," her husband soothed.

"I know," Kenna said without missing a beat. "I wasn't complaining. I loved our wedding."

"Me too," Aleck agreed.

"I think it was his curiosity about Carly that tipped the scales for him showing up," Slate said.

Carly glanced at Jag's teammate. She didn't know the man too well. "Me?" she asked.

"Yeah. He's busting his ass to figure out who was working with your ex. I'm not surprised he wanted to meet you."

Suddenly, Carly wondered if she measured up to the mysterious man's expectations.

"Before he left, he told me how much he liked you," Jag said, reading her mind.

"He did?"

"Said he was going to 'stop fucking around and solve this shit.' And that's a direct quote. That doesn't mean he wasn't putting the effort in before now, just that meeting you made it even more personal."

Carly nodded.

"I think it was the hug," Mustang said, grinning.

"I can't believe you did that!" Lexie shook her head. "He still

scares the hell out of me. No way would I have ever made that move."

Carly shrugged. "It seemed like the right thing to do at the time. If I'd thought about it, I probably wouldn't have done it."

"Well, for what it's worth, I think that man needs a woman's touch more than anyone I've ever met," Elodie declared.

"Jody," Kenna said with a nod.

"Who?" Carly asked.

"Jodelle. The woman who we all think Baker's interested in," Lexie said.

"All right, we're going," Mustang declared. "We aren't going to stand around and gossip about Baker's love life."

Carly laughed, as did the other women.

"Party-pooper," Elodie grumbled, hooking her arm with her husband's.

The group headed down the stairs toward the parking lot. Carly waved at her friends and said she'd be in touch soon.

The second the door shut behind Jag, he said, "I know you're hungry. I figured we could stop on the way back home. You craving anything or you want me to pick?"

This man. He was always so in tune with her. "You pick," she said easily.

Jag nodded and pulled out of the parking lot and turned right to head back toward Honolulu.

"I know I said it before, but I had a very good time today," Carly said.

"Good."

As they drove, she quietly studied Jag...and realized she loved him. She wasn't all that surprised at the revelation. She'd never felt as close to a man as she did with him. He was everything she'd ever wanted in a partner. It was almost a scary thought,

because she didn't want to do anything to fuck things up between them.

Intellectually, she knew she wasn't at fault for how things ended up between her and Shawn. That was all on him. He was the asshole, as Jag was so fond of telling her. But a small part of her couldn't help but worry it was at least *partially* her fault. That somehow, she'd made him change the way he had.

As if he could feel her negative thoughts, Jag reached for her hand and said, "I enjoy spending time with my friends, but I can't wait to get home and just chill with you."

Her doubts disappeared in a flash. "Same," she said fervently.

It was time. Time to show him how much she wanted him. If he didn't make a move to sleep with her tonight, Carly would. She wanted this man, more and more every day. She was so ready to be with him in every way a woman could be with a man.

Instead of being nervous about her decision, Carly felt as if a weight had been taken off her shoulders. Tonight, she'd make love to her man and tell him exactly how she felt about him. It was a risk, but one she had a feeling would pay off tenfold. She wanted to spend the rest of her life with Jag, and the rest of her life would start tonight. She couldn't wait.

CHAPTER SEVENTEEN

Carly sighed in frustration. Nothing had gone the way she'd hoped after leaving the ranch. They'd stopped and had a late lunch on the way home, and Carly had thought she and Jag were on the same wavelength as far as intimacy went.

But when they got home, he seemed to withdraw. They still snuggled on the couch, but he didn't even try to make out with her. When Carly tried to entice him to touch her by practically shoving his hand under the hem of her shirt, he'd gotten up to get them refills on their drinks.

She was beginning to get a complex...but she wasn't giving up. Not yet.

Remembering the advice Kenna had given her about climbing on top of him when he came to bed, Carly decided that would be her next attempt. She'd make it very clear that any reticence she might've once had was long gone.

She headed into the bedroom around the same time she

usually did. When she changed, she wore the usual oversized shirt, but felt a little racy leaving off her underwear.

As she lay in bed waiting for Jag, Carly knew she was being stupid. She and Jag were both adults. She should just talk to him. Tell him outright that she wanted to make love. But for some reason, she couldn't. Maybe it was fear of rejection. Maybe she was a bit intimidated by Jag, sexually. She obviously still had a bit of insecurity when it came to intimacy. But that didn't mean she didn't want him. She did.

So she was going to take control. Make sure Jag had no reason to doubt she was ready for sex. Her heart raced in her chest, and she smiled. She'd left the bathroom light on, as usual, and couldn't wait to finally fulfill some of her fantasies tonight.

Half an hour later, Jag entered the room. He was quiet, as usual, so as not to wake her. But Carly definitely wasn't asleep. She'd even touched herself while thinking about the night to come, making sure she was slick and ready for her man.

Jag went into the bathroom and Carly heard the water come on. She pictured him brushing his teeth and pulling on the loose cotton pants he usually wore to bed. When she'd first started sleeping with him, she'd been relieved he wore the long pants. It made her feel more comfortable.

But she was ready for him to ditch them. She wanted to feel his legs against hers. Wanted to have better access to his cock. She *craved* him. Now that she'd decided to make the first move, Carly was hornier than she could ever remember being with another man.

Jag came into the room and headed for the bed. He climbed under the covers and she immediately turned, snuggling into him as she usually did. She smiled when his arm went around her.

This was her favorite part of the day. Lying with Jag, being held tightly by him, safe and secure.

But tonight, she felt more than contentment. She inhaled, bringing his scent into her lungs. She thought about how amazing he was. How considerate. He loved to surprise her, pamper her. Being with him made her feel cherished, which wasn't something Carly had ever felt before.

Taking another deep breath, she moved, shifting up to her knees, then throwing one leg over Jag's body.

He inhaled sharply in surprise, but didn't say anything.

Carly rested her palms on his chest, loving the way the scant chest hair scraped against her sensitive skin. She was straddling his belly, and she blushed knowing he could certainly feel the wetness between her legs. She shifted backward a bit, hating that the waistband of his cotton pants was between them.

"Hey," she said in a low tone that she hoped sounded more seductive than nervous. "I didn't think you'd ever come to bed."

He was staring up at her with a look she couldn't interpret. Carly also realized that he hadn't touched her. His hands hadn't gripped her hips like she'd imagined him doing. A pang of doubt snuck into her brain, but she forged on.

"Thank you for today, it was the best I've had in a very long time," Carly told him. "And I can think of the perfect way to end it." She gyrated her hips a little. "I want you, Jag. I'm more than ready for us to move our relationship to the next level. You've given me plenty of time, and I appreciate it. You mean more to me than anyone I've ever been with. You've been my friend, my rock, my knight in shining armor, my cheerleader. Now I want you to be my lover too."

Carly held her breath as she waited for Jag to move. To sit up and hold her against him as he told her how happy he was. Or

maybe he'd put his hand on the back of her neck and haul her down so he could kiss her.

But to her surprise, Jag did none of those things. He did nothing at all. He lay under her, still as a stone.

"Jag?" she asked tentatively after a tense silence, more confused than ever.

"Get off."

Carly blinked in surprise. "What?" she whispered.

"Get off me," Jag repeated in a tone she'd never heard before. It wasn't really angry, it was more...distressed?

Carly was so startled, she could only sit atop him and stare.

Then Jag finally moved. His hands went to her waist, but not to pull her closer. He moved her aside and shifted out from under her. Then shot off the bed as if she had some deadly communicable disease.

She watched in disbelief as he stalked to the bedroom door and left without another word.

Carly was sure she could literally feel her heart breaking. She'd never been as stunned or hurt as she was in that moment. Not even after the first time Shawn had struck her. She'd actually expected that from him, after experiencing the anger he'd stopped hiding from her.

But rejection from Jag was the *last* thing she'd expected. It came completely out of left field.

She felt incredibly stupid. She brought her legs to her chest and hugged them, resting her cheek against her updrawn knees. Tears fell, but no sound left her lips.

God, how could she have been so wrong? How had she misread his signals?

No. She hadn't. She was completely sure of that. They made out a lot. He touched her all the time, holding her hand, wrap-

ping his arms around her, kissing her forehead. She'd felt his erection when they'd made out, she hadn't imagined that. And when they were out and about, when he wasn't keeping his eyes on their surroundings to make sure there weren't any bad guys lurking about, he was looking at her with what she'd assumed was affection. Even love.

Just hours ago, she'd come to the realization that she loved him. Was she that bad at reading men? She'd obviously been wrong about Shawn, but she'd just started getting her confidence back, and a large part of that was because of Jag. Had he been playing her all this time?

Carly had too many questions, and no answers. Just the echo of his words in her head.

Get off me.

She was humiliated—and suddenly wanted nothing more than to leave. Looking around, Carly saw the suitcase she'd packed when she'd first come to his apartment, sitting on the floor just inside his closet.

Without thinking about what she was doing, she leaped up and frantically searched for her clothes. She began to stuff the bag with her things without bothering to fold them. Her only thought was to protect herself from further hurt. To leave. To get away from Jag's sudden coldness.

The bag was full way before she'd finished putting all her things in it and Carly struggled to zip it closed. She was crying so hard now, she couldn't see what she was doing. Frustrated and distraught, she sat back on her heels and sobbed silently. The last thing she wanted was to give Jag the satisfaction of knowing he'd broken her.

Before long, her sorrow morphed into anger. How could she let another man get to her like this? She'd honestly thought Jag

liked her, maybe even loved her. He was apparently a master manipulator, even more skilled than Shawn. Had he laughed about her with his friends? The thought was like a dagger to her heart.

Well, fuck him. Fuck *all* men. She was really done this time. She was going to find a nunnery to join. Move away from Hawaii, even though she loved living here, and start over somewhere else. Maybe Maine. That was as far from here as she could think to go.

But before she left, she wanted answers. Wanted Jag to look her in the face and tell her what she'd done to make him turn on her so horribly. Explain what the hell he was thinking and what he'd gotten out of stringing her along.

She'd never, *ever* admit that she'd fallen in love with him. She'd take that to the grave.

Wiping her face clean of the tears she'd shed, Carly stood. She knew she was probably blotchy and her eyes bloodshot, but that couldn't be helped. She would confront Jag, find out what the fuck his problem was, then go home. Back to her own apartment. She'd be fine. Threat or no threat, she'd rather take her chances on her own.

Her mind made up, and determined to tell Jag off, she took a deep breath before marching out of the bedroom and into the hall. The only illumination in the apartment was the light over the stove that Jag left on just in case she needed something in the middle of the night. He'd said he didn't want her to trip over anything and hurt herself.

Mentally, Carly snorted. What a crock of shit.

She stomped into the living room, ready to tear into him— but stopped dead in her tracks. She didn't know what she'd

expected him to be doing, but she hadn't thought he'd be sitting on his couch, slumped over with his head in his hands.

He didn't look angry. Didn't look like he was anxious for her to leave.

He looked utterly broken.

Carly tried to maintain the anger that had blazed through her veins just seconds ago, but it was impossible...despite still wanting to scream at him, tell him what an asshole he was, that he was throwing away the best thing he'd ever had.

She loved Jag, even though he'd just crushed her. She couldn't simply turn that off. And something was seriously wrong.

"Jag?" she whispered.

He didn't respond.

Carly realized for the first time that she was still only wearing his oversized T-shirt. It came down to her thighs, but she was still naked underneath. She felt decidedly underdressed for his confrontation, but it was a little late to go back and change now.

She took a step closer to the couch and realized that Jag was shaking. Trembling so hard she could see it from where she was standing. And Carly knew without a doubt that he hadn't simply rejected her to be cruel.

Swallowing hard, her anger dissipated. She was more worried now. She contemplated going back into the bedroom and grabbing her phone so she could call Mustang, or Midas, or someone. But then Jag spoke.

"I'm sorry," he said, his voice anguished.

Jag was her rock. Her pillar of strength. He was supportive and sweet, always complimenting her and pushing her to carry on. But right now, he was completely defeated.

"What's wrong?" she asked.

Jag shook his head in his hands. He hadn't looked up at her. "I can't do this. I thought I could...but I can't. It's impossible."

Carly's heart broke a little more at his words, but she refused to leave until she found out why he was acting this way. "Do what?" she asked, her own voice trembling a bit.

"Have a relationship. I want to. *God*, do I want to. But I'm too fucked up. I can't do this to you."

Carly wanted to cry again, but this time not for herself. It was for the man who was obviously agonizing over something deeply troubling. Tentatively, she walked toward him and gingerly sat on the edge of the couch. Three feet separated them, but it might as well have been a chasm. How had they gone from being as close as two people could be, to this?

"You aren't fucked up," she said quietly.

He snorted. It was a harsh sound, and when he lifted his head and looked at her, even in the dim light she could see the wetness on his cheeks.

Jagger Bennett was crying?

Carly's fear spiked. Whatever was wrong, it was big. Huge.

"When we were at Aleck's wedding, you said something to me. You probably don't remember, but you said that I have no idea what it's like to be vulnerable. Do you remember that?"

"Yeah," Carly said. "You told me that I'd be surprised." At the time, Carly had blown off his response, thinking there was no way a man like Jag, a decorated Navy SEAL, a man who demanded respect with just a look, could ever feel as vulnerable and exposed as she did.

Jag stared off into space. "Are you leaving?" he asked.

Carly scooted a little closer. "I was," she said honestly. "I packed my bag and came out here to tell you that I thought you were a jerk."

He nodded as if he expected that answer. But his shoulders hunched over a little more and he seemed to deflate right in front of her. "You should go," he agreed. "I'll call Mustang or someone to pick you up."

"Talk to me, Jag," Carly begged.

She honestly didn't think he would. She sat next to him silently in the mostly dark room, praying he'd tell her what was wrong. But when ten full minutes passed without either of them saying a word, she sighed and stood.

She made it to the hallway before he finally spoke.

"It started when I was eleven."

Carly turned and stared at the man she loved, the one who'd broken her heart. Now she had a feeling it was about to break for different reasons. Her feet were moving without her telling them to. She walked back to the couch and sat down. She'd wanted him to talk to her, but now she was terrified about what he'd say.

In a million years, she wouldn't have expected him to say what he did next.

"She was seventeen, and my dad hired her to babysit me. She lived a few houses down from us. Bridget Smith. Such an unremarkable name for someone so fucking evil."

Carly tentatively reached out and touched Jag's forearm. He moved so fast she squeaked in surprise as he latched onto her hand as if it was the only thing keeping him from drowning.

He kept speaking.

"She was fun. Let me stay up way past my bedtime, watch R-rated movies, and I could eat whatever I wanted. I loved when my dad went out with his buddies and she got to come over. I didn't realize she was...grooming me.

"One night, she told me she'd brought over a special movie

for us to watch. We went into my bedroom and sat on my bed. She sat with her back against the headboard, and she settled me in front of her. It was a porno. I was scared at first...I knew it was wrong...but she told me not to worry, that my dad was gone and we wouldn't get into trouble."

"Holy shit," Carly breathed. "How old were you?"

"Twelve," Jag said with no emotion in his voice.

Carly was having a hard time wrapping her mind around what she was hearing. But everything he'd hinted at was beginning to make sense now. She'd always thought it was odd that he hadn't had any girlfriends, that he didn't have more sexual experience, but she was beginning to understand.

"We started watching porn together every time she came over. And she began to touch me. I got my first erection with her. I was so confused because her touch felt good, but also dirty at the same time. When I was thirteen, she took my virginity. Gave me a hand job until I was hard, then forced me to lie on my back and...and she had sex with me. I just lay there, terrified out of my mind, watching as she got herself off on top of me. It was almost as if I wasn't there. She didn't even look at me. It felt like I was one of the sex toys I'd seen in the movies she made me watch."

Jag's words were coming faster now, as if he was purging all the darkness he'd held inside for years, since the sexual assault.

"I didn't want to be with her, but she gave me no choice. She was older, had been messing with my head for years. She laughed at me, told me I was pathetic. Then she'd force me onto my back and stroke me until I got hard. She never wanted me to touch her, never showed me affection. She just grabbed my dick and got me hard before she climbed on top."

"When did it stop? Did you tell your dad?" Carly asked softly, wishing she knew what to say.

Jag snorted. "I didn't tell anyone. I was too ashamed. Felt too fucking...*unclean*. But my dad found out because he walked in on us one night. He came home early from bowling, or poker, or the strip club...wherever he was, and saw her raping me."

"Did he turn her in?" Carly asked.

"No. He shut the door without a word," Jag said, voice flat. "After she left, I waited for him to ask if I was all right. To tell me he'd never let her hurt me again. But instead, he slapped me on the back and said I was a *stud*. Told me how proud he was of me for banging an older chick."

Carly wanted to throw up. This just kept getting worse and worse.

"I was too old for a babysitter by then, but she kept coming over when my dad went out. I don't know if he set it up because he was proud of his fourteen-year-old son having sex with a woman who'd just turned twenty, or if she watched for him to leave at night. But she just seemed to know when he was gone. I kept telling her I didn't want to have sex, but she'd just grab my dick through my pants and tell me of *course* I wanted to fuck. All guys did.

"My grades started to slip. I distanced myself from my friends, because I felt so goddamn dirty. They were starting to get interested in girls, and I had no interest in doing what Bridget was doing to me with *anyone*. I never wanted to be at home, because I was afraid she'd come over if I was, but I didn't want to be around anyone either.

"One day, just after my fifteenth birthday, she came over like usual. She reached for my dick the moment the door closed behind her. I was fucking mortified that the sight of her made

me hard. She'd conditioned me to get an erection just by *looking* at her. But I'd had enough. I punched her. Hard. I was going through a growth spurt and starting to fill out. I told her to get out and never come back or I was calling the police.

"She laughed. Said no one would ever believe me because she was a woman. She threatened to tell everyone that I raped *her*. I knew she was right. She told me to get my fucking ass into the bedroom. So I did. That was the last night she raped me. I think she realized she wasn't going to be able to control me for very much longer. I saw her here and there after that, but we never spoke to each other again."

"Fucking bitch! God, I want to beat the shit out of her. Ruin her goddamn life! Wait—can Baker find her and do that?"

Jag turned to look at her for the first time, and Carly was stunned to see his lips twitch.

"What in the world are you laughing at? This is not a laughing matter!" she seethed.

He sobered. "I know. And...I think I knew this was how you'd react."

"How could I not? Jag, she fucking raped you! First, that's child abuse, and child porn, and endangerment, and probably a hundred other things. But second, you were a *child*!" Her voice rose. Carly knew she sounded a bit hysterical, but she couldn't help it. The thought of *Jag* being abused like he'd been made her utterly crazy. "And I can't believe your dad was proud. What an asshole! I'm serious about making her pay. They should *both* pay. I don't care that it's been a few decades. She can't get away with that shit scot-free!"

"God...I love you," Jag whispered.

Anything else Carly was going to say blanked from her mind. "What?"

"And that's why you need to go."

Carly shook her head in confusion. "I'm not leaving."

"You have to. I can't do this. I'm fucking broken, Carly. The second you threw your leg over me, I froze. I was that thirteen-year-old kid again. I won't sentence you to living my hell with me."

She shook her head again. "If you think you can tell me that you love me and you're breaking up with me in the same breath, you're crazy."

"Angel," Jag said, "it's *because* I love you that I have to let you go."

"No," Carly said succinctly.

"No?" he echoed.

"I love you too, Jag. And when you love someone, you don't give up on them just because things are complicated. You stood by me when I needed you the most, when I was a complete wreck of a human being, and there's *no way* I'm leaving you. What if the roles were reversed and it was me sitting here, telling you a babysitter raped me for years and my mom thought it was great that I was getting some? Would you be disgusted? Would you think less of me? Would you leave me?"

"You know I wouldn't," Jag said.

"Then why the hell do you think I will? Jag, what happened to you was terrible. And it *was not your fault.*"

"I freaked out on you," Jag said dejectedly. He was looking down at their still clasped hands, refusing to meet her eyes.

"Yeah, you did," Carly said bluntly. "But you had a damn good reason. I should've just talked to you. Told you I wanted to make love. Instead, I thought it would be a good idea to take control. Obviously, that wasn't exactly the best way to go about trying to

be more intimate with you. But, Jag...what did you think you were going to do? Keep that secret to yourself forever?"

He shrugged. "Yes?"

They were silent for a long moment.

"Here's what we're gonna do," Carly finally decided, sitting up straighter and putting some force behind her words. "We're gonna go back to the bedroom and get some sleep with you holding me, just like you do every night. Tomorrow, we'll find a good therapist for you to talk to."

Jag shook his head. "No."

"Yes," Carly insisted. "You need to talk to someone about this. You've kept it inside for way too long. You need to purge it, purge *her*. Again, if someone assaulted me, you'd insist on me getting help. Admit it."

He nodded.

"There's nothing wrong with getting help, Jag."

"Men don't get raped," he whispered.

"That's *bullshit*. Maybe it doesn't happen as often as it does to women, but she had sex with you against your will. That's rape, even if you got hard. Sometimes women get wet when they're raped, that doesn't mean they enjoyed it or wanted it. It's a natural reaction of the body."

Her voice lowered. "Please don't let this break us up. I need you, Jag. Nothing's changed with my situation. You make me feel safe, but more than that, I love you. You're everything I've ever wanted in a partner, and nothing you've said tonight has changed that for me. You need to be in charge during sex? Fine. I can handle that. For the rest of our lives, if necessary."

He looked up then, and Carly could see the desperate hope in his eyes. "I don't want you to feel sorry for me."

Carly laughed. She couldn't help it. "Feel sorry for you? Jag,

242

you're a badass Navy SEAL. Generous, funny, considerate, amazing, and a hundred other adjectives. The last thing I feel is sorry for you."

"I didn't mean to make you cry," he said, bringing his hand up and brushing his knuckles against her cheek.

"I know."

"Did you really pack your bag?"

"Yeah."

"Good."

"Good?" Carly asked.

"Yeah. I never want you to be afraid to go where you want and do what you think is right. If I fuck up, you *should* want to leave. You're too good to stay with anyone who doesn't treat you like you're the most important person in their life."

Carly pressed her lips together so she didn't start crying again.

"I'm so sorry," Jag said. "I never meant to taint you with my past. I thought I had it under control...but obviously, I don't."

Carly brought their clasped hands up and kissed his knuckles. "Will you come back to bed?"

After a moment, Jag nodded slowly. He stood and pulled Carly up beside him. But instead of heading for the bedroom, he pulled her into his arms. She went without hesitation. She snuggled against him and could hear his heart beating under her ear.

"I love you," Jag whispered into her hair.

"I love you too," Carly responded.

"And for the record...I *want* to make love to you. So goddamn much. I just...my feelings about sex are complicated."

Carly could understand that after hearing about what he'd been through. "We'll figure out how to make things work together." She tilted her head up and looked at him. "I love you

because of who you are, not because of sex. We can still be intimate without sex."

He looked skeptical. "You'd stay with me even if I couldn't make love to you without having a nervous breakdown?"

"Yes." Her answer was simple and heartfelt.

A look she couldn't interpret entered his eyes, before his expression became resolute. "I'll talk to someone. I want to be the man you deserve."

"You already are," she told him, grabbing his hand and leading him toward their room.

Jag was worth fighting for, and now that she knew what he'd survived, she was more than determined to win. Bridget fucking Smith would *not* win. No way. Jag was stronger than that bitch.

Carly was also going to find a way to talk to Baker and get him to track down Jag's rapist...without telling him what had happened to his friend. It was nobody's business but theirs. But she wanted the bitch to pay for what she'd done to the man Carly loved.

They crawled back under the covers together, and Carly was suddenly exhausted. She'd run through a gamut of emotions in just the last hour and felt as if she could sleep for days.

Jag pulled her into his arms and kissed her forehead. "I love you," he whispered.

"I love *you.*"

They didn't say anything else, and if Jag's hold on her was a little tighter than usual, neither of them commented on it.

Carly had been stunned to learn what had happened to her man, but she knew he'd be able to work through it. He was the strongest person she'd ever met, and they loved each other. That would get them through whatever life threw their way.

CHAPTER EIGHTEEN

Jag hadn't *ever* wanted Carly to know what had happened to him. He was afraid she'd look at him differently if she knew. But the morning after he'd freaked out and almost lost the best thing that had ever happened to him, Carly wandered into the kitchen, gave him a long, heartfelt hug like she did every morning, and mumbled under her breath about needing coffee.

She hadn't acted differently toward him. If anything, Jag felt as if they were even closer after his confession.

That morning, he'd called his commander and told him he needed to speak with a psychologist. To his credit, Commander Huttner hadn't asked why, hadn't told him to man up or some other bullshit. He'd simply given him some time off to do what he needed to do.

He probably thought Jag was experiencing post-traumatic stress from one of the many missions he'd been on, and he was happy to let him go on thinking that. The military had gotten

better about encouraging their members to get therapy when they needed it.

Now it was five days since he'd freaked out on Carly, and Jag had already been to two sessions with the psychologist. It was unbelievable, but he felt as if a weight had been lifted off his shoulders already. Jag was well aware that it would take more than a couple hours to ease his psyche, but the fact that his secret was no longer his to bear alone went a long way toward helping him come to terms with what happened. He should have sought help years ago.

The truth of the matter was, he'd been a kid when he was abused. And his therapist confirmed that Carly was right, his body's natural reactions didn't mean he was complicit in what Bridget had done. He was still working on the guilt he felt for not standing up to her sooner, but hopefully, with time, that would pass as well.

His relationship with Carly, however, was more solid as ever. She loved him. Jag couldn't help but smile when he remembered hearing those words back for the first time. He was afraid of intimacy. Of having sex. But he wanted Carly. He'd need to be in control when they finally made love, and he knew Carly wouldn't mind.

He'd just finished working out with his team and was sitting in his car in the parking lot at the Naval base, getting ready to drive home to shower and change. When his phone rang, Jag was so startled, he jumped. He shook his head wryly. Some badass SEAL he was. He'd been so lost in his head, he'd totally blanked.

"Jag here," he said after he clicked on the phone.

"It's Baker. Your woman called me yesterday. Said she needed a favor."

Jag was a bit stunned. He hadn't thought Carly was serious

about calling Baker, but obviously she was. "Let me guess... Bridget Smith?"

"Bingo. You want to tell me what this is all about?"

"No," Jag said. He wasn't about to get into what had happened. It was hard enough telling Carly and his therapist. He wasn't at a place yet where he could confess to his teammates or Baker, no matter how close he was to them.

"All right. Just tell me this—does Carly have a good reason for wanting me to ruin this woman's life?" Baker asked.

Before the other night, Jag might've said no. Might've avoided anything having to do with his past, just wanting to keep it buried. But he couldn't pretend he didn't love how protective Carly was of him. And after talking with the psychologist, and Carly, he merely said, "Yes."

"Consider it done."

Jag wondered if he should feel guilty over what was about to be unleashed on Bridget...but he couldn't.

"I might need some more info. Bridget Smith is pretty damn vague. I'm good, but not *that* good."

"What kind of info?" Jag asked.

"Age, where she grew up, that kind of thing."

"She'd be around forty-two or so today. Grew up in my hometown in Oklahoma."

"Went to the same high school as you?" Baker asked.

"Yes."

"Okay. I might call in some help on this one, I know a guy in Colorado who's really good at finding people. But I didn't call just to talk about that."

Jag braced as his friend continued.

"I dug up some more info on Jeremiah Barrowman."

"Keyes's friend who works at the country club," Jag said.

"Yup. Seems he has a pattern," Baker went on. "Fucks up, apologizes, gets back into a woman's good graces, then does the same damn thing he did before."

"Like hit them?"

"No. Like mind-fuck them," Jag said. "He makes them think they're slowly going crazy. I talked to two ex-girlfriends and they both said he definitely had two sides. One was nice and gentlemanly and extremely remorseful, and the other was almost psychopathic. His favorite thing was sneaking around outside their homes at night, making them think an intruder was trying to get inside. The women would freak out, call him, and he'd come over to save the day. Then he'd come back the next night and do the same thing.

"One of the women put up a camera without telling him and caught him red-handed. He apologized, saying he was just worried about her living alone and wanted to make sure she was taking every precaution. He was convincing enough that the woman took him back. Only for other weird shit to start happening. Things were moved around in the house, but nothing was taken. He denied it was him. Then she started getting threatening emails. She eventually discovered it was Jeremiah and broke up with him."

"So you think his apology to Carly when he showed up at Duke's was bullshit?" Jag asked.

"Probably. All of Keyes's buddies knew he was obsessed with Carly. He openly talked about getting revenge on her for dumping him, even mentioned how he planned to teach her a lesson. But of course, no one admits to believing he was truly serious. But Jeremiah is now at the top of my list of people who would probably drop everything to help scare the shit out of her."

"And the boat?" Jag asked.

"Still working on that. There are a lot of fuckin' private docks and boats on this island," Baker said. "And there are a lot of people who go to the Waialae Country Club who Jeremiah could've borrowed from that night. It's slow going interviewing the members with boats, but I'm working on it."

Jag owed Baker. Huge. It was obvious he was frustrated that he hadn't already nailed down Keyes's accomplice, but he was doing everything in his power to make sure whoever it was didn't get away with finishing the plan. "Carly's supposed to work later this morning. In your opinion, is she in danger?"

"She's been in danger since she broke up with that asshole," Baker said bluntly. "But if you're asking if she's in *more* danger than she's been the last few months, the answer is, I don't think so. But I still don't have a good feeling about the situation."

"What does that mean?" Jag asked, semi-alarmed.

"Just that this has gone on too long. If Keyes had an accomplice, the asshole has been very patient. But I'm betting he's getting anxious to finish what Keyes started. Everything within me says this isn't over. That someone's biding their time. Just tell Carly to keep her eyes open for anything unusual."

"More unusual than seeing Keyes's friends everywhere?" Jag asked in frustration. "I swear she's run into them more now than when she was dating the fucker. Just the other day, Gideon Sparks dropped off two envelopes at Duke's. One for Carly and one for Kenna. They had year-long passes to the Honolulu Zoo inside and some bullshit note about how sorry he was about everything that had happened. How he wanted to try to make up for some of the trauma they'd gone through."

"No shit?" Baker asked.

"No shit," Jag confirmed. "And Beau Langford sent her a gift

certificate for a free sunset cruise that embarks out of his marina. As if she'd ever get in a boat within ten miles of that asshole."

"Yeah, not a good idea. I'll look into both men, maybe pay them another visit to see what their motivation was."

"Carly already called Detective Lee and told him about both. He said he'd talk to them."

"Yeah, but I'm thinking I can get more info out of them than he can. I'll do my best to make sure they forget Carly exists."

"Thanks."

"All right, I'm gonna jet, just wanted to make sure everything was all right with you and Carly and make sure her request was legit."

"It's legit," Jag found himself saying.

Baker was quiet for a moment, then he shocked the shit out of Jag by saying, "You're a damn good man, Jag. Carly's lucky to have you." Then he clicked off the connection and left Jag sitting in his car, staring at his phone.

Shaking his head, wondering how the hell Carly's blood-thirsty request had led to Baker giving him a pep talk, Jag started his engine and backed out of the parking spot, anxious to get home. He'd be late getting to work, but he didn't give a shit. He was going to take his time and have breakfast with Carly, as usual.

He wished he could spend the day with her, but that wasn't possible. There had been another kidnapping of school children in Nigeria. This time it was nearly five hundred boys. Boko Haram was at it again, and the United States had offered any help to the Nigerian government that they needed in order to track down the group and get the children back. The SEALs were neck deep in researching the area where the boys

had disappeared, in case they were sent in to assist in the recovery.

Jag didn't want to leave, not now, but the thought of what those boys' fates would be if they weren't found struck a little too close to home, and he wanted to help get them back to their families.

He drove home a little too quickly and took the stairs two at a time as he ran up to his floor. The second he entered his apartment, he smiled. It smelled like cinnamon rolls. He kept telling Carly that he couldn't eat that kind of junk in the morning before work, but she simply shrugged and baked stuff anyway.

"Morning," Jag said as he walked into the kitchen.

She turned and smiled at him, and Jag melted. This was what he wanted. Carly smiling at him like that for the rest of their lives. He'd do anything to make that happen. *Anything*. The fact that she'd accepted what had happened to him, that she hadn't stormed out after he'd treated her like shit, was a minor miracle. He hadn't realized until afterward how close he'd come to losing her. He hated that he'd hurt her, but she didn't hold a grudge and things were now even deeper between them.

He stalked over to her, and Carly's smile widened as he got close. He wrapped an arm around her waist and yanked her against him. She stumbled, but the laughter that left her lips as her hands landed on his chest let him know she wasn't frightened.

She was still smiling when his lips landed on hers. He couldn't wait another second to touch her. She tasted sweet, as if she'd been sampling the icing that was supposed to go on the cinnamon rolls when they came out of the oven. But within seconds, everything but the feel of her against him and her lips under his faded into the background.

He kissed her with all the love he had in his heart. All the gratitude that she was the woman she was. All the relief that she'd been able to overcome her reticence when it came to dating.

They were both breathing hard when he pulled back.

"Um, wow," Carly said, staring up at him with wide eyes.

"Morning," Jag said softly.

"Did you have a good workout?" she asked.

Jag shrugged. "Mustang kicked our asses extra hard today, probably to make a point that he knew I'd slacked off the last few days."

Carly rolled her eyes. "Oh, a few days off of work. Yeah, you're such a slacker."

Jag chuckled. Then he sobered. "Baker called me this morning."

Carly blushed and asked lightly, "He did?"

She knew why Baker had called him, but was obviously trying to play it off. "Yup."

She hesitated when he didn't say anything else, then finally asked, "Are you mad?"

"Mad that you're trying to protect me? That you're blood-thirsty in your desire for revenge? No."

"It's not revenge," she said immediately. "It's justice. Jag, what she did was not only morally wrong and evil, it was *illegal*. And I can't help but think if she did it to you, she's done it to other boys. I want her to pay. Not for ruining your life, because you're amazing and you being as successful as you are is a big 'fuck you' to her. But for her being a horrible, awful person."

Jag couldn't help but smile.

"So? What'd you tell Baker?" she asked. "More importantly, what'd he tell you? Did he find her yet? Has he shut down all her

bank accounts, put viruses on her computers, gotten her fired and all that stuff yet?"

"Good Lord, woman," Jag said in surprise. "Seriously?"

"Oh, yeah," Carly replied with a nod and a hard look in her eyes. "It's not enough, not nearly enough for what she did, but it's a start."

Jag ran his hand over her hair and shook his head. "He wanted to know if your request was legit. Basically, wanted my approval."

"What did you tell him?" Carly asked when he didn't immediately continue.

"I gave him the green light."

Satisfaction filled her eyes. "Good."

Jag knew he had to tell her everything else Baker had mentioned, but he had other things on his mind at the moment.

"I want to make love to you," he blurted—then cringed at how abrupt that sounded.

But Carly merely smiled and seemed to melt into him further. "Yeah?"

"Yeah. Tonight."

"If you're asking if that's okay with me, it definitely is," she said. Then she sobered. "But I want you to be sure you're ready. I accidentally brought back a lot of awful memories for you the other night, and the last thing I want is for you to do something you're not ready for. It's only been a few days, Jag—"

"I'm ready," he told her. "I regret what happened because I hurt you, but honestly, I'm also *glad* it happened. It forced me to finally face my past and take steps to move on. With you. You are *not* that bitch who hurt me. I love you, Carly, and there's nothing I want more than to show you how much. I can't

promise I won't have setbacks, but I know being with you will be nothing like it was with her."

"You weren't 'with' her," Carly said fiercely. "And you're right, it won't, because I love you and you love me and I'd never, *ever* hurt you. I don't expect or want you to be perfect in bed, Jag. I just want *you*."

"So...tonight?" he asked.

"Yes. A hundred times yes."

They smiled at each other. Jag closed his eyes for a moment, wondering how he'd gotten so lucky. Then he felt her hand on his cheek. He opened his eyes and got lost in the ocean-blue depths of her gaze.

She went up on her tiptoes and brushed her lips against his. It was a brief caress, but Jag still felt his cock twitch. It was obvious he wasn't going to have any issues getting hard, which was a relief. He'd gone through a period years ago where he couldn't get aroused no matter what he did to try to stimulate himself.

"Jag?" she asked softly.

"Yeah?"

"You stink. You need to shower."

He laughed. "Not surprised, considering how many burpees I did and all the running up and down the beach Mustang tortured us with this morning."

But Carly didn't pull away from him. She just smiled.

"Angel? If I'm gonna shower, you need to let go of me."

"Fine," she mock-huffed before slowly backing away. "By the time you get back out here, the cinnamon rolls will be done."

"I can't have carbs and sugar for breakfast," he reminded her.

"Right, because that's only for us mere mortals," she joked.

"Fine. I'll make your protein shake. You can wash down your cinnamon roll with it." She winked.

Jag laughed out loud once again as he turned to head down the hall to the bedroom.

"Jag?" Carly called out.

He turned. "Yeah?"

"Love you. And I'm so damn proud of you. Tonight's gonna be amazing. Unforgettable."

Her words made him feel complete. "Yes, it is," he agreed. "I hope you're ready for me," he warned. "It's been a long time since I've been with a woman...and I have a feeling I won't be able to get enough of you."

At least ten feet separated them, but Jag still felt the electrical current that he'd felt the first time he met her. He glanced down and saw her nipples, hard under the cotton T-shirt she had on.

"Bring it," she said with the same chin lift he used with his friends.

Jag wanted nothing more than to stalk back into the kitchen, throw her over his shoulder, and haul her into the bedroom. But he needed to get to work, and Kenna would be there to pick her up soon. So he merely smiled and forced himself to walk away.

After showering and changing—and eating not one, but two cinnamon rolls, along with his protein shake—Jag had to get going. No matter how much he wanted to stay and hang out with Carly, he had a job to do.

Carly walked him to the door, and he couldn't resist pulling her into his arms once more.

"Be careful at work today," he said.

Her head tilted as she looked up at him. "I will, but...do you know something you aren't telling me?"

"Not really," Jag said. "When I talked to Baker earlier, he said he's dug up some more stuff on Jeremiah, stuff from his past that's concerning. We both agree it would be good if you kept an eye out for him and if you see him, immediately let me know."

"I will," Carly promised. "I feel more comfortable being out of the apartment, but every now and then I still feel as if I'm being watched. Maybe I'm just being paranoid, but..." Her voice trailed off.

"Don't discount your feelings," Jag told her. "I can't tell you how many times paying attention to something that simply felt off has saved our butts when we're on a mission."

Carly nodded.

"You're still carrying the pocketknife I gave you, right?" Jag asked.

"Yes."

"And the handcuff key?"

Carly smiled, nodding.

"And you're paying attention when you're walking, not looking at your phone?"

"Yes, Jag. I swear."

He took a deep breath. "I'm sorry, it won't always be this way. There will be a time when you can relax and not worry about someone jumping out from behind a car or something."

"I know," she said with only a hint of concern in her voice. "It's taking a while, but I'm slowly getting more confident about being able to protect myself."

"Good." Jag hated that she'd had to learn the hard way how important it was to always be aware of her surroundings, but he'd rather she be prepared and ready for anything than be caught unaware.

"Anything in particular you want for dinner?" she asked.

Jag shook his head. "Just you."

Carly grinned. "I think that can be arranged."

"Be safe today," he said again.

"You too."

"Nothing too dangerous about sitting in a conference room all day," Jag said wryly.

Carly shrugged. "You never know."

"True. I love you, angel."

"Love you too."

"Text me when you get to Duke's and when you get home. Please."

"Of course." Carly tightened her arms around him, hugging him hard.

Jag put a finger under her chin and tilted her head up, kissing her. It wasn't a short kiss either. It was a prelude to what was going to happen later that evening. By the time he pulled back, they were both panting.

"I can't wait to make you mine," he whispered.

"I already am," she retorted.

Jag smiled and forced himself to step away. "Have a great day," he said.

"You too."

Jag adjusted his erection after his apartment door had shut behind him and took a deep, calming breath. He was ready for tonight. It felt as if he'd waited his entire life for Carly...and he was determined to make sure she knew it.

* * *

The man sat in the parking lot of the apartment complex where the bitch was staying. He'd been watching her for weeks, waiting

for a chance. He hadn't minded so much when she'd holed up in her own apartment, because it gave him pleasure to know she was too terrified to leave. Wondering who might still want her dead.

But as time went by, and after she moved in with the fucking boyfriend, she'd gotten more and more confident. She wasn't scared anymore.

It was time for him to make his move. Had to put all the lessons Shawn had taught him to use. Show Carly that she was nothing. Make her understand that she'd had everything with Shawn, and she'd thrown it away.

Everything was planned, he just had to find the perfect opportunity to grab her. Glancing at his watch, the man scowled. He was going to be late for work...again. His boss wasn't very happy with him at the moment. His perfect record was thoroughly shot. Another thing to blame Carly for.

He was late so much because he'd been following *her*. Waiting to strike.

He almost had his chance the other day, when she'd gone to the grocery store by herself, but there had been too many people in the parking lot. Too many witnesses. He needed to get her alone.

A car pulled up to the front entrance of the complex, and the man growled low in his throat. It was that cunt who'd killed Shawn, with the guy her asshole millionaire husband had hired to drive her and the bitch to work in Waikiki.

There was nothing the man could do today, since she'd be surrounded by people at Duke's. There wouldn't be an opportunity to snatch her there. And the boyfriend always picked her up. But his time was coming. He had to be patient just a little bit longer.

Once the bitch was in his clutches, she wasn't getting away. He was too smart; even smarter than Shawn, in some ways. He had everything planned perfectly. Looking down at the bag on the floor of the passenger seat, he smiled. He was ready at all times now. All he needed was one minute, and she was his.

That new boyfriend should be thanking him. She'd ruin his life just like she did Shawn's. He was doing the world a favor by eliminating her.

"Don't worry, Shawn. She's gonna pay for what she did. To you *and* to me. Mark my words."

After a happy Carly got into the car and it pulled away, the man turned on his engine and eased out of the parking lot before heading to the interstate. He'd have to come up with another excuse as to why he was late, but he wasn't concerned.

"Just a little longer," he murmured as he drove. "This will all be over soon."

CHAPTER NINETEEN

This had been the longest day ever. Carly was fidgety and impatient and more than ready for her shift to be over. All she could think about was Jag and what they were going to do tonight.

"What's up with you?" Kenna asked when they were thirty minutes out from quitting time. "You've been kind of weird all day."

"Nothing," Carly said.

"Bullshit. Spill," Kenna ordered.

Carly couldn't keep the smile off her face. "Jag and I just have...special plans tonight."

She didn't need to explain. Kenna squealed a little and clapped her hands lightly. "Yay! Are you nervous?"

"No." And she wasn't. After everything that had happened between them, sex with the man she loved more than life itself wasn't anything to be nervous about. She hoped and prayed everything would go smoothly for Jag's sake, but she wasn't

overly worried about that. She'd experienced Jag's increased confidence firsthand in just the last week.

She *had* been worried about his first session with the psychologist, about all the horrible memories he'd have to relive, wondering if they'd make him reticent to touch her sexually. Instead, the opposite seemed to happen.

Jag had touched her more in the last several days than he had in the last couple of months. He seemed more...secure in his masculinity. He kissed her longer and harder, his hands lightly roamed her body when they lay down to sleep. He smiled easier, laughed more. It was as if the weight of the world was beginning to lift from his shoulders.

No, Carly wasn't nervous in the least, she was excited about what making love might do for their relationship.

Kenna tilted her head as she studied Carly. Finally, she said, "I'm happy for you. Jag's really great. Kind of quiet...but I have a feeling you're helping him slay his demons."

"Who said he has demons?" Carly asked a little defensively.

Kenna shrugged. "It's fairly obvious...but not in a bad way. He's relaxed a lot since meeting you. It's a good thing, Carly. I'm not judging or anything."

Carly forced herself to chill. "I know, sorry. And he *is* great. I literally don't think I would've been able to make it through what happened without him."

"Order's up!" one of the cooks in the kitchen yelled, making both Kenna and Carly jump in surprise.

Kenna chuckled. "Jeez, he loves to do that," she complained.

"Yup." At one time, being startled like that would've sent Carly into a panic attack. She was proud that she could laugh it off now.

Glancing at her wrist, she saw that she only had twenty-five

more minutes before she was done. Jag had texted earlier. The guys were working later than usual, and Aleck had arranged for the car service to pick up both her and Kenna.

Carly knew the time would come when she needed to start driving herself to work, but for the moment, she was content to keep things as they were. She was getting better, less frightened to be out by herself, but she also didn't want to rush things. Baker was still working on uncovering who was helping Shawn, and the last thing Carly wanted to do was be one of those "TSTL" heroines in some of the romance books she liked to read.

Thinking about romance made her thoughts return to Jag. She couldn't stop the smile from forming on her lips.

"Oh, Lord, don't go daydreaming again," Kenna complained. "Get your order out, woman."

Carly smiled. "You're just jealous," she taunted.

"Nope. Really happy for you, actually. But knowing you're gonna get some tonight makes me want to show my man how much I love *him*."

Carly rolled her eyes as she put two chicken sandwich meals on her tray. She turned, balancing the tray on her shoulder, and looked at her friend. "Probably a good thing for all of us to make sure our men know how much we love them. I have a feeling they're gearing up to be deployed again."

Instead of disagreeing, as Carly had hoped she might, Kenna nodded. "Yeah, I'm getting that impression too."

For a second, Carly felt the familiar panic begin to rise within her, but she pushed it down. She didn't want to think about being on her own without Jag to lean on, to make her feel safe, but she vowed to never put more stress on him than he might already feel leading up to a mission. She'd be fine. She had close

friends, and if she felt she was in danger, she'd just hole up in Jag's apartment until he either returned or she felt brave enough to venture out again.

"Everything'll be okay," Kenna soothed, putting a hand on Carly's free arm.

She nodded. "It will," she agreed. Then smiled at her friend before turning to head into the dining room to deliver the meals. She wasn't going to think about Jag leaving. It was inevitable, but she didn't have to make herself sick wondering when or how long he'd be gone. This was a part of her life now, and she needed to prove to herself, and Jag, that she was strong enough to handle it.

For now, she wanted to concentrate on moving their relationship forward. And tonight was going to be the first step toward the rest of their lives.

The anticipation was thick in the air, but Carly did her best to ignore it. She'd put some chicken breasts in the oven when she'd gotten home from work, taken a shower, shaved her legs, and made sure to put on more of the cherry blossom lotion than usual, because she knew Jag loved it so much.

When he'd finally gotten home, they ate dinner, talked about how their days went, and generally tried to ignore the desire building between them.

But the second the dishes were put away, Jag backed Carly against the kitchen counter. He took her face in his hands and stared at her.

Carly grabbed hold of his wrists and held on as she met his gaze.

"You ready for this?"

"Yes." There was absolutely no hesitation in her voice.

"Me too," Jag said with a small smile.

Carly returned his grin. He'd showered when he'd gotten home and changed into the cotton pants he usually slept in. He wore one of his Navy T-shirts, and her fingers itched to slide under the hem and touch him skin-on-skin. But she kept her hands where they were. Jag needed to be in control tonight.

Without another word, he leaned down, kissed her hard and fast, then took her hand in his and headed out of the kitchen.

Knowing she had a goofy smile on her face, Carly followed eagerly. He led them into the master bedroom and didn't stop until they were standing next to the bed.

"I've got condoms," he blurted. It was almost cute how nervous he looked.

"I'm on the pill," she informed him.

"Yeah, I know. I've seen them in the bathroom."

When he didn't say anything else, Carly said hesitantly, "We don't have to use condoms if you don't want to. I'm clean, haven't been with anyone since Shawn, and you better believe I got myself tested when I broke up with him, just to be sure." She knew she was babbling but couldn't make herself stop. "So, I can't get pregnant. Well, I mean, there's always a chance, the pill isn't one hundred percent effective, but it's also not the right time of the month for me anyway. If you're not comfortable with that, we can use a condom." She forced herself to shut up.

Jag took a deep breath. His pupils were dilated and he looked as if he was one second away from throwing her on the bed and having his way with her...which Carly was more than all right with. "I've never... She always put a condom on me before...you know."

Carly nodded and smoothed her hands over his chest.

"It always felt as if she thought I was dirty," he admitted.

"You aren't," Carly reassured him gently. "And for the record, I've never made love to a man without a condom. It would be a first for us both."

At that, Jag relaxed a fraction. "Sex without protection can be messy for a woman," he said quietly.

Carly figured he'd learned that from the porn movies the bitch had forced him to watch. She pushed down her anger at the thought. This wasn't the time for that. She smiled at Jag. "I'm not worried."

In response, Jag's hands went to the hem of the blouse she'd put on after showering. It was pale green and had a deep V-neck. It showed off her cleavage and made Carly feel sexy. Slowly, she raised her arms over her head, making it easier for him to remove the garment.

She arched her back a bit as she stood in front of him—and loved the look of lust that flickered over his face as he drank her in. Carly was on the shorter side, but she'd always had curves. She'd filled out even more after moving in with Jag and starting to eat well again. Her boobs were more than a handful...and she couldn't wait for Jag to touch her.

"Can I take off my bra?" she asked, not wanting to do anything that might make him think about *her*.

Jag licked his lips and nodded. He hadn't taken his eyes off her chest. Reaching behind her, Carly undid the clasp and let her bra fall to the floor. It felt naughty to be half-naked in front of him when he was still fully dressed, but it also felt right.

His hands rose and slowly covered her breasts, squeezing slightly. Carly sighed and arched her back even more, pressing herself into him.

"Fuck," Jag whispered, closing his eyes briefly. "You feel amazing."

He smoothed his hands down her body, fingers slipping under the leggings she'd chosen because they were easy to remove. He met her eyes then, and what Carly saw made her squirm. She could barely see the brown she'd grown to love because of his dilated pupils. He was breathing hard through his nose and the calluses on his hands felt deliciously rough against the skin at her hips.

He ever so slowly pushed her leggings and underwear down her legs. She kicked them both off when they fell to her ankles. She was now completely naked in front of him...and it felt so erotic. A little scary too, but in a good way.

"You're so beautiful," Jag said reverently as he fell to his knees in front of her. "Spread your legs, Carly."

She did as he ordered without hesitation. This somewhat bossy lover was very different from the almost broken man she'd seen the other night. She much preferred Jag this way.

His palms massaged up and down her thighs, his gaze locked on her pussy. Carly didn't know what to do with her hands, afraid to trigger him, so she kept them at her sides. Jag's fingers moved higher and higher with each pass, and she held her breath, praying he'd touch her.

"You're wet," he said softly as he continued to simply stare.

"Yes."

"You like this?" he asked.

Carly nodded.

He stared up at her. "Why? I haven't even touched you."

"Because you're just so...I've never..." Carly was having trouble putting her thoughts into words. "I like it when you take control."

"Me too," Jag said with satisfaction and a hint of relief. "You want me to touch you?"

"Please."

"You smell amazing," he sighed, instead of doing what she wanted. He leaned forward and inhaled sharply. "Like ambrosia and cherries."

Carly had no idea what the hell ambrosia smelled like, but she wasn't going to ask.

Jag moved closer and brushed his nose against her closely cropped pubic hair. She gasped in anticipation and swayed.

His hands were there immediately, holding onto her hips, steadying her.

She felt his tongue against her hip bone...then against her wet folds. She spread her legs even farther, needing him.

But Jag didn't continue his exploration. He stood. Voice almost guttural, he said, "Lie back on the bed, feet flat on the mattress, knees out."

Carly shivered. Holy fuck, he was hot like this. She hurried to obey. The second she was in position, he climbed onto the mattress without taking off his clothes. Her belly clenched. For a second, she wondered if there was something wrong with *her* for getting off on being so vulnerable for him. He definitely held the power right now. Not taking off his shirt or pants, ordering her into position...it all made his control over her more than clear.

He held her gaze as he shuffled toward her on his knees. Then he put his hands on her inner thighs and pushed her legs even farther apart.

Carly knew she was soaking wet. Her nipples stood up on her chest as if begging for his touch. She squirmed.

"Stay still," he warned, and Carly immediately froze.

He settled on his stomach between her legs and used one of his hands to pull her lips apart.

"Jag," she whimpered.

"Shhhh. I've never seen this up close and personal before..."

Carly bit her lip and her head fell back on the pillow. If Jag wanted to examine her, she was going to let him. He could do whatever he wanted.

At the first touch of his finger, her head came back up. She couldn't *not* watch him.

He licked his lips again as he ran his index finger around her clit, slowly. She jerked when he touched the sensitive nub, and saw him smile.

"You like that."

It wasn't a question, but Carly answered anyway. "Oh, yeah. Definitely."

Jag took his time, learning what she liked and what made her writhe under him. He eased his finger inside her body, thrusting slowly a few times, and Carly moaned. When he removed his finger, he studied it for a moment, glistening with her juices, before putting it in his mouth.

It was one of the hottest things Carly had ever seen. The look of ecstasy that crossed his face when he tasted her would be burned in her memory forever. Then, as if he couldn't wait another moment, his head dropped and he licked her with one long swipe.

Carly bucked.

He did it again, lapping up the copious amounts of her excitement leaking from between her legs. It felt good...but when he tentatively sucked on her clit, Carly squeaked.

He looked up as if to reassure himself that the sound was one

of pleasure and not something else. Carly nodded at him. "More!"

He smiled briefly before lowering his head.

The next few minutes were some of the best of Carly's life. No one had ever made her feel the way Jag did. As if she was going to come out of her skin. He seemed to know exactly how much pressure to apply to her clit to drive her crazy, but not send her over the edge.

"Jag, please!"

"Please what?" he mumbled against her sensitive skin.

"Make me come. I *need* to."

"I like you like this," he said, lowering his head.

"Jag..." Carly whined.

He chuckled, and the warm puffs of air against her pussy were both heaven and hell.

His fingers slicked between her lips once more, spreading her excitement up to her clit and lightly caressing it. "You're soaking wet. And it's all for me." He sounded somehow smug and in awe at the same time.

"Uh-huh," Carly murmured.

"I want to watch you orgasm," Jag said. "I've never seen it. Not from someone I've cared about, that is."

His words alone almost made Carly go over the edge. She both hated and loved that she would be his first in some very important ways. "I'm close, Jag. Please!"

Instead of lowering his head, he flattened his hand on her lower belly and used his thumb to manipulate her clit. At the same time, he inserted two fingers from his other hand inside her body. He began to thrust in and out while strumming her clit.

Carly's hips shot off the mattress and she groaned. He

continued to finger fuck her, and Carly couldn't keep still. She thrust against his fingers over and over as a keening sound she'd never heard before escaped her throat.

It was too good. Too much. Almost overwhelming.

"That's it. Almost there," Jag said, his voice gruff. His eyes dark.

Then his fingers moved faster, rocking in and out of her soaking folds as he increased the pace of the flicking on her clit. Carly's hips stopped moving in midair and she hung there for a moment as she stood on the edge of the precipice of pleasure.

Then she was flying. Her heart beat out of control and she forgot to breathe as she experienced the most intense and out-of-control orgasm she'd ever had in her life.

Jag's fingers slowed, but he never stopped caressing her as she continued to shake. When she finally sagged back down to the mattress, Jag removed his fingers from inside her and lowered his head.

He licked her over and over, eagerly, as if he couldn't get enough of her taste. Every time his tongue brushed against her sensitive clit, Carly jerked.

Just when she didn't think she could stand another moment of his touch, when she was once more ready to lose it, Jag rose to his knees. He ripped off his T-shirt and shoved his sleep pants over his hips. For a second, Carly didn't think he was even going to take the time to remove them totally, but then he fell to one hip and jerked them off.

His cock was long and hard. Thick. She'd felt it against her when they were sleeping and when they made out, but she'd never seen it. Carly wanted to touch him. Wanted to drive him as crazy as he'd made her, but she forced herself to remain still.

Jag once more pushed her thighs apart as he scooted closer.

They both moaned when the tip of his cock brushed against her soaking folds.

"You ready?" he asked as he took hold of the base of his cock and squeezed.

"Yes," Carly said, succinctly and clearly.

She held her breath as he moved even closer.

* * *

Jag couldn't think straight. He licked his lips and tasted Carly there. He could've spent all night worshiping her, tasting her, watching and feeling her explode on his fingers and mouth. It was the most amazing thing he'd ever felt. So wet. So tight. But he wanted it all. Wanted everything from her.

This was nothing like it had been with Bridget. *Nothing.* It was more. So much more.

Being with someone he cared about, loved, made every touch, every moan, every kiss more exciting. He'd never *felt* so much as he did right this moment. Had never felt as if he didn't get inside her, he'd literally die. The excitement and anticipation racing through him as he looked down at her was nothing like he'd ever experienced.

Jag was well aware that not having to use a condom was a gift. He'd heard enough sailors and friends bitching about the things to know how much more he was about to feel, since he was bare. It was almost overwhelming to think about, but he wanted this. Needed it.

Holding the base of his cock tightly to prevent himself from prematurely coming, Jag inched closer to Carly. Her legs were spread wide and he could smell her arousal. She'd squeezed his fingers so tightly when she'd come that he

couldn't help but think about how it would feel around his cock.

For the first time in his life, he let himself go with a woman.

He didn't feel guilty or dirty for being hard. He didn't feel like this was wrong, or like she was using him. He wanted to fully experience the moment, not close his eyes and pray it would be over soon.

He notched the tip of his cock inside Carly's folds and felt a spurt of come erupt from the tip. He squeezed himself harder, praying he could hold off long enough to get inside the woman he loved.

He wasn't a virgin in the strictest sense of the word, but what Bridget had forced him to do didn't count. He understood that now. And the two women he'd been with in all the years since had been farces compared to what he was feeling right now. He'd basically shut off all emotion and gone through the motions to get through those encounters.

This was where he was meant to be. Here with Carly. Next to her. Inside her. He felt loved. Reborn. He wasn't going to mess this up.

He wanted—no, *needed* to feel her come around his cock.

With a renewed sense of control, Jag slowly pushed all the way inside his woman until his balls brushed up against her. Then he reached down and grabbed one of her ass cheeks and pulled her open, so he could get inside even farther.

It was unbelievable. The most pleasurable thing he'd ever felt in his life. Wet and hot and tight. He could almost feel Carly's heartbeat around his dick. That was fanciful, of course; that wasn't how things worked. But Jag didn't care.

He realized that he'd closed his eyes, and he opened them to stare at the woman under him. She was lying completely still,

letting him do whatever he wanted to do to her. Jag had never loved anything or anyone as much as he did Carly. She understood. Knew he needed to do things his way.

"Okay?" he croaked.

"Okay," she reassured him with a small smile. "More than okay. You're...huge, Jag. You feel so good. I'm so full..."

Her words made Jag smile. "Yeah?" he asked, experimentally pulling back then quickly thrusting inside once again. If he had his way, he'd never leave. He wanted to stay inside her forever. The realization was unbelievable and mind-blowing.

Mentally chuckling about his crazy thoughts, he turned his attention back to Carly. He wanted to make this good for her. He leaned over, putting his hands by her shoulders, and began to slowly thrust in and out.

Her hands came up and gripped his biceps, digging her short nails into his skin. "Oh, yes! That feels so good," she said softly.

Jag liked this. Liked being on top. Liked knowing he was in complete control. Needed it. Her legs wrapped around him, feet digging into his ass, but despite that, he knew she was at his mercy.

For a moment, he felt guilt for that thought.

But then she whimpered and thrust up to meet him.

"Faster, Jag!"

He shook his head. No, if he went faster, he'd lose it and come. And he wanted this to last much longer. So he continued his slow and steady thrusts.

But eventually, while he knew what he was doing felt good for Carly, he realized she wasn't anywhere near another orgasm.

Experimentally, he thrust into her harder.

She cried out, and he moaned at the way her tits jiggled. So he did it again. And again. The harder he fucked her, the more

Carly came undone beneath him. This was all new to Jag. New and thrilling, and he catalogued her every response, noting what she liked and what she loved.

She thrust up into one of his lunges, whimpering when his pelvic bone hit her clit. Jag belatedly understood that if she was going to come again, he needed to stimulate the sensitive little button. He put all his weight on his left hand and snaked his right between them. The position was awkward, and his thrusts faltered as he tried to rub her clit and fuck her at the same time.

"I can do it," she breathed, but Jag shook his head. A vision of Bridget flicking her clit as she rode him flashed in his brain, and he did his best to push the image away.

"No," he said, harsher than he wanted.

Carly immediately nodded and put her hands over her head.

Jag felt bad for practically yelling at her, but her submissive position made another pulse of come spurt out of his cock. It made him slide even easier in and out.

Instinctively, Jag jerked up and sat back on his heels, grabbing Carly's hips and pulling her ass onto his thighs. He couldn't thrust well in this position, but that was probably for the best at the moment. He was way too close to coming.

"Jag?" Carly asked, but he didn't answer. Couldn't because his jaw was clenched too tightly. The sight of his cock buried inside her pussy was erotic as hell. He'd never been as turned on as he was at this moment.

All his life, he'd felt as if his abuser had broken something inside him. That she'd made sure he'd never feel passion or lust or desire, ever.

But it turned out he wasn't broken after all. Carly was his salvation, and there was no doubt his libido had roared to life because of her.

Using two fingers, he began to massage her clit. Hard.

The second he touched her, Carly jerked and let out an adorable squeak. He grasped her hip with his free hand and held her against him as he worked to make her come. She squirmed in his lap, but he didn't let up. He needed to see and feel her come more than he wanted to come himself.

It didn't take long. She was already primed and ready. He saw her stomach muscles tighten and her thighs clenched around his hips. She let out a screech as her orgasm overtook her.

Jag threw his head back and clenched his teeth as her body strangled his cock. He'd never, *ever* felt pleasure like this.

He couldn't hold back his own orgasm. He forced his eyes open and stared down at where he was joined with Carly as his cock flexed deep inside her. He could feel the come churning up from his balls as he exploded. He groaned loudly, bombarded by sensation.

He came longer and harder than he ever remembered doing so before. Something about being with Carly, being inside her, feeling her pleasure all around his cock, and seeing her cheeks and upper chest flush as she orgasmed, fueled his own pleasure.

He held her against him, not ready to leave her body yet. She had to be uncomfortable, with her back arched the way it was, her hips hoisted onto his lap, but Jag couldn't let her go.

Sweat dripped from his temple and he wiped it away with his shoulder. He felt as exhausted as if he'd just been through one of Mustang's killer obstacle courses, but at the same time, he was hyped up and ready to conquer the world—because he'd just made love to his woman.

Carly sighed and stretched her arms over her head. She smiled shyly at him. "That was...incredible," she said softly.

Jag's cock twitched inside her, and she giggled.

"Seriously?" she asked.

"I think you've created a monster," Jag rasped, his voice sounding rusty.

He braced himself over her, keeping his hips locked to hers, and lay down, putting a hand on her lower back and anchoring her to him as he moved to his side. It was an uncomfortable position, as one of her legs was under his and he couldn't snuggle her as easily as he liked.

Without thought, Jag rolled to his back, taking Carly with him.

She stilled as she looked down at him. "Is this..."

"It's fine," Jag said when her voice trailed off. "You aren't her. I have no idea how the fuck I could ever think this was anything remotely like before."

He urged her to relax, and he sighed in contentment when her nose brushed the side of his neck as she cuddled into him. He could feel her hard nipples against his chest as she shifted, getting comfortable, and wetness coated his balls.

This was what he'd been missing in his life. Carly. He'd been missing *her*.

"If I get too heavy, move me," she said sleepily.

It was way too early for him to go to sleep, but he had no problem with Carly using him as a pillow. "No way in hell are you too heavy. You're perfect," he told her softly.

She snorted, but didn't protest. "Jag?"

"Yeah, angel?"

"That was okay? You didn't have any bad moments?"

"None," he reassured her. "You..." His voice cracked and he cleared his throat. Overcome with emotion, he took a moment to swallow hard and get control of himself before he continued. "I love you," he told her.

"I love you too. So much. If you decided you didn't want to be with me anymore, it would destroy me."

"Not happening," Jag said sternly. After a moment, he asked, "I didn't hurt you?"

She chuckled against him. "Not even close."

"It'll be better next time," he reassured her.

She snorted again.

"Seriously. I came way too fast. I wanted to last longer."

Carly lifted herself off his chest a bit, which made his cock twitch inside her once again. She shifted her hips, but he didn't slip out of her. "It was a huge turn-on that you came right after I did."

"You have no idea how fucking amazing you feel around me," Jag said in awe.

She smiled shyly again. His gaze went to her tits, brushing against his chest hair. "Next time I'm gonna play a little more," he told her.

Carly eased back down to his chest. "Okay."

"Okay?" he asked, needing to hear her acquiescence again.

"Yup. As far as I'm concerned, you can do whatever you want, whenever you want."

Jag's cock twitched again.

He felt her lips smile against his skin. Turning his head, Jag kissed her temple. "Why don't you take a nap. When you wake up, I'll work on my endurance. Does it bother you that I'm still inside you?"

"No, not at all. But...things might get messy."

"Awesome," Jag breathed. He couldn't think of anything better than having his come leak out of her. It was a Neanderthal thought, but he didn't even care.

"I hate what happened to you," Carly said softly, "but I can't

help but be pleased you're experiencing pleasure like this for the first time. With me."

"Me too. There's no one I'd rather have as my mentor than you."

Carly chuckled again, then shifted, getting more comfortable.

Several minutes went by, and when Jag felt small puffs of air from her mouth against his sensitive skin, he sighed in contentment.

He never thought he could get to this place. But here he was, lying under a woman and perfectly content to do so.

"Thank you," he mouthed silently to the woman who owned his heart before he finally closed his eyes. He had plans for Carly, and he wanted to make sure he was rested.

CHAPTER TWENTY

Carly lounged on the couch, staring into space with a small smile on her face. The last week had been...a revelation. Jag was everything she'd ever wanted in a boyfriend, but never thought she'd have.

He'd been late leaving for work after PT just this morning, because she'd been lazy and hadn't gotten out of bed by the time he got home.

After he'd fucked her into a pile of goo, he'd said he couldn't resist the temptation of her in his bed, naked and sleepy. Carly was more than all right with that. He'd left her still in bed, trying to recover, with a satisfied smile on his face.

Jag may not have had much experience when it came to sex, but he was a fast learner. Carly had never been with a man as determined to make sure she orgasmed each and every time they made love. He paid attention to every little move and sound she made, and if he didn't think she was enjoying something, he'd immediately change up his technique.

Last night, he'd said he wanted to try letting her be on top at some point. Carly wasn't eager to rush that. His reaction was still pretty clear in her mind, and they had plenty of time to work up to it. Besides, she was more than enjoying Jag being in control.

He'd seen the psychologist a couple more times, and he told Carly the other night that he was angry at himself for not doing so earlier. What happened to him was a big part of who he was today, but he was finally dealing with it.

Stretching, Carly smiled when she felt a twinge of soreness between her legs. Her phone vibrated next to her with a text and she reached over to pick it up.

Kenna: I just wanted to tell you how proud I am of you. I know this is coming out of left field. I was thinking about how well you're doing and it almost made me cry. Love you.

Tears sprang to Carly's eyes after reading her friend's message. Truth be told, Carly was proud of herself too. She'd come a long way from the terrified woman huddled in the corner in her bedroom, hiding in her apartment, too scared to step foot outside. She wasn't quite back to the woman she'd been before Shawn, but that was all right.

Carly wasn't sure she *wanted* to go back to being the slightly naïve person she'd been. Thanks to the self-defense lessons with Elizabeth, and getting tips from Jag and his friends, Carly felt stronger. If Shawn had kidnapped her a few months ago, instead of Kenna, there was no way she would've had the inner fortitude to do what her friend had. She would've been paralyzed with

fear, and Shawn would either have succeeded with his evil plans or she would've been blown to bits along with him.

It was easy to armchair quarterback what she might do now if Shawn was still alive and tried to snatch her, but she wanted to think she'd be able to get away from him somehow. She never went anywhere without the small bottle of pepper spray in her purse, and she made sure to always wear shorts or pants with pockets so she could carry the pocketknife Jag had given her. She'd learned a lot of ways to use her body—elbows, knees, even her head if necessary—to get someone to let go of her so she could run like hell.

That was one of the things Elizabeth hammered home in every session. The goal was to get away from an attacker. Not stay and beat him up. *Get away.* Facts showed that once a bad guy got someone in a car, the chances of the victim surviving went down at least fifty percent. Elizabeth also said one of the best weapons a woman, or anyone, had was their voice. People who were up to no good didn't want any attention brought to what they were doing. So even if an attacker told you not to make a sound, nine times out of ten it was better to scream your head off.

Of course, Elodie had to go and ask what happened if they *weren't* in a public place. She was probably thinking about what had happened to her when her life was threatened in the middle of the ocean, where no one would have heard her if she'd screamed.

Elizabeth's answer was to tap her temple with her finger. "Then you have to be smarter than your attacker."

It was a simplistic answer, which Carly didn't really think would actually help in a life-or-death situation, but she understood Elizabeth's point. Panicking wouldn't help. And if there

wasn't anyone around who could help, it would be up to the victim to help themselves.

Shaking her head, not wanting to think about such depressing things, Carly typed out a response to Kenna.

Carly: Thanks. I wouldn't be doing nearly as well without your help. I admire you a hell of a lot, woman. Even before I really got to know you, I looked up to you. Love you.

Kenna sent back an entire string of emojis in response, and Carly could only laugh. It was such a Kenna thing to do. She was about to put her phone back down so she could go back to daydreaming about Jag when it rang, scaring the shit out of her.

Chuckling at her over-the-top reaction, she answered.

"Hello?"

"Oh, thank God you're there. This is Alani. I need your help."

"What's wrong?" Her boss sounded frazzled, which was very unlike Alani. She was usually unflappable, so something major had to be up for her to be calling so early, and sounding so out of sorts.

"Today's our inspection from the health department. Usually I'm not concerned. We do everything we're supposed to and if we're cited for something, it's super nit-picky and isn't a big deal. But the new manager was on yesterday, which you know, since you worked with him. He's been good for the most part, and he's great with asshole customers, but today's delivery of supplies just arrived. Robert placed the order for the first time by himself yesterday. I have no idea what happened, if he got interrupted or

was distracted or what, but instead of two cases of lettuce, he ordered *twenty*. We're also overwhelmed with broccoli. There's no way we can use fifty-five heads!"

"Holy crap, seriously?" Carly asked.

"Yes!" Alani practically yelled. "Normally, I wouldn't care. I'd probably even laugh it off. But we also got our monthly order for hula pie supplies. There's no space in the refrigerators for all the extra produce. If the inspectors get here and see that stuff sitting around, not properly stored, we're gonna get hammered. Even if I explain what happened and told them we aren't going to serve the stuff that's not refrigerated to customers, they might not believe me."

"What can I do to help?" Carly asked. She felt awful for her boss. Alani was an amazing manager and it wouldn't look good for her if Duke's got a low score from the health department on her watch. Even if it wasn't her fault.

"I hate to even ask this, because I know it's not something you're going to be comfortable doing, but I tried calling a few others and everybody already has plans."

"It's okay, Alani," Carly assured her.

"I called Food For All, and they said they'd be happy to take the extra lettuce and broccoli. The Barbers Point location is closed today, but they said the downtown building was open and could take the extra food."

Carly nodded. She remembered Lexie and Ashlyn saying the other day that they'd be closed most of today because they were doing a mobile food drive downtown. The goal was to bring attention to the need for donations and to try to humanize the homeless in the area. Kenna and Elodie were also going to help, as well. Carly had wanted to go, but she knew it would be too much for her. She felt awful about sitting at home while her

friends were out doing good deeds in the community, but she vowed to make up for it somehow.

"I'd never normally bother you this early, but the inspector usually shows up around ten," Alani went on, her voice rising with her anxiety. "If I can get the excess food out of here, I think we'll be okay, but I can't leave."

Carly stood up and headed for the bedroom to change. "I can be there in about half an hour," she told her.

"I owe you *so* hard," Alani said, the relief easy to hear in her tone. "Pull up right outside the hotel, I'll come out there and meet you so you won't have to park in the garage. I think I can get the extra stuff into about three boxes. That'll fit in your car, won't it?"

"We'll make it fit," Carly reassured her.

"Thanks again, Carly, you're a lifesaver! Seriously."

"I'll see you soon," she said.

"Bye."

Carly clicked off the phone and grabbed a tank top from the drawer. She stood there for a moment, staring at Jag's dresser. He'd moved his stuff around and cleared out two drawers for her. It was still a little hard for her to believe things were going as well as they were, but she was deliriously happy and wasn't about to question it. She put on a bra and pulled a black tank over her head. She decided to wear pants, as the weathermen were predicting rain later that afternoon and there was a pretty good breeze outside right now.

After slipping on the khakis, Carly grabbed a pair of flip-flops and headed for the bathroom. She ran a brush through her hair and tied it back with a scrunchie. She took a moment to stare at herself in the mirror. She barely recognized this woman from the one she'd been a few months ago. Her face had filled

out a little from eating regular healthy meals and she no longer had dark circles under her eyes.

She felt like a new person, and she loved who she was right now. She wasn't going to ever go back to the scared, withdrawn woman she'd become after Shawn's insane kidnapping plot.

Whirling around, Carly headed for the front door of the apartment. She grabbed her purse and the pocketknife she always put on the small table near Jag's front door. Once she was sitting in her little Ford Escape, she took a deep breath. Her adrenaline was coursing through her veins, which was ridiculous, considering the situation. She was just going to drive into Waikiki, pick up the produce, drop it off at Food For All, then come home. But Alani's desperation had seeped into her psyche, making her flustered and eager to get to Duke's before the health inspector.

That didn't mean she would be stupid. Taking her phone out of her purse, Carly sent a quick text to Jag. She knew he was in meetings all day—very serious meetings, if the little he'd told her about what was going on was any indication. Carly didn't know the details, but it was looking more and more likely that he and his team would be going on a mission soon. Still, the last thing she wanted to do was leave the apartment without telling anyone.

Carly: I'm headed out for a bit to do a favor for Alani. Don't worry, I've got my pepper spray and my knife. I'll text when I get home. Love you.

· · ·

Shoving her phone back into her purse and putting the car in reverse, she backed out of the space and headed out.

* * *

He couldn't believe Carly was actually leaving...*by herself!*

He'd waited so long for this moment, and it was finally happening. She didn't have her boyfriend with her and none of her fucking girlfriends were here.

It was time. Time to get this done. He was ready, had been for weeks. He had all the supplies and the boat was on standby. Even better, it was supposed to storm later. Everything was setting up perfectly for him to finally finish what Shawn had started.

All he had to do was follow her and wait for an opportunity to make his move. And he had no doubt it would work. It had to.

"It's happening, buddy," he said out loud as he followed the bitch from a discreet distance. "She's finally gonna pay for everything she did to you."

Anticipation flowed through his veins. He could barely contain his excitement. This was going down. Today. Now.

Carly Stewart was going to die—and he couldn't fucking wait to see her face when she realized what was about to happen.

* * *

Picking up the extra produce had gone smoothly. Carly had called Alani to tell her she was in the area and when she arrived at the Outrigger Hotel, Alani had been waiting. She had a cart holding three large boxes, and they quickly got them loaded into

Carly's car. One box fit in the trunk and the other two went on the back seat. Alani had hugged her tightly and thanked her profusely once again. Then Carly had headed downtown to Food For All.

She hadn't counted on there being some sort of event going on in the area. Even though it was early, there were people *everywhere*. Vendors were lined up on the sidewalks and some streets were even blocked off.

Swearing because she wouldn't be able to simply pull up outside the food pantry and quickly drop off the boxes, Carly headed for the closest parking garage. She was going to have to make three trips in order to deliver all the food. The thought of walking back and forth, amongst the hundreds of other people on the streets, made her break out in a cold sweat.

For a moment, Carly thought about going home and texting Lexie to tell her she had the food donations, and ask if maybe she could pick them up. But the second she had the idea, she dismissed it. First of all, Lexie was busy at a Food For All booth. Carly hadn't thought to ask if there was an actual *event* in conjunction with her friends being downtown today.

Secondly, there wasn't room in the fridge at Jag's apartment for all the food, and if she left it in her car all afternoon, in the blazing sun, it would wilt and probably go bad. The thought of wasting all that food didn't sit well with Carly. Not with the number of people who could use a healthy meal.

So she sucked it up and pulled into a parking space in the garage. She'd had to go all the way up to the top floor to find a spot, as there were so many people downtown for the festival, not to mention those here for their normal workday.

Carly sat in her car, gripping the steering wheel for a full five minutes, trying to work up the courage to get out and head

down the stairs to the food pantry. She had no doubt they were busy and might not be able to spare anyone to come help her, but...she'd go find out.

The sooner she got out of her car, the sooner she'd be done with this and on her way home.

Hating how weak she felt when just this morning, she'd congratulated herself for her bravery, Carly took a deep breath and pushed open the car door. She could do this. It was crazy to think someone was going to jump out and kidnap her at any second.

She'd taken two steps away from the car when a man appeared out of nowhere.

Carly yelped in surprise and took a few stumbling steps backward.

"I'm so sorry! I didn't mean to startle you," the man said.

When she recovered, she realized she knew him.

"Gideon...What are you doing here?" It was Shawn's friend. The one who worked at the zoo. She'd seen him a few times in recent months, and hadn't gotten any negative vibes from him... but she was still cautious. What were the odds he would be here, now, in this parking garage?

He wore his familiar tan overalls. She wondered if he had any other clothes, because it had been a long time since she'd seen him in anything other than the zoo uniform he always seemed to wear.

"The zoo has a booth at the festival," he said with a shrug. "I'm coming to do a shift, but didn't realize how crowded things would be. I just parked over there," he said, gesturing over his shoulder vaguely with a thumb.

Carly relaxed a fraction. "Oh, yeah. It's crazy."

"What are you doing here? You going to the festival?"

"No," she said a little too loudly. Taking a deep breath to calm herself, Carly explained, "I'm dropping off a donation to Food For All, but like you, I didn't know it would be this crowded so early. I couldn't get to the actual building, so I had to park. I've got three boxes I need to bring down there, but thought I'd go ask for help."

Gideon nodded. "Ah, that makes sense." He looked toward her car and obviously saw the boxes in her back seat. "Those are pretty big boxes. You want my help? We could bring two boxes down now, then come back for the last one. I can take it down for you, since I'm staying to work at our booth anyway."

Carly couldn't help feeling slightly relieved. Gideon wasn't exactly a person she'd choose to be around, but it was better than walking around by herself, feeling vulnerable. At least she knew him, even if he'd been Shawn's friend, and he hadn't said or done anything to make her suspect he held a grudge. If anything, he'd gone out of his way to put her at ease.

Even now, he kept a respectable distance, not crowding her.

At this point, Carly just wanted to get the hell out of this garage, away from all the people milling around on the streets. And she couldn't deny the thought of only making one trip down to Food For All sounded really good right about now. If she took Gideon up on his offer, she could be back in her car and on her way home in ten minutes. Tops.

"Okay," she said before she could change her mind.

"Great. It's a very nice thing you're doing, donating food, I mean," Gideon said.

Carly nodded and headed for her trunk. She'd still had her keys in her hand, positioned to hurt someone if they attacked her, and now she stuck the key in the lock to open the trunk.

She leaned over to grab the box—and something hit the back of her head. Hard.

Carly let out a muffled grunt and found herself falling. She hit her face on the edge of the trunk and practically bounced off. But she didn't hit the ground.

"I've got you," Gideon said.

For some reason, his words sounded funny. Carly squinted at him as he lifted her into his arms. He wasn't a large man, about Jag's height, but he had the strength to carry her without too much trouble.

He was walking away from her car, but Carly was having trouble keeping her eyes open. Her head was throbbing and she felt as if she was going to throw up. It wasn't until she felt something against her back that she opened her eyes wide. Gideon was laying her down on something. Turning her head, she was confused for just a second.

Then everything finally registered.

Gideon had hit her. And now he was putting her inside a trunk.

Gideon Sparks was the man they'd been looking for all along. The mild-mannered zoo worker was kidnapping her!

Carly opened her mouth to scream, but before she could make even the smallest sound, Gideon's fist flew forward and struck her face. She passed out and knew no more.

CHAPTER TWENTY-ONE

Jag was exhausted. He and the rest of the team had worked through lunch as they scoured maps and intel to try to figure out where Boko Haram might have stashed the kidnapped boys. There weren't a lot of choices in the area, and five hundred people or more weren't exactly inconspicuous.

The Nigerian military was scrambling to rescue the boys, and there was a chance Jag's team would be sent out without too much notice, and they needed to be ready.

Around three-thirty in the afternoon, they'd gotten word that the boys had been found and a rescue attempt was in progress. They'd sat in the conference room, tense and silent, as reports trickled in.

By four-fifteen, most of the boys had been rescued with minimal casualties, and would be returning to their families as soon as possible.

It had been a roller coaster of a day, and all Jag wanted to do

was go home and see Carly. She had a calming effect on him, whether it was when he got too far inside his own head and couldn't shake his past, or if he'd just had a bad day at work.

Once the team was released, Jag pulled out his phone to check his messages, his first opportunity to do so. He hoped to find something from Carly. She had a tendency to send him cute texts throughout the day, letting him know she was thinking about him or just to chat about something or other.

Today he only had one text...and it had been sent more than eight hours earlier. She said she was helping Alani and that she'd let him know when she returned home.

But she hadn't. She hadn't even said where she was going in the first place, just that she was doing a favor for her boss.

"Aleck!" Jag yelled, jogging to catch up to his friend. The team had separated after exiting the building, all heading to their own vehicles.

Aleck turned. "What's up?" he asked.

"Have you heard from Kenna today?"

"Yeah, why?"

"Was Carly with her?"

Aleck shrugged. "Not that I know. She was going downtown with Lexie and Elodie to do that Food For All thing."

Jag turned and stuck his fingers in his mouth, whistling loudly. It was the easiest and fastest way to get the rest of the team's attention.

Within moments, the guys were headed his way. As soon as Mustang was within earshot, Jag asked, "Has Elodie seen Carly today?"

Mustang looked confused, but shook his head. "I don't think so. Elodie said she got home not too long ago. Said she was tired, but that the day was good."

"Midas?" Jag asked.

"No. What's up?"

"Maybe she went to see Monica?" Jag asked Pid almost desperately.

"Mo was working at the Head Start Center all day. What's wrong? Where's Carly?"

"I don't know if anything's wrong," Jag said, but his gut was screaming at him. "She said she was headed out and that she'd text when she got home. But she never did. And she left around eight this morning."

"Maybe she forgot," Slate suggested.

Jag shook his head forcefully. "No way. You guys know how she is. If she says she's going to do something, she does it."

"Nobody panic," Mustang ordered. "Have you tried to call her, Jag?"

Feeling stupid because he hadn't, Jag didn't respond, but lifted his cell and clicked on Carly's name. He waited as the phone rang in his ear. Once, twice...it rang five times then her voice mail clicked on. Jag clenched his teeth and hung up, then immediately called back. The same thing happened. Five rings, then her sweet voice message sounding in his ear.

"Hey, babe. You heard from Carly today?" Aleck had called Kenna before Jag had hung up. "Right, no, it's all good, I was just wondering. I'll see you soon, yeah?" He clicked off the phone and shook his head.

"Shit! This is bad," Jag said, feeling an overwhelming sense of doom.

"I'll follow you home. Maybe she's there and she got sick or something and just forgot to let you know she's home. She could be sleeping," Mustang said.

Jag realized his friend was trying to be positive, but deep

down, he knew his and Carly's worst fear had come true. The mystery accomplice had made his move.

Carly's life was in danger—and she was possibly already dead.

Without another word, Jag turned and ran toward his Jetta. Mustang was right, he had to make sure she wasn't at home before calling in reinforcements. Detective Lee had to be informed that Carly had disappeared. The police might not be willing to take a missing person's report since she hadn't been gone even twelve hours yet, but maybe the detective could get things moving along, given her situation.

Whether or not the police got involved, Jag needed to get a hold of Baker. If there was anyone who could help them find Carly, it was him. He'd been questioning and shadowing Keyes's potential accomplices for weeks. He had to have a clue. He *had* to.

Driving way too fast toward his apartment complex, Jag's hopes were dashed when he didn't see Carly's vehicle in the parking lot. She wasn't here, he knew that without having to go upstairs and check. Yes, she could've had car trouble and taken a taxi home, but she would've texted him and told him what was going on if that was the case.

So the questions now were...why, exactly, had she left the house? Where was she going? What happened when she got there? And where the hell was she now?

He slammed his car into park but didn't bother getting out. Carly wasn't upstairs and he didn't want to go up there and feel the emptiness of his apartment. Memories of her would overwhelm him and he wouldn't be able to think straight. Carly was depending on him to find her, and he wouldn't rest until he did just that.

He saw his team gathering outside his car out of the corner of his eye, but all Jag's attention was fixed on his phone. He clicked on Baker's name and the second the other man answered, Jag spoke. "Carly's gone. He got her. We need help finding her."

* * *

Carly moaned. Her head was pounding and her face felt as if it were on fire. She had no idea why she hurt so much...but in seconds, it all came back to her.

Her eyes flew open but they wouldn't focus. The overwhelming urge to puke came over her and she turned on her side and wretched. Her belly clenched as she purged everything in her stomach.

When she'd finished throwing up, she heard something. Turning her head gingerly, she looked to her left.

Gideon was sitting at the back of what she now realized was a boat...and he was laughing.

"So fucking pathetic," he snarled.

Carly finally realized that part of the reason she was throwing up was because of the boat, and she always got seasick when she was on the water. Even if it was the smoothest day ever, she still got green.

Today was definitely not a smooth ocean day. Carly had no idea how fast they were going, but the small boat was bouncing as it flew over the water. There was no wheelhouse to protect them from the spray of the waves or from the rain.

And it was pouring. Rain lashed against her face, feeling like tiny stings from insects. Gideon didn't seem to even notice the

weather. He had one hand on the tiller, steering the engine behind the boat, and was smirking like a lunatic.

"It's about time you woke up, fucking lazy bitch. I've been waiting hours for you to wake up. I didn't even hit you that hard, but you've been unconscious for-fucking-ever. I could've thrown you overboard already. But I wanted you to be cognizant of what was happening—and why."

Panic rose within Carly and her breath momentarily paused in terror. This was literally her worst nightmare come true. She was alone with Gideon, someone who obviously wanted to do her harm, had *already* done her harm. She didn't know what his ultimate plan was, but it couldn't be good.

She sat up...and looked down at her leg in confusion when it didn't move easily.

Gideon laughed again. "You aren't going anywhere until I want you to," he told her with a nasty grin.

Carly stared in surprise at the kettle bell that was attached to her ankle by a sturdy-looking rope. There was only one reason Gideon would've tied a heavy weight to her leg. She looked over the side of the boat at the rolling waves, and another bout of nausea had her bending over to throw up once more. This time all that came out was bile.

Carly's heart was beating a million miles an hour. She was completely on her own...and these were probably her last few minutes on Earth. Gideon was going to kill her. She knew that as surely as she knew her name.

The lessons Elizabeth had pounded into her surged to the front of her brain.

Fight. If you can't get anyone's attention, you'll have to use your own smarts to try to get out of the situation. Whatever you do, you cannot give up. If you do, your attacker wins.

The very last thing Carly wanted was for Gideon to win. No way in hell.

Her mind cleared as if a set of curtains had been thrown back. She didn't know what she was going to do, but giving up wasn't on the list.

Maybe she could tackle Gideon and push him overboard. She could then drive the boat back to shore. She had no idea where they were, but if she turned in the opposite direction they were going now, she was bound to run into land at some point.

Or maybe she could pick up the weight tied around her leg and hit him over the head with it, knock him out and, once again, take control of the boat.

Different scenarios spun in her head as she tried to figure out what to do.

"I can see you thinking." Gideon smirked. "Might as well stop, your poker face is shit. You can't outwit me. You're too goddamn stupid. I have no idea what Shawn even saw in you. You're fucking *pitiful*, and he told us all about how much you sucked in bed." He snorted. "The thought of you even attempting to satisfy a man like Shawn is ridiculous."

"If I was so bad, why'd he care so much when we broke up?" Carly couldn't help but ask.

"Because he did you a favor!" Gideon yelled. "He was willing to take you under his wing, teach you."

"Teach me what?" Carly asked.

"How to be a *real* woman. How to satisfy him. How to be a fucking benefit to society instead of a goddamn leech. You were an *embarrassment*. All he ever tried to do was make you a better woman, and you threw that in his face! It wasn't your place to decide when the relationship was over. Shawn wasn't done with you."

Carly stared at Gideon in disbelief.

He looked absolutely terrifying right now. The rain had soaked him through and his thinning hair was slicked back on his head. His face was red and his eyes bloodshot. He looked as if he was two seconds away from absolutely losing it.

Gideon took a deep breath and continued speaking. "He was my mentor. Taught me everything I needed to know about women. He even helped me find one. We had her all picked out, I'd started grooming her to be mine, just like Shawn did for you. She was young, impressionable, and she *liked* me," he said in a dark, low tone. "But after Shawn died, she didn't understand why I was so upset. Couldn't help me. And without him, I didn't know how to make her come to heel. She left me. Just like you did to Shawn. It's all your fucking fault! You shouldn't have left him! If you hadn't, I'd still have my own woman. She'd be trained by now. Would do whatever I asked. Cook, clean...open her legs whenever I demanded. It's *your fault*! Yours!"

Jesus. Shawn was teaching him how to manipulate a woman. How to reel her in and denigrate her and make her feel as if she had no other options but to stay with the man abusing her. She knew Shawn was an asshole, but had no idea he was *that* big of one.

And Gideon?

Gideon was fucking *insane*.

Deciding she needed to do whatever she could to mollify the man, Carly said, "I didn't know. I'm so sorry he's dead."

"Your fault!" Gideon screamed, repeating himself. "It's *your fucking fault*! But you'll learn. If it's the last fucking thing you do."

"Learn what?" Carly couldn't help but ask. The words just popped out, and she immediately wished she could take them back. The last thing she wanted was Gideon trying to "teach

her" how to please a man. If he tried to rape her, she'd somehow find a way to rip his dick off and feed it to the sharks. The thought of anyone so much as *touching* her after she'd been with Jag made nausea rise up once more. But this time she held it back, focusing all her attention on her kidnapper.

She couldn't think about Jag right now, she needed to figure out a way to outsmart Gideon. She was *not* a stupid little girl, like Shawn thought. She was a grown-ass woman who was going to show this asshole *exactly* how smart she was...as soon as she thought of a way to get out of this predicament.

"Look how worthless you are. How fucking pathetic," Gideon growled. "You'll learn your place. You're nothing but a useless bitch—and you're gonna die. And once you do, I can start over, put all of Shawn's teachings to use and find my own woman again. I'll make Shawn proud of me."

Carly's breath caught in her throat as Gideon lifted his hand and pointed a gun. He'd obviously been holding onto it the whole time, but she'd been too focused on other things to notice. It looked...funny to her. Not like the pistols Jag owned, or the guns she'd seen on TV. The barrel looked longer, a little wider.

"When I decide we're out far enough, I'm gonna shoot you with a tranquilizer. It won't kill you right away, but it'll make you damn sleepy. At least that's what it does to the lions I use it on." He laughed loud and long, sounding unhinged. "It's calibrated for their body weights, so there's a good chance you'll be knocked out quick. Then I'm gonna throw you overboard. You'll sink like a rock. You can try to hold your breath, but it'll be no use. You'll be too tired, too overcome by the tranquilizer. And instead of inhaling air, all you'll get is water in your lungs.

"You'll sink all the way to the bottom of the ocean, where

sharks and fish will feast on your flesh until you cease to exist. And you'll spend every goddamn second of your last conscious minutes wishing you'd been a better woman. Willing to satisfy and please Shawn. Then you'll spend eternity in *Hell*, with all the other women who thought they could control their men. Women who should've been subservient!"

Gideon was fucking looney tunes. How he'd been able to hide it from Detective Lee, Baker, her and Jag, and everyone he worked with, Carly had no idea. But one thing was very clear. If she didn't do something right now, she would die exactly how Gideon described.

She shifted, and something bit into her thigh...

Her pocketknife!

An idea began to form in her head.

Glancing around carefully, she couldn't see much of anything. The rain was falling in thick sheets, obscuring Oahu, which she assumed was behind them. And while she didn't know exactly what time it was, it was getting dark. If she could get away, the night would help her stay hidden.

The one positive thing in her mind was that Gideon could only take her as far as the gas in the engine would allow. He had to save enough to get back. And while it had been a while since she'd trained for any kind of race—years, actually—Carly trusted her own swimming ability more than she did the man sitting at the back of the boat.

The vessel they were in wasn't fancy. Didn't seem to have any kind of GPS that she could see. There weren't any life jackets or life rings. No railings around the edge of the boat either. It literally looked like some kind of cheap, oversized rowboat. Whoever Gideon had borrowed it from obviously didn't use it

for any long-distance excursions. They probably used it to fish or took it out to snorkel near the shore.

Gideon continued to rant and rave about what a horrible person she was and how she was going to die a painful death, just like Shawn had. How he was going to find an eighteen-year-old girl and mold her into a submissive, perfect woman. But Carly ignored him. She worked out in her head what her next steps should be. She had no idea if her idea would work, but she literally had no other choice. She wasn't about to sit here and let Shawn's fucking friend shoot her with a tranquilizer and throw her overboard. If she was going into the water, it would be on her own timetable.

And that time was—now!

Taking a deep breath, Carly swiftly grabbed the kettle bell and using all her strength, she threw it—and herself—over the side of the boat.

As she suspected, she took Gideon completely off guard, too busy listing all her faults. She heard the boat continuing on course, moving farther away. It would take him a moment to stop the boat and turn around.

One thing Gideon had gotten right was the fact that she would most definitely sink as soon as she landed in the water, thanks to the heavy weight around her ankle.

Moving quickly, she reached for the pocketknife. More thankful than she could say that Jag insisted she always carry the thing, Carly did her best to open the blade while also holding onto the kettle ball. She barely managed. Knowing it was only a matter of time before she ran out of breath, she frantically sawed at the rope. Somehow in her panic, she cut her palm when she grabbed the rope instead and dropped the kettle ball, to keep the material taut, hoping to cut more easily.

For a terrified moment, she thought the knife wasn't sharp enough, that the rope was too thick, that she was going to sink to the bottom of the ocean just as Gideon had planned.

But she sawed away—and the rope finally cut through.

Desperate for air, Carly swam for the surface as fast as she could, clutching the knife, not wanting to drop it since it was literally her only defense if Gideon got close again. She popped up and inhaled a large breath, promptly coughing and choking from a wave that washed over her head.

Unfortunately, her coughing let Gideon focus in on her position when she surfaced, and he quickly turned the boat in her direction.

Fuck!

He lifted the gun and fired as he got closer. Carly couldn't hear the pop of the air mechanism, but she felt something brush against her arm before she was able to duck under the water.

Knowing her only chance was to get as far away from Gideon as possible, and to use the storm to hide her whereabouts when she came up for air, Carly reluctantly dropped the knife. She hated to let it go, but she needed both hands to swim underwater as fast as she could.

When her lungs felt as if they were going to burst, she spun to her back and surfaced, figuring it would be harder to spot her if just her face appeared above the waves, instead of her entire head. She took several deep breaths before sinking back down, turning over and doing the breaststroke underwater once more.

She did that over and over, not even looking for Gideon. All her focus was on staying underwater for as long as possible and swimming as hard as she could. And when she did come up for air, putting only her nose and mouth above the water.

Time had no meaning. She could've been swimming for

minutes or hours. But the next time she surfaced, Carly took a chance and looked around for Gideon.

All she saw was water. No boat. No Gideon with his dart gun aimed, ready to shoot.

It was both a satisfying moment and a terrifying one. She was all alone, somewhere in the ocean, with no idea where she was, in the middle of a storm.

A wave crashed over her head and Carly sputtered and spit out the saltwater that had gotten into her mouth.

And quickly, another terrifying realization hit.

Now that she'd stopped moving...her limbs felt uncoordinated. And she was dizzy.

Not only did she have a head wound, and probably a concussion, but the dart Gideon had shot *actually hit her*.

She had to assume it had only nicked her. Otherwise, Carly knew she'd be dead right now. If it fully sank into her skin, she'd have felt it, and she would have been knocked out long before now. But enough of the drug had gotten into her system that she felt woozy, and yes...tired as hell.

Determination filled her. She wasn't going to give Gideon the satisfaction of failing. No. She needed to get back to Oahu so she could tell the detective, and Baker, and everyone else that it had been Gideon who'd kidnapped her.

She wasn't going to die. No fucking way. She'd made it this far, all she had to do was swim to shore. Piece of cake.

Carly did her best to stay positive as minutes ticked by, but the longer she swam, the more thoughts of defeat tried to sneak into her psyche. The rain stopped, which was good, but darkness fell. She had no way of knowing if she was even swimming in the right direction. For all she knew, she was headed out to sea instead of toward safety.

But she didn't stop. Just kept moving her arms and kicking her feet.

Just when she didn't think she could go another inch, when the desire to close her eyes and let sleep overtake her had become too much to resist...Carly's knees scraped against something in the water.

Even through the pants she was wearing, whatever she'd run into *hurt*. She cried out in pain and reached for her knee. She promptly scraped her hand next, clearly on whatever had cut her knees. Coral? No...rocks.

Black lava rocks.

Looking around, Carly spotted the outline of a dark shape to her left. An island! It wasn't Oahu, but at that moment, Carly didn't care if it was freaking Russia.

Moving carefully so she didn't cut herself any more than she already had, Carly managed to drag herself onto the rocks at the edge of the island. They were sharp, and she was thankful she was wearing khakis, even though they'd felt like they weighed a hundred pounds in the water. She collapsed onto her stomach, with no strength to go farther.

It didn't matter. She was out of the water and had escaped from Gideon. When the sun came up, someone would come, maybe a fisherman, and she could get their attention and finally go home. The waters around Oahu were normally filled with boaters at all hours, but the storm had sent them all for cover.

But tomorrow...tomorrow would be different.

Now that she was safe, as safe as she could be for now, Carly allowed the tranquilizer to finally take effect. She was unconscious in less than a minute.

She didn't hear the birds who lived on the island, squawking to each other, warning the others of an intruder on their terri-

tory. She didn't feel the occasional crab walking over her body as they searched for food in the crevices between the rocks.

And she didn't hear the faint motor of a lone boat in the distance, riding back and forth through the water as its operator desperately searched for his escaped pray.

CHAPTER TWENTY-TWO

Jag followed Mustang out of the police station to his friend's pickup. He remembered Elodie had named the piece-of-shit vehicle Ben, but that little detail couldn't make him smile right now. Nothing could.

As soon as they realized no one knew where Carly was, they'd gone to the police station to meet with Detective Lee. He'd been concerned about Carly's disappearance, but without knowing who Keyes's accomplice was, he had nothing to go on as far as finding her. He was as much in the dark as Jag and his team. He'd put out a BOLO for her car and reassured Jag and the rest of the team that every officer would be on the lookout for either her or her car.

Gritting his teeth, Jag looked up at the sky through the truck's window. It was pouring rain. Lightning lit the darkening sky every now and then and he couldn't help but wonder where Carly was. What she was thinking. If she was all right...

He shook his head. No. She *was* all right. She had to be. The alternative was unthinkable.

"We'll head back to your place. Slate's not as good with electronics as you are, but maybe he's found something on the security cameras," Mustang said. "We'll check in with Baker, he said he was on his way down from the North Shore. We'll also keep calling Alani. I know Lee said he would stop by Duke's himself, but Carly said she was doing a favor for the woman, so she's definitely who we need to start with."

Jag nodded, but he was having a hard time concentrating. He was ninety-nine percent certain they wouldn't find anything useful on the security footage. Whatever had happened to Carly had gone down somewhere other than at their apartment. He didn't know how he knew that, it was just a gut feeling. And her boss wasn't at work, and so far hadn't answered her cell.

They needed to find her car, that would at least give them a starting place. The detective would check the parking garages around Duke's and Waikiki, but that would take time. Even though Oahu was small in terms of actual square milage, there were still almost a million registered vehicles on the island. And finding Carly's among them was akin to trying to find a needle in a needle stack.

They needed a miracle.

As they drove back to his apartment complex in silence, Jag thought about a conversation he'd had with Carly. She'd told him that no matter what happened, she wouldn't ever give up. That she'd fight to the death if need be, because she now had something to fight for...him.

He was suddenly very thankful for the self-defense lessons and the talks they'd had about how she could protect herself. Her purse was gone, which meant she had the pepper spray he'd

given her. And he hoped she also took the pocketknife when she left.

Jag took a deep breath. He'd been so proud of her for finally feeling comfortable enough to venture out on her own...and then this had to happen.

"He was watching her," he blurted.

Mustang looked over at him, but didn't say anything.

The more Jag thought about it, the more sure he was. "Other than a couple quick trips to the grocery store, she hasn't been anywhere by herself in months. If I wasn't with her, it was one of the girls. The car service took her to work and she was surrounded by people there too. I think he was biding his time. Watching and waiting for the chance to snatch her."

"You're probably right," Mustang said.

Jag wanted to yell in frustration. One part of him shamefully wished Carly wasn't so strong, that she'd clung to him a little longer. But that would've only postponed the inevitable. Then again, maybe if she'd still been frightened of going out by herself, Detective Lee or Baker would've figured out who was gunning for her before much longer.

"It won't do you or her any good to beat yourself up," Mustang said. "Trust me, I know how you're feeling right now. When Elodie disappeared, I didn't know if I could forgive myself for not keeping a closer eye on her. For underestimating the Columbus family. You just have to have faith. Carly's out there, and we're gonna find her."

Jag nodded, but deep down he had his doubts. He knew what the statistics said. That if a missing person wasn't found within twenty-four to forty-eight hours, they were probably dead. And the timetable was even quicker for women. Their only saving

grace was that whoever had her, probably wanted to make her suffer like Keyes had planned.

And it made Jag feel physically sick to have to hope that was the case.

But he and Carly could deal with whatever happened to her. He just needed her back in his arms, alive and in one piece.

Baker was exhausted. Mentally and physically. And he felt an immense amount of guilt. He should've put more pressure on Shawn's friends. Should've worked harder to figure out who he was looking for. And because he hadn't, Carly was missing.

It had been a long time since he'd gotten so...attached. Baker might not be an active-duty SEAL anymore, and his team might be long gone, but Mustang and his friends had become his new team. Their women were sweet. Down-to-earth, welcoming, and damn funny. He genuinely liked them.

They were also extremely prone to landing in trouble. If they were his, he'd probably lock them down and never let them leave the house.

His thoughts briefly turned to Jodelle. He'd suppressed a lot of emotions over the years; it was the only way to deal with the things he'd done and seen.

But Jodelle was even more closed off than he was.

On the surface, she was open and friendly. Feeding and looking out for the local surfer boys. But she was a kindred spirit, and Baker had known it the first time he'd met her. They both kept their true emotions on lockdown. She was his soul mate. He had no idea how to reach her, however. She had walls around her heart even taller than his own.

Shaking his head, Baker realized he'd been standing on the sidewalk outside of Theo's studio apartment for several minutes. The formerly homeless man had become a fairly close friend. He was genuine and never held back what he was feeling or thinking. Baker had started bunking with him when he was on this end of the island and it got too late to head home.

He needed to get some work done, and Theo's small apartment was the perfect place to do it. The little apartment was quiet. And as much as Baker liked Jag and the team, they'd all be extremely keyed up right now, and he needed to briefly recharge to figure out who'd grabbed Carly and where they might've taken her.

Knocking on the door, Baker got no answer, but it didn't take him much to get inside the apartment. Theo wasn't there, which wasn't exactly unusual. The man might have a safe place to lay his head now, but old habits were hard to break, more so for Theo. The mentally challenged man needed routine, and more often than not he went back to his old stomping grounds and slept on the streets.

Lexie wouldn't be happy to know what Theo was doing, and Baker didn't plan to tell her. She and Theo were close, and she'd done all she could to keep him safe. That was enough.

Baker planned to shower and lie down for thirty minutes to clear his head before he headed back out. He *had* to find Carly. He couldn't fail.

He forced himself to go back over everything he'd learned about Shawn Keyes's friends. He was still leaning toward Jeremiah being the culprit. But he couldn't discount Luke. He was an asshole, just like his father had been, and he'd definitely worshipped his dad.

Baker had just stepped out of the small shower and gotten

dressed when the door opened. Theo had returned—and he looked extremely agitated. The second he saw Baker, his eyes widened and he yelled, "Baker!"

"What's wrong, buddy?" he asked.

"Bad things are happening!"

Baker froze. It wasn't so much what Theo said, but the emotion behind his words that made him realize this wasn't something in Theo's head. "Take a breath," Baker ordered. "That's it. Another. Good. Come here and sit down and tell me where you've been, and what's going on."

Theo nodded and did as Baker ordered. He shuffled over to the couch. His clothes were dirty and his hair needed a good washing, but now wasn't the time to gently chide the man for sleeping on the streets again. Baker frequently told him it wasn't safe, but Theo did what he wanted. He was a grown-ass man, even if he didn't have the same mental capabilities as others his age.

"First, are you all right?" Baker asked.

Theo nodded.

"Good. Now tell me what has you so upset."

"I went downtown," Theo said. "I heard Lexie talking about the festival. I like festivals. There's lots of booths and food."

Baker nodded.

"I took the bus. I didn't walk," he said a little defensively.

Baker knew Lexie had gotten on him about walking all the way downtown. It took almost the entire day, and she hated to think of him going so far on foot. She'd gotten him a bus pass so he could go back and forth between downtown and Barbers Point safely.

"Okay, buddy. No problem."

"I ate some food, talked to some friends. Then got tired,"

Theo said. "I wanted to take a nap, but all my usual places were too crowded."

His agitation increased again, and Baker reached out and grasped Theo's hand. "What did you do? Did you find a good place to sleep?"

Theo shook his head. "No. The garages were all too busy. Too many people. It was loud and I couldn't find a good place. I had to come back here on the bus and it was crowded. A man started yelling at me. I didn't like him. So I got off at the next stop and I got lost. I couldn't find the right bus to bring me back. I had to walk. I'm tired and I don't like it. And the girls are upset and Carly's missing!"

Theo was almost crying by the time he finished speaking. Baker hated that he was so upset, but he honestly didn't have a lot of time to calm Theo.

"I'm sorry, buddy. It sounds like you haven't had a good day."

Theo shook his head vigorously. "No. Not good day. Too many people and cars. Everywhere. On sidewalks, on the bus, in the parking garage."

With another mention of garages...Baker was anxious to try Alani again. Jag had called Duke's immediately after discovering Carly was missing, because she'd said she was doing a favor for her boss. But the manager had already left the restaurant and no one could get a hold of her. He needed to talk to the woman. She was the only one who could give them a starting point to find Carly.

He pulled out a twenty-dollar bill and handed it to Theo. "Why don't you head down the street to that noodle place and get yourself an extra-large order?" he suggested.

And just like that, Theo's bad mood seemed to evaporate. "Yeah! I like noodles!"

Without another word, he headed for the door.

Baker pulled his phone out of his pocket. He dialed Alani's personal cell phone.

For the first time since Carly's disappearance, she picked up.

She was surprised to hear from him—and even more shocked to learn that Carly was missing. "Missing? Holy crap! I'm so sorry! I was at the gym and had my phone turned off so I wouldn't be interrupted in the middle of my workout. I just turned it back on and was about to call Jag after seeing his missed calls. Carly was nice enough to do me a huge favor so the health inspector wouldn't find Duke's in violation. Too much food was ordered, and she picked it up at Duke's and was going to take it to Food For All," she told him.

"Which one? The downtown one or out here in Barbers Point?" he bit out.

"Downtown."

Baker's mind was racing. "Okay, thanks. If you hear from her, will you let Jag know?"

"Of course."

"Thanks." Baker clicked off the connection and immediately dialed Food For All's downtown location. He hung up a few minutes later...after learning that, while they'd been expecting Carly, she'd never arrived with the food.

Baker surmised that she must've been grabbed somewhere between Waikiki and downtown. It was possible someone had run her car off the road, but he didn't think so. There would be witnesses if that happened. And after hearing Theo say how crowded downtown was with the festival going on, how many people and cars there were, whoever grabbed her could have easily used the chaos to go unnoticed.

Setting up his laptop and frantically clicking the keyboard,

Baker hacked into the security cameras downtown, estimating the time Carly might have been there based on when Alani said she'd stopped at Duke's. He knew he should call Jag, but he wanted to have something to tell the man when he did, not give him any false hopes.

It took a while—way too long for Baker's peace of mind—but eventually he found what he was looking for. In one of the parking garages, he saw Carly's vehicle arrive. She had to drive around for quite a while to find an empty space.

But it was the vehicle behind hers that had his full attention.

She'd had to go all the way to the top floor. The footage was a bit grainy, but Baker clearly saw what happened. A man got out of the car that had been following Carly's. They had a short conversation. When Carly turned toward the trunk of her car, the man hit her. Baker didn't know if she was knocked out or just disoriented, but the man carried her to his car and shoved her in the trunk.

It was a shit piece of luck that, even though downtown was crowded, no one had been in the garage with them when he'd made his move.

While the footage wasn't the best, Baker easily recognized the man who'd kidnapped Carly. He knew everything about every single one of Keyes's friends.

Gideon Sparks drove a tan Cadillac which matched the vehicle that had been following Carly, and there was no doubt—with his pot belly and familiar uniform—that it had been Sparks who'd snatched her.

Determination rose within Baker. The man was better than he'd given him credit for. He hadn't even been near the top of Baker's suspect list. He was a loner, didn't have a lot of friends, and as far as Baker knew, didn't have a boat. But there were

many ways to get access, and obviously he and Carly's ex had done so for their nefarious plot that had gone so wrong.

Baker didn't know what the motive was for Sparks, but it didn't matter. The man had Carly—and he needed to let Jag and the others know what happened. The more eyes they had on the lookout for Gideon Sparks and his car, the better.

Jag was more hyped up than he'd ever been during a mission. He couldn't sit still. He couldn't do anything but worry about Carly. She could literally be anywhere. There were thousands upon thousands of acres of wilderness on the island where she could be dumped, miles and miles of water. And now it was nighttime.

He shivered at the negative thought of her lying somewhere, in the dark, hurt...or worse.

"She's alive, she has to be," he whispered in an agonized tone. His team was scrambling to find any scrap of information that could help them track her last steps. Slate was arguing with her cell phone provider, trying to convince them to tell him the last location where her phone pinged, to no avail. Alani still hadn't answered the last time they called, Pid was trying to get access to traffic cameras, and the other guys were also on their phones, doing what they could to try to get a hold of Shawn's friends to verify their whereabouts.

It all felt like too little, too late.

When Jag's phone rang, he looked down, praying it would be Carly calling to tell him she was fine. That she'd gotten a flat tire and had no cell reception somewhere. It was almost crushing to see Baker's name on his screen.

"Jag."

"Gideon Sparks," he said without preamble.

It took a moment for Jag's brain to catch up with what his friend was saying. "What?"

"Gideon snatched her from a parking garage downtown. I finally reached Alani—her phone was off—and she explained the favor. Took a while, but I found her car on security cameras and watched Sparks knock her out and put her in his trunk."

Jag gestured frantically to his teammates. "Fuck. What was the favor?"

"She was bringing food from Duke's to the downtown Food For All. Even with all the people being around for the festival, Sparks grabbed her in a parking garage. No one else was around."

"Shit! Has anyone talked to Sparks today?" Jag asked his teammates.

They all shook their heads.

"What's going on?" Mustang asked. "Is it him?"

"Baker saw him take Carly on security feeds," Jag said. "Baker's headed downtown to where her car is located."

"Tell him we're splitting up. You, me, and Aleck will go to Sparks's place. Pid will call Detective Lee. Midas and Slate will meet Baker at the parking garage. The zoo is closed right now, but if we don't find Sparks, we'll check in with his coworkers first thing in the morning when they open. And if we *do* find Sparks...we'll take him to Slate's house for a chat." Mustang's tone was deadly and determined.

It was a risk to basically kidnap a man so they could interrogate him, but everyone was done fucking around. They'd get Sparks to tell them exactly what he did with Carly, by any means necessary, then they'd get her back.

"I heard him," Baker said in Jag's ear. "We need Sparks alive if Carly isn't with him," he warned.

Jag nodded even as bile rose in his throat. "I know." Too much time had passed. Carly had been snatched hours ago. When Carly had needed him most, he'd been clueless and sitting in a fucking meeting, his phone turned off. And now she was out there somewhere, with someone determined to do her harm. And on top of everything, it was fucking raining like a bitch again, after a brief break in the storm.

"Keep me updated," Baker ordered.

"Will do. Thanks." Jag owed the man. Again.

"Later," Baker said, ending the connection.

Jag quickly told his teammates what Baker had said and he felt better at seeing the looks of determination on their faces. He was relieved Mustang was sending him to Sparks's house. If Carly was found, hurt—or worse—he needed to be there.

* * *

Jag was more than frustrated.

He was in agony.

Last night, he'd been so sure they were on the verge of finding Carly. They knew who had taken her, what Sparks's car looked like, and everyone was looking for her.

And yet here it was, almost ten o'clock the next morning, roughly twenty-four hours after she'd gone missing...and they were no closer to finding Carly *or* Gideon Sparks than they'd been last night.

Jag hadn't slept. Neither had any of his friends. Even the women had pulled an all-nighter at Kenna's condo, worrying and calling anyone they could think of to spread the word about their missing friend.

The Honolulu Zoo was opening in minutes, and he, Aleck,

and Mustang were on their way. Jag was more than ready to talk to some of Sparks's coworkers to see if they could get any more insight on the man. Baker had spent the night digging deep into the bowels of the Internet for every scrap of information about Sparks he could find.

What he'd discovered hadn't made them feel any better. There had been a restraining order taken out on Gideon several years ago, but his last name was misspelled, which was why no one had found it before now. A nineteen-year-old girl, who'd grown up in foster care—and who looked eerily like Carly...blonde hair the same length, blue eyes—had requested the order after dating Gideon for a few months, then breaking it off. The order had claimed he was stalking her since their breakup, and she was scared for her life.

The restraining order even mentioned Shawn by name. The woman had also been scared of Gideon's friend, of how much influence he had over her ex-boyfriend.

Baker also found out that Sparks and Keyes had spent a lot of time together in the weeks before Shawn died. Their phones had pinged in the same places almost every night, credit card receipts proved they'd eaten and drank at the same bars.

Baker had apologized to Jag over and over, but Jag didn't blame the man for not finding the missing pieces before now. Sparks had hidden his tracks amazingly well. He was either extremely smart or very lucky.

But with every minute that passed, Jag's anxiety rose. It had been too long since Sparks had grabbed Carly. It wasn't likely she was still alive—and the thought made Jag want to throw up and fucking kill Sparks with his bare hands. The thought of him touching Carly was repugnant.

When Mustang pulled into the parking lot for the zoo, it was

instantly apparent that something was going on. There were two ambulances and almost a dozen police cars in the lot, parked haphazardly.

Mustang had barely stopped his truck before Aleck and Jag jumped out and were running toward the entrance.

An officer stopped them and wouldn't let them through the gates. Jag was about to lose his shit, and probably do something that would jeopardize his career at the same time, when Mustang held out his phone to the officer.

"Take it. It's a Detective Makanui Lee. He wants to talk to you."

The policeman looked confused, but thankfully took the phone from Mustang.

Jag barely held on to his composure.

After just seconds, the officer handed the phone back to Mustang and nodded, stepping back. "He authorizes you to go in, but says to stay out of the way," he warned. "Don't get involved in the current investigation."

Jag still didn't know what the fuck was going on, but he didn't hang around to ask. All he cared about was getting to Sparks. He ran inside and headed for the lion habitat. It didn't escape Jag's notice, however, that it was the same direction where all the commotion seemed to be coming from.

He stopped short at the yellow police tape that had been strung outside the tall fences surrounding the lion enclosure. Aleck stopped an EMT who was headed back toward the parking lot with an empty gurney. "What's going on?"

"Someone went insane and entered the enclosure. The lions apparently didn't like someone encroaching on their space and... well, you can imagine what they did."

Jag's breath hitched in his throat. Not Carly. God, not the woman he loved.

"Is she alive?" Mustang asked, obviously on the same wavelength.

"It was a zoo employee, could tell by what was left of the uniform. Accessed the premises with his own key and security code, before opening hours. And no, he's definitely *not* alive," the EMT said with a shudder. "We could barely even tell it *was* a 'he.' Those lions were pissed way the hell off for some reason. I don't know if they were provoked before he went in or what. Cops have already requisitioned the security cameras, so they can provide more info. Anyway, I'm guessing things are gonna be shut down here for a while. The other zookeepers are still trying to wrangle the agitated cats away from what's left of their morning meal."

The man was super chatty, which Jag was thankful for. This obviously wasn't a normal call for him, and he was probably still trying to deal with what he'd seen.

The EMT walked away, and Mustang held up a hand. "We don't know that it was Sparks."

"Of course it was," Jag said, his shoulders slumping. "Who else would it be?"

"But why?" Aleck interjected. "There has to be a reason he'd decide to kill himself. He was pretty fucking smart. He fooled Baker, the cops...all of us. Why would be take Carly, do whatever he did with her, then kill himself? He certainly wasn't feeling guilty about what he did."

A spark of hope flared within Jag. "The only reason I can think of for Sparks offing himself...is if he fucked up and she somehow got away."

Mustang nodded. "I agree."

"She's alive," Jag whispered, scared to say the words too loudly. "He fucked up, she got away, and he knew he was going to get caught."

"And didn't want to spend his life behind bars. Decided to go out his own way," Aleck speculated with a nod.

"Probably trying to be more dramatic than Keyes," Mustang said with disgust.

"Well, I'd say he accomplished that," Aleck returned dryly.

"But where's Carly?" Jag asked.

That was the million-dollar question. They might know who took her now, and from where, but not what Sparks had done with her.

Carly lifted her head and couldn't hold back the moan. She hurt. All over. Her head was still throbbing and every muscle in her body screamed in pain as she moved. Pushing herself up, she immediately regretted it as her hand felt as if it were on fire. Looking down, she saw a slice through her palm that definitely needed stitches.

She vaguely remembered cutting herself with the knife as she'd sawed at the rope holding the weight to her body. She still had the remnants of said rope hanging off her ankle. She couldn't tell what time it was, but the sun was almost fully over the horizon. She'd survived the night.

Smiling, despite the amount of pain she was in, Carly couldn't help but feel overwhelming relief. Gideon might've kidnapped her, but she'd outsmarted him and escaped. She was damn proud of herself. Of course, she wasn't out of danger, but

as long as she didn't have someone else determined to drug and drown her, she thought she was doing pretty well.

Sitting up and shifting on the uncomfortable lava rock under her ass, Carly assessed her situation. The island she'd found was nothing more than a jagged mass sticking up in the middle of the water. It was maybe fifty meters long and twenty meters wide. And it was covered in bird shit. There were no trees, no source of fresh water, nothing but birds staring at her accusingly, as if they were pissed she'd disturbed their peace.

The sky was overcast and it looked like it was going to start raining again at any second—but the best thing Carly had ever seen was the outline of a mountain in the distance. She wasn't that far from land. She assumed she was looking at Oahu, but couldn't be sure. If it had been a sunny day, there probably would've been lots of people on the water already, fishing, snorkeling, and simply enjoying a beautiful Hawaiian day. But because it was crappy out, Carly didn't see anyone.

She couldn't be bitter. The storm had saved her life last night. It seemed fitting that Gideon had lost her in a storm, when Shawn had failed at killing Kenna in the same kind of conditions.

Carly thought about getting back in the water and swimming to shore, but she knew distances could be deceiving, especially in this kind of weather. It could be one mile or ten, and while she might be able to make it a mile, there was no way she'd be able to go any considerable distance.

Her best bet was to stay put and wait for someone, anyone, to go by.

Then she had the awful thought that maybe Gideon was still out on the water looking for her. Wanting to make sure she'd

died. The last person she needed to flag down was the man who wanted her dead.

Shaking her head, Carly refused to believe she'd made it this far, only to be recaptured. Gideon was probably back at home, thrilled that he'd succeed in finishing what Shawn had started. The man was certifiably insane. She hadn't done anything to him —or Shawn, for that matter. There was absolutely no reason for Gideon to hate her so much.

But what was clear was that Shawn had been grooming him just as he'd once done to her. He obviously got off on manipulating people, and he'd taken Gideon under his wing and done the same, just in a different way. When she'd broken things off with Shawn, it had apparently angered Gideon just as much as it had her ex. They'd both taken her rejection as a personal affront. It didn't make a lot of sense, but nothing about Shawn or Gideon did.

Carly scooted farther up on the rock and did her best to hobble to a flatter part of the island. It was excruciating to walk on the sharp rocks in her bare feet, but the alternative was her death, so she sucked it up and did what she needed to. The amount of bird crap was almost impressive. The stench, though, left a lot to be desired.

She was extremely thirsty, in pain, stuck on Bird Shit Island... but she was alive. Things could be far worse.

Carly settled down on a spot that seemed to have a little less bird crap than the rocks around it and hugged her knees to her chest. She didn't care how long she had to sit here, she wasn't going to die. No way. Not after everything she'd been through.

Kenna and the rest of the women were probably completely freaked out. Then her thoughts turned to Jag...and she almost

cried. He was probably going out of his mind with worry. He'd move heaven and earth to find her. He and his team. She had no doubt they'd figure out what happened. She imagined their apartment being a kind of central hub for the search. The guys would all be stone-faced, concentrating on their phones and computers.

They'd track her movements. Alani would tell them that she'd been at Duke's and had picked up the produce to bring to Food For All. They'd figure out that she never did drop off the food, and they'd find her car in the parking garage...but then what? How would they know Gideon was the one who took her? And how would they know he took her out on a boat?

Panic nearly overwhelmed her, but Carly shook her head. No, she had to stay positive. Jag was smart. One of the smartest men she knew. He and his teammates would find her. She just had to be patient.

Her mind strayed to what had happened to Jag when he was a kid. He must have been so terrified and confused every time his babysitter came over. But he ultimately didn't give up. He'd been so strong, and Carly wanted to be just like him. Make him proud of her. And in order to do that, she had to stay alert so if a boat *did* go by, she could get their attention and get back to Jag.

As the minutes passed, it got harder and harder to be patient, to stay positive.

Trying to swim to shore felt more and more like the best option. The last thing she wanted to do was spend another night on this rock. Not that she remembered the first night, but still.

Just when she'd decided that she couldn't wait anymore, that she was going to have to rescue herself and swim to Oahu, Carly heard something.

At first, she thought she was hallucinating. That it was just wishful thinking that had her hearing a motor.

Then she nearly panicked again. What if it was Gideon coming back? She was a sitting duck, and she knew without a doubt he wouldn't mess around with a tranquilizer dart this time. He'd probably choke the life out of her before taking her back out to sea and making sure she sank to the bottom.

Through the misty morning, even as she tried to calm herself, Carly saw something orange and white cutting through the waves. It wasn't coming toward her—which made her panic for an altogether different reason.

The Coast Guard boat was slowly moving through the water parallel to the island, as if it was looking for something...or someone? Carly barely dared to hope that maybe they were looking for her. Maybe they were just on a routine check of the waters around the island. But in the end, it didn't matter what they were doing, as long as they found her.

Carly stood up, barely able to stay on her feet, and began waving her arms over her head and screaming as loud as she could. It was unlikely anyone would be able to hear her over the motor, the sound of waves against the rubber-hulled boat, but if there was even a one-percent chance they'd notice, she'd yell until she was hoarse if that was what it took.

For a terrifying moment, she thought the boat was going to keep on going. That whoever was onboard hadn't seen or heard her.

Then, miraculously, the clouds parted momentarily—and sunlight shone on the rock. As if a flashlight was pointing straight down on the island where she'd been marooned.

The Coast Guard boat made a sudden turn...in her direction. Carly didn't stop waving her arms and shouting, not until a loud air horn sounded from the boat. She swayed on her feet as the boat came closer and closer.

They'd seen her. Thank God!

Carly cried without any tears falling. She was too dehydrated. But she also couldn't help smiling. She'd done it. She'd beat Gideon *and* Shawn. She wasn't the pathetic bitch they thought she was. She might be younger, but that didn't mean she was an idiot. Carly was proud of herself.

She dreaded what was sure to come when she got home. There would be interviews with the detective, probably reporters desperate to hear her story; she'd have to face Gideon in court, and she had a feeling she might relapse when it came to trying to gain back her independence.

But with Jag at her side, she could do anything.

Jag. God, she couldn't stop thinking about how worried he had to be.

With that thought fresh in her mind, the first thing she said when a young man wearing an orange life jacket, blue hat, shirt, pants, and waterproof boots climbed out of the boat and came toward her was, "Call Jag!"

"Carly? Carly Stewart?" the man asked as he gently gripped her arm.

She nodded. "Please! I need to call Jag!"

"We'll get a hold of whoever you want once we get you onboard. Can you walk?"

"Yes," Carly said, but when she tried to take a step, her body refused to cooperate. Her knees buckled and she would've gone down hard if the Coastie hadn't caught her.

"I've got you," he said.

The man and two of his boatmates got her off Bird Shit Island and onto their boat. She was placed on a bench and given a warm blanket. Then someone placed a bottle of water in one of her hands and a phone in the other.

Carly was more relieved than she could say that Jag had made her memorize his number. He'd said there might come a time when she needed to dial it rather than just click on his contact. And he was right. Of course.

With her fingers shaking, she pushed the buttons to his number.

"Jag. Who is this?"

She closed her eyes. She'd never heard a better sound in her life than Jag's voice.

"It's me," she eventually croaked. Her voice was shot from screaming to try to get the Coast Guard boat's attention.

"Carly? Holy shit! Is it really you?"

"Yeah."

"Where are you?! Are you okay? What happened?"

She wanted to answer all his questions, but her throat closed up and she was too overcome with emotion.

"Carly? *Talk to me!*" Jag shouted.

All Carly could do was hold the phone out to the young man who'd come onto the island to get her. She heard him talking to Jag, but she suddenly couldn't keep her eyes open any longer. She was done. Emotionally. Physically. Mentally. All of it. But she'd made sure that Jag knew she was alive, so he wouldn't continue to worry.

Apparently, that was all she needed to do before her body finally gave out and she gave in to the unconsciousness slowly overtaking her.

CHAPTER TWENTY-THREE

Jag sat next to Carly on his couch but couldn't manage to make himself let go of her. From the second he'd heard her voice, he'd been desperate to get to her. To see for himself that she was all right. He'd arrived at the hospital even before the Coast Guard helicopter had landed with Carly.

Mustang had told the nurses that Jag was Carly's fiancé, and they'd let him go into her room after the ER doctors examined her.

She'd been exhausted. She had a bandage on her hand, a bruise on her face, and scrapes on her arms and knees. Jag had never seen anything as beautiful as Carly in that moment.

It had taken a few hours before they'd been allowed to leave. The doctors wanted to keep her at least one night, but Carly insisted on signing herself out.

Mustang had driven them home, and after a short and emotional visit with all their friends, they were finally alone. He

loved their concern and happiness over Carly's return, but he needed to have her to himself for a while.

Jag stood, then leaned over and gently picked her up. She didn't protest, simply snuggled into him as he carried her into their bedroom. He lay her on the bed and sat next to her, taking a deep breath.

"I'm okay," Carly said softly.

Jag swallowed hard. "I need to see for myself. May I?" he asked, reaching for the buttons at the front of the shirt she was wearing. She'd changed out of the scrubs she'd been given at the hospital as soon as she got home.

Carly nodded, and Jag quickly and efficiently stripped her out of his oversized button-down. He felt no physical desire at the moment; his fear was still too raw. He just needed to check her over from head to toe.

She lay quietly as he examined her. There were bruises on her torso and her arms were scraped, most likely from the lava rock on the island she swam to. He couldn't see the wound on her palm, since it was bandaged, but he'd seen it at the hospital. It looked fairly gnarly, but was a clean cut and would heal fine. His eyes continued down her body, noting the scrapes on her knees, cringing at her swollen feet and the gouges on the tender soles, again from walking on the sharp lava rocks.

His gaze went back up her body and finally rested on her face. The doctor had to shave a bit of hair at the back of her head, so he could clean and put in a few stitches from where Sparks had struck her. She also had a bruise on her cheekbone, from where she'd said Gideon punched her to knock her out.

She was truly lucky to be alive after being bashed over the head with the expensive, heavy flashlight that had been found in Sparks's car, being grazed by a tranquilizer dart made for lions,

almost sinking to the bottom of the ocean, and then spending the night out in the elements.

But she *was* alive.

Jag could see the emotion in her eyes, and it made him want to cry. He'd come way too close to losing her. But his Carly was tough. She hadn't survived because of anything he'd done. No, she'd done it all on her own. She'd saved her own damn self—and he couldn't be prouder.

"Come here," Carly said, holding out her arms.

Jag took off his shirt before he lay down next to her. He pulled her into his arms and reached down and eased the comforter up and over them. After a moment, he realized that he was shaking...and Carly was smoothing a hand over his chest and murmuring gently.

"It's okay. I'm here," she said.

God. This woman.

"You're amazing," he whispered.

She shook her head. "No, I think I'm just stubborn."

Jag barked a quiet laugh. "I'm sorry—" he started, but Carly shook her head and went up on one elbow.

"No, don't do that."

"I have to," he said. "You were taken right out from under my nose. We had no idea where you were. Detective Lee was the one who contacted the Coast Guard and asked them to be on alert, just in case. We were going to make Sparks tell us where you were, but he killed himself. We had nothing to go on. You could've been *anywhere*."

"You would've found me," Carly said.

Jag couldn't believe she still had just as much confidence in him as she had before getting snatched. All he could do was press his lips together and shake his head.

"Jag, seriously, the only reason I survived was because of you. First of all, I knew you'd never rest until you found me. Second, I thought about what you went through as a child, and how strong you were, and knew if I could have a fraction of your strength, I'd be okay. Third, everything you ever taught me about personal safety ran through my head. If I just sat there and let Gideon carry out his plans, I would've been dead for sure. So, I ran through my options and decided I'd rather take my chances with the sea.

"Fourth, I remembered all the stories you told me about Hell Week and how the only thing that kept you going was a positive attitude. Fourth...wait...fifth? I lost count. Anyway, I had that knife in my pocket that *you* insisted I carry with me. I have to admit, I thought it was overkill at first, but I'll never doubt you again. It saved me. I would've run out of air if I couldn't cut off the weight Gideon tied to me.

"I also fucked up in a lot of ways. I never should've let Gideon get close to me in that parking garage. I let down my guard because he seemed so...unassuming. He was being nice, and saying the right things, and I trusted him when I shouldn't have. I took my eyes off him for a split second and that was all the chance he needed.

"Please...I can't deal with you feeling guilty because you didn't physically show up to get me off that island. Or because you couldn't make Gideon tell you where I was. You might not have been there in person, but every minute of the time I was with Gideon—well, when I was conscious, that is—you *were* with me. Without you, I would've been a basket case in the bottom of that boat, and he would've succeeded in finishing Shawn's plan. You gave me the strength to fight back. To not give up."

Jag closed his eyes and did his best to get a handle on his emotions. He shouldn't be surprised how well she was taking what had happened. That she didn't blame him, the detective, or his SEAL team. They'd all let her down, and yet by some miracle, she still didn't blame them.

His eyes opened, and he pulled her against him once more. She went willingly and snuggled close.

"Marry me," he whispered.

"Of course," she whispered back.

Jag wanted to laugh. She didn't sound surprised, didn't get all giddy and excited. She accepted his proposal calmly, as if it was a foregone conclusion that he'd ask and she'd say yes.

"I don't have a ring, but I'll get one," he told her.

"Don't care," was her response.

"We can have any kind of wedding you want."

"Duke's," she said without lifting her head from his shoulder. "I want to get married on the beach at Duke's. Anyone who's there for a meal can attend. Hell, anyone on the beach can come too. I want hula pie for our cake, and I want Paulo to officiate. He's already got the license and everything, I heard him talking about it once. He'll be hilarious...and that's what I want. For everyone to laugh and have a good time."

"Done," Jag said.

"I want to wipe out any lingering bad energy from that beach after what Shawn did. I want to rub it in his face, wherever he is, that he didn't win. In fact, that he lost spectacularly. He didn't break me. Didn't break Kenna. Instead, because of what he did, he brought me to *you*, and now I'm happier than I can ever imagine being."

God, Jag loved this woman.

"Can I ask something?"

"Of course. Anything," Jag said.

"Will you tell me about Gideon? I know you must've talked to Detective Lee. Will you tell me what you found out about everything he did? How he managed to trick everyone?"

Jag didn't want to. He wanted to lie there and never think of that fucking asshole ever again, but Carly deserved to have her questions answered.

"The cops haven't found a suicide note or anything yet. I'm guessing he didn't leave one. Based on the security footage, he provoked the lions, teasing them with their morning meal, not giving it to them. They were extremely agitated when he walked into that enclosure. It didn't help that he was holding the raw meat they received in the mornings. He didn't die fast." Jag was extremely happy when he heard that last bit from the police.

"I have to admit that I feel a little bitter, knowing I won't get to face him. Don't get to show him that he didn't break me. But he got what he deserved."

Jag wasn't so sure about that, but he let it go. "Apparently he borrowed the boat from one of his coworkers at the zoo. The man thought Sparks was into fishing, never thought twice about letting him take the boat out whenever he wanted. It wasn't moored at a marina or anything, which was why Baker couldn't find security video of him at any marinas. It was simply tied up in a private inlet near the man's house, and Sparks could come and go without anyone seeing him or being suspicious.

"A woman came forward after she saw the news about what happened. She was the one who got the restraining order against him. She was very young at the time, on the verge of losing her apartment and flat broke. Sparks played on that, most likely with Keyes's encouragement. He helped her out, she let down her guard. Then he changed, began to manipulate her. Belittle her."

"Like Shawn did to me," Carly said quietly.

"Yeah. We think Shawn got some kind of sick thrill out of teaching a socially awkward loner like Gideon how to fuck with women's heads. We can only speculate at this point, but I assume Gideon was more than willing to help with the plan, to thank Keyes for his *mentoring*. Especially after you took out the restraining order, just like the girl he'd dated. And when Shawn died...he probably just cracked. Couldn't handle it. All his dreams of having a woman of his own had gone down the drain because he needed Shawn to help him manipulate others. You were the only person he could blame."

Jag stopped speaking and held his breath as he waited for Carly's reaction.

"That's...so sad," she said after a moment.

It *was* sad. Pathetic, tragic, and fucked-up, but sad.

"And the island I managed to wash up on really *is* called Bird Shit Island?" she asked.

"Apparently. Its real name is Mōkōlea Rock. But locals call it Bird Shit Island because, well...you know."

Carly snorted. "I know." Then she tentatively asked, "So...it's really over?"

Jag's arms tightened, and he had to force himself to relax. "It's over," he reassured her.

He felt her sigh in relief against him, her warm breath caressing his neck.

"Okay."

"Okay?" Jag asked, wanting to make sure she wasn't just humoring him.

"Yeah. I want to put Shawn, and Gideon, and everything about that damn relationship behind me. I want to move on. To marry you, to get back to the person I was before all this

happened. I made some mistakes, but I didn't deserve what happened to me."

"No, you didn't," Jag agreed.

She tilted her head back. "Are you and the others going to be headed out on a mission soon?"

Jag frowned in confusion. "No, why?"

"Because you were in all those meetings. Something major was happening, and I just figured you'd be leaving soon. You told me that's how it works, that sometimes you guys spend hours and hours going over intel, then you'd be deployed."

Jag nodded. It was hard to believe that forty-eight hours previously, the only thing on his mind was the kidnapped boys in Nigeria. That seemed like a lifetime ago. "I can never guarantee we won't be sent out at a moment's notice, but the thing we were researching was resolved without us having to lend our assistance."

Carly sagged against him. Jag hadn't realized how worried she was about him leaving until right that moment.

"Good."

Jag brought a hand up and smoothed it gently over her head. "I love you," he said softly. "I swear I lost ten years off my life when I realized you hadn't texted to let me know you got home safely."

"I'm sorry," she said.

"No," Jag told her with a shake of his head. "Don't be sorry. What happened wasn't your fault. It was that asshole's."

"We need to watch that movie. Soon," Carly said.

Jag chuckled lightly and nodded. "Okay."

"Is Baker okay?" she asked after a minute.

Jag sighed. "I don't know."

"He didn't do anything wrong. I know for a fact he worked his ass off to find me."

"He did," Jag agreed. "But he doesn't like to fail."

"Oh, good Lord, he didn't fail," Carly protested. "He was the one who found that footage of Gideon hitting me and stuffing me in his trunk!"

"He doesn't see it that way."

"I'm gonna talk to him," she said firmly. Then her voice softened, and she added, "But not right now. I'm comfortable."

Jag nodded against her. He'd been afraid he'd never have this again. Never be able to hold her. Sparks could have terrorized her much more than he had. Could've assaulted her. The last thing he ever wanted was for her to go through what *he* did. The helplessness, the degradation, the pain. What had happened to Carly was bad enough. If Sparks had touched her, Jag knew neither of them would be dealing with what happened as calmly as they were right now.

"I'm looking forward to the barbeque at Kenna and Aleck's place this weekend."

Jag smiled. That was such a...normal topic of conversation. Carly had just gotten out of the hospital, she was probably still in a good deal of pain, and yet she was putting what happened behind her. She was fucking amazing.

"Me too."

"Elodie said she was going to go all out," Carly said.

Jag could feel her smile against him. "Which means we're all gonna eat extremely well."

"I can't wait to taste those burgers the guys are always talking about."

"She's got a magic touch. I think I'm envious of Mustang."

"Hey," Carly protested, poking him in the stomach. "I can cook."

"Of course you can," Jag said immediately, knowing better than to contradict his woman...not if he wanted her to ever cook again in the future.

"But not like she can," Carly added. "Jag?"

"Yeah, angel?"

"I love you. So much. And I'm not scared of it. I thought I'd be wary of falling in love for a long time, after everything that happened, but I know without a doubt that this is where I'm meant to be. I had to experience everything I did with Shawn, and even with Gideon, so I could end up right here. I'd go through it all over again if it meant being with you."

Jag was nearly overwhelmed with emotion. But he under-stood what she meant. He wouldn't change anything about his own life if it meant being with Carly. It was a startling thought. For so much of his adulthood, he'd been so bitter about what he'd gone through. But now? He understood that he'd had the experiences he did in order to be the man Carly needed. "I love you," he managed to whisper.

Carly nodded against him and let out a long breath. "I think I could sleep for days," she murmured.

"Me too." Jag felt exhaustion pulling at him. He'd been awake for more than thirty-five hours. The adrenaline spiking through his veins had helped him stay on his feet, but now with his woman safe and sound in his arms, Sparks dead, and knowing Carly would marry him, he felt himself crashing.

The last thing Jag remembered was inhaling deeply and smelling Carly's sweet cherry blossom scent. She was finally free of her past, and all that lie ahead of them was a beautiful future.

* * *

Carly didn't know what woke her up later, but when she looked at the clock, she saw that it was only three in the morning. She'd slept deep and hard, safe in her man's arms, but now her conscience nagged at her. She knew she could close her eyes and go back to sleep easily, but there was something she needed to do.

Surprised when she was able to slip out of Jag's arms without waking him, Carly tiptoed to the door and headed into the living room. It was obvious Jag had suffered while she was missing, and she vowed to do whatever she could in the future to help him get over what had happened.

Her phone was sitting on the kitchen counter, where Jag had left it when they'd gotten home. His teammates had retrieved it from her car after locating it in that parking garage. She picked up the cell and saw she had several text messages from her friends. They were all expressing their gratitude and happiness that she was home. Even Monica had sent a short text letting her know how relieved she was that she was all right, which meant the world to Carly, because she knew the other woman wasn't exactly a "texter."

Kenna had also started a group text about what everyone should bring to the barbeque that weekend and was being her usual bossy, organized self.

Carly would respond to all her friends later, but first she had more important things to do. She didn't even hesitate to click on the name in her contact list. It was late, or early, but she instinctively knew it wouldn't matter.

"You all right, Carly?" Baker said quietly when he answered after only one ring. "Where are you?"

"I'm fine," she said softly, sinking down onto the couch. "I'm home."

"Then why are you calling?" Baker asked.

"Where are *you?*" she countered.

He sighed. "I'm sitting on the beach up here at the North Shore."

"If you're sitting there obsessing about what you think you should've done differently to find Gideon or to prevent what happened, I'm gonna be pissed," she told him.

But he didn't laugh. "It was my fault, Carly."

"That's such bullshit," she insisted. "Do you control what everyone does or says these days? Because I didn't get the memo."

Baker was silent on the other end of the line, so Carly continued.

"I know everyone is kind of scared of you, and that you're this big bad former SEAL who everyone relies on when shit hits the fan, but you're human, Baker. You eat, drink, and shit the same way we all do...unless you don't and no one's told me...but that's neither here nor there. The only people to blame for what happened are Shawn and Gideon. No one else. You aren't Superman. You couldn't have prevented what happened."

"I should've figured out that Gideon was the accomplice," he said quietly, the agony easy to hear in his voice.

"How? Osmosis? The guy was sneaky and smart. It's likely he tailed Jag and me for months, and we had no clue. And there was no way you could've interviewed every single one of his coworkers and people he saw on a regular basis to find out about the boat he borrowed. If he was the only suspect, then maybe you could've seen behind the bullshit façade he showed the world, but he wasn't. There were plenty of other people you

were looking into. I'm not good at math, but if there were a hundred friends and acquaintances you had to investigate for each of the people who were close to Shawn, it would've taken you forever."

Baker grunted. Carly was taking that as a good sign.

"You want to know why I'm up right now?"

"Yes," Baker said immediately. "You should be asleep. Is your head hurting?"

"Not my head. My heart," Carly told him. "I just *knew* my friend was blaming himself, and there's no need. As I told Jag earlier tonight, I would go through the same thing all over again if it meant I ended up exactly where I am right now. Let it go, Baker. Please. No one thinks less of you because you didn't figure out Gideon was Shawn's accomplice before he took me. Not me. Not Jag. Not anyone. Cut yourself some slack. If you don't, I'm gonna continue to lose sleep, and I'll probably get a complex and be paranoid and won't be able to function. I'll lose my job and become a burden on society."

Carly was laying it on as thick as she could, and to her relief, she finally heard Baker chuckle.

"Right, wouldn't want that."

"I'm serious. Get over yourself. That's an order."

"Yes, ma'am. Now how about you march your ass back to bed and rest? I'm guessing your head is throbbing and it probably wouldn't hurt if you took another pain pill."

Carly laughed. "I will, if you march *your* ass back to your own bed and get some sleep. It's not safe on the beach this time of night...or morning."

Baker chuckled again. "Right. I'm a surfer dude. The beach is my second home."

"Whatever. Then go back to your first home and sleep," Carly told him.

"I will. Carly..."

"Yeah?"

"Thanks."

"You're welcome."

"Later." Baker hung up without another word.

Carly stood to do just as he suggested, to snuggle back in bed with Jag, but jolted in surprise when she saw him leaning against the wall just inside the hallway that led to the bedroom.

"You scared me," she said.

"Baker?" Jag asked, nodding to the phone she'd just put down on the coffee table.

Carly nodded.

"He good?"

She shrugged. "I don't know. I hope so."

"He's good," Jag said firmly, then held out his hand.

She walked toward him and took it, sighing in contentment when Jag pulled her against him.

"How'd I get so lucky?" he murmured into her hair. But he didn't give her a chance to answer his question. He turned her and hugged her against his side and walked them back into the bedroom. He got her settled under the covers once more, then went into the bathroom. He came back out with a pill in his hand and a glass of water.

Carly wasn't surprised he was on the same wavelength as Baker when it came to the meds. She took it without complaint, and when Jag got back into bed, she curled against him once more.

"Love you," she told him.

"I'd be upset that you snuck out of our bed to call another

man, but it's one of the things I love so much about you. That you constantly think and worry about others. I love you, angel."

Carly smiled. She thought she'd left the room without waking him, but she should've known better. She sighed in contentment and closed her eyes...and was asleep again in less than a minute.

EPILOGUE

Jag watched Carly as she walked along the beach and laughed with Kenna and Lexie. The barbeque was just what they'd all needed. Carly felt much better, and her various cuts and bruises were already on their way toward healing. Amazingly, she seemed to be putting her horrible experience behind her much faster than the rest of the team.

They all struggled with the fact that they hadn't been able to prevent what happened, or even find her once she was taken. But Carly being Carly, she'd still thanked them profusely and so far showed no signs of PTSD. It was early days, but he was optimistic.

Jag turned his attention back to his phone and re-read the article for the tenth time...the one that Baker had emailed him a link to earlier that morning.

It wasn't long, merely a paragraph or so, from yesterday's edition of a small-town paper, but it held enough information to satisfy Jag.

. . .

Local resident Bridget Smith was arrested today after police received an anonymous tip that she was the owner of a popular child pornography website. When police executed a search warrant of her premises, they discovered a thirteen-year-old Brooksfield boy, Adam Beaufort, who'd disappeared from the area more than a year ago. He was being confined against his will in Ms. Smith's basement. He's been reunited with his family and charges are pending against Ms. Smith for kidnapping, rape, and several other allegations. The investigation into the disappearance of two other local boys is also pending, and sources say it's possible Smith was involved in both. We'll have the full story tomorrow on Adam's reunion with his family.

His woman would be thrilled to know that Baker had followed through with her request to make Bridget pay for what she'd done to him all those years ago. He could only guess the anonymous tip had come from the retired SEAL.

On one hand, he was relieved that Bridget was behind bars, but another part of him felt guilty that he hadn't spoken up years ago. Maybe if he had, countless other boys wouldn't have been victimized.

"Hey," Mustang said as he approached Jag.

Doing his best to put the past behind him once and for all, Jag turned toward his team leader. "Hey," he echoed.

"Is Carly as bummed as the other women that Baker didn't show up today?"

"A little," Jag said with a smile.

"This isn't his kind of thing," Mustang said.

"Nope. But Carly understands that."

"Yeah. Elodie too. They've kind of adopted him though."

They both chuckled. The thought of anyone 'adopting' Baker was humorous.

"Incoming," Mustang said under his breath.

Jag looked up and saw Carly heading his way. She stole his breath with how beautiful she looked. Her blonde hair was down and blowing in the breeze coming off the ocean, and the wide smile on her face was something he swore he'd never take for granted.

"Burgers will be ready in about five minutes," Mustang said before nodding at Carly and turning to head back to the grills, where his wife was making her popular hamburgers...and attempting to keep the other guys from "ruining" them.

"You look happy," Jag observed.

"I am. It's a gorgeous day. The sun is shining. I'm with my friends, and the man I love has his eyes on me. What else could I ask for?"

Jag hadn't planned on doing this right now, but he couldn't help himself. "How about a ring to go with that proposal I made the other night?" he asked, pulling a box out of his pocket.

Her eyes got wide as she stared at the box. Jag opened it to reveal the emerald-cut aquamarine surrounded by small diamonds, and reached for her hand.

Carly stood stock still as he slid the engagement ring down her finger.

"Breathe, angel," Jag said with a small chuckle.

That seemed to shake her out of the trance she was in. Carly squealed and threw her arms around his neck. He laughed and spun her in a circle before putting her on her feet once more.

"I'm not gonna want to wait," he warned. "So you should probably talk to Alani and figure out a time that'll work out."

"I will!" Carly said happily. "Oh, Jag. I love it!" She held her hand out, gazing adoringly at her ring.

"I love *you*."

Carly hugged him once more. "I love you too. So much!" Then she asked, "Can I show the others?"

He laughed. "Of course. Go. I know you're dying to."

Carly leaned up, kissing him hard and fast, then turned and jogged toward everyone standing around the grills, salivating over Elodie's burgers.

Jag stood back for a second, soaking in the moment. Seeing Carly happy and vibrant went a long way toward banishing all the negative thoughts consuming him just months ago. She was surrounded by the other women, and they were all hugging and congratulating her. Even his friends were smiling.

When Carly turned and gestured for him, Jag didn't hesitate. She was the best thing that ever happened to him, and he'd spend the rest of his life exactly where he wanted to be...right by her side.

* * *

Ashlyn was standing near the front doors to Aleck and Kenna's condo complex as she waited for the taxi Robert had called for her. Slate exited the building and seemed surprised to see her.

"Hey, what's up?" he asked.

Ashlyn gestured toward the long drive. "Waiting for my taxi."

"Why didn't you say something? I can take you home."

"It's fine. I didn't want to bother anyone." Ashlyn had taken a

taxi to the barbeque that afternoon because she wasn't sure if she was going to drink or not, and she didn't want to drive if she got tipsy.

"I'm taking you home," Slate said firmly. He turned around to go back inside, probably to tell Robert that he could cancel the taxi.

Ashlyn sighed at his high-handedness. But the more she hung out with Slate and the other guys on his team, the more she realized being overprotective was just a part of who they were. Slate couldn't help it. So there was no point in protesting.

He strolled back out, and Ashlyn couldn't help but admire—for the millionth time—how good-looking he was. She'd had her eye on him for quite a while, ever since she'd first met him in fact...despite all the protests otherwise to her friends. She wanted to think he was equally interested. But so far, neither of them had made a move to do anything about it.

Without a word, Slate took her elbow and steered her toward the parking lot and his Chevy Trailblazer. Her skin tingled where he touched her, and Ashlyn couldn't keep the smile off her face as he held the passenger door open for her.

"What's that smile for?" Slate asked.

"Nothing," she said immediately.

He stared at her for a moment as she buckled herself in, then shut the door.

The ride to her apartment was comfortable, and for once they weren't sniping at each other. When Slate pulled into her parking lot, he put the vehicle in park and turned off the engine, twisted toward her. "I was thinking..."

"Dangerous," Ashlyn teased.

Slate rolled his eyes. "You want to go out sometime?"

She stared at him in surprise for a long moment, waiting for him to start laughing or something. When he didn't, she asked, "Seriously?"

"Yeah. We hang out all the time already. I like you, even if I *do* think you take too many chances with your safety. And yes, I know you're careful when you deliver meals, and I know you're perfectly able to look after yourself, but I still worry because there are a lot of assholes out there. I thought that maybe you might...you know...want to hang out sometime. Without the others around."

Ashlyn grinned. "Yes."

It was Slate's turn to look surprised. "Really?"

"Yeah. But I don't want anything serious," she added quickly. "Don't think you can make up some excuse to move me into your house, or think that I'm going to fall madly in love. I wouldn't mind hanging out and...you know. But I'm not looking for a relationship anytime soon."

"'*You know*'?" Slate repeated.

Ashlyn grinned wider. "Sex. Friends with benefits...that kind of thing."

Slate returned her grin. "I'm perfectly all right with that."

"Good."

"It's still early," Slate mused. "You want to come over to my place and watch a movie or something?"

"We could go up to my apartment," Ashlyn said. "I've got Netflix."

"Netflix and chill?" he drawled, one brow quirked.

Ashlyn's nipples peaked. She was more than ready to sleep with Slate. She'd been hot for him for what seemed like forever. And she liked sex. A lot. Missed it. Wouldn't mind breaking her

cold spell with the hot Navy SEAL. "Oh, yeah," she said, a little more breathy than she'd intended.

Slate's eyes dropped down her body, and she liked the way he was looking at her a hell of a lot. He climbed out of the car and walked around to her side. When Ashlyn hopped out, he shut her door and immediately backed her up against it. The metal was still warm from the earlier sunshine.

He leaned close and took her lips without a word.

Ashlyn threw her arms around his neck and held on as he kissed her with all the pent-up sexual tension they'd been tiptoeing around for months.

When he finally lifted his head, Ashlyn could feel the dampness between her legs.

"Nothing serious," he murmured as he studied her.

"Nothing serious," she echoed.

Then Slate wrapped an arm around her waist and they walked toward the entrance to her apartment building.

Her friends were gonna die when they heard she and Slate were finally acting on their attraction. They'd probably go overboard and assume they'd get married in a week or something, since they were all madly in love with their own SEALs. But Ashlyn was more than satisfied to merely hook up. She was practical, and they were too different to actually end up together in the long run...but in the short term? Ashlyn was all for casual dating and sex.

She couldn't keep the smile off her face as Slate led her up the stairs.

* * *

Ooooh, I have a feeling Ashlyn isn't going to be able to keep

things as "friends with benefits" for long. Especially not when she learns what secret Slate is keeping. Get it now! *Finding Ashlyn*

If you want to LISTEN to Finding Carly, you can get the audio HERE.

Want to talk to other Susan Stoker fans? Join my reader group, Susan Stoker's Stalkers, on Facebook!

Also by Susan Stoker

SEAL Team Hawaii Series

Finding Elodie
Finding Lexie
Finding Kenna
Finding Monica
Finding Carly
Finding Ashlyn (Feb 2023)
Finding Jodelle (July 2023)

Eagle Point Search & Rescue

Searching for Lilly
Searching for Elsie
Searching for Bristol (Nov 2022)
Searching for Caryn (April 2023)
Searching for Finley (Oct 2023)
Searching for Heather (TBA)
Searching for Khloe (TBA)

The Refuge Series

Deserving Alaska
Deserving Henley (Jan 2023)
Deserving Reese (May 2023)
Deserving Cora (Nov 2023)
Deserving Lara (TBA)
Deserving Maisy (TBA)
Deserving Ryleigh (TBA)

SEAL of Protection Series

Protecting Caroline

Protecting Alabama

Protecting Fiona

Marrying Caroline (novella)

Protecting Summer

Protecting Cheyenne

Protecting Jessyka

Protecting Julie (novella)

Protecting Melody

Protecting the Future

Protecting Kiera (novella)

Protecting Alabama's Kids (novella)

Protecting Dakota

SEAL of Protection: Legacy Series

Securing Caite

Securing Brenae (novella)

Securing Sidney

Securing Piper

Securing Zoey

Securing Avery

Securing Kalee

Securing Jane

Delta Force Heroes Series

Rescuing Rayne

Rescuing Aimee (novella)

Rescuing Emily

Rescuing Harley

Marrying Emily (novella)

Rescuing Kassie

Rescuing Bryn
Rescuing Casey
Rescuing Sadie (novella)
Rescuing Wendy
Rescuing Mary
Rescuing Macie (novella)
Rescuing Annie

Delta Team Two Series

Shielding Gillian
Shielding Kinley
Shielding Aspen
Shielding Jayme (novella)
Shielding Riley
Shielding Devyn
Shielding Ember
Shielding Sierra

Badge of Honor: Texas Heroes Series

Justice for Mackenzie
Justice for Mickie
Justice for Corrie
Justice for Laine (novella)
Shelter for Elizabeth
Justice for Boone
Shelter for Adeline
Shelter for Sophie
Justice for Erin
Justice for Milena
Shelter for Blythe
Justice for Hope

Shelter for Quinn
Shelter for Koren
Shelter for Penelope

Ace Security Series
Claiming Grace
Claiming Alexis
Claiming Bailey
Claiming Felicity
Claiming Sarah

Mountain Mercenaries Series
Defending Allye
Defending Chloe
Defending Morgan
Defending Harlow
Defending Everly
Defending Zara
Defending Raven

Silverstone Series
Trusting Skylar
Trusting Taylor
Trusting Molly
Trusting Cassidy

Stand Alone
Falling for the Delta
The Guardian Mist
Nature's Rift
A Princess for Cale

ALSO BY SUSAN STOKER

A Moment in Time- A Collection of Short Stories
Another Moment in Time- A Collection of Short Stories
Lambert's Lady

Special Operations Fan Fiction
http://www.AcesPress.com

Beyond Reality Series
Outback Hearts
Flaming Hearts
Frozen Hearts

Writing as Annie George:
Stepbrother Virgin (erotic novella)

ABOUT THE AUTHOR

New York Times, *USA Today* and *Wall Street Journal* Bestselling Author Susan Stoker has a heart as big as the state of Tennessee where she lives, but this all American girl has also spent the last fourteen years living in Missouri, California, Colorado, Indiana, and Texas. She's married to a retired Army man who now gets to follow *her* around the country.

She debuted her first series in 2014 and quickly followed that up with the SEAL of Protection Series, which solidified her love of writing and creating stories readers can get lost in.

If you enjoyed this book, or any book, please consider leaving a review. It's appreciated by authors more than you'll know.

www.stokeraces.com
www.AcesPress.com
susan@stokeraces.com

facebook.com/authorsusanstoker
twitter.com/Susan_Stoker
instagram.com/authorsusanstoker
goodreads.com/SusanStoker
bookbub.com/authors/susan-stoker
amazon.com/author/susanstoker

CPSIA information can be obtained
at www.ICGtesting.com
Printed in the USA
BVHW090733061022
648739BV00001B/8